"PUT ME DOWN. I CAN WALK FROM HERE."

The Villa Thessalo lay just ahead, a pleasant, foursquare building with pots of riotous red geraniums gracing the entry.

He did not comply, only went up the steps, pushed open the door, and carried her inside. The dim coolness soothed her heated face.

"Mr. Trentham—"

"Hush." He tightened his hold on her and mounted the treads without faltering. He lowered her and Caroline uncurled her fingers from around his neck.

"Thank you," she said softly, meaning it with all her heart. His attention and concern, the absurd way he had carried her down the cliffs—it was not something she was accustomed to, but it was a great kindness.

"The pleasure was mine." And to her surprise, he smiled.

The expression nearly stole her breath. Mr. Trentham's smile was dazzling.

It was a good thing he so rarely smiled.

All He DESIRES

ANTHEA LAWSON

ZEBRA BOOKS
Kensington Publishing Corp.
http://www.kensingtonbooks.com

ZEBRA BOOKS are published by

Kensington Publishing Corp.
119 West 40th Street
New York, NY 10018

All Kensington titles, imprints, and distributed lines are available at special quantity discounts for bulk purchases for sales promotion, premiums, fund-raising, educational, or institutional use.

Special book excerpts or customized printings can also be created to fit specific needs. For details, write or phone the office of the Kensington Special Sales Manager: Attn.: Special Sales Department. Kensington Publishing Corp., 119 West 40th Street, New York, NY 10018. Phone: 1-800-221-2647.

ISBN-13: 978-1-4201-0457-8
ISBN-10: 1-4201-0457-8

First Printing: November 2009
10 9 8 7 6 5 4 3 2 1

Printed in the United States of America

This book is dedicated to our first readers—
Ginger, and the ORWA critique group

Chapter 1

Crete, March 1848

Caroline Huntington was falling.

The distance from saddle to ground took on a dreadful expanse as her horse reared. Flung backward, heartbeat doubling in her throat, she clutched at the pommel, but the smooth leather slipped beneath her palms. For a sickening moment she hurtled down through empty air. Then the earth rushed to meet her, clouting her head and sending a rough pain jolting down her outstretched arm. She swallowed, sudden darkness hovering at the edges of her vision. From far away she heard the throb of hoofbeats receding.

"Help . . ." It came out a moan, and who would hear? She had left the village far behind, drawn too far up the track by the promise of a dazzling view from the hillside, the scent of dusty herbs in the clear air.

How quickly the world had upended. One moment riding above the olive groves, the next . . .

She drew in a shaky breath and tried to sit, the world spinning at the motion. There was no sign of her skittish mount, no sign of any other living creature besides herself. The air was still and quiet, the late-afternoon light fading to red even as she lay on the path. She was alone, a stranger surrounded by silent hills.

Her arm hurt far too much, the ache magnified by the throbbing in her head. Would anyone find her out here? She thought of her uncle back in London, her brother—they were so terribly far away. Her mind veered from the notion she might never see them again. No. She only had to get up and start walking, keep breathing through the pain, but she felt tired, so tired. . . .

When she opened her eyes again the world had darkened and there were stars above her, cold and distant. She stared at the sky as the constellations spun and wavered. The ground was hard and chilly beneath her, and the joint of her elbow felt as though it were on fire. Clenching her jaw she forced herself to her knees, then made a staggering lurch that brought her to her feet. Her legs seemed barely connected to her body and she fought for balance, breath scraping her throat. The world tilted, then steadied.

Right arm cradled close, she began to pick her way back down the path. Every step jarred and made her want to sit down again, or better yet, lie down and give in, but she pressed her lips together hard and kept on. One step. Then another. One breath. Then another.

She did not know how long she had been walking, but the stars had come down to earth and seemed to dance in front of her. She blinked, blinked again, and the points of light resolved into fires. No, torches. She could hear voices, calling something that sounded like her name.

"I'm here!" she cried, lifting her good arm, eyes hot with relief. In moments they were there, her rescuers, dark-eyed olive farmers, talking excitedly and waving their torches.

"Caroline! Thank heavens we found you." Maggie Farnsworth pushed to the fore, her normally neatly coiled hair straggling from its pins, her face lined with worry.

How odd. When had her traveling companion ever appeared less than tidy? Caroline swayed and Maggie caught her.

"Quick, someone help me," Maggie called. "She's about to collapse."

"Allow me to assist you." A silver-haired gentleman with a French accent stepped forward, reaching for her.

Caroline flinched. "Not my elbow—"

"Pardon me, mademoiselle. We must get you to a doctor immediately." He turned and shouted in Greek. Two men hurried back down the track, their torches leaving smears of light against the darkness.

"Manolis will bring the cart," the Frenchman said. "It will not be long."

"Thank you, Monsieur Legault," Maggie said. "Your assistance tonight has been invaluable. When Miss Huntington did not return from her ride . . ." Her breath caught on the words.

"There now. We foreigners must look after one another, is it not so? Though without the help of these good men we would not have found your friend."

"But we did. We did." Maggie supported Caroline, holding firmly to her uninjured arm. The flames reflected off Maggie's gold-rimmed spectacles. "When you had not returned by supper, I knew something was wrong. The owners of the villa directed me to Monsieur Legault, and he helped organize the search."

Caroline swallowed. "I'm so glad." She leaned against her friend and closed her eyes. How could she have been so thoughtless, so careless? She would make it up to Maggie, somehow.

"Ah," Monsieur Legault said. "Here is the cart. It will not be comfortable, but the aid we seek is not far."

Maggie led Caroline to where the rustic vehicle waited. "I would not think a village of this size boasted a doctor," Maggie said. "How fortunate."

The Frenchman smiled, though there was something cautious in his expression. "We shall see. Come."

The cart rolled forward over the rough track, and it did not take long for Caroline to fall into a hazy, pain-filled daze. The night sky, the flaring torches, the jolting ride wove together into a disjointed tapestry. She did not realize they had halted in front of a cottage until Maggie coaxed her upright and helped her from the cart.

Monsieur Legault went to the door. He pounded, and pounded again until at last it was opened by a figure who remained in the shadows. Caroline blinked, her vision still blurred. A tall man, she thought.

"What do you want?" His voice was gruff.

"Mr. Trentham, we require your help." The Frenchman waved to where Caroline stood, supported by Maggie. "The mademoiselle is injured."

The man shook his head. "I cannot help you." He began to close the door, but Monsieur Legault set his foot in the jamb.

"I ask you not to be stubborn. She is hurt—she must be seen."

The shadow moved closer to the light. He *was* tall, his hair the color of night. The torchlight painted hollows under his cheekbones and cast his uncompromising nose in sharp relief. He did not look like a doctor, not with his creased clothing and untamed hair, a scowl making his face even more forbidding. When his gaze moved to her, Caroline *felt* it, a nearly physical sensation, like standing under a storm cloud just before the fury of wind and rain lashed down. She shivered.

He regarded her for several moments, measured by the rapid beat of her heart. His eyes seemed black in the flickering light. That intent gaze moved down to her dusty boots, then returned to her face.

At last he turned to the Frenchman. "The woman is on her feet. She looks well enough. Take her to Rethymno." He stepped back and made to close his door again.

"You must help us," Monsieur Legault said, a pleading note in his voice. "Rethymno is too far, and you know how little talent the doctor there has."

"Enough to care for an injured arm. Good night."

"Wait!" Maggie stepped forward, bringing Caroline with her. "You cannot refuse—you are English!"

"Oh?" He paused with one hand on the door frame, his lips twisted as though he had tasted something bitter. "I don't see that it signifies."

"Of course it does. This is Miss Caroline Huntington, the niece of the Earl of Twickenham. How can you consider yourself a gentleman if you turn her away?"

"Who says I consider myself a gentleman?"

Caroline took an uneven step forward, ready to add her voice to the argument, but the world tilted. She heard Maggie gasp, but Monsieur Legault was quicker. He spun, bracing Caroline before she fell.

"You see?" He glared back at Mr. Trentham. "It is more than her arm."

The dark man said nothing for a long moment, then with a curse he turned on his heel and stalked back into the cottage. Light from inside spilled across the threshold.

"Come, little one." Monsieur Legault aided Caroline into the cottage while Maggie followed behind.

"Put her in there." Mr. Trentham gestured down a short hallway but made no move to follow.

Caroline allowed herself to be led and was dimly aware of sinking down on a bed, of Maggie removing her riding boots and helping her lie back. The room whirled behind her closed eyelids.

"Do not worry at Mr. Trentham's manner," Monsieur Legault said in an undertone. "He was a very skilled doctor—even if he refuses to acknowledge it."

"Why is that?" Maggie asked.

"He will not speak of it. But your companion, she is in good hands. Come, madame, you must sit too—the events of the evening have unsettled you. Look, you are trembling."

Caroline heard her friend's sigh, the weary rustle of skirts settling. She wanted to apologize, but all strength had left her.

Her head hurt, and it was easier to simply lie still, eyes closed, and try not to imagine what would follow. Would she have to return to England? Maggie would insist on accompanying her, but that was unthinkable. Her friend's mission in the Mediterranean would have to be abandoned if she did so—and it would be Caroline's fault.

"I see you've made yourselves at home."

She opened her eyes to see Mr. Trentham standing in the doorway. His dark hair looked as though he had roughed his hands through it before entering the room. It gave him a wild, untamed air.

"Really, sir." Maggie started to rise, but he waved her back to her seat.

"Calm yourself, Mrs. . . ."

"Farnsworth," she supplied.

He gave a nod, then turned his scowl toward Monsieur Legault.

"*Bien,*" the Frenchman said. "I knew we could rely upon you, Mr. Trentham."

"You presume too much." The black-haired man stalked to Caroline's bedside. He moved with an almost imperceptible limp, favoring his left leg. He bent and looked into her eyes, forcing her to meet his gaze. Caroline stared back into deep indigo—the color of the sky after sunset, just before it shades into night.

"My elbow," she said, trapped by his gaze. "I landed on my arm when I fell."

"Here?" He set two fingers to the inside of her elbow, where the fire burned.

She flinched. "Yes."

He took her hand and she felt the roughness of his palm. "Can you move your fingers, Miss Huntington?"

She could, her fingers brushing lightly against his.

"Good." Despite the difficult introduction and his obvious unwillingness to care for her, his touch was gentle.

Steady competence radiated from his hands, an odd contrast to the rest of his demeanor.

"The blood flow doesn't appear to be compromised, but your elbow . . . Take a deep breath."

Caroline obeyed as his large hands moved up her arm. When he touched the joint she stiffened in pain and could not help her quick, indrawn breath, but she refused to give voice to the lightning slicing through her. She would bear whatever came in silence, for Maggie's sake.

His touch moved back down to her wrist. "Move your fingers again. Yes, that's it. Any tingling? Loss of feeling?"

"No." It came out a strained whisper.

He glanced up. "Mrs. Farnsworth, I require your assistance."

Maggie came and stood at Caroline's shoulder. Her face was pale and she was breathing quickly. "I am not certain—"

"Grasp her arm here, above the elbow. Firmly. I am going to apply a downward pressure and lever the arm so the bones can return to their proper alignment."

"Lever the arm?" Maggie's voice was faint.

Mr. Trentham looked impatient. "That's generally the accepted procedure to reduce a dislocated elbow."

"Shouldn't you administer something for the pain?" Maggie sounded as though she were the one in need of medication.

Caroline glanced at her friend. "I will be all right." She forced a smile past the throbbing ache.

"Please, Caroline. I can't bear the thought of you suffering." Maggie swallowed.

A sudden, dangerous edge leapt into Mr. Trentham's voice. "She said she would be all right."

"You don't know my companion as I do," Maggie said. "She won't admit . . ."

He leaned forward and stared into Caroline's eyes. A ghost of something like panic shadowed his expression. "I do not run an apothecary. And I do not administer medications." His tone was harsh. "You have no right to ask."

"Mr. Trentham." Monsieur Legault spoke from his place at the end of the bed, his voice soothing. "A small dose of laudanum. It will not hurt, surely. She seems to be in some difficulty."

"Please." Maggie's voice held a touch of desperation.

Caroline wanted to argue that she could bear it, but she was not certain she could. Just the thought of him straightening her arm brought her perilously close to tears.

Mr. Trentham stood, hands balled into fists. "You don't bloody know what you're asking."

Tension vibrated from him, and Caroline was reminded again of a storm about to break free, some elemental force barely chained.

"Now, my friend," the Frenchman said softly.

"No." The doctor spun, mouth tight and furious, and strode hurriedly from the room.

Chapter 2

The door banged against the wall in Mr. Trentham's wake, the noise underscoring the shocked silence that descended. Maggie turned a distressed look to Monsieur Legault, but he only shook his head. No one spoke.

Long minutes passed, and it did not seem at all certain Mr. Trentham would return. Caroline began to think the strange man had fled into the night, abandoning them.

Then, as abruptly as he had left, he returned, carrying a brown glass bottle and a spoon. After opening the cap, he wetted the tip of his finger with the medicine and tasted it, then thrust the bottle into Maggie's hands.

"Here. If you feel it's essential, you administer the dose."

"But . . . how much would you recommend?"

"None. The outcome is upon your head." He made for the door again, then paused and looked over his shoulder. "One spoonful."

Maggie poured out a measure and gave it to Caroline. The bitter liquid tasted dreadful, but she was beyond caring.

"How long until it takes effect?" her friend called.

"Soon." Mr. Trentham's voice from the other room was strained.

Caroline listened to the sound of his pacing until it became impossible to concentrate. The room seemed to be filling up with soft white clouds, or perhaps it was her head filling up—she was not sure. Either way, it was a welcome whiteness. The pain felt muffled and very far away.

"Miss Huntington?" Mr. Trentham's words pierced through the clouds. He had returned to stand at the bedside.

She blinked. "I . . . I am ready. I think."

"Good. Mrs. Farnsworth, take hold of her arm."

Caroline closed her eyes. There was a gentle, steady pull and someone screamed.

"Madame!" The urgency in Monsieur Legault's voice made Caroline open her eyes, but he was not speaking to her. Both he and Mr. Trentham were kneeling on the floor, the younger man supporting Maggie.

"For pity's sake." Mr. Trentham lightly slapped her cheek. "Wake up, Mrs. Farnsworth. Let me remind you that you are not the injured one."

Caroline giggled; she could not help it. The two gentlemen glanced up at her.

"I'm glad you feel no pain, Miss Huntington. Do not attempt to move your arm. I will splint it—as soon as I manage your squeamish friend." Mr. Trentham frowned down at Maggie, who still lay unmoving in his arms. "Legault, you'll find brandy in the cupboard beside the sink. I think Mrs. Farnsworth requires a restorative."

The Frenchman rose. "Will she be all right?"

"She's fine—though useless for nursing. As soon as she regains consciousness I'm sending her back to the village with you. Kindly ask if Madame Legault will come in the morning to tend to Miss Huntington's needs. And now, sir, if you will have the courtesy not to faint, you may assist me in splinting her arm."

Alex Trentham stood in the doorway, watching until the lantern-lit cart carrying Mrs. Farnsworth and Monsieur

Legault dipped down the path and out of sight. His shirt was damp with perspiration. The night air was chill, but he did not retreat from it. There was nowhere to go. His solitude had been torn away, his peace disturbed—he had had a patient thrust upon him—it was all one great, bloody nightmare. He glanced back at his bedroom, the irrefutable evidence asleep in his bed.

Damn Miss Huntington for carelessly injuring herself. Damn Legault for his insistence. And damn his own miserable history for haunting him here, over a thousand miles from England.

He slammed the door against the darkness outside. There was nothing to be done now—except wait, observe her condition, and get her out of his house as soon as she could be moved. When she had gone he would forget, once and for all. He must never allow this to happen again.

Legault had left the brandy on the sideboard. Alex poured a glass and went to the kitchen table, which was pushed against the wall and had wooden crates stacked beneath it. He took a long drink, then removed the cloth draped over his latest project.

Bones, compliments of Legault's archaeological dig. Large ones and small, the remains of the ancient inhabitants of this island, markers of a civilization buried for centuries. Legault dug them up and Alex pieced them together. There was much that bones could reveal to a trained eye: the age of the deceased, whether their lives had been ones of brutal labor or pampered ease.

There were distinct advantages to working with the dead. The souls had fled and there was nothing he could do to harm them. Nothing at all. Alex lifted his glass and drained it, then selected a metacarpus and held it to the light. A number at the bottom, inked in his own neat hand. Setting it aside, he made a notation in the book that lay open beside him.

"Hello?" Miss Huntington's voice drifted from the bedchamber, soft and uncertain.

He held very still, willing her to fall back asleep. But no, he heard her stirring, and then she called again. "Is anyone there? I'm so thirsty."

He pushed back his chair and fetched a cup, filling it. The soft light of the lamp he carried preceded him into the bedroom, illuminating his—no, he would not call her his patient. Her brown hair was loose against his pillow, her eyes wide and dreamy. The flame pricked glints of gold in her brown eyes, gilded strands of her hair.

"Hello," she said. "Are you an orphan?"

"I beg your pardon?"

She gave no response, still clearly under the effect of the laudanum. Thank God she had suffered no ill effects from the dose. For a terrible moment he had been so afraid . . . but she was safe. And had shown a great deal of courage. In the morning there would be pain, but tonight her face was open and serene.

"I've brought water." He set the cup down and slid one arm behind her shoulders, boosting her up. The bedcovers slipped down, revealing a silken white chemise that followed the curve of her breasts, and Alex felt a sudden leap of physical awareness.

He had not practiced the role of physician, nor seen a woman in a state of undress, in a very long while. The detachment that used to serve him so well was gone. It was impossible not to notice her feminine shape, the smooth column of her neck, the softness of her full lips as he held the glass against them. The scent of her. Despite himself he dipped his head, inhaling. Her warm weight rested against him, the softness of her hair brushing against his throat.

"Drink." His throat felt tight.

She took a long, thirsty swallow. "Good," she said, a single drop of water glinting on her lower lip. "How did you lose your parents?"

It was a question asked in innocence, and he felt oddly

compelled to answer. "My father died years ago, and my mother . . ." He barely allowed himself to remember what his life had been, before. "She was alive when I left."

She laid her head against his arm, and he let go the shreds of memory. With steady hands he helped her lie back, then pulled the covers up, restoring her modesty—though that brief contact with all that was warm and female still flared within him, not so easily obscured.

She sighed. "I suppose your mother abandoned you. Maggie says some do. I wish I had known mine."

She seemed determined to share confidences. Alex pulled a chair over and settled himself next to the bed. It was unlikely she would recall anything of their conversation in the morning—there was no harm in it, and he could humor her until she fell asleep again. Her secrets were safe with him. And despite the disruption she had caused she was here now, and a part of him sorely missed having company—some conversation to keep back the dark night.

"What happened to her?" he asked gently, as much to escape his own thoughts as to learn hers.

"She died giving birth to me—a life for a life, I suppose." Her expression was tinged with sorrow. "And then my father, when I was a young girl."

"So you are truly an orphan."

"Yes." A delicate shiver ran through her.

He took her good hand in his, wanting her to feel less alone. "I know loss as well. The world changes forever." His own words surprised him—he had never spoken like this.

She met his gaze and he recognized in her amber-flecked eyes an expression he had seen often in his own mirror.

"Then we understand one another, sir. That is a rare thing."

"Is it?"

"Yes." Her face was serious.

Her warm hand gripped his, and Alex felt it, a tenuous connection. It frightened him beyond words, made him want to shove his chair back and leave her, to retreat far enough to stretch that slender thread to the breaking point. But he remained where he was.

When would he ever experience this again—the chance to sit in the lamplight and hold a beautiful woman's hand? And she was beautiful, her eyes brimming with memory, her hair falling free, her hand strong and alive and holding on.

"You should rest now," he said, his voice thick with an emotion he did not understand.

She drew in a deep breath and let it out in a sigh. "Yes."

A few moments later her eyelids drifted shut, but she did not release his hand, and he made no effort to free himself.

Grey light seeping from behind the linen curtains woke him—that and an ache in his leg that protested his spending the better part of the night in a chair. Miss Huntington was deeply asleep, the hand that had held his through the dark hours now curled, relaxed, against the pillow. For a long moment he gazed at her, marking the regular rise and fall of her breath, the healthy color, the serenity her face held in dreaming.

Muttering an oath, he levered himself out of the chair and walked stiffly to the front room. He should have spent the night beside the fire, wrapped in blankets, not dozing beside some woman who meant nothing to him.

He was forever outside that world of sweetness. It was his fate, and here on Crete, the birthplace of ancient myths, fate was something that could not be escaped. It could only be endured. The pain in his leg reminded him, the sharp twinge returning him to reason with every step.

Miss Huntington would be gone soon enough, and he would be glad to see her go.

The ancient bones on his table gleamed hard and white in the growing light. With quick steps he crossed the room and drew the cover over them.

Chapter 3

Caroline woke with a dull throbbing in her arm. Everything around her was white and drenched with light. It took several moments for her eyes to adjust, to realize she was lying in a bed, whitewashed walls beyond. A soft length of linen hung from the single window, the thin fabric filtering the sunlight that poured into the room.

Where was she? Would the pain engulf her if she lifted her head? No, at least not too badly. Her right arm was wrapped and bound into a sling. Carefully, using her legs and good arm, Caroline inched herself up on the pillow. The sheets felt wonderfully soft against her bare legs. She glanced down, relieved to see she was clad in her chemise—not completely naked in some stranger's bed. She eased up a trifle more, ignoring the buzzing in her head, until she could see past the bed linens.

This was obviously someone's bedroom, but a very plain one. No bright hangings on the wall or knick-knacks adorning the top of the spare wooden bureau. The room was without decoration but for a small ceramic vase painted with a motif of bulls on the bedside table. It seemed the room of someone who had stripped life down to the bare essentials. Not ascetic, though—she had to admit the bed was quite comfortable. There was a door made of planks that had been smoothed and oiled to a golden luster. It was a very beautiful door, she decided.

Memory came flooding back. She had been injured and brought here. How long had it been? Days? Panic bolted through her. Where was Maggie? Had the boat for Malta sailed without Caroline?

She struggled with the sheets and levered herself up, fighting the wave of aching dizziness her movements triggered. Keep breathing. She pressed her lips tightly together.

Beyond the half-open door a man was sitting at a table writing, his face in profile to her. He looked stern, with his thick dark hair and sun-bronzed skin, like a warrior on some ancient fresco. Stern, but familiar . . . Yes, she remembered now. The unwilling doctor with the careful hands. Mr. Trentham.

"Sir, I beg your pardon," she called. Her voice emerged more quietly than she had expected, but he heard. He glanced up and she was startled once again by the intensity of his gaze.

"You're awake." He closed his book and rose from the table, expression both grim and relieved as he entered the room. "Is there much pain?"

"A small amount." She would not admit how the room had begun to spin. "What day is it? Would you help me rise?"

His brows drew together and he made no move to assist her. "Do you recall what happened? Your friend told me she thought you had been thrown by your horse. Riding out alone—why is it tourists behave so foolishly when they leave home?"

"I'm not a tourist," she protested, but it was not true. She had accompanied Maggie to the Mediterranean to help with her friend's orphanage project, but *she* was the one who had insisted they detour to Crete for a holiday. A week to revel in the sun and antiquity of the island—it seemed now to have been quite a foolish idea after all. "Where is Mrs. Farnsworth?" Surely Maggie would not have abandoned her here.

"You're lucky they found you. And no doubt Mrs. Farnsworth will be arriving soon, as she has every day, to check on your condition."

Her condition . . . "Is my arm broken?"

"No. You dislocated your elbow." A frown marred the strong lines of his face. "I've splinted it, but am more concerned about the injury to your head. You've been unconscious for nearly two days. Do you know who you are, where you are?"

"Of course I do. I'm Caroline Huntington, and I am in some cottage on Crete."

He made no reply to that, only leaned in and placed his hands on either side of her face, the touch unexpectedly gentle. His hands were warm, and this close she caught the scent of him: soap and sage, and beneath that, something deeply male. She swallowed as he held her still, his gaze moving from one eye to the other.

"Difficult to tell how severe the concussion is." The feel of his touch lingered as he lifted his hands. "You'll have to go slowly—bed rest for at least a week."

Caroline gave a small shake of her head and regretted it as the whirling redoubled. "That's impossible. I need to accompany Mrs. Farnsworth to Malta. She has an important meeting to attend in the capital."

"Valletta?" He raised one brow. "Unlikely."

Irritation banished some of her pain. "I do not appreciate your skepticism, sir—and I will not take orders from a reclusive Englishman masquerading as a Greek olive farmer." She bit her lip. It was an unkind thing to say, but he could at least consult her before making pronouncements regarding what she could and could not do. She softened her tone. "Whatever are you doing here, so far from anything that could be called civilization?"

"That is none of your concern." He took a step back. "What does concern you is that both your arm and your head are in need of mending."

"If you will fetch my clothing . . ."

He made a sharp gesture of negation. "You are not well enough to travel across the room, let alone to Malta. I have tended you, Miss Huntington—reluctantly and at some personal cost. The only fee I require is that you rest until you are fit for travel."

Caroline returned his frown. What a contrary man. Her head hurt and he was beginning to annoy her. Besides, clad only in her chemise with the coverlet providing little concealment, he had her at a distinct disadvantage.

"The only reason I'm not fit for travel is that someone has made off with my clothing! There will be competent medical care in Valletta. Malta is a British protectorate after all. I am certain Mrs. Farnsworth can—"

"Mrs. Farnsworth is useless as a nurse." He folded his arms. "I cannot release you into her care, certainly not for a sea voyage."

"Malta is only—"

"Enough. Believe me, I would be happy to see you go, if my conscience would permit it."

"What do you propose? That you keep me here as a captive in your . . ." She felt her cheeks flame. It would not do to end the sentence with the word *bed*. Covering her confusion, she pleated the covers with her good hand, then finally met his deep blue eyes. "Sir, please fetch my clothing. While I appreciate your concern, I assure you I would make a most disagreeable captive. If you insist on imprisoning me, I will be forced to contact the authorities."

"Damnation!" His mouth thinned at the corners. "You're not my captive—you were forced on me—and I've no doubt you can be disagreeable. You've already demonstrated that fact."

He kept his gaze locked with hers a moment longer, then turned and strode to the wardrobe. With a yank, he threw the door open and pulled out her wrinkled riding habit and crinoline. "I have no desire to hold you here against your will, but I will not help if you insist on reinjuring yourself. Here." He tossed her clothing beside her on the bed, then stalked out of the room, closing the door forcefully behind him.

Caroline drew in a deep breath. Good riddance. She had

feared he would insist on standing by, and the thought of him watching as she dressed sent another blaze of heat into her face. At least she had finally made him understand she was well enough to clothe herself.

One-armed, she pushed back the covers and scooted herself down the bed. As long as she did not jostle her right arm it was bearable. She reached for her crinoline and shook it free of the dress, but there was no way she could pull the dratted thing on one-handed while lying down. There was nothing to do but to stand.

The tiled floor seemed terribly far away. She swallowed and fought for balance. Think of Maggie. If her foolish injury jeopardized the project in Malta, how could she ever face her friend again? Maggie had been focused on nothing but the orphanage in Valletta for months. They could not miss that meeting.

A moan escaped as her feet touched the floor, and for a moment she thought the dizziness would prevail. She pressed her lips tightly together and leaned—nearly collapsed—against the bed frame, knocking the bedside table as she did. The small vase on the table teetered, and Caroline could only watch as it tipped over the edge to shatter on the floor beneath. She hoped it had not been very dear to him.

"Miss Huntington?"

"No—don't come in! I'm all right."

There was a censorious silence. He was no doubt standing just outside the door, waiting for her to admit defeat. Well, he would be waiting a very long time. She did not think much of his treatment, one moment professing she had to rest and stay abed, the next flinging her clothes at her and bidding her dress herself when he did not get his way. What an impossible man.

Now, to don the crinoline. She dragged it off the bed and managed to put first one bare foot through, then the other. The cloth felt thick and unwieldy, threatening to slip off as she inched it up with one hand. There. She was shaking from the effort and could feel perspiration dampening her forehead, but she had done it.

The dress next. She reached, but it slithered out of her grasp to huddle on the floor. Poor thing—she knew just how it felt. Very well, she would pick it up. Just bend over and—

She let out a cry and grabbed at the bedcovers as her vision swam, darkness filtering her vision and pulling her down. The bedroom door slammed open, and Mr. Trentham was there, catching her in his arms and cursing under his breath.

"Stupid, stubborn woman."

Despite the rough words he lifted her gently back to the bed. With one move he stripped the crinoline off, leaving her legs bared to the thigh. Before she could protest the immodesty of it he pulled the covers up, then laid the back of his fingers against her cheek, his expression unreadable. "Don't move." He then left the room.

No need to caution her. She was not certain she could move even had she wanted to. Caroline closed her eyes. She almost wished she *had* lost consciousness—anything to elude the horrible feeling in her head.

Faint sounds came from the room beyond, dishes clinking together, a chair scraped across the wood-planked floor. She heard him return but could not manage to lift her lids.

Perhaps she *had* pushed herself too far. But really, a week in bed? It was out of the question. She had promised to *help* with Maggie's orphanage project, not make it impossible for her friend to succeed.

"Drink this."

She opened her eyes to see him holding out a clay cup. "What is it?"

"Water." He slipped one arm behind her and held the cup to her lips. "You've exhausted yourself."

He set the cup down and tucked the covers closely about her, then gathered up her clothes and returned them to the wardrobe, making no mention of her failure to dress. In fact, he did not speak at all as he fetched a broom and swept up the broken vase. Caroline watched him from behind heavy, half-closed lids—the unyielding set of his lips, the pull of his shirt against the strong muscles of his arms. . . .

Blast it. Alex paced, more concerned about Miss Huntington than he wanted to admit. She was weak and seemed intent on doing herself harm. He had not expected she would have been able to sit up, let alone actually get out of bed and tumble to the floor. Her strength of will surprised him. He had been a fool to let her try to dress herself alone, but something about the woman goaded him unreasonably.

Hold her captive? Not bloody likely.

Still, temper or no, the image of her clad only in her chemise would not leave him, nor the feel of her soft curves against him, her naked legs. . . . He swallowed. Now that she had regained consciousness he needed to get her out of his bedroom, and out of his house, as soon as possible.

The sound of the mule-drawn cart creaking up the hill interrupted his thoughts. He ran a hand over his face and went out to the stoop. His home—chosen for its seclusion—had never seen so many visitors. It was patently impossible to work with her under his roof.

The gnarled olives on one side of the cottage cast dappled shade over his garden: sunflowers and pole beans and a scatter of wild poppies mixed in with the rioting greens. Beyond, hills ran down to the sun-spangled blue of the Mediterranean, with a distant glimpse of the village nestled between the cliffs and the sea.

There was Manolis driving his ramshackle cart, which always looked as though it would go to pieces if it hit a stone. Somehow, though, it never failed to make the journey up the dusty, winding track to his door. The serious Mrs. Farnsworth sat on the bench beside him.

Alex straightened his shoulders and stepped out into the

light as she disembarked, tweed skirts uncreased from her ride up the hill, her sand-colored hair neatly in place and not a smudge on her gold-rimmed spectacles.

"Good day," he said.

"Is it?" Her voice was shaded with worry. "How is Miss Huntington?"

"Awake at last." *And perfectly stubborn.*

The anxious lines on Mrs. Farnsworth's face eased. "I am much relieved to hear it. Thank you for caring for her so capably, Dr. Trentham. We are scheduled to depart for Malta on Monday's boat, and I am sure she has told you of the importance of our project. The orphans there . . ."

He gave her a stern look. "I have explained to her, and I will explain to you. Miss Huntington will not be traveling for some time yet, and certainly not on the next boat."

Mrs. Farnsworth paused at the doorstep. "Oh dear. But it is essential—"

Alex caught her elbow. Surely Mrs. Farnsworth would be more reasonable than her younger companion. "What is essential is that Miss Huntington makes a full recovery. You are responsible for her welfare here, are you not?"

"Not precisely." She gestured with one hand. "We are traveling together, but Caroline is not my employee, nor my dependant. She has a will of her own."

That much had been amply demonstrated. He tried again. "You must make her understand. She cannot embark for some time yet."

Distress settled around the corners of Mrs. Farnsworth's eyes. "But the nature of our errand is urgent. You have no idea how difficult it was to obtain an interview with the governor. If we are not there at the appointed time . . ." She pulled away and stepped into his house. "That appointment *must* be kept."

Alex pressed his lips together and gestured Mrs. Farnsworth to the bedroom. Perhaps seeing how weak her companion was would make the woman see sense.

Miss Huntington's face was pale, but her expression warmed when she saw her friend. "Maggie! I'm so sorry about all of this."

Mrs. Farnsworth hurried to the bed. "Don't be sorry. I am so glad to see you're awake and recovering." She set her hand lightly on her friend's shoulder. "Whatever shall we do? The doctor says you are not fit to travel to Malta, and I cannot possibly leave you."

"We will . . ." Miss Huntington stopped and glanced to where he stood in the doorway. "Mr. Trentham, I desire a private word with Mrs. Farnsworth, if you would be so kind."

How easily she dismissed him, as if his bedchamber were her private domain, and he nothing more than an unwanted errand boy. He gave a curt nod. "Ten minutes." He strode out of the room.

Her voice followed him. "Mr. Trentham."

"Yes?"

"Please close the door behind you."

Alex shut the door on the two women, resisting the urge to slam it. Of all the irksome . . . He left the house for the sunshine outside, but not even the fresh, salt-edged air could ease his irritation with Miss Caroline Huntington. He could tell she was plotting something in there with her friend. Perhaps they needed a demonstration of where, exactly, the limits of her strength lay.

Manolis waved to Alex from where he had pulled his cart into the shade. The cart driver was eating his lunch: flat bread, a white slab of feta, and oil-cured black olives. Alex went to join him and leaned against the side of the cart. He studied his cottage, sturdy and serviceable with thick, earthen walls washed white to reflect the summer heat. Moving Miss Huntington to the village would do much to restore his refuge.

"Manolis, could you transport the Englishwoman to the village as you brought her here the other night?"

"The road is steep and rocky." The older man gave him a

curious look. "She is so bitter then that you do not want the taste of her in your home?"

Involuntarily, Alex recalled the warmth of her hand in his as she spoke through the laudanum that first night, the way her unbound hair spread across his pillow. He frowned. "It is best if she recuperated at the villa."

"I see." Manolis inclined his head. "Perhaps she is too much like honey, and *iatros,* you deny yourself the sweetness of life."

"Life is not sweetness." The words sounded harsh even to his own ears. Yet he could not banish the image of Miss Huntington in her thin chemise as he had lifted her that morning, nor forget the feel of her body pressed against his.

Perhaps there was sweetness in life—but not for him.

He pushed away from the cart. "Come in the early afternoon. Sweet or bitter, I will have Miss Huntington out of my house."

The two women glanced up, startled, as he entered the bedroom without knocking. "Starting tomorrow the two of you will have all the privacy you desire. I am moving you back to the village, Miss Huntington."

"Oh?" Her brown eyes lifted to his. "Of course, it's welcome news. I will be able to assist Maggie—and she can help me."

Mrs. Farnsworth nodded, then added, "It is for the best, especially as you appear to be an unmarried man, Mr. Trentham." Her voice was firm, but she flushed after delivering the words.

"Maggie is right," Miss Huntington said. "It would be unseemly for you to keep me here any longer than is necessary." She dropped her gaze to the coverlet, and he guessed she, too, was remembering the events of the morning.

"Then it is agreed. Manolis will move you in the cart—tomorrow. But I warn you, it will be a difficult ride down. You'll need to be well rested, and be tended to afterward. You're in no condition for extended travel."

The two women shared a glance, then Miss Huntington laid her head back against the pillow. "I trust this will work out for the best. For all of us."

Chapter 4

London, March 1848

Lord Reginald Huntington paused at the top of the steps outside his club and turned the collar of his greatcoat up against the rain. Behind him the doorman bowed good night, then pulled the mahogany doors closed, sealing away the warm light and polished comfort. Reginald turned with exaggerated care and made his way to the line of carriages waiting at the curb. Not that he felt the cold, at least not physically. More than enough whiskey burned through his blood to keep the night at bay.

It was the knowledge of his father's latest betrayal that chilled him. His cousin Caroline was going to become his sister! The old man was going to formally adopt her.

It was a fate he would not wish upon his worst enemy—no, it was *precisely* the fate he would wish upon his worst enemy. The insufferable chit. His father would do well by her, providing a dowry and annual income and leaving Reginald—the heir—with a substantially reduced portion. His cousins had wormed their way into his father's affections and the old man had treated them as his own. Reginald scowled. Better than his own.

Where was his bloody carriage? He squinted into the

darkness, finally locating it near the back of the line. His driver, bundled against the pervasive drizzle, climbed down to open the door without so much as a "Good evening, sir." The fellow kept his head bent and whisked away the step before Reginald even had a chance to settle himself. He had half a mind to call him back and remind the scoundrel who it was who paid his salary, but the carriage had already lurched into motion.

He settled back onto the leather seat and closed his eyes. It was sour, the knowledge that he had never been enough for his father. But life was sour. The real problem was the reduction of the Twickenham estate. Given his father's fondness for Caroline, her portion would be substantial.

Which was most unfortunate, since Reginald had already pledged nearly the entire inheritance as security for his loans.

The carriage veered around a corner. Damn his driver, was the man drunk? Reginald raised his fist and pounded on the carriage roof.

"By God, watch your driving! Why aren't we there?" He pulled back the curtain and peered out at run-down buildings crowding a narrow, dirty street. Windows were cracked and boarded, and the few pedestrians out in the rain looked bent and ragged. Not a neighborhood he would wish to visit even by daylight, and certainly not a neighborhood they should be passing through on the way to his town house in Grosvenor Square.

A needle of fear pricked him and he wrenched on the door handle. The door was fixed shut from the outside.

"Stop at once!"

In response, the driver whipped up the horses, sending the carriage careening through the back alleys of London. One wheel went up over the curbstone, jolting Reginald to the floor. He braced himself against the corner and kicked repeatedly at the door, splintering the wood beneath the fine-tooled leather, but it would not give. The coach slowed, then halted as he gave one last kick, sending the door flying open.

"Well, well. Look who's being a feisty lad." Figures loomed in the opening, one holding a lantern. The light showed a blunt-nosed man wearing an unfriendly smile and a garish green waistcoat. "Lord Huntington, I presume."

Reginald slowly sat upright, taking in the menacing faces, the yellow-wheeled cab parked behind them. Fear laid a clammy hand on the back of his neck. He swallowed and made a show of straightening his clothing. "You are mistaken. The name is Crawford. Anthony Crawford."

The man raised the lantern. "Crawford, is it. Well, Mr. Crawford, why would you be riding in Reginald Huntington's carriage in the wee hours?" He turned and spoke to the driver. "This is Huntington's carriage, isn't it?"

"Aye, the driver said so hisself before I knocked him down and took his clothes."

"If that is the case," Reginald said, "then I must have entered the wrong carriage by mistake."

"Did you? Well then Mr. *Crawford,* it's a bigger mistake than you know. Our employer told us to deliver a message to the occupant of this carriage," said the man with the lantern.

"What message is that?"

"Come out here and we'll tell you."

Reginald backed against the seats. "I think not." He kept his voice steady. "The weather outside is positively dreadful. Besides, I am tired and drunk, and unlikely to remember much of your message. Perhaps you can call on me at a more propitious time."

"Perhaps you can stop your yammering." The man turned to one of his companions. "His lordship wants us to call on him another time. Jenks, are you free for Tuesday Tea with Lord Reginald?"

"I'll have to check me datebook. No, no, I've a luncheon with the Queen on Tuesday." The laugh that followed sent an unpleasant shiver up Reginald's spine.

"Well then." The blunt-nosed man slammed his fist into his open palm. "We'll have to deliver our message as scheduled."

The lunge through the carriage door came an instant sooner than Reginald expected. He twisted aside, but hard hands yanked him from the coach.

"Here now." The man called Jenks fetched him up against the wheel. "Glad you decided to join us, yer lordship."

The other men snickered, and Reginald ceased struggling. The odds were so far out of his favor that it was belittling to even try. "Very well. Say your piece."

"Oh, our message ain't in words." Jenks plowed his fist into Reginald's midsection. He doubled over, breathless, as blows rained down. He covered his head and dodged as he could, but soon enough ended up on the ground, a warm trickle of blood scoring down his cheek.

"Tsk, tsk," Blunt-Nose said. "Seems you've ruined a fancy set of clothes. Hard to get bloodstains out of fine linen, I hear." He bent and grinned into Reginald's face. "Now listen. Our employer has heard some disturbing news about your inheritance. Seeing as you owe him a fair bit, he wanted to make sure you understood how serious he views the situation."

Reginald wiped his mouth and stared straight into the man's muddy brown eyes. "I assure you, whatever rumors your employer has heard are unfounded. You may tell him I will see to the matter."

"That's what the boss is afraid of, seeing how last time you said *that* you went chasing off to Africa. That's not going to happen again."

"Let me take care of it."

The other man turned his head and spat on the ground. "You'd better be quick about it. Our employer ain't going to wait for you to muddle things this time. He's sending someone to handle it, ain't it so Simms?" He tipped his head to Blunt-Nose.

The man smiled. There was no mirth in the expression.

"Time for a bit of game hunting, I think. I hear those Mediterranean islands hold plenty of good sport."

Reginald lifted himself off the unswept cobbles. "What are you saying?"

Simms gave him an unpleasant grin. "Only that it might not be healthy for your cousin to come between the boss and his interests. And it might not be healthy for you to let that happen—if you get my drift." His booted foot caught Reginald squarely in the ribs. As he gasped for air, the other men hauled him up and flung him back into the carriage, which set immediately into motion.

He lay on the floor gasping as the vehicle jolted over the cobbles. They could not threaten him like this—him or his family. Much as he disliked his cousin, she was *his* cousin, to deal with on his own. There had to be some way to stop Caroline's adoption. He had to find a way. His life depended on it.

The carriage halted again and Reginald braced himself for another encounter, but there was only the shifting weight as his driver dismounted, followed by the sound of running footsteps fading into the night.

Crete, March 1848

Caroline lay quietly, trying to will away the aching in her head. She should be feeling far stronger. Maggie needed her, and right now she was hardly able to sit up. One thing was certain, though: no matter how weak she might actually feel, she could not reveal it to Mr. Trentham. If he thought her unfit to travel to the village today, she would become his captive. She could not afford his interference. Once she and Maggie reached Malta she would rest, but not before.

Besides, being here was not truly restful. She was too aware of his presence—his footsteps as he crossed the front room. Even now she could tell he was coming to the bedroom. A quick knock at the door, and he entered. His dark hair curled over his collar and his simple shirt was open at the neck. She tried not to stare at the tanned skin revealed there. Did the man not own a cravat?

"Manolis will arrive soon." He strode to the wardrobe and gathered her clothing. "We'll have you convalescing in your rooms at the villa before suppertime."

Convalescing. She hated that word. But now that she was about to leave she did owe him her gratitude.

"Mr. Trentham." She lifted her eyes to his. "Thank you. I know I have been a burden, and I shan't forget your kindness. You are a skilled physician."

He looked away. "I did very little. Thank Legault. I would have sent you away."

"All the same, you did care for me. I know your presence here will be of great benefit to the people of the village. I have always thought England should produce more doctors and send them out to teach and heal. Like you. Imagine the benefit to the people of this village if it had a clinic with you at its head." She smiled.

Heavens, she was starting to sound like Maggie. First, a boarding school in London, now she was converting doctors with a missionary-like zeal. She glanced up at him and her smile wilted at the harsh look on his face.

"I am no longer a doctor, Miss Huntington." His voice was tight. "This village needs no clinic because it has no physician. You are the last person I shall treat."

Caroline returned his frown. "What? You will turn away those in need? If that is your attitude, then perhaps the villagers should expand the cemetery. They will no doubt need the extra room." It was difficult to fathom how a man with his obvious skills could retreat here and do nothing. "Why are you here on Crete, Mr. Trentham, if not to help?" She did not understand him at all.

He laid her dress and crinoline on the bed. "There was no

doctor here before I came, and there will be none after I am gone. I thank you to not rest the weight of the world on my shoulders, Miss Huntington."

Something in his tone, some underlying shadow, made her hold her tongue when she normally would have pursued the argument. This man carried a burden; she could feel it, though she had no idea what it possibly could be, or why he would feel compelled to carry it all the way to Crete.

Finally he cleared his throat. "I apologize that there is no woman to help you dress. Madame Legault will not be accompanying Manolis, as we need to keep the cart as light as possible for the journey down."

"You mean to say *you* will be helping me dress?"

"Would you prefer to wait for Manolis instead?"

"I think not! I can do it myself." Caroline lifted her chin. "You are an unmarried man—it's beyond proper. Just help me to my feet, Mr. Trentham."

"You're not—"

"Please." She looked directly into his dark blue eyes. He stared back and she could hear her own heartbeat thudding. "If I cannot, I will call for you. I promise."

He studied her face for a long moment, some turmoil behind his eyes, as if he was inwardly debating with himself. Finally he nodded. "You will let me know immediately if you need aid."

"Yes. I trust you'll be waiting outside the door again, ready to spring to my rescue."

"I am not your knight errant, Miss Huntington. Call for help before collapsing this time."

He slipped his arm behind her. Caroline took a breath and swung her legs over the side of the bed. The world started spinning, but she bit her lip, determined. She was grateful to have his arm bracing her, strong and steady.

There, she was on her feet! She gave him a weak grin.

He did not smile back. His gaze was fixed on her, serious and intent. "Any dizziness? Can you stand alone?"

"I'm well," she lied.

He carefully withdrew his support. "Then I will leave you to dress."

She took a steadying breath as the door closed behind him, then reached for her crinoline. It was easier to pull on this time, though the fabric bunched about her hips and would not lie straight. One-armed, there was little she could do about it—and the dress would cover it anyway. It was tricky trying to keep her balance, hampered by the bulky petticoat as she lifted first one leg then the other to step through the skirt of her russet riding habit. She had to stop and swallow furiously midway through but kept the sickness at bay—just.

"Miss Huntington? Are you still well?"

"Um. Yes, quite all right," she called back. "I just need another moment or two." She had to get her good arm through the dratted sleeve, and it was like trying to catch a fish barehanded. There. Her left arm slid through and she shrugged the dress up to her shoulder. Oh dear. Caroline drew the fabric around her other arm. There was no way it would fit through the sleeve, not in the sling, but perhaps the dress would fasten closed around it. Ah, the dratted buttons. There was no way to do them up without help.

"Mr. Trentham?"

He was through the door and beside her in an instant, hand at her elbow. "Good. Still on your feet, I see."

"I make it a habit not to collapse more than once a week. However, I do need assistance with my buttons. Would you?" She presented him with her back.

He was silent for a long moment and she could feel a flush come to her cheeks. The dress was barely covering her, one shoulder completely bare, the thin cotton of her chemise doing not a thing to make her feel less vulnerable. It was quite immodest, but what choice did she have?

She felt him take hold of the fabric and pull gently. Her

injured arm was trapped uncomfortably against her side and she froze, anticipating pain. He stopped.

"I need to make some alterations," he said. "Stand still."

Perhaps it was the command in his voice or the absurd nature of the situation, but she trembled a little and obeyed.

He slipped the shoulder of her dress off and Caroline clutched the neck of the bodice just as it began to slide down. "Ah . . . what are you doing?"

"Fixing your dress." He took the empty sleeve in his hands and tore, ripping it free of the bodice.

She stared at him for a shocked moment before finding her voice. "Sir! You've ruined a perfectly good dress!"

"You have ruined a perfectly good arm." His face was stern, but she thought she glimpsed the barest light of humor in his eyes. He dropped the sleeve to the floor, then turned his gaze on her, studying her form.

Heat scalded her face.

"One more adjustment, I think." His hands skimmed her side and took hold of the dress. Caroline held her breath at the sound of tearing cloth as he ripped the seam open. "That should do," he said.

"I would think so." She felt quite unsteady. "You owe me a new riding habit." Imagine, him tearing her dress to pieces while she was still in it!

He eased her sling through the rent he had made, then turned her and drew the dress closed. "There. Not the height of fashion, but serviceable enough." His fingers worked deftly up her back and he brushed her hair away from her nape to do up the final buttons. The touch of his hands left a fleeting warmth.

Caroline glanced in the mirror mounted on the wardrobe door, noting the pinkness in her cheeks. "My dress looks like it has been mangled by wild beasts, and my hair . . ." It was a fright, cascading loose and untamed over her shoulders. She swayed.

He slipped one arm around her waist to steady her, then guided her back to the bed. "Sit."

Caroline tried not to cling to him as she lowered herself, but the edges of her vision were beginning to blur.

"I'm not certain we should attempt to move you." His breath ruffled her hair. "You are still too weak."

She stiffened. "I can hardly remain here." Not alone with him. And certainly not if she and Maggie were to make the boat to Malta.

He studied her for a long moment, the shadows returning to his eyes. "Very well. Let's see what I can do about your hair."

The right side of her head was tender, but he was gentle as he combed. She sat motionless under his touch as he plaited the strands and tied off the braid.

"There. You look quite the thing, Miss Huntington."

"For a beggar's ball, perhaps. You seem to have missed your calling as a lady's maid."

"It's good to know I have a profession to fall back on, should I ever require one." He helped her recline against the pillows. "Conserve your strength. You'll need it for the journey down."

She must have slept, for it seemed moments later that Mr. Trentham returned, though the sun was slanting through the bedroom window in the way of afternoon light.

He offered his arm. "Manolis is here. Let's get you to the cart."

Caroline rose, glad for his support as the room teetered, then righted itself. A few careful steps and she was across the bedroom threshold. The room beyond was a confused blur of rustic furniture and a brightly colored rug. All her attention was focused on the simple act of moving one foot, then the other, of keeping her balance while the floor slanted beneath her.

"Oh!" She lurched forward and the world tilted crazily.

Mr. Trentham's arms instantly came around her, steadying her. No longer in imminent danger of falling, she closed her eyes and leaned against him, trying to absorb some of his strength.

"Almost there," he said. "A few more steps."

The cart was waiting, the back filled with bedding. He eased her in, considered for a moment, and frowned. "I'll fetch more blankets. I want you as cushioned as possible."

"I am not such a fragile parcel," she began, but he had already turned and gone. And she had to admit she did feel rather breakable.

"There is no telling the *iatros* what he can and cannot do," the cart driver said from his perch on the bench.

"What does it mean? *Iatros?*"

"Mm . . . one who cures others. I do not know your word for it."

"Doctor," Caroline supplied. "Although it seems he does not care to be called that. I wonder why." The more she felt returned to herself, the more curious she became about the mysterious Mr. Trentham.

He returned, arms laden again with cushions and blankets. "There. The best we can do." He braced the pillows around her and rolled the blankets to support her arm. "Try to keep from moving."

"Perhaps you could have found a better-sprung cart."

"This *is* the better-sprung cart." He nodded at the driver.

"I have the best cart on the entire coast," Manolis said. "It hauls only the finest olives and fish." He sent her a wide grin. "Hold on, little fish. We go now." With a lurch, the cart began moving down the narrow track.

Caroline braced her feet against the weathered backboard. Her legs would be tired by the time they arrived, but she felt secure. If only the dizziness would not rise every time they bounced over a stone.

The driver turned to look back at her. "She is well, *iatros,*" he called.

"Good. I'll be right behind you."

At first it was quite bearable. The slanting sun felt warm and lazy on her limbs, and the gentle rocking of the cart lulled Caroline into a half doze. The nearby hills folded down to the sea, and Mr. Trentham rode his rangy brown horse behind the cart. He was a splendid rider, she noted, watching him guide his mount one-handed down the rough track. He did not sit his horse so much as become part of it. In her sleepy eyes the figure became a centaur, the torso of a man, the body of a horse, following along a track that skirted the cliff's edge and the bright sea.

A jolt roused her, the flash of pain making her cry out. They were descending steeply and the track had become much rockier. Caroline grit her teeth as the wheel jarred again.

"How are you holding up, Miss Huntington?" Mr. Trentham had guided his mount beside the cart and was watching her intently.

She forced a smile. "Splendidly. How much longer?"

"Another mile." He urged his horse forward and bent to speak to the driver. Caroline squeezed her eyes closed, concentrating on simply breathing, trying to block out the spinning sky, the roaring in her ears. The cart moved more slowly now, rocking and tilting like a boat in rough seas. The ride would never end—she was sure of it.

The cart was rounding a curve when suddenly it canted sideways. She heard the sharp crack of wood splintering, and the world skewed. The blackness in her head turned to a sickening maelstrom and she shrieked as the bedding slid around her, carrying her in a landslide of fabric until she fetched up hard against the side of the cart. Mr. Trentham was shouting but his voice grew more and more distant until everything went blessedly quiet.

"Miss Huntington?" His voice sounded worried.

She opened her eyes. She was lying on the ground beside the tipped vehicle and his face hovered just above hers, mouth tight. She blinked, trying to focus on his blurred features. Velvety blackness trailed around her senses—warm and dark and comforting. *Just let go,* it urged. *Retreat from the pain.*

"Damn it, Miss Huntington!" His hands cupped her face. "I don't need you unconscious."

Her eyelids fluttered open and she dredged up the strength to speak. "Caroline. If you are going to swear at me, then call me Caroline."

"Good girl." The lines bracketing his mouth eased.

"I'm not a girl." It was the best she could manage, but already she could feel the lovely soft darkness retreating. "Oh, but I feel sick. . . ."

He lifted her to her knees and supported her, while Manolis came quickly with a jug of water. Dear heavens, she was shaking so badly she could scarcely manage a sip. It would have been dreadfully humiliating had she the energy for such emotions.

"There now." Mr. Trentham held her gently. Below, the blue eye of the Mediterranean winked boldly under the sun. She let her head fall against his shoulder. It was enough just to breathe in his embrace. A tiny sigh escaped her.

"Just a little farther." Gathering her closely against him, he stood, bearing her in his arms.

She let out a small breath, but he did not seem uncomfortable holding her so. It was not worth protesting, so she slipped her left hand around his shoulder and held on.

Manolis had unhitched his mule from the cart and was fastening splintered pieces of wooden wheel across the animal's back.

"Oh," she said. "Is that what happened—did the cart break?"

"Yes, the wheel." Mr. Trentham's voice thrummed against her.

Manolis checked the burden and nodded. "I will meet you in the village, *iatros.* The steps are too steep for my mule." He gave them a wave and set off down the track.

"Is he abandoning us?"

"Hardly. The village lies just below, but the cart track circles all the way around. There are steps cut into the cliff, leading directly down. I'll carry you."

"Carry me? The whole way?" She swallowed.

"Never fear, Miss Huntington. I promise not to drop you into the sea. Now, hold tight."

She took a deep breath, hoping it would make her lighter. He strode out confidently, the slight hitch in his walk barely noticeable.

"Better?" His breath brushed her cheek.

"Yes." Anything was better than being joggled about in the cart again, and there was something rather pleasant about being held in his arms.

Caroline tried to ignore the pressure in her head and concentrate instead on the unaccustomed sensation of being carried: the splay of his hand across her ribcage, the strong arm supporting her legs, the warm breadth of the chest she lay against. He moved nimbly, navigating the uneven steps cut into the stone and obviously taking care to jolt her as little as possible. Halfway down he paused. The afternoon sunlight reflected off the water and warmed the whitewashed buildings of the village below. She glanced up into his face, noting the set of his jaw, the drop of perspiration trailing down his lean cheek.

"We could rest. . . ."

"Almost there." Though his breathing had deepened, he spoke without apparent strain. "Think of your nice, soft bed."

The steps widened and gentled as they entered the village. A few men greeted the doctor casually, as if he carried injured Englishwomen through the village on a regular basis.

"Put me down. I can walk from here." The Villa Thessalo lay just ahead, a pleasant, foursquare building with pots of riotous red geraniums gracing the entry.

He did not comply, only went up the steps, pushed open the door, and carried her inside. The dim coolness soothed her heated face.

“Mr. Trentham—”

“Hush.” He tightened his hold on her and mounted the treads without faltering.

“There you are!” Maggie hurried into the hall and flung open the door to Caroline’s rooms. She did not seem to think it odd that Mr. Trentham was carrying his patient. “The bed is just there. Let me fetch some water.”

He lowered her and Caroline uncurled her fingers from around his neck.

“Thank you,” she said softly, meaning it with all her heart. His attention and concern, the absurd way he had carried her down the cliffs—it was not something she was accustomed to, but it was a great kindness.

“The pleasure was mine.” And to her surprise, he smiled.

The expression nearly stole her breath. Mr. Trentham’s smile was dazzling.

It was a good thing he so rarely smiled.

Chapter 5

Alex climbed back up the cliff steps, wishing the brisk evening breeze could carry away his thoughts, sweep away the feeling of Caroline Huntington's body printed against his. A useless hope. Nothing short of a wild *souroko* wind would be able to scour that sweet sensation from him—and part of him was glad.

A wicked part of himself, one that yearned for something he could never have, that had welcomed the opportunity to touch her. She was a beauty, headstrong and spirited even in her present condition. Thank God she was out of his house. Not that he didn't trust himself to behave as he ought—as a gentleman should—but spending time in her company was going to prove increasingly difficult.

He would need to tend her for several weeks yet, and he was already struggling to maintain his professional façade. It felt like little more than a thin veneer over his more turbulent self. He was half tempted to let her go through with the scheme he suspected she had brewing . . . but no. Selfish desires aside, it could do her irreparable harm if she traveled again so soon. His mind and body would have to make their peace—at least until Miss Huntington had left the island for good.

He untied Icarus from the thin olive tree that had sheltered the horse through the afternoon. "Good lad. We'll get you home, and a handful of oats as thanks for waiting."

The horse nudged him with his wide, soft muzzle, and Alex swung up into the saddle. He had no doubt sleep would evade him even more than usual this night, chased away by the memory of Miss Huntington nestled in his arms. Body pulsing, he bent low and urged his mount into a canter.

"Caroline? Are you awake?" Maggie's voice was low, her footsteps soft as she moved about the room.

"Good morning." Caroline levered herself up with her good arm, blinking away the last wisps of dreaming. Her head still hurt, despite the full night's sleep. She had almost forgotten what it was like not to ache. Heavens, her body was taking its own sweet time. She hated to think Mr. Trentham had been right. Not that she had the luxury to remain an invalid, even had she felt the inclination. The boat for Malta departed tomorrow and, sick or well, she would accompany Maggie aboard. She could do nothing less for her friend.

"Have you begun to pack?"

"Not yet," Maggie said. "Dr. Trentham was by earlier and said he would come back when you were awake. After yesterday he is quite set against you exerting yourself. If he saw our trunks out, well . . . No need to let him know our plans."

She went to open the shutters and Caroline blinked against the sudden brightness. White and blue. A perfect Mediterranean day, full of clear dry light and the scent of curing olives. On the small balcony bright geraniums stared boldly back at the sun and a light breeze riffled the surface of the bay beyond. She scooted herself up a bit more, closing her eyes as the room tilted then steadied.

Maggie sent her a worried glance. "Are you truly feeling well enough to travel? I'd hate to jeopardize your health for the sake of my mission."

"A temporary light-headedness, that's all." She hoped the smile she gave Maggie was reassuring.

Her friend pushed her spectacles up her nose, seeming less convinced than Caroline would like. "At any rate, the doctor said you should try to eat." She took up a tray and brought it to the bedside. "It's some of the local delicacies. Figs and honey-sweetened yogurt, and this lovely bread, spinach pie, olives, and black tea." Maggie frowned down at the tray. "It's hardly the type of food an invalid needs, but there was no porridge to be found."

"It smells delicious—much better than porridge. If I can't explore Crete, at least I can taste it." Caroline took up a piece of bread.

Maggie watched her, a frown creased between her brows. "You do seem pale. Perhaps I can change the meeting—"

"You are starting to sound like *him.*" She could not help the touch of exasperation in her voice. "And you can't change the meeting—you know better than I how difficult it was to arrange. The Governor of Valletta will not think better of your project if we do not appear on time." She took a bit more bread and softened her voice. "I am a trifle worse for the wear and limited to one hand, perhaps, but I will manage—there is simply no other option."

Her friend's expression remained serious. "Doctor Trentham is concerned for you—as much as I have been. And he is a doctor of some skill. Perhaps we should listen to him."

"Maggie . . ." She paused at the sound of voices outside the window. Mr. Trentham's low, strong tone was unmistakable. "Oh! He's here." She pinched her cheeks to raise a healthy color. "Put another pillow behind me, if you will."

A minute later he knocked and Maggie opened the door.

"Good morning." Mr. Trentham strode into the room, bringing the sage-laden scent of the hills with him. He went to Caroline and fixed her with the intent look that was becoming so familiar.

"Miss Huntington, I'm glad to see you appear somewhat rested despite the knocking about you took yesterday. Travel can be hazardous—especially to someone still recovering." He bent and gazed into her eyes, his fingers gently exploring the side of her head.

Caroline fixed her thoughts on feeling well, trying to ignore the fluttering in her stomach. He placed a hand on her forehead, his palm warm and slightly rough.

"Hmm. You do not seem feverish, nor chilled." He turned to her friend. "Has she eaten?"

"Yes, doctor, with some appetite."

Caroline blushed. Maggie made it sound as though she had licked the plate clean.

"Good." He returned his attention to her. "I know you think you cannot miss the boat to Malta, but after yesterday you should see how little able you are to make that journey."

"Mr. Trentham—"

He held up one hand. "There is another solution. I'm surprised you and Mrs. Farnsworth haven't thought of it."

"Oh?" She lifted her brows. "What is that?"

"Mrs. Farnsworth can continue on while you stay here and recuperate. When she is finished pleading for the orphans of Valletta, she can return and collect you."

Caroline blinked. "But I . . . She needs me. Don't you, Maggie?" She sent her friend a glance. Left here, under Mr. Trentham's care? It was a disturbing thought.

"She doesn't need you as much as you need to heal." His voice was inflexible.

Maggie stepped forward, a considering look in her eyes. "The idea certainly has merit."

It certainly did *not.* Caroline swallowed. In any case, the argument was moot. They would both be on the ship tomorrow and be done with Crete and Mr. Trentham forever. The thought sent a twinge through her, a fleeting sense of something lost. Still, she would not let Maggie leave without her. Although the safety of their plan lay in convincing him otherwise. They would only need to pretend to agree with his idea.

Caroline widened her eyes at Maggie. "Mr. Trentham is right." She silently urged her friend to play along. "It is your project after all, and while I came along to assist, you will do a splendid job without me."

Which was, in fact, nothing but the truth. Maggie was a considerable force—articulate and formidable when it came to championing her charitable missions. She had helped Caroline a great deal with her boarding-school project in London. All the more reason why, aching head notwithstanding, it was only right that Caroline return the favor. No matter what she told the erstwhile doctor.

Maggie pressed her lips together. "Very well."

Mr. Trentham looked taken aback. Clearly he had not expected them to agree so readily. Caroline hoped he had not noticed how unconvinced her friend had sounded. She smiled sweetly at him. "If we have no choice, then we can only make the best of it."

"Well," he said, recovering with surprising grace, "I'm glad you're seeing sense at last." His deep blue gaze rested on her. "Now that that's settled, it's time to meet your new companion."

The room went utterly silent.

Caroline felt her eyes widen in shock. "My new *what?*"

"Miss Huntington, credit me with a shred of sense. You cannot stay here unchaperoned. With Mrs. Farnsworth leaving, you'll need someone to care for you, provide company, and assist you. You don't expect *me* to sit at your bedside and take dictation, do you?"

Caroline bit her lip. "You've considered all the details, haven't you?" How very vexing of him. It would be that much more difficult to slip away tomorrow if she had to contend with a chaperone.

He turned and strode to the door. "Pen," he called, "you may come in now."

A young woman stepped into the room. Her face was downcast and partially hidden by an old bonnet that had been exposed to too much weather. A lock of blond hair had escaped its confines. She wore scuffed high-laced boots and her dress was patched and seasons out of fashion, not to mention too short at both the hemline and sleeves.

"Miss Briggs," Mr. Trentham said, "allow me to introduce Mrs. Farnsworth, and her friend, Miss Huntington. No doubt Madame Legault has told you something of her."

"Hello," Caroline said. This little sparrow of a girl seemed half inclined to take flight at any moment.

Miss Briggs looked up, and Caroline revised her estimation of the girl's age upward. Though she looked thin and fragile, Miss Briggs was not a child, but a young lady.

"Pleased to make your acquaintance," Miss Briggs said. Her deep brown eyes were a curious contrast to her pale hair and complexion. She hesitated, then plunged ahead. "I hope . . . that is, it is very kind of you to allow me to assist you. I will do my best for you, I promise." The words came out in a rush.

"Of course you will." Caroline felt a pang. It would be difficult for Miss Briggs to do her best when she would not be there.

"I hope so." The girl twisted her fingers together. "I want to do a good job for you. I can take dictation, and, um, have a splendid hand, as my father . . ." She halted, her gaze focused downward once again.

Caroline shot a glance at Mr. Trentham, unsure if she should ask further. He shook his head infinitesimally and stepped forward to take Miss Briggs's arm.

"I'm sure the two of you will be a comfort to each other. Thank you for coming to meet Miss Huntington, Pen. You can take up your duties tomorrow."

"Yes," Caroline said. "Tomorrow afternoon." Guilt twisted inside her as the girl's brown eyes sought hers for reassurance. How would this fragile miss feel when she came to the room only to find it empty? She seemed so trusting, it felt wrong to make promises Caroline did not intend to keep. Miss Briggs dropped a curtsey before allowing Mr. Trentham to show her out.

Caroline looked to Maggie, but before they could speak the doctor returned. His dark hair was ruffled as though he had just run his hands through it.

"Explain, if you please," Caroline said. "What was that about her father? Miss Briggs seemed on the verge of tears when she spoke of him."

He let out a slow breath and shook his head. "Tragic. He's a talented scholar of ancient languages, Greek especially. Came out to do translations for Legault, and brought Pen with him. Unfortunately, the fellow is also a drunk and a cad. He left Crete—abandoned her with the Legaults in order to pursue a Sicilian woman of extremely poor reputation."

"The poor dear," Maggie said. "How long ago?"

"Four months."

"Four months!" Caroline said. "And he has not returned in that time?"

"No." His mouth was tight. "Nor sent word. The Legaults have done what they can, but they are busy with the excavation."

Sympathy squeezed Caroline's chest. "Was there no one to come help? To take her home?"

"Apparently not. We offered to pay her passage back to England, but Pen said she did not know where she would go. Madame and her husband are planning to take her with them to Paris once the excavating season here ends, but that will not be for some months yet."

Nowhere to go. Caroline could only imagine how difficult it must be for Miss Briggs, stranded on Crete, abandoned by her father. A place must be found for the girl in England. She frowned.

The thought that she, too, would be abandoning Miss Briggs on the morrow cast a shadow across her heart.

* * *

In the early dawn light Caroline sat up and carefully swung her legs over the edge of her bed. Only a touch of dizziness marred her balance. Her elbow ached, but it was well splinted. She rose to her feet and smiled in triumph. Mr. Trentham had underestimated her. Unfit for travel, indeed. And Miss Briggs . . . well, Caroline had asked Maggie to pen a letter promising to send for her. It was all they could do for the girl at present.

She had begun piling dresses on the divan, one-handed, when Maggie came in.

"Caroline! You ought to have waited for me."

"Don't fret, Maggie. Can you reach that hatbox? It keeps eluding me."

Her friend gave her a worried look. "Do reconsider. I think Mr. Trentham's plan is a good one."

"I can hardly let you go off without me. I feel perfectly well, and if I stay here I'll go out of my head with boredom."

Lips closed tight, clearly refraining from further argument, Maggie fetched the box and helped stow the few hats from the wardrobe.

"There, those are the last of my things," Caroline said. "Are you ready?" The question was rhetorical; no doubt Maggie had been up since well before dawn, each item of clothing neatly folded and stacked within her valise.

"Of course. Why don't you rest a moment while I go see about our conveyance down the coast." Lamplight flashed off her spectacles. "Are you certain you feel well enough to travel? I still think—"

"I feel quite able." Her voice did not falter on the lie. If Maggie knew, well, Caroline would not make her friend choose. She had the uncomfortable thought that Maggie might indeed abandon her here if forced to make a decision. The woman's projects came first, as indeed they should. Still, it was imperative that they leave as quickly as possible. She did not think that Mr. Trentham or Miss Briggs would come calling until the afternoon, but it was best not to take chances.

As soon as her friend departed, Caroline unlocked her knees and sank back onto the bed. It had taken increasing effort not to show how soon she had tired. She closed her eyes, but that only increased the slow spinning darkness in her head. Drat it. Maggie did not need to know that once the first surge of determination had worn off she had begun to feel unsteady.

It was some time before she heard her friend's crisp footsteps returning, and Caroline was grateful for the extra chance to rest. She sat back up and assumed an expression of cheery determination. The look on Maggie's face as she entered the room, however, did not bode well. The crease between her brows had deepened and she was frowning.

"What is it?" Caroline asked, uneasiness running through her.

"It's quite vexing. I have been informed there are no vehicles for hire anywhere in the village! The arrangements I made yesterday afternoon seem to have unraveled."

"Dear heavens, how could that be? What about horses?" She tried not to think what a few hours on horseback would do to her already throbbing headache.

Maggie shook her head.

"Mules? Wheelbarrows?" Caroline heard her voice rising. "Manolis and his cart?"

Her friend pressed her lips together. "I tried everyone, Caroline. They all refused. And the old cart driver was nowhere to be found."

"How utterly troublesome!" She rose to her feet, irritation lending her energy. "We *must* make the boat, and we cannot walk all the way down the coast. Surely someone—"

"No one will." The deep masculine voice sounded more than a little annoyed.

Caroline whirled, hand at her breast, then swayed as her senses teetered. "Mr. Trentham! I beg your pardon, don't you ever knock?"

He strode into the room and halted. Arms crossed, he surveyed the stack of luggage with a look on his face that made her shiver.

"Mr. Trentham, I—"

"No need to explain. What you are doing is beyond obvious. I suspected as much with you two twittering conspiratorially." He paced forward to stand directly before her, his displeasure a palpable heaviness in the air. "Sit down, Miss Huntington, before you fall down. Much as I might like the thought of having your troublesome self gone from here, my conscience cannot allow it."

Caroline lowered herself back onto the bed and willed her legs to stop trembling. Part of her knew he was right—her head was spinning terribly again—but it burned to admit defeat. It was too humiliating, to be caught trying to escape, to be the focus of those storm-darkened blue eyes. She took a wavering breath.

"Mrs. Farnsworth." He nodded to where Maggie stood, holding the hatbox in front of her like a shield. "Assist Miss Huntington back under the covers. I will be driving you—without your companion—to catch the boat to Malta. See that you have everything you need." He turned on his heel and left, the uneven reproach of his footsteps echoing down the hall.

"Well." The air in the room was growing more breathable. Caroline gave her friend a tremulous smile. "You don't suppose I could stow away in your trunk and put pillows in the bed instead? No, Mr. Trentham would notice it was bolsters under the covers, and not me."

"Oh, Caroline." Maggie helped her lie back. "You have not been forthright about your condition. Truly this is for the best. I would never be able to forgive myself if I had spirited you away to your harm." She took Caroline's hand and held it between her own hands. "Your support means a great deal to me. I will be able to feel it when I speak for the children and the orphanage. But you must promise to follow the doctor's orders, or I shall be forced to stay here to see that his instructions are carried out myself."

Caroline blinked, then could not help smiling at the determined look on Maggie's face. "If you are as convincing with the Governor of Malta, I've no doubt you will have a school approved and built within a fortnight."

Her friend squeezed her hand. "Everything will turn out for the best. I will be back before you know it. And you will do well for Miss Briggs, if I know you. I believe a divine hand guides us, Caroline. Consider that you may be here for a purpose."

Caroline felt a wry bubble of humor rise. "Perhaps my purpose here is to torment Mr. Trentham."

Maggie gave her a smile bright with relief. "If so, you seem to be succeeding marvelously."

"You do indeed," Mr. Trentham said, entering the room with Miss Briggs in tow. He nodded at the girl. "I'll leave you two to get acquainted. I trust Mrs. Farnsworth is ready to leave?"

"Yes," Maggie said. "Take care of yourself, Caroline. I will see you soon."

Caroline met her friend's eyes. "Do write, please."

"Of course." Maggie marched to the door, then paused. "And you—concentrate on getting well."

"I will. Safe travels." Caroline tried to keep her tone cheerful, despite the emptiness opening up inside her. Being left behind was always the most difficult thing.

She listened to the tap of her friend's heels down the stairs, the sound of voices, the jangle of bridle and creak of wood. She hoped Mr. Trentham had come up with some better form of transport than Manolis's old cart. The port of Agia Galini was three hour's travel down the coast. Three hours, and then Maggie's feet would leave Crete's shores, while she was forced to stay. Though she had to admit, it was her own foolish fault.

Miss Briggs had gone to the window. She waved once, then turned back to Caroline. "They're off. Mr. Trentham is sending Pavlos and Eleni with her to Malta."

"Who?" She fastened on the distraction.

"Brother and sister. Twins, actually. They've recently been complaining the village is too small, so, um, Mr. Trentham arranged for them to accompany your friend." Miss Briggs ducked her head and removed her hideous bonnet.

Caroline drew her gaze from the window and studied her new companion. Another welcome distraction. She had not been left entirely alone, after all. Miss Briggs was here, and Mr. Trentham had made it clear he was not going to neglect her. The knowledge cheered her, more than it ought.

"Let me fetch you some water, Miss Huntington." Miss Briggs poured a glass from the blue ceramic pitcher on the table and brought it to Caroline.

"Thank you." Truly, if anyone had the right to feel lost and alone it was Miss Briggs, abandoned here so far from home. It made Caroline's own problems dwindle nearly to insignificance. Maggie would return for her, and it was not as if she were cut off from her own family, her home. As soon as she recovered she would be free to leave. Caroline drew in a deep breath and released it, letting some of her own disappointment go.

"Please sit, Miss Briggs. Tell me something of yourself."

The girl perched on the edge of the chair beside the bed, hands clasped tightly in her lap. "I, ah, I don't know what to say. To tell. About myself."

Caroline gave her an encouraging nod. "You are from London?"

"Yes." The girl fell silent.

"Well, that's good. So am I." She did not want to press, at least not quite so early in their acquaintanceship. It seemed Miss Briggs had come from difficult circumstances. "Tell me about your education." There was a trace of lower-class accent in the girl's voice, but nothing pronounced.

Miss Briggs glanced up, a bit more animation touching her face. "My mother was a governess and, um, she made sure I had proper schooling. Although my ancient languages are not very good."

"Nor are mine! Thank heavens we don't have to converse in Latin. Although I'm sure the local dialect is a challenge in itself."

The girl gave a self-deprecating shrug. "After some time it's understandable enough."

"It would appear I'll be here long enough to make a start at it. Although there are things on Crete I would rather do."

"Such as?" Interest glimmered in Miss Briggs's soft brown eyes.

"I wanted to come here because of the myths. I was hoping to see the cliffs Icarus flew from. Or visit the cave where Zeus was born, though it's doubtful I'll see it, now."

"I have visited it. Mr. Trentham took us there." Miss Briggs's voice dropped. "They say you can hear the ghosts of all those who have prayed to him sighing in the winds around the cave."

"Did you?"

She shook her head.

"It sounds wonderfully eerie." Caroline considered the girl a moment. "But how did you become acquainted with Mr. Trentham?"

"Monsieur Legault gives him the bones, from the dig. He puts the bits back together and tries to tell if the person was old or young, had injuries, and, um, perhaps how they died."

"Delightful." Caroline should have known he had such a morbid hobby. "Perhaps I should be worrying a bit more about being under his care."

"Oh, not at all." Miss Briggs gave her an earnest look. "He is very well thought of, even though he does keep himself aloof."

"I'm much relieved to hear it. I'd hate to think he was only waiting for me to expire to see how badly my arm is fractured."

That surprised a smile from her new companion, a lopsided grin featuring an engaging gap between her front teeth. "Oh, no. Mr. Trentham is very kind."

Not kind enough to escort Miss Briggs safely back to London, however. "At any rate, he has brought you to me. But please, call me Caroline. This situation"—she glanced wryly down at the covers—"hardly warrants formality."

"Then you must call me Pen." The girl ducked her head once more. "But you are tiring, and Mr. Trentham gave me instruction that you were to rest."

"No doubt. He probably tells his bones that, as well."

"I'll just keep my journal then, while you nap." Pen rose and fetched a battered book and pencil from the satchel she had brought, then sat at the table and began to write.

Caroline lay back against the pillows. "Pen, will you write some letters for me? Now that I am on Crete longer than anticipated, I must inform my uncle and brother immediately." And she would have to confess her injury, though she would make light of it. She was going to be fine, after all, and there was no sense in worrying them needlessly.

"Of course, miss, after you wake."

She closed her eyes and tried to think of home, but instead the image of Mr. Trentham came unbidden. The shadows in his dark blue eyes, his disheveled hair. The care he took with her, despite his obvious reluctance: the gentleness of his hands, the utter competence as he tended her.

She was far away from everyone she knew and loved, with Maggie growing ever more distant, yet somehow she did not feel afraid.

The sound of Pen's quiet humming followed her into sleep.

Chapter 6

London, April 1848

Reginald pushed open the door to his father's study. The old man was there, working at his desk. He glanced up and set his pen down as Reginald marched into the room.

"Father. I do believe there's something you've been meaning to tell me." He set his hands on his hips. "The little matter of the new *daughter* you intend to acquire."

Lord Denby sighed and removed his spectacles. "You have heard about the adoption plans, then. I am sorry I did not tell you sooner, but the petition process is a long one, and I wanted to be certain everything was in order first. I am not deliberately keeping secrets from you, you know."

The devil he wasn't. Reginald knew what his father thought of him, had seen the frown on the old man's face, which he had quickly hidden when Reginald had entered the room. Ever since his father had taken Caroline and her brother in he had felt it—the subtle message that he, Reginald, was lacking. At first he had fought against it, but it had become easier with time to just accept the fact, to become in actuality what his father had thought him. And in a way it was satisfying—he was fulfilling his father's expectations at last.

"I've never been enough for you, have I? Better to just

replace me with someone more biddable, someone more decent?" He sneered the words.

"Enough!" His father stood. "I am not considering adopting Caroline in order to replace you, Reginald. This is something I have been considering for months. She deserves to have a place, a full place, in our family."

"Yet she will take only *half* my inheritance. I suppose you want me to be grateful for that, and for giving me a sister."

"You are my heir, heir to an earldom. Nothing can diminish that! And if you do not consider her as a sister"—Lord Denby shook his head—"it is not for lack of opportunity. Both she and her brother have long treated me as more than simply their guardian. I intend to bring her formally into the family—where she belongs."

It was too damned much. "She belongs as a vicar's wife in some rustic hamlet! I can't believe you would throw over your own flesh and blood like this."

"You have never understood—"

"I understand perfectly." Reginald forced his hands to unclench. "You plan to adopt Caroline, whatever I may feel about it." Why couldn't his father just give the chit a dowry and marry her off? The man was too sentimental for his—or the family's—good. Certainly too sentimental for Reginald's good, as his recent violent encounter with his creditors had proved. He still felt a faint twinge in his ribs every time he drew breath.

"It is for the best. You will come to understand that in time, when the weight of the title rests on your shoulders." Lord Denby's lips tightened. "Meanwhile, I suggest you reconcile yourself to the idea."

Not bloody likely. He would have no shoulders for a title to rest on if something wasn't done to stop the adoption. But it was clear he was going to get no further here. He gave the old man a cold stare. "I see how it is. Good day . . . Father."

Back straight, he left the study. He had not thought he could change his father's mind, but some barely acknowledged part of him had hoped his feelings would influence the old man. Rubbish.

He collected his hat and cane from the butler and let the heavy doors of Twickenham House shut behind him. He would, as usual, have to rely upon his own devices. And if it ended up causing his father pain, well, he had brought it on himself by insisting upon such a foolish course of action.

"To my club," he directed his driver as he entered the coach, after first giving the man a hard stare to determine it was indeed *his* driver. The day was advanced enough that when he arrived there was a good chance he would find Viscount Keefe there. The man was predictable in his habits, and, luckily for Reginald, those habits seemed to be worsening.

He leaned back, propping one ankle across his knee. His father had been given his chance. Now it was Reginald's turn, and the plan he had concocted was brilliant, if he said so himself.

Once at the club he selected a table positioned just at the edge of the shadows, but close enough to the center of the room that he was still clearly visible. Wouldn't do to be too inconspicuous, not when he wanted Keefe to seek him out. Reginald had no doubts he would. A few judicious words dropped into the right ears assured the man would come to him.

It did not take long. He sipped his whiskey and watched as his target casually made his way over.

"I say, Huntington, may I join you?"

Reginald waved to the other chair. "Be my guest." He studied the tall, well-proportioned man taking a seat across from him. Viscount Keefe—golden, handsome, popular with the ladies, and possessed of a particular weakness.

The perfect tool.

Reginald signaled the waiter. "What are you drinking, Keefe?"

"The same, thanks." The viscount crossed his legs and affected to look nonchalant, but spoiled the effect by drumming his fingers lightly on the tabletop. "I've heard some interesting things about you recently."

"Interesting? In what way?" Reginald kept his voice bland.

"Well . . ." Keefe leaned forward. "Aside from some gossip about an opera dancer, word is you are about to embark on a very lucrative financial venture."

"Perhaps." He smiled inwardly. The rumors he had seeded had indeed reached the proper ears. The potential lure of easy money had done its part to pull Keefe in.

"Dash it all, Huntington, do you have to be so secretive? You know I consider you a friend."

He knew no such thing, but if Keefe wanted to imagine they were friends, so much the better. "Why so interested? Doesn't your family give you an ample allowance? I can't imagine you'd want to be involved in my little schemes."

Of course he knew full well the viscount was in nearly as much difficulty as he himself was, financially. It was not easy to maintain a certain lifestyle on what the older generation considered a proper allowance. Certainly his family provided for him, but Keefe's tastes had begun to far outstrip his income.

Due primarily to his secret vice. Opium. Opium of the quality and quantity the man seemed to crave was not cheap. Ultimately it would devour him. But not, Reginald hoped, before the wedding.

"I am interested, actually." The golden-haired man gave him a smile full of charm and bright, even teeth. "My income could stand to be fattened up a bit. And, frankly, a man likes some independence from the dictates of family."

Reginald nodded. "Family is one of the great curses of a man's life."

"Too true." Keefe knocked back the rest of his whiskey. "My dear papa, under pressure from Mother, is going to tie off the purse strings if I don't procure a mate this coming

Season. As if I had either the time or inclination to go chasing down a suitable chit. Blasted inconvenient."

Excellent news. Reginald concealed a smile behind his raised glass. "Dreadful news. Any prospects?"

"God, no. Though I need to start looking. There must be some well-heeled heiresses about. Can't put it off any longer. In fact, Papa has already cut back my incidentals a bit more than is comfortable."

Reginald set his glass down and leaned forward. "This may be our lucky day, Keefe. You need a suitable wife and income, and I know someone on the marriage mart whose value is about to rise. Significantly. Best of all, nobody else knows."

The viscount's green eyes sparked with interest. "Go on."

"Think of it, my friend. You can be first off the mark, wooing and winning the prize before the competition has even caught the scent."

"Who is she? You must introduce me immediately."

Reginald held up his hand. "If I tell you her name and give you the key to her heart, I'm going to want something in return. This information doesn't come cheaply."

"What's your price?" Keefe ran his fingers back and forth over the leather armrest, though he kept his voice cool.

"Thirty percent of the dowry."

The viscount frowned. "That's a steep price."

"It's a rich dowry."

"Then why don't you marry the chit yourself if she is so well endowed?"

Reginald shuddered. Perish the thought he ever be shackled to that do-gooding harpy. "The truth is, she would not have me. But you . . . With my information there is little doubt she would be eating from your palm within a fortnight."

"I've had my success with the fairer sex." Keefe smiled his even smile.

"Then there's nothing to lose. If she won't have you, you spend nothing but the effort of wooing. If she will have you, then your father restores your allowance, you gain control of her income, and you get to keep two-thirds of her dowry. What do you say?"

"Twenty-five percent."

Reginald hid his amusement. "You insult me." He made to stand.

The viscount, a flash of panic in his eyes, waved him back. "Sit down, sit down. I was jesting. Thirty it is. But who is she? I won't have her if she's hideous in appearance or manners—though you wouldn't suggest such a woman, would you?"

"No. She's not a remarkable beauty, but passable. You'll find it easy enough to sow your seed there. And I'm sure I needn't remind you that beauty is fleeting, but a substantial annuity brings joy for a lifetime."

"It does, indeed. Now who is it?" The man was drumming his fingers again.

"Caroline Huntington. My cousin. She's going to be adopted by my father."

Comprehension flashed through Keefe's eyes. For all his dissipated ways, the man was no fool. "Ah. Made part of the family. With part of the family's fortunes attached."

"Indeed." How it galled.

Keefe nodded. "I've seen your cousin—tolerable-enough looking. And the Huntington fortune—even a fraction of it—is quite respectable. I imagine I could take on some 'regular' expenses here and there."

"Very practical—for both of us." Reginald lifted his glass. "To romance."

"To wooing and winning." Keefe followed suit.

"To substantial annuities." Their glasses came together with a satisfying clink. "I've no doubt you can court my cousin successfully. Especially as I will provide you with details of her habits. Blind her with kisses, marry her, and install her out in the country somewhere. Before long you'll be back in Town, living the merry life."

And Reginald would benefit, far more than 30 percent of the dowry. Keefe was a scandal waiting to happen—a big enough one to discredit even the most charitable-minded of chits. Although the timing had to be just right, so Reginald could save his own skin while getting his damned cousin out from underfoot.

"I'll call on your cousin at her earliest convenience."

"There is one problem."

Keefe rubbed his fingers along the armrest. "I thought you said there were no other suitors."

"There are none. But Caroline is abroad just now, in the Mediterranean. She's expected home quite soon. Be assured, I will notify you immediately upon her return."

"The sooner the better. I can't stave off my tailor's bills much longer." Those emerald eyes glinted as Keefe rose. "I await your word. Good day, Huntington."

"Good day, indeed."

Crete, April 1848

Alex set the woven basket down and straightened his coat, then rapped on the door of Miss Huntington's quarters.

"Pen?" her clear voice called from inside.

"Not Pen," he replied.

"Mr. Trentham. One moment. I wasn't expecting . . ."

He heard rustling from within, and a sound that could have been the scraping of a chair. Finally, after several moments she bade him enter.

He was pleased to find her resting in bed—not attempting to sweep cobwebs from the ceiling, or organizing the villagers into a volunteer fire department, or engaging in whatever other endeavors might pop into her head.

"You're here rather early to inspect my arm, aren't you?" she asked, the covers pulled up to her chin.

He went to set the basket on the table, but the surface was covered with stationery, correspondence and, oddly, sheets of paper with numerals written large.

"There has been a change in plans. Madame Legault needs Pen this afternoon, so it has fallen upon me to play nursemaid."

"You?" Her fingers tightened on the blankets. "It's not necessary. I assure you, I will do quite well on my own."

He set the basket down and looked at her more closely. Her color was good, her eyes were clear, but there seemed something peculiar about her, or more accurately, the shape she made beneath the coverlet. It appeared bunched in odd places, and her toes raised the blanket in two sharp points.

He stepped closer. "Have you been spending adequate time resting, Miss Huntington?"

"Oh, yes." Her eyes were wide. "Just as you advised."

"Is that so?" He bent and with a quick tug whisked the covers off the bed.

"Mr. Trentham! Why—" She reached for the blankets, but it was too late.

"Yes. I know. An outrage. And do you always wear full skirts and *shoes* beneath the bedclothes?"

She laughed then and blushed most charmingly. "You have, quite literally, uncovered my secret, sir. I'm afraid I am incapable of lying about during the day. I know—I've been a terrible patient—but if you do not let me outside, I shall have to throw myself out the window, upsetting all those lovely geraniums in the process!"

He tried, without real success, to keep a stern look on his face. "It's obvious to me that leaving you unsupervised would be utter folly. What with you leaping into and out of bed, diving out the windows, perhaps even turning somersaults."

"No, not somersaults. They make me dizzy."

"It's a good thing I had the foresight to plan an outing to distract you from such mischief."

She looked up at him, interest sparking in her brown eyes. "An outing?"

"If you feel strong enough."

"Yes, yes, of course I feel strong enough. How fortunate that I find myself pre-dressed for an outing." She offered him her hand, and he helped her rise to her feet, where she teetered for a moment before recovering her balance. "Let me just fetch my pelisse and hat." She moved to the wardrobe and handed him her pelisse, turning so he could drape it about her shoulders. One-handed, she fumbled at the catch.

"Let me fasten that for you."

It should have been a matter-of-fact enough thing, closing the pelisse, and yet suddenly it was not. Her hair smelled of rosemary, and his hand was so close to her throat that he could not help but be aware of the delicate pulse there. For a bare second his fingers brushed against her skin.

She stilled, heightened color touching her cheeks. "Would you help with my hat as well? I have yet to master the art of tying a bow single-handed."

She tipped her chin up, bringing their faces close. Too close. Her eyes were wide, fixed on his, and he had to force his fingers to move. What would those soft lips, so near his own, feel like? Warm. Delicious. He had to fight to keep from bending, laying his mouth over hers and tasting for himself. . . .

He finished tying the ribbons and stepped away, then gestured her toward the door.

Outside the sun was dazzling, reflecting off the whitewashed walls of the village. She stopped on the doorstep and sighed, then closed her eyes as she lifted her face to the light. The breeze teased a strand of hair against her cheek, and Alex felt a sudden, insane impulse to reach and tuck it behind her ear. He gripped the basket handle tightly and turned his head toward the sea.

"Where are we off to, kind sir? And what is in your basket?"

"We are having a picnic at the seashore." It suddenly seemed a frivolous and foolish thing to do.

A smile tilted across her face. "A picnic sounds just the thing. And any respite from my rooms is very welcome."

"Take my arm—the going is uneven in places." And though his steps might be uneven as well, he suspected she would need the support.

As they walked she leaned more heavily upon him at times for balance. He forced the doctor to the forefront, viewing her with the clinical detachment that had once been effortless. From the rhythm of her steps, he guessed she had not been completely truthful about the extent of her vertigo. Still, the improvement was noticeable, and she did not seem to be tiring as they reached the wave-swept sand that ran flat and even from the edge of the rocks to the sparkling turquoise of the Mediterranean.

"Pen is spending the afternoon with Madame Legault?" she asked. "Am I right in thinking Madame took the girl under her wing after her father left?"

"Yes—although it is you, Miss Huntington, who seems to be restoring her spirits. Whenever I see her she talks of nothing but your projects."

She glanced at him. "I think assisting me makes her feel strong, and keeps her from dwelling too much on her unhappy situation. And in truth, her help is quite invaluable."

"She did mention you dictate reams of letters." He thought back to the papers in her room. "But I saw more than correspondence on your table. Do you have Pen practicing her numbers?

"Ah. She did not tell you about my arithmetic project with the village children?"

Alex felt a smile lift the corner of his mouth. "No. Perhaps because she knew I would only remind her that you should be resting, not setting up a school." The woman was incorrigible, but somehow he could not begrudge her this. Not with the sun glinting off the sea, the scent of sweet herbs in the dry air.

"Well, I *am* having Pen do most of the teaching, if that sets your mind at ease."

"Marginally."

"The girl has quite a talent for it. It's a skill that could serve her well in her future."

"I don't think Pen has much considered her future," he said. How could she, waiting here abandoned, hoping her father would return? An event that seemed less likely with each passing month.

"Well, I have."

"That doesn't surprise me." He assisted her over the low ridge separating the main beach from the smaller shore, watching intently. Any moment now she should catch sight of it.

"Goodness!" Miss Huntington halted, surprise and pleasure lacing her voice. "How perfectly lovely. Is that for us?"

"Yes." Satisfaction flared through him at her delight. He gazed at their destination trying to view it through her eyes.

A makeshift pavilion stood on the shore. Lengths of white cotton billowed in the breeze on three sides, while the fourth was open to the sea. Through the cloth he glimpsed a woven mat covering the sand, cushioned chairs, and a small table, ready for the luncheon he carried. It was a haven, a place apart. A place, he hoped, that would amuse his reluctant charge. He did not inquire too closely of himself why that should be important.

Had he made it too elaborate? But she did need a shade for her fair skin, and a comfortable place to rest.

"This is far more than a rustic picnic." She tucked her good arm through his as they made their way down the beach to the shelter. Once inside, she settled on a chair and gazed about like a newly crowned queen surveying her realm.

"You look comfortable."

She turned to him, eyes dancing with amber lights. "It's delightful. I promise to be a model patient from here forward."

For a moment Alex could not see a patient before him at all, only a woman, vibrant and whole in the sunshine, smiling up at him. He took a step toward her, then caught himself, changed course to set the basket on the table.

"No more thoughts about diving out the windows, then—although you do have a balcony."

"Are you suggesting I tie my sheets together and lower myself one-handed from it?" She was laughing at him. "It's maddening to be able to see everywhere and be able to go nowhere. Although"—she glanced about her once more—"this is certainly somewhere, and a fine somewhere at that. I have always loved the shore, perhaps because we lived far from it. It seems so exotic."

"I grew up by the sea." It was a harmless enough admission.

"How delightful! To be able to beach-comb whenever you wanted. Did you find many treasures?"

"I don't remember. And it was not peaceful and tame like this. Storms would blow in that no sane person would want to be out in." He shut his teeth over more words, slamming the doors of memory shut. He would not, must not, go back there, even in thought.

His hands trembled as he opened the basket, and he had to fight off the sudden urge to flee back to the safety of his cottage. No. No, he was here—on Crete. This was a different sea, a different sky, and Miss Huntington was here as well, speaking to him, her voice a quiet melody. He let the sound of it wash over him, carrying him back to the present.

". . . had any number of fantastical items in his collection," she said. "My grandfather was always fascinated by the natural world. Why, he discovered an entirely new species of flower in Tunisia. Last year my brother, James, was able to go collect it." She paused and looked over the blue waters. "Which way is Tunisia from here? Straight across?"

He squinted across the waves, grateful for the distraction. "No, Egypt is to the south. Tunisia is that direction." He pointed to the right. "As is Malta."

"Malta." She shaded her eyes with her hand, and he knew she was thinking of Mrs. Farnsworth.

He began setting out their luncheon. "I hope you like the

local food. I'm afraid cucumber sandwiches were in short supply this morning."

She left off scanning the horizon and turned to face him. "Oh, I do, very much. I'm glad there's no gruel with treacle anywhere on the island."

"Happily, living here means an escape from English cooking. Although eventually one tires of olives. Sometimes I long for a nice brisket of beef with boiled potatoes."

"Mr. Trentham." There was something cautious in her voice. "How long have you been here? On Crete?"

Alex pulled a loaf of bread out and set it next to the pale slab of goat cheese. He took a long moment before answering, calculating the seasons in his head. The answer surprised him. "Three years."

"Three years? But, what about your family, your friends in England?"

He frowned, shoulders tight beneath his coat. "There is nothing, and no one, for me there." What he had done ensured it.

"I truly doubt that," she began. "You seem—"

"Miss Huntington"—he jabbed his thumb into an orange and began tearing the peel off with sharp movements—"if you are eager to speak of England, then do so. Tell me about your family." Anything to deflect her interest.

He could feel her watching him as he finished peeling the orange and divided their lunch onto the plates set out for them.

"My family." She shifted in her chair.

He handed her a plate, then took the opposite chair and concentrated on ripping his bread into bite-sized chunks.

She ate an olive, then at last answered him. "My parents died when I was quite young, and my brother and I were taken in by my uncle."

Yes, he recalled their conversation that first night, when she had named herself orphan. "Did he treat you poorly? Is that why you champion the cause of orphans?"

"Heavens no! Uncle Denby has been nothing but kind

ever since he made us part of his family. No," her face grew pensive, "I have been awarc for a long time that there are others far less fortunate than myself."

"Why make it your mission to help them?"

She gave him a thoughtful look. "What are we here for if not to make things easier for one another? I find myself in a position to help. It would be remiss of me not to do so."

"That's very noble." He poured two glasses of water and set hers beside her plate. She reached, placing her hand over his before he could pull away. Startled, he glanced into brown eyes dark with concern.

"Mr. Trentham, I have found that sometimes it helps to speak about one's troubles. If you need to . . . well, please consider me a friend."

Her skin was warm, and for a brief moment he was tempted not to move away from her touch—but no. The last thing he wanted was to see her turn from him, disgust and horror in her eyes. It was his burden to carry. Alone.

He pulled away. "Thank you. Talking does not help me."

"Very well." She took up her glass and drank, staring out at the sea once more.

The strained silence between them slowly eased as they sat. The sunlight playing in the light fabric of the curtains, the constant hushing of the waves, slowly chased the darkness back. It did not belong here, in this day, in this place.

Her voice laid itself over the quiet, her tone pensive. "I don't think helping others when I can is noble. More that it's right, and human. But we needn't speak of that." She turned to him, a determinedly bright look on her face. "Tell me about working with Monsieur and Madame Legault. Has the excavation turned up any treasures?"

If she wanted to steer the conversation onto safer ground he was happy to follow. They had already skirted too close to the edge.

"If you mean fabulous caches of gold and jewelry, no.

There have been some fine pottery jars"—he would not mention the one she had inadvertently shattered—"and a few items of beaten silver and bronze. I don't think Legault is interested in finding treasure, which is odd for a man who likes to dig in the dirt. Although he does think there are other possibilities scattered about the island."

"I'd imagine he is right. After all, Crete is the birthplace of Zeus, the home of King Minos, the Minotaur, the labyrinth."

Alex shook his head. "King Minos is just a myth, Miss Huntington. I doubt his palace, or any sort of labyrinth, actually exists."

"But certainly they do!" She leaned forward. "What seems to us to be ancient legend must have some basis in actual history. Something mystical must still linger in the Cave of Zeus. Pen tells me you have been there."

"Yes. It's a few hours' ride from the village."

"I was hoping to see the cave before—well, before this happened." She lifted her splinted arm, a rueful expression on her face.

"It's an interesting place. The locals still bring offerings, as they have done for generations. There's a feeling of great antiquity there."

Miss Huntington nodded, listening intently, and despite himself Alex found the afternoon brightening once again. He went on to describe his visits to the cave, and thought that, in the retelling, it had indeed been a place of mystery.

"But I am keeping you from dessert. Have you tried the local version of baklava yet, Miss Huntington?"

"I haven't. It looks . . . sticky. But delicious," she said, eyeing the honey-drizzled triangles.

"Both." He offered her one of the delicate desserts.

She took a tentative bite, then a look of bliss crossed her face. "Oh . . . it's like tasting pure sunlight." Her tongue flicked out, chasing a stray bit of pastry from her lip, and he abruptly forgot what they had been talking about.

Honey. Her hair holding glints of it, tawny flecks in her eyes. He was certain she would taste of it, and the urge to go to her, lift her in his arms and savor her mouth with his own was nearly overwhelming.

"Thank you for the most agreeable afternoon." She let out a pleased sigh. "It was so *good* to get out of my rooms."

He cleared his throat. "Then we'll have to see it happens more often."

Although he feared he had not been the most agreeable company—alternately brooding and enthralled. Still, if she was happy then the picnic could be counted a success. He stood, tucked the used dishes back into the basket, and brushed the crumbs from the table. The lads would be along later to dismantle the pavilion, though perhaps he would have them wait a few days so Miss Huntington could return. He could picture her here again tomorrow, reading a book and drinking tea. "Now, though . . ."

"Yes." She glanced at the sky, where orange streamers of clouds preceded the dusk. "Time to go back."

He held his hand out to her and she set her good hand in his, smiling. "See how obedient I am? Not even dragging my heels in the sand."

"Most impressive. You'll be fully cured in no time." And on her way back to England.

He raised her hand to his lips, a courtly gesture, and she stilled, her breath indrawn as he brushed his lips across her skin. Heat flashed through him, and he lingered too long, but he could not help himself. Her hand was soft and he yearned too much for that softness. At length he straightened and tucked her hand into the crook of his arm, not meeting her widened eyes.

The sun slanted low across the beach as they made their way back toward the village. At length Miss Huntington looked over her shoulder and he followed her gaze to the pavilion, white cotton gilded nearly to gold, a swirl of gulls calling overhead, the wavelets running up, and away.

Chapter 7

"Pen!" Joy bubbled through Caroline as she leapt to her feet. "The letter you just brought—it's from Maggie. She did it! She's convinced the governor to approve her orphanage in Valletta."

Pen flung up her arms, scattering the wildflowers she had been arranging. "Hurrah! What splendid news, Caro."

Caroline laughed, then rather quickly sat back down as the room began to spin. When it stilled she picked up the letter again. "I'm so pleased."

Her spirits felt lighter than they had for, well, for longer than she could remember. This enforced break on Crete was not all bad. She had been able to keep up her correspondence with Pen's help, and her new companion was blossoming like one of the wildflowers outside. And now, the news that Maggie had met with success. She drew in a deep breath. Her injury had not, after all, caused her friend's project to fail—although Maggie had cautioned in her letter that she would have to remain on Malta a while longer to ensure the project got off to a smooth start.

Caroline was glad to hear she would not be immediately collected from Crete. Certainly, it was better she remain on the island another few weeks. She was not fully recovered, and she doubted Mr. Trentham would let her go until she was. And, to be honest, she did not want to go.

When he had kissed her hand it had sent an odd thrill through her, a warm swirl that had uncurled from her feet and swept through her, leaving her exhilarated and confused in its wake. Even now the back of her hand tingled with the memory.

"Grand news for a grand day," Pen said, bending to gather up the strewn flowers. She had come in, arms full of sweet herbs and wildflowers picked from the hillsides, and set about making jaunty bouquets. Now the rooms were scented with chamomile and sage, splashed with color from the poppies and iris.

"This one for the balcony, I think." She took up her last jar of flowers and went out to the narrow terrace. With the days growing warmer they left the door open wide, and the comfortable sounds of village life drifted up. "Caro, come look," she called. "I think someone new has arrived. A European."

Caroline went to join Pen. True enough, there was Manolis, his cart filled with luggage and oddly shaped bundles. Beside him on the seat was a stocky, muscular-looking gentleman, wearing a large hat that shaded his features. As they watched, the cart turned near the fisherman's cottages and disappeared toward the olive groves.

"So it appears. No doubt we'll discover more soon—in a village this size everyone knows everyone else's business."

"No question of that. Look, here comes Mr. Trentham." Pen leaned over the balcony, waving broadly.

Spotting them, he lifted a hand in return. When he reached the villa he swung smoothly off his mount.

"Care to descend, Miss Huntington? It's a lovely day for a stroll on the beach."

"Yes! Give me a moment." She hurried back inside, swept up the letter and tucked it into her pocket. Her times outside with him were precious, and she would not give them up for anything.

Pen pulled a shawl from the wardrobe and draped it over Caroline's shoulders. "Enjoy your walk. I'll just tidy up here while you are gone."

Caroline found Mr. Trentham waiting for her at the foot of the stairs. He offered his arm. "To the shore?"

"Yes—and I have the most marvelous news to report." She could not help grinning at him. "But . . . I think we will wait until we reach the pavilion." She wanted him to read the letter himself.

"Hmm. Let me guess. You've purchased a forge and are going to teach the village boys blacksmithing?" His tone was dry, but she caught the flash of amusement in his eyes.

"Hardly." She pretended to ponder. "Although, the idea has merit." She laughed at his expression, then stepped around a tumble of rocks. "Mr. Trentham, I believe someone new has come to the village. Pen and I saw him from the balcony, riding with Manolis."

"Another English tourist apparently—a sportsman by the look of the gear he brought. We've had a plague of tourists through here of late." The corner of his mouth lifted.

"If I *was* a tourist, then I certainly no longer feel like one. Not when I know half the villagers by name—and you have no idea of how much I see from the balcony."

"Oh? What do you see from your perch?"

"I see the fishing boats go out on the morning tide, when the sea is smooth like a mirror. I see the priest walking with his spotted dog, and of course Manolis going back and forth with his cart. Did you know Young Georgios was promenading about yesterday with an enormous fish he had caught? Hoping Maria would notice him, I suspect."

"It sounds quite crowded." His tone suggested he preferred the peace of his isolated cottage.

She bit her lip. It was not good for him to hold himself so apart, removed from even the simple joys of friendship. She could see how loneliness had tarnished him and could not help but notice how he was beginning to brighten the more time he spent with others. Whatever secrets he held, surely they could be eased by sharing.

They had arrived at the pavilion, which had begun to list to the left. Today the cotton fabric was pulled wide, the sun sprawled over the chairs. She sat and drew the letter from her pocket. It seemed fitting that she had saved the news to share with him here, in their private sanctuary.

"See what arrived in the post?" She held it up. "A letter from Maggie, and—well, you must read it yourself, Mr. Trentham."

"I can hardly read it with you waving it about like a fan." He caught the pages from her and seated himself. As he read an errant smile teased the edge of his mouth, softening his features. Why, he looked quite handsome like that, with the wind lightly ruffling his hair.

"Excellent." He looked up, a spark in his usually somber eyes. "So, the orphanage will be built. Mrs. Farnsworth has succeeded in her mission. And you are mending nicely. Here, not on Malta." He folded the letter but did not hand it back, only gave her an expectant look, one eyebrow lifted.

"What? You are waiting for me to say how right you were?" She tried to sound indignant, but her joy in sharing the good news spoiled the attempt. "Very well. You were right, Mr. Trentham. And you needn't look so self-satisfied about it."

He leaned back in his chair, lips curving up in an actual smile. "One must savor these little moments."

Something inside her unfolded at his words. She did not think he let himself enjoy much in life. It was important he could take pleasure in this.

"Though, I must confess," he said, "I was never clear on why Malta needed an orphanage to begin with."

"Well, there is Valletta, garrisoned by British soldiers for over thirty years."

"Yes, I comprehend that part."

She leaned forward. "But do you comprehend the children those men have sired? Children whose mothers have brought their infants to the gates and left them there, hoping the soldier who fathered them would take them in, see them raised as one of the privileged, one of the ruling class? The men almost never do—realistically, how can they? Many of the children must fend for themselves on the streets."

"I see." His dark blue eyes were fixed on hers. "And are there no orphans in London who need your help?"

She nodded. "More than enough."

The image rose once again in her memory's eye. The pale, pinched face of the girl dressed in rags, sheltering a younger child in her arms, both of them shivering in the chill winter rain. Caroline had glanced out the carriage window when the vehicle stopped because of some obstacle farther up the street and seen them.

Her cousin Reggie had, too. "There," he had sneered. "Orphans. That is you, Caroline, but for my father's generosity. You belong there. With them."

The words had struck deep. Without thinking, she had wrenched open the carriage door and splashed across dank puddles. Her cousin called after her, but she ignored him and pulled at her cloak pin. It gave and she tugged the garment off, the cold air sudden and unfriendly with nothing between it and her skin but the fine wool of her dress.

"Here." She held the cloak out to the girl, and it was like looking into a distorted mirror. Brown eyes dull with hunger and cold, chapped lips and cheeks, hair that lay lank and uncombed across thin shoulders. Caroline shivered from more than the chilly air. Reggie was right—this could have been her.

The girl stared at her and the child in the circle of her arms whimpered. Then, in a motion too quick to follow, the girl snatched the cloak and scuttled with her charge into the mouth of the alley. Caroline peered into the thick darkness, but they were gone.

"Fool." Hard fingers gripped her arm as Reggie pulled her back toward the carriage. "You've cost my father several pounds, and for what? What did you expect? A curtsey and song of thanks? Their kind don't know the meaning of the word."

Caroline pulled away and hurried up the carriage steps. "I didn't expect any thanks."

It was true. Giving the girl her cloak had made the world a kinder place in some small way. But giving away her cloak was not enough—not nearly enough.

Was helping with a new orphanage in Valletta enough? Or funding the school in London? Would she ever be able to give enough to erase that stark image haunting her memory?

"I contribute in London." She answered Mr. Trentham's question. "With Maggie's help, I've established a school, and have plans in motion to do more. But there are other people, other organizations that can help there. The children of Valletta have no one."

"They do now."

The warmth in his voice nearly undid her. She had expected more questions, more arguments—people almost never understood. It was easier to remain comfortably uninvolved, to argue and intellectualize the subject. If half the energy people spent avoiding the problem was actually put to use trying to fix it . . . Throat tight, Caroline gazed out at the sea.

He did not press her. Silence unfolded around them, but it was an accepting one, a peaceful quiet that did not need words. At length she drew in a deep breath and turned to find him watching her, something akin to understanding in his eyes.

"I've no doubt you have touched the lives of many, Miss Huntington. Thank you for sharing the news that Mrs. Farnsworth was successful in such an important undertaking." He slipped off his chair, knelt beside her. "Now let's see how successful we've been at helping this elbow mend."

Caroline lifted her arm, letting his large, gentle hands take the weight. It was a familiar business, yet today she felt breathless as he unwrapped the bindings, the pressure about her arm easing as he unbound the splint. The last strips came away, leaving an almost painful awareness as her skin was bared to the sunlight and air.

He cupped her elbow, carefully feeling around it. His fingers hit an especially sore place and she drew in a sharp breath.

"Tender?" He looked up at her, black hair falling into his eyes. "Yes, I'd expect so. But the swelling is almost gone."

She swallowed. "How long until we can remove the splint for good?"

"Soon." He set the splint against her skin again and began rewinding. When he was finished he took her hand, setting his palm against hers. "Push against me—yes, like that. Hmm. You'll need to strengthen the arm. Healing takes time."

More time. But somehow the thought did not seem so dreadful anymore. Now that she knew Maggie had succeeded on Malta, she did not mind tarrying here. The project in London called, but not loudly. The warm sun of Crete, the slow pace of the village had worked its alchemy upon her. She felt loosened in a way she never had in England—like crystallized honey that had warmed enough to flow smoothly.

And there was Mr. Trentham. She had to admit, she was not unmoved by him. Every day she woke and considered the number of hours before he would arrive at her doorstep, tried to suppress the way her heart jumped when she caught sight of his figure.

He was still holding her hand, his warm fingers close about hers. She deliberately kept her gaze on the water, content—more than content. The pulse of the waves became the pulse of her heart, a steady thrum centered on the feel of his hand against hers. Her breath was the breath of the wind, a sudden, vast feeling, as though she were a part of the sky, the water, the light glancing on the waves, part of this man beside her.

At length he released her. "We should return."

She was sorry to go.

"I was thinking," he said, when they had almost reached the villa, "tomorrow we could range farther afield, if you are feeling strong enough."

"Certainly I am. An outing would be grand. May I ask where?"

He shot her an amused look. "You may ask—but I prefer to keep my surprises."

"How vexing of you!" She smiled up at him. "It will have to surpass the pavilion, you understand. I am becoming accustomed to a certain caliber of surprise."

"It will meet your expectations," he said, then firmed his lips, as if keeping himself from saying more. He remained silent until they reached the door.

"Well, good afternoon, Mr. Trentham."

"Miss Huntington." He paused, something flickering in the depths of his eyes.

The falling light played in his dark hair, and she turned to face him, aware of a sudden hush in the air, as though a dome of quiet had descended over the two of them. His gaze dropped to her lips and he leaned forward. Heat rushed through her, and a quickening anticipation. . . .

"*Iatros!*" A man stepped out onto his stoop and hailed Mr. Trentham, and the moment was broken.

Mr. Trentham held up a hand in greeting, then stepped back, making her a slight bow. "Good afternoon. I shall see you tomorrow."

She watched as he strode up the street, something she could only name as yearning pushing through her, wrapping round her heart, strong and sweet and uncomfortable, like a stolen sip of brandy.

Chapter 8

The next morning Alex tethered his horse outside the villa, then hailed Manolis, who was coming down the street with two more mounts. "Excellent. Tie them here. I'll be leaving with the ladies shortly."

The older man smiled. "It is good to see you in the sunshine, *iatros.*"

"It's sunny nearly every day." But he knew what Manolis meant.

It was irrational, the good humor that had settled over him. His past had receded, the memories of what he had done distanced from this place and time. What was important was *now*: the kestrels swooping overhead in the clear, dry air, the day unfolding before him, full of promise. The brown-haired woman waiting, whose smiles were like balm and honey, whose company he had begun to enjoy far more than he should. Still, there was no harm in turning his face to the light she held, as a cold man might warm himself before a fire. It was not as though he were trying to claim that fire for himself, or coax it into burning on his own hearth.

He whistled to himself as he mounted the stairs two at a time. Pen opened the door immediately at his knock. He looked over her shoulder, catching sight of Miss Huntington in the next room.

"Hello, Mr. Trentham." Pen grinned at him. "We're nearly ready. Where are we going?"

"It's a surprise, but one you'll know soon enough." He could not swear to it, but the girl seemed more presentable these days. The anxious expression had faded from her eyes, and there was something different about her dresses. "Will you run down to the kitchen and see that the supplies I asked for are ready? Have them taken out to the horses."

"Of course—and I think I know where we're going." Her look turned conspiratorial. "It's a grand idea." She gathered up her shawl and bonnet and slipped out.

"Miss Huntington?"

"Come in." She was standing before the wardrobe, wearing the dress he had first mangled, the russet color bringing out echoes of autumn in her hair. The sleeve had been remade, as had the right sleeves of all her dresses, a panel of fabric enlarging them enough to accommodate the sling. She smiled and warmth kindled through him, all the way to his soles.

"I'm looking forward to our mysterious adventure today," she said.

"You feel well enough to ride?"

"Ride? Absolutely!" Her smile widened. "That means we're going some distance. I'll be ready in a moment. Although—did Pen just step out?" She glanced down at the pair of boots she was holding.

"Allow me to help."

"Yes, you'll have to. One-handed lacing is quite impossible." She went to the nearby chair and sat, then pulled her skirts up slightly and held out one stockinged foot. Her cheeks held a blossom of color that had not been there moments before.

He took up a boot of finely tooled leather and went on one knee before her, near enough that the scent of her teased his senses. Soap and flowers, and the warmth he identified as simply her—the fragrance had become familiar since that first night she had arrived at his doorstep. Although his sheets had been laundered straight away, sometimes late at night he imagined he could still catch her scent there, elusive and lingering in the folds of cotton.

He loosened the laces and spread the boot wide, holding it open for her to slip her foot into. For a moment her heel caught, and he slid his hand around her ankle, guiding her. She let out a faint breath.

Soft, warm . . . Without conscious intent his hand moved up her calf, her silk-clad skin intoxicating—and Alex was abruptly aware that he was caressing her leg in the heated darkness beneath her skirts. It drowned out all his other senses, that touch, that desire to keep on touching.

He dropped his hand, scorched. Forced himself to tie up the laces, though his fingers felt barely under his control. One boot safely on. Now the other.

He would not, would *not,* allow himself to caress behind her knee, though it was only the lift of a finger away. He would not imagine what lay beyond that knee, the pale, curving softness of her thigh. . . .

"Finished." He rose to his feet, feeling as though he had been standing too close to a raging fire, the heat assaulting his skin even as the flames beckoned him closer.

"I did say once before that you had missed your calling as a lady's maid." Her voice was uneven, her cheeks pinker than before.

"I'm surprised you trusted me after the damage I did to your clothing last time."

"I do trust you."

Which only made things worse. He was no longer entirely sure he could trust himself. "Come. Pen is waiting."

She accepted his help in rising, her gaze finally meeting his. The amber flecks in her eyes shone like glints of gold and her lips were parted.

"Thank you."

It had been his pleasure, and a guilty one, but if he read her aright he was not alone in the pleasure. It was heady, seeing the flush of awareness on her open face. Heady—and impossible.

Alex stepped back, made himself release her hand. He did not deserve the touch of this beautiful, spirited woman—but that did not mean he didn't desire her. Desperately. Since she had arrived he had begun to *feel* again. It would hurt when she left. Deep inside, all his old pain was still there, waiting to rise up and engulf him. Dormant now, it needed only the spur of a new loss to overwhelm him again. He knew it, and still he could not manage to lock himself away.

They emerged from the villa to find Pen mounted and waiting. A satchel of provisions bulged behind the saddle.

"That's rather a lot of supplies." The girl shot a glance behind her. "We're only going to be gone part of the day, aren't we?"

"Yes. But we're going to have company for lunch." Alex moved to assist Miss Huntington into the saddle. She had paused, reins in one hand, and was regarding her mount.

"You needn't fear," he said. "Agalma is a steady beast."

Pen laughed. "Steady? She's the slowest horse on the entire island. You'll be lucky if she doesn't decide to lie down and take a nap—with you on her."

"Do you have so little trust in my ability to ride?" Miss Huntington asked Alex.

"I don't lack confidence in your horsemanship, just the ability of your head to withstand a repeated concussion. Up you go." He boosted her sideways into the saddle, trying not to think about her trim ankles, the soft skin of her legs. His hands tightened with the memory of touching her. Miss Caroline Huntington. He turned and swung himself onto Icarus. "We're taking luncheon to the excavation, Pen. Do you think we'll be able to pry the Legaults from their labors?"

"I'm sure we can. Oh, and I guessed it. It's a splendid idea." She urged her horse forward.

"Another excellent surprise." Miss Huntington smiled at him.

"Tell me more about the site. Pen says the Legaults came across the place some years ago and organized an official excavation?"

"Semiofficial at best. The Turkish authorities keep an eye out, but so far they have not interfered. Of course, if Legault discovers something marvelous—inscribed tablets of solid gold or a cache of jewelry—they would quickly become interested."

"Is that likely?"

"It's an old Roman ruin, built upon an even older village. As you yourself said, who knows what secrets the earth will yield."

She glanced up the track, a wistful expression on her face. "I'm glad to have the opportunity to visit this excavation everyone talks about."

He smiled to himself, imagining her reaction when she saw the ranks of marble statuary, the baths and basilica, the small open amphitheater. There were treasures aplenty, though they might not be as tangible as gold coins.

"Mr. Trentham," she said after they had ridden on. "What about the bones? Pen says you piece old bits of skeleton together."

"The artifacts only tell part of the story. I lend my knowledge of human anatomy to Legault so he may better understand the people who lived here."

"Yes. Your training as a doctor. I've been wondering—"

"Old bones are hardly a fitting subject for such a day." And could lead them into dangerous conversation. He would not allow the past to mar the present. Catching Pen's eye, he nodded to her to take his place riding beside Miss Huntington. "I'll check the road ahead."

This was Crete at its best, before the heavy summer heat pressed down like an iron over the island. The breeze was fresh, and white and brown herds of goats were scattered over the hills, the sound of their bells carrying faintly in the spring air. Alex squinted up at the sun. They were making good time, despite Miss Huntington's slow-footed mount.

Another half hour of gentle riding and they crested the

plain. The ruins ahead were visible now, and Miss Huntington let out a low cry of pleasure.

"Look at the pillars, the amphitheater. . . ."

He could not hold back a smile. "You are not disappointed then?"

Her eyes were alight, her generous mouth curved. "I'm not in the least disappointed. I can hardly wait, in fact. Go, you wretched beast." She kicked her heels against Agalma's sides and the long-suffering horse lumbered forward.

It did not take long to reach the cluster of canvas tents that marked the Legaults' camp. During the winter months they took rooms in the village, but the temperate springtime saw them moving to the site to be closer to the work, before the stifling summer heat ended the season.

Alex slid from Icarus and tethered him to the remains of a weather-worn column. Pen followed suit, no stranger to the site herself.

"Miss Huntington." He went to assist her.

Smiling, she set her good hand on his shoulder and let herself slip forward into his arms with serene confidence. He closed his hands about her waist and braced her descent against him. It was not deliberate, but he could not help holding her against him an extra heartbeat. Then two. The wind hushed through the cypress, bringing with it the fragrance of herbs and cedar.

This was getting to be a damnable habit. He took a step back. "Let us go make our greetings to the Legaults."

She turned toward the tents, not meeting his gaze, though an awareness of how close their bodies had just been seemed to pulse in the space between them. "I see Pen has lost no time in doing just that."

They joined the girl under one of the striped awnings, where she was engaged in animated conversation with Madame Legault.

"Alex, good day to you!" the Frenchwoman said, rising,

then bestowed a kiss on each of his cheeks. "And Miss Huntington as well. Welcome." She held out her hands. "Let me look at you, *cherie. Oui,* much improved! Such color in your face, and your eyes are sparkling. Monsieur Trentham has done wonders with you."

The color Madame had remarked on seemed to deepen as Miss Huntington nodded. "I am feeling better daily."

"And who would not, with such a handsome doctor to tend them?" She smiled. "But let us go pull my husband from the dirt and make ready for luncheon."

They found Monsieur Legault directing his workers in the middle of the excavation. He greeted them cheerfully, remarked also on Miss Huntington's improved health, and promised to join them soon. They left him busy with a measuring stick in a trench, calling admonishments in Greek for his men to be careful with the wheelbarrows.

"Let's spread blankets in the shade of the grove," Pen said. "Then it will be a properly rustic picnic."

"That is very well for you young persons," Madame Legault said, laughter in her voice, "but I will have them fetch a chair for my old bones to rest upon. And pillows for you as well. Even youth needs comfort."

Pen found a suitable place and flapped the blankets open over the grasses. "Anyone who accompanies her husband on his expeditions *and* writes up all the field notes could not possibly be thought of as old."

"Well, perhaps not so ancient then." Madame shot a wry glance at the girl. "But let us see what delicacies you have brought. Once my husband catches the scent of food he will be here *tout de suite.*"

The workmen brought chairs and carried a table out from one of the tents, and soon there was an elegant dining area set up. Alex was quietly amused. No matter how rustic the surroundings, Madame Legault lent an air of refinement to any undertaking. She even wore perfume at the dig, no matter how impractical the notion. The delicate aroma of violets wafted about her.

"Unearth our bounty, *ma petite,* so we may entice my husband to stop his labors." She settled herself in one of the chairs and Alex seated Miss Huntington across from her.

Pen opened the satchel. "Olives, of course, and bread. Oh, and my favorite." She pulled out a packet of rolled leaves. "Dolmades."

"I haven't tried them." Miss Huntington took the packet, held it up to her nose and sniffed. "Hmm. As long as there is baklava I will be content."

"Dolmades are stuffed grape leaves—they're delicious." Pen continued setting bundles on the table until there was an impressive picnic laid out.

Alex was glad to see they had not forgotten the honey-drizzled sweets. He had expressly asked that baklava be included.

"Here comes your husband now," he said, seeing Monsieur Legault approaching from the dig, "just as predicted."

"*Bonjour*—let me greet you properly, now that I am no longer so covered in dust." The Frenchman made the rounds, giving the women the traditional buss on the cheeks. He knew Alex well enough to substitute a firm handshake instead. "I have brought us something to drink."

He lifted the jug he carried and gave it a flourish, then poured five goblets of *retsina,* the yellow wine glowing in the light.

Miss Huntington picked up her glass and wrinkled her nose slightly, then took a cautious sip. "Heavens! It's very . . . unusual."

Alex took a swallow, the piney taste lingering in his mouth. Not his preferred beverage either, but quite fitting here among the ruins.

"Retsina." Monsieur Legault held his glass up, sending the golden liquid swirling. "It's an acquired taste. In ancient times they sealed the wine into amphorae with a mixture of plaster and pine resin. Inside the narrow-necked container, the wine took on the flavor of the sealant, and *voilà,* a new beverage was born." He tipped his glass to them. "To new experiences in exotic places—and the courage to savor them."

Alex raised his glass along with the others. Miss Huntington's eyes met his for an unguarded instant, and then she drained her glass.

"Oh!" She puckered her lips like someone who had tasted a lemon, then smiled. Her reaction drew much laughter, and Alex, to his surprise, found himself laughing along.

Madame refilled his glass. "Mr. Trentham, I think the retsina agrees with you, for I believe that is the first time I have heard you laugh."

He shook his head. Surely he must have laughed before. "Well"—he lifted his drink again—"to new experiences."

"Tell me about the excavation," Miss Huntington said. She leaned forward, listening intently as the Legaults spoke of the dig.

Alex watched as she savored the tastes: goat cheese, Pen's esteemed dolmades, the oily cured olives. She had an openness and curiosity that was captivating. The sun slanted through the leaves overhead, caressing her cheek and teasing out the highlights in her hair. But even more than her beauty, it was her warmth of spirit that drew him to her so powerfully. He had laughed, damn it, and he knew it was not wine that had unlocked his laughter.

"Oh! Mr. Trentham, you do not know of our newest discovery," Madame turned to him. "Four days ago we began unearthing the walls near the amphitheater. It is the Roman baths—quite delightful. Tell them, Henri."

"Frescoes—very well preserved." He waved his napkin to emphasize. "It is thrilling to uncover them from the earth, after so long. Although we must keep canvas sheets over them, once finished, so as not to distract the workmen."

"Distract them?" Miss Huntington took another bite of her baklava.

Alex shifted in his chair. He had a notion as to why, and Madame Legault's next words confirmed it.

"They are quite sensual in nature." A mischievous light flashed in her eyes. "Beautiful examples of the art. You must go view them after luncheon. Though perhaps Pen is still too young."

Pen giggled and Madame gave the girl a gentle smile.

Sensual frescoes? Alex coughed. "I really don't—"

"The historical perspective is quite fascinating," Monsieur Legault said. "No matter their subject matter, they are spectacular examples of the fresco art form."

"You will not want to miss seeing them," Madame said, nodding. "They are *magnifique!*"

Miss Huntington's eyes were bright with interest. "Certainly we shall go."

Alex shot the French couple a sideways glance. "How 'sensual' are these frescoes? Perhaps they should not be viewed in mixed company."

"Ancient art is always worth seeing." Madame tossed her head, a touch of impatience evident in the gesture. "You English can be so . . ."

"I have viewed the Elgin Marbles," Miss Huntington said. "Some would argue they are of an explicit nature, and I am hardly the worse for it. I would very much like to see the frescoes."

Madame Legault gave her an approving look. "You are a sensible young woman, not so prudish as Mr. Trentham. I am certain you could appreciate the artistry of the frescoes. Some of them are quite inventive. It is refreshing, the views the ancients took, and then so splendidly realized in plaster and paint."

Dear God, he could only imagine what the Legaults had unearthed. Call him a rake, but he was deeply curious to see how Miss Huntington would react. The desire he tried to ignore hummed loudly through his body.

When there were only crumbs left, Monsieur Legault pushed his plate away. "I regret I cannot accompany you, but I must return to work. The time to excavate is short, with summer approaching. Thank you for the most excellent company and luncheon. Enjoy your afternoon here." He rose and smiled at them.

"I will come with you, Henri, or my notes will fall too far behind." Madame Legault stood and joined her husband. "But please, the rest of you stay as long as you like. Mr. Trentham, you know the site well enough to show Miss Huntington about." The mischievous look returned to her eyes. "Do not neglect our newest find! *À bientôt.*" She slipped her arm through her husband's and, heads close together, they left their visitors to enjoy the dappled shade of the cypresses.

Alex looked at the others. A slight blush rested on Miss Huntington's cheeks.

Pen yawned widely and lay back on the blanket. "The retsina is making me sleepy. You two go on while I rest." She tucked her arms behind her head and closed her eyes.

Miss Huntington looked at Pen, her eyebrows pulled together in a slight frown. "Are you sure you don't wish to see the new discoveries?"

The girl opened one eye. "I'm sure. I am too young—and too full. Although I expect you to tell me about them when you return."

Alex rose and offered Miss Huntington his arm. "There is much worth seeing, even if we do not view the frescoes." After all, that was the reason he had brought her here.

Her expression touched with shyness, but nonetheless resolute, she took his arm. "I think our hosts would be disappointed if we did not at least take a look."

They walked in silence, and he was too aware of her as they made their way through the excavation. The light breeze pressed her skirts against her legs. Just how explicit were these frescoes? The Legaults, in their enthusiasm for the past, might well see the artwork differently from someone less enraptured by its antiquity.

"As a man, I would assume . . ." Miss Huntington cleared her throat and began again. "I neglected to ask whether you have some experience with the style of artwork we are going to see."

"I suppose you don't mean the effect of paint over plaster."

"Um. No." Her fingers tightened fractionally on his arm. "I mean the kind depicting the human form partially clothed."

"Is that what you think we are going to view?"

She blushed again, not meeting his eyes. "That is what I would surmise from the conversation at luncheon."

"I've known the Legaults for some time and don't believe they would have swaddled the frescoes with canvas if they merely depict the partially clothed human form. They are from Paris, after all."

She glanced up at him, her eyes widening with understanding. "You mean . . ."

Desire leapt in him, seeing her thus, her breath indrawn, lips parted. It was a moment before he gained enough control to speak.

"We should return." He forced the words out.

"No." Her voice was soft, but her eyes were sparkling. Not with outrage, as he might have expected, but with something else. Curiosity? "I—I would like to see the frescoes."

"It's not advisable." Especially for him. The edge of distraction was drawing perilously near.

"I assure you I will do my best to appreciate them on their artistic merits. Besides, our hosts expressly urged us to go." Bold words, belied by the color on her cheeks. Their gazes held a fraction too long, and then she looked away, her throat moving as she swallowed.

They skirted the edges of the amphitheater, the olive branches hushing in the breeze like echoes of ancient applause.

Miss Huntington admired the features he pointed out, but they both were distracted, her polite murmurs masking a growing tension between them. He tried not to envision the subject matter of the frescoes. Surely the Legaults would not have encouraged their viewing if the paintings were too explicit.

Their steps slowed as they reached the edge of the newest excavation, a wide trench dug into the ground, containing the canvas-draped walls. Bare earth was heaped on the far side, and a ladder gave access to the site. No turning back now.

Alex descended, then beckoned her to follow. It was impossible not to admire her shapely backside as she went down the ladder. He reached, steadying her about the waist as she took the last few rungs. The fine wool of her dress was soft under his palms—but not as soft as he imagined her skin would be.

He drew in a deep breath and released her. She turned to him, smiling, and then they moved to stand beside the wall. The sun was bright on the draped canvas, while beneath lay shadowed mystery.

Her arm brushed against his as she raised her good hand to move the cloth aside, then seemingly thought better of it. Her fingertips only brushed the canvas before she lowered her arm again. "Perhaps you had better."

Half his attention on her, he reached and slowly pulled the cloth open. A rounded arm, a swath of blue garment, dark almond eyes in an oval face—the fresco was revealed.

Miss Huntington let out a breathy laugh. "I hope you are not disappointed, Mr. Trentham, but I do not find myself shocked in the slightest. I have seen more explicit depictions in garden statuary and fountains."

The painting showed a woman reclining against a basin, the lower half of her body draped in a blue cloth. Her rounded arms were revealed, the gentle swell of her hip, but the image owed more to art than eroticism. Relief warred with regret. Madame Legault was likely chuckling to herself even now at the joke she had played on him.

Miss Huntington leaned forward, her arm brushing his as she bent to better view the painting. "It's amazing how the pigments have been preserved through the centuries. The details—look at the shadows here, in the folds of the cloth."

"Lovely." He was more interested in watching her, but it was true, the image before them was a fine example of ancient Roman art.

"Let's see the others." She moved down and drew the canvas aside. "Oh," she said, then made no other movement.

He stepped up and looked over her shoulder. Heat flared through him as he saw what had caused her reaction. The image was faded but clear, and there was no mistaking what it showed. A well-endowed woman, quite naked, being caressed from behind by a man. One hand encircled her breast, while the other rested lower, directly over her . . . dear God.

Alex swallowed. Erotic indeed. He was suddenly, blindingly aware that he stood behind her at almost the exact same angle, that he had only to reach around and cup her breast to echo the image painted on the wall before him.

She stared at it a long moment, her breathing quickening as she studied the image of a woman being caressed. The warm scent of her skin was like inhaling brandy fumes. He glanced down and could not help notice her nipples pricking up against the bodice of her dress. She wet her lips and stood as if entranced.

With a muffled groan he looked away, his own arousal spurred even further by the evidence of hers. Sweet torture. His hands ached to touch her as the woman before them was being touched, to rekindle that ancient desire.

"Very . . . lifelike," she said at last. Her cheeks were flushed and she seemed to make a deliberate point of not meeting his gaze.

"I don't expect you've seen garden statuary that echoed this theme."

"Ah, no. I'm sure I would recall if I had."

He had to smile at her response. "Come." He offered his hand, but she was already turning to the last canvas and lifting it aside.

Oh, bloody—

"Miss Huntington . . ." The painting was beyond everything proper. No wonder the Legaults had covered it. He opened his mouth but could not summon any words. She had taken an involuntary step back—her body pressed against him, her hair lightly brushing his throat.

"Heavens!" Shock and excitement laced her voice. "Whatever are they doing?"

He cleared his throat. "Bathing." It was a patent lie, but how the hell was he supposed to explain? His cock strained against his trousers.

She tilted her head. "I suppose she could be bathing a part of him. Though why she should be kneeling with her face so very close to his, er, his manly parts—"

"Stop." His voice was tight.

She continued, her breathing coming even more quickly. "And this one beside it—now she is the one being bathed. Though why her legs should need to be spread so wide . . ."

Without thinking he turned her, enfolded her in his arms. She came without hesitation, her clear brown eyes, damnably full of desire, of curiosity, searching his. He was vibrating with need, her arousal an unbearable spur.

There was nothing else to be done. Alex lowered his head and kissed her.

Chapter 9

Dear heavens. Mr. Trentham's lips came down over hers in a gesture that seemed inevitable, as if they had been moving toward this kiss from the moment they had met. It was a wildness of sensation, a shiver that ran through her entire body from the place their mouths touched. Caroline trembled, as though she were made of nothing more substantial than air and light, and gave herself up to it.

His kiss was warm and firm and as perfectly commanding as the rest of him. She obeyed—she could do nothing less—as he enfolded her in his arms and pressed her close. All her thoughts fell away, and she was falling, falling up, into the sky.

It was as though she had been waiting for this feeling for years; the sense of rightness, of completion, was like a key turning in a lock. Her body was swept with tickling flame, the impossible breathlessness of being fused so closely against him, the hardness of a male body so different from her own. So wonderfully different.

The kiss was over far too soon. To her dismay he set her at arm's length, his expression shuttered, though his breathing came as fast as her own.

This would never do. Not at all—not if she wanted him to kiss her again. Which she did, rather desperately. Kiss her and . . . other things, things she had seen pictured quite recently.

Her bosom tingled at the thought. She stepped forward until her skirts brushed his trousers.

"Miss Huntington." His voice was rough. "You would do well to keep your distance."

"Why?"

"Because you don't know where this will lead."

She set her palm to his shirtfront, feeling the heat of his skin, the hard muscles beneath the cotton. Immediately his hand encircled her wrist, his grip hard, inexorable—but he did not pull her hand away. She stared up into his turbulent blue eyes, his body strung taut.

"You may find far more than you've bargained for." His grasp on her wrist loosened and he set both hands to her shoulders, holding her in place—to keep her from coming closer, or from moving away, she was not certain which.

"I've been kissed before," she said.

She *had* been kissed before—once. She recalled the occasion with clarity. The garden party where Charlie Burnham had shown her the rose arbor and then clumsily embraced her, his lips sliding from her cheek over to her mouth. It had been a rather damp experience, as he seemed unsure what the desired effect ought to be, or how to achieve it. Afterward, she'd surreptitiously wiped her face with her handkerchief. The experience had left her utterly dissatisfied. Surely there had to be something more.

Alex had just shown her there was—very much more. If only he would kiss her again.

"Let me demonstrate exactly the danger you seem so determined to court." His voice emerged as nearly a growl.

A shiver of anticipation went through her as he stared at her a long moment, then bent his head, capturing her mouth with his. A wild, womanly part of her rejoiced, a part that kindled when his mouth descended over hers, that knew enough to name the spark in his eyes as hot desire.

This was an altogether different kind of kiss from the first.

Possessive and hungry, as though something in him had broken free of restraints, a fierceness in the way his lips took hers. His fingers laced through her hair, while his other hand moved to her back and pressed her tightly to him.

His tongue licked at her lips, as though he tasted something sweet and must devour every trace of it. It was shockingly intimate, but even more so when he nudged her mouth open with his and swept his tongue inside. Hot and wicked. She dug her fingers into his shoulder to keep her balance while new sensations stormed through her.

He nudged her a step back, mouth still covering hers, until she was against the wall, her splinted arm useless at her side. The stone at her back, Alex over her, pressing against her, his body heavy and insistent, kissing her like a starving man with a feast set before him.

The first kiss had been a sweet breeze. This was a hurricane, seizing her far off course, the uncharted sea a tumult, her senses whirling. He circled his tongue around hers and she gasped from the pleasure of it, the fierce current of desire that poured from him straight into her, as though she were drinking it from their open mouths, fused together. It was heady—far stronger than any liquor she had tried, and blurred her mind ferociously until there was only the feel of his body hard against hers, his hand tangled in her hair, the impossible tempest of their kiss.

She would not have remained standing but for him pinning her against the wall. Then he dropped his hand to her breast and she gasped aloud. Sparks showered through her and she was filled with hot confusion. She squirmed beneath his hand and he pulled back, abruptly breaking their kiss.

Both of them were breathing raggedly, and her heartbeat pulsed through her in waves. She flattened her palm against the stones and stared up at him, dizzy and overwhelmed.

"Is that what you want—to be taken like some wanton against a ruined wall?" His voice was hard, but there was something desolate in his eyes. "What then? Could you look me in the face the next day, Caroline Huntington? Would you think well of me—of yourself?"

"No." The word emerged as a thin whisper. Despite her yearning for him, it was too much, too soon.

"Say it again."

"No." Stronger this time. She pushed herself upright.

"I didn't think so." He stepped away. "Be careful what you ask for."

Throat dry, she watched him gather his self-control and wrap it around himself like a tattered cloak. He had not meant to kiss her then, at least not at first, but he thought she had been affected as much as he.

Dear heavens. Alex had kissed her, and nothing would ever be the same.

He climbed the ladder, held his hand out to help her up the last few rungs but did not offer his arm as they silently made their way back. Concentrating on her footing, she tried to calm the jumbled whirl of her thoughts. Alex. Kissing her. It was the thing that shone brightest, despite his attempt to frighten her away.

Alex jammed his hands into his pockets and paced beside Miss Huntington, ignoring the twinge in his leg. Damn him for a fool—but at least at the end he had made her see she was trifling with things better left alone. If only she would keep her distance, he would be able to subdue the beast of desire she had set free in him.

It was encouraging that she did not try to draw him into conversation as they walked back to the picnic site. Truly, he did not need this complication, this thunderous unbalancing of his life she had wrought. Nothing good could come of it. Far better he had stopped her now, no matter that the world seemed greyer, the hollow inside himself echoing.

Pen was still dozing. She opened her eyes halfway as they approached and smiled a dreamy smile at them.

"It's really too comfortable, Caro. Here." She patted the nest of cushions beside her.

"If you insist." Miss Huntington took a seat on the blanket beside her friend. "Perhaps a short rest. Thank you for the company, Mr. Trentham." She did not look at him, and he pretended what he felt was relief.

"I'm going to talk with Legault," he said. "Come find me when you wake." He hoped the Frenchman would have more bones for him—anything to take his mind from kissing Caroline. Though he knew it would not be that simple.

A dusty half hour later Pen hailed him. He looked up from the newest finds Legault had unearthed to see her approaching, Miss Huntington lagging several steps behind.

"I'm going to show Caroline the basilica. Would you care to join us?"

"Not now. I'm examining something for Monsieur Legault." He squinted at the sky, judging the sun's position. "Collect me on your way back. We should be riding out soon." He kept himself from glancing at Miss Huntington. No need to act like a besotted schoolboy.

Pen nodded. "We won't be long. Come on, Caro." She frowned over her shoulder at him as they left.

This time he did watch as the ladies headed for the perimeter of the excavation. Perhaps he ought to join them; he could not concentrate on the delicate bones Legault had directed him to.

He was setting his tools aside when the sharp crack of a shot, followed by a woman's shriek, split the lazy air. He was running before his mind had finished identifying the sound. Dread pushed his heels hard against the uneven ground as he sprinted forward, air rasping his throat. Where were they? Bloody hell, why had he let the women out of his sight?

He rounded the corner of the ruined basilica. Empty. But there— Was that a flutter of calico near the jumbled stones? Yes. They were there among the trees, Caroline's arm about Pen. Both of them still standing.

Relief poured through him.

"What happened?" He fetched up hard beside them. "Caroline, are you all right? Pen, you're bleeding." He took the girl's chin, turning her face to see the long scratch down one cheek.

"I was standing by the wall when there was an explosion of some sort." Pen's voice was shaky. "Then I pushed Caro into the cypress."

"It was a shot," Caroline said, her face pale.

"Here." He thrust his handkerchief into her hand. "See to Pen. It's a cut, not a graze. The bullet must have ricocheted off the wall." He whirled and scanned the brush. "What kind of idiot is out here shooting?"

Caroline shook her head. "That shot came far too close to Pen."

"And to you." He caught sight of movement beyond the trees. "Stay here."

He dodged through the cypresses, fury and fear a tight knot in his throat. There. A skulking figure in the underbrush. Alex burst from the trees and launched himself at the fellow, knocking the rifle from his hands.

"I say!" It was an English voice. "What the devil are you about?"

Alex grabbed a fistful of the stranger's coat and drew him forward. "I'm asking you the same. What in bloody hell are you doing with a gun out here?"

Muddy brown eyes set over a blunt nose blinked at him. "After pheasant, of course. Had a lovely fat one—or nearly did. Went to ground just there." He jerked his head toward the trees.

"Your shot went astray." God, when he thought of how close it had come to Caroline, to Pen. He shook the man. "You nearly struck one of my companions."

"Never say so!" The man pulled his hat off. "Had no idea anyone was about. None at all."

"Who are you, anyhow?" Alex released his grip on the man's coat, part of him wishing the fellow had offered more resistance. It was difficult to release his own anger when faced with such easy capitulation.

"Mr. John Simms, sportsman at large." He offered a meaty hand.

Alex stared at him a moment, then took it. He did not expect the bruising force that accompanied Mr. Simms's handshake but applied equal pressure in return.

"You're the new arrival, then. I advise you to keep clear of this area—it's the site of an archaeological excavation. In fact"—he bared his teeth in something he hoped did not in the least resemble a smile—"I advise you to give up shooting altogether. It can be a dangerous sport."

Something flashed in the man's eyes before he dropped his gaze and turned his hat about in his hands. "Aye, I see that well enough. The game hereabouts is tricky. Better luck fishing, maybe."

"Indeed. Good day, Mr. Simms."

The man replaced his crumpled hat, then bent and retrieved his gun. "My apologies for startling you. See you about the village, I suppose."

Or not. Alex wanted nothing to do with him—and most certainly did not want Caroline or Pen anywhere near the man. Something in his manner was decidedly off. Alex watched, arms folded, as Simms took himself off. Just before he descended from view the sportsman turned and gave a jaunty wave.

Alex waited until he was out of sight, then returned to the women. Pen's cheek had stopped bleeding, and Caroline seemed to have collected herself.

"A hunter," he explained briefly, voice tight. "His shot went astray. I dare say he won't be shooting on the island again." He should have confiscated the man's rifle. If he heard of Simms using it again, he would not hesitate to do so. "Come, let's bid the Legaults farewell."

Past time they left the excavation. He would not feel easy until the women were safely back in their rooms at the villa.

Chapter 10

Caroline did not care to admit it, but the next day she was content to rest. Clouds had rolled in from the south, borne by North African winds. A light spattering of rain made it easier to pull a lap robe over herself and spend the morning with her copy of *Jane Eyre: An Autobiography,* by Currer Bell.

The book had been published only last year, and there was much speculation as to whether the author was male or female. She suspected female and had read the novel a half dozen times, taking pleasure in the tale of an orphan far less fortunate than herself who in the end gains true happiness.

She turned a page but could not concentrate on the story—not when another story was spinning inside her. Alex's kiss and the way it had made her feel. She could not stop replaying it in her mind, could not stop wishing that he would kiss her again, today. And the next day. And the one after that. She traced her lips with the tip of her finger and closed her eyes, trying to evoke the vivid flames he had lit within her.

Where would it lead? She pushed the question away. It did not matter, not while she was still here, on Crete. Despite his warnings, she knew she was safe with him. Alex would never press her past her consent.

A brusque knock at the door made her smile and drop her hand from her mouth. "Come in, Mr. Trentham."

He strode in, shoulders darkened from the rain, drops caught in his raven black hair. "Good afternoon." His expression was serious, but it lightened as he moved into the room, as though seeing her wrought a subtle transformation in him.

Certainly it worked a powerful one in her. She rose and set her book aside, then, unsure, folded her good arm under her sling. Yesterday had been impetuous, but standing here, facing him in her own rooms, awkwardness settled between them. This was not a secluded site decorated with highly improper illustrations, where a kiss would be a simple, inexorable thing.

He cleared his throat and waved her to the nearby chair. "Sit. Let me take a look at your arm."

So it was to be the doctor, not the lover. Not that she had expected . . . well. She did not know what to expect, but no matter how he might insist he was only her physician, they were more than that. Friends at the very least—and how unanticipated that was. A wry smile tugged her lips. She never would have imagined becoming fond of this dark and taciturn man, this reluctant doctor of hers.

Swallowing back the hope that sprang up every time, she unhooked the sling and offered her splint for inspection. Three weeks since her fall. It seemed an eternity. She felt completely different, as though the Caroline Huntington who had tumbled from her horse was barely the same woman who sat here now, acutely aware of the man standing before her.

He unwound the linen, each layer freeing her until he reached the splint and lifted it away, then set his fingers to the exposed skin of her elbow and pressed. "Any pain?"

"No." She blinked in surprise. "None at all."

"Hmm." He took her hand in his and extended her arm. "How about now?" His hair fell across his forehead as he bent over her, focused on his task.

She tried to concentrate on how her arm felt, but it was nearly impossible. Awareness of him hummed through her, as if the two of them were engaged in a quiet, formal dance, his touch guiding her movements. She felt her breathing deepen, as though they were dancing in truth, her hand placed lightly in his as he whirled her through some candlelit ballroom.

"Miss Huntington?"

She glanced up at him, recalled his question. "A faint ache, that's all."

He released her hand and moved to stand behind her. "Raise your right arm straight out to the side. Yes, like that." He slipped his hands beneath, supporting her. "Very good. Now relax."

That proved easy enough, as her muscles were amazed and trembling to be put to use again. Goodness, she had not expected to become weak in such a short time. Alex moved her arm forward and back, then, seemingly satisfied, laid it in her lap, leaning over her as he did so.

Sudden heat washed her. His head was bent very close and the familiar scent of him—sage and something essentially male—tingled her senses. She held still, afraid to move, nearly afraid to breathe.

His voice was low and deep. "I think we've reached a milestone, Miss Huntington, don't you?"

"Yes." It came out a whisper.

She sensed his gaze and turned her head. Their faces were bare inches apart. She leaned forward, yearning to set her lips against his, to sigh in his breath, to learn the taste of him.

"Miss Huntington." His voice carried a soft warning, one that she chose to ignore. It took a mere inclination of her head to bring her mouth to his.

Softly at first, she brushed her lips across, exploring the feel of him. His mouth was like silk, the skin of his face slightly rough, and the contrast made warmth kindle deep within her. The curve of his lower lip was irresistible. She nibbled gently, darting her tongue out to taste him.

Alex held still, but she felt a tremor run through him as she lifted her hands—both hands—and threaded them through his hair, bringing his mouth firmly against hers. A current of something sweet and exciting ran through her, igniting her to boldness. She flicked her tongue out, tasting him, heard his breathing speed as she licked the crease of his lips.

Then his mouth parted, his tongue met hers, and she was ablaze, a sudden wildfire sweeping through dry grasses. He held himself away from her, letting her control the kiss, though she could feel his hands gripping the chair to either side. It was a heady feeling. She slid one hand to the back of his neck and slanted her mouth, discovering how easily their mouths fitted as the kiss deepened.

An odd, aching pulse began to beat through her, spreading from her center. She breathed in time to it, let her tongue twine against his, obeying that primal rhythm. It was glorious—it was not enough. She recalled the feel of his body against her, craved it, then abruptly remembered where that had led. She pulled back, hands still woven through his hair.

His eyes remained closed a moment, and when he opened them she saw the same hunger she felt. She wanted him to rise, to sweep her tightly against him and kiss her once more, but instead he sat back on his heels.

"Alex." Her hands slipped to his shoulders.

He took her hands in his, held them firmly. "I have good news for you."

The thought that he was going to kiss her senseless faded as he watched her intently. She raised her brows. "You're going to let me order a forge for the village after all?"

A smile darted across his face. He turned her hands over, his thumbs rubbing her palms. "Almost as good. The splint is staying off. You'll only need the sling now."

It was hard to concentrate on his words, she was so distracted by him caressing her hands. The meaning took a moment to penetrate, and when it did she jerked her head up.

"Truly? I am healed?" Joy and dismay moved through her in waves. Healed. She had wanted nothing more for the last weeks, and yet . . . She bit her lip. She did not want to leave Crete, leave Alex. Not now, with something just begun between them.

"No—not fully healed. You need to rehabilitate your arm, regain your strength and range of motion. Do you swim?"

"Yes, of course." Her brother, James, had insisted she learn.

"Tomorrow after lunch, then. I know a bay that will suit admirably."

"Caro!" Pen's light voice called outside her door. "I've brought the post."

Alex released her hands and rose in one smooth motion. No more stolen kisses. She tried not to sigh too loudly as she called for Pen to come in.

"Letters from London!" The girl hurried into the room, brandishing a packet. "Oh, hello, Mr. Trentham." Her bright eyes darted to the piece of wood lying on the table. "Goodness, is that Caro's splint?"

"I was thinking of framing it as a memento of my adventures here," Caroline said. "What do you think?"

"If it were me, I'd fling it into the sea. How wonderful that you are rid of it at last. But here," she handed Caroline the letters, "you can open them yourself!"

She could not help smiling at her young friend. It was remarkable how the girl was blooming. She seemed to stand a little taller, and since Caroline insisted they take their meals together, Pen was losing her birdlike frailty. Food always tasted better in company, and they had yet to exhaust their many topics of conversation—most especially Mr. Trentham and his mysterious past.

He was from the north of England, and he had a brother. That was all Pen had been able to glean, though she had pestered the Legaults for details.

Pen and Caroline entertained themselves by fabricating wild histories for him. He was the disinherited son of a duke, banished for falling in love with a serving maid. He was a spy for Her Majesty, keeping an eye on the Ottoman Empire from this advantageous post. He was a smuggler, formerly employed by the East India Company—oh, the list went on. Yet somehow none of the stories ever seemed to fit, and Alex remained an enigma.

Caroline shot him a quick glance, running her fingers over the letters on her lap. "Such a blessing, being able to open my own correspondence. Oh, happy day."

"Indeed." A smile rose in his eyes, though his lips remained unbent. "I'm glad I could be here to witness this historic moment."

"Well, it is a treat. Even with the reliability of the P&O line, this is the first correspondence from home I've received since my injury."

"Then I'll leave you to it." Alex inclined his head. "Until tomorrow, Miss Huntington. And don't forget your bathing costume."

"Bathing costume?" Pen asked.

"Mr. Trentham is determined to throw me into the sea tomorrow."

The girl laughed. "The swimming is lovely here. But Madame asked me to join her tomorrow afternoon—unless, of course, you need me."

"I think I can manage to keep Miss Huntington from drowning." Alex bowed, a glint of something mischievous in his eyes. "I will see you tomorrow."

Caroline watched him go. Wherever was her bathing costume? Likely deep in one of her trunks, the voluminous dark blue dress packed away after her injury. It was not terribly becoming, but that could not be remedied. As for Alex—would he go shirtless? Perhaps she would be able to see the strong muscles of his arms and chest, slick with water. . . .

"Aren't you going to read your letters?"

"Of course." Forcing her breathing to slow, Caroline shook free of daydreaming and turned to her correspondence. "This one's from my uncle."

She read it, feeling his concern clearly even through the scrim of pen on paper. The last letter she had posted had been full of reassurances that she was nearly healed and would soon be on her way back to London. It had been mostly optimism, but she had needed to ease his worry.

Next, a letter from the Ladies' Auxiliary Board. She would read it over, then forward it to Maggie. She scanned the text, then read it again more carefully, a thread of anxiety winding through her.

"Is something wrong?" Pen asked, perceptive as usual.

"No—at least not yet. I can't tell precisely, but . . ." She felt her brows pull into a frown.

Vague allusions to other projects the board was considering, the reassurances they found her and Maggie's work of value—but there was something in the tone of the letter that did not seem right. Most dismaying, however, was the postscript scrawled at the bottom from their ally within the organization, Mrs. Thorne. *Advise you return posthaste. Dispensary funding in jeopardy.*

"What's the dispensary?" Pen had come to stand beside her and was reading over her shoulder.

"Maggie and I intend to expand the Twickenham School—the charity boarding school I told you of—and add a place to treat illnesses and make medicines available. It's a pressing need in the poorer neighborhoods."

Pen nodded. "It seems an excellent idea."

"It is—and we thought the board agreed. But now I'm not so sure." It was a string tying her to London, and tugging. "Fetch my lap desk, and I'll compose a reply." With Maggie so involved with the project in Valletta, Caroline would have to take the lead in London. Although it was difficult to argue persuasively for the project from such a distance.

Pen held up a last package. "What's this? It looks intriguing—from a place called Somergate."

"My brother's estate." Caroline took it, spirits lifting a

notch. It contained a brief, concerned note from her brother, and a much longer letter from his wife, Lily, plus a watercolor sketch of a purple hyacinth in bloom.

"Oh," Pen said, "that is lovely."

"Yes, my brother married a talented artist. Lily is about to publish a folio of her botanical illustrations, and she always includes a little something in her letters. Last time it was a sketch of a teacup, though she prefers flowers."

"I do, too. But I never was much for drawing them." Pen pursed her mouth and sent a considering look at the bouquet on the table.

Caroline mentally added art lessons to the already long list of things she would like to provide the girl. She set Lily's letter aside and regarded her companion. "Dear Pen, I have been thinking."

"Oh?" The girl tilted her head.

With the reminders of her life in London, her thoughts about Pen's future had crystallized into determination. "Come with me when I return to England. Now that Maggie is delayed indefinitely on Malta, I'm in need of a traveling companion. Besides, I would miss you terribly if you had to stay behind on Crete."

"Really?" Pen's eyes opened wide. "I could go with you?"

"Of course. I would like nothing more—if you find it agreeable." The Legaults had expressed a willingness to take her back to Paris with them, but Pen was an Englishwoman. She would thrive best rooted in her home soil. Would the girl refuse? Caroline laced her fingers together. She did not think so, but . . .

"I do, I find it most agreeable!" Then Pen's expression dimmed. "But perhaps it isn't the best idea after all."

"And why is that?" Caroline leaned forward, willing her to agree.

The girl bit her lip. "I'm not certain what my situation in London would be. And if—when—my father returns for me, he would wonder. . . ."

"Then Mr. Trentham and the Legaults can tell him where you have gone, and that you're safe and well. You can leave a letter to him in their care." Pen would be far better off making her own life than waiting here indefinitely for a man as negligent and unreliable as her father. "I will help in whatever way I can." She set her hand on the girl's shoulder. "In fact, I am in need of a secretary. It strikes me that you would fit that position exceptionally well. May I offer you permanent employment?"

"Oh, Caro! What a dear friend you are." The tears in Pen's eyes spilled over. "I don't dcscrvc you." She pulled her sleeve across her cheeks and leaned into Caroline's embrace.

"We all deserve the best, Pen. All of us."

The next day saw a return to warm breezes and sunshine, and Caroline felt a mounting anticipation for her afternoon swim with Alex. Anticipation that slowly curdled to frustration as she searched in vain for her bathing costume.

"I can't find it anywhere—and this is the last valise."

Pen looked up from the stack of garments she was refolding. "Likely Mrs. Farnsworth finds herself in possession of two." She sounded exasperatingly calm.

"But—" Caroline felt upset, all out of proportion. She had nurtured such hopes for the outing.

"Caro, don't fret." Pen rose, a chemise draped over her arm. "We'll devise something you can swim in. Don't you think this will work?"

"A single chemise?" She shook her head, then thought a moment. "Perhaps two, layered together, with the skirts split and bloused around my ankles. That ought to preserve my modesty well enough and still allow some freedom of motion." And most important, enable her to spend the afternoon with Alex.

A quarter hour later she laughed at herself in the mirror, her calico walking dress oddly bulky and bunched over the makeshift bathing costume. Hardly the alluring picture she had wanted to present, but it would have to do.

"We can mend your chemises once we leave Crete," Pen said. "We'll have time on the way back to England." The girl had clearly embraced the idea. Every other word she spoke today was *England.* "But Madame is expecting me, and I see Mr. Trentham is waiting below. Enjoy your swim!"

"Tell him I'll be down directly."

Outside, Caroline found her placid steed tethered beside Alex's glossy chestnut. She shook her head in feigned dismay. "I did hope you'd find me a livelier mount. I trust we haven't far to go."

"A short way down the coast. There's a cove that's warm, even in spring. Up you go." He boosted her into the saddle, swung up onto Icarus, and led the way—at a very tranquil pace.

It was not too long, perhaps a half hour, when the horses made their way down a boulder-strewn incline and she saw the cove. Sheltered by a curving line of hills that tapered into the sea, the turquoise water gleamed and beckoned, hushing quietly on the sand. Another few minutes' ride saw them to the beach.

"Here we are." He reined Icarus beside a lone tree filled with creamy blossoms and dismounted.

Caroline let him lift her down. The feel of his hands at her waist was distractingly pleasant, although he released her as soon as her feet touched the sand.

"What is that lovely smell? It seems I should know it."

He wound the reins around a limb of the tree, then looked up into the branches. "Almond blossoms." He reached and broke off a spray, presented it to her.

"Thank you, good sir." She laughed. "And here I thought you had no feelings for me." She batted her eyelids in an exaggerated fashion.

The corner of his mouth twitched. "Milady, your bath awaits."

She looked out over the bay. "It's a marvelously large tub. However do you heat it?"

"Come and see." He strode down to the sea, then trailed one hand in the frothy waves that pushed up onto the sand. When he straightened she thought he was smiling.

"How is it?" she called.

"Perfect."

He peeled off his coat as he came back toward her. Like the locals, he went without a waistcoat, and the white expanse of his shirt made Caroline blink. She stared at the sun-bronzed skin at his throat.

"I presume you brought your bathing costume?"

She flushed. "I, ah, seem to have misplaced it."

"Really." He looked at her, something flickering in his eyes. "I didn't take you for a nude bather, Miss Huntington. How . . . provocative."

She shivered. The thought of being naked in front of him sent a curious prickling over her skin. "Ah . . . I have something I think will do. Instead."

He nodded, then stood watching her, hands on his hips.

She slipped her arm from her sling, untied her bonnet, then began pulling pins from her hair, conscious of his gaze on her. The act of taking down her hair had never felt so intimate. Each loosened strand moved in the light breeze, brushed across her face and hands. She gathered it up, fingers beginning to plait it into a braid.

"Leave your hair down," he said, his voice compelling. "It's beautiful."

She stilled. "Very well." Pen could help her comb the tangles out later. She set her fingers to the buttons of her blouse, then glanced at him. "It's rather ungentlemanly of you to watch."

A grin unfurled across his face, feral edged, nothing she had seen on him before, though his eyes held the same heat she recalled from their kiss by the frescoes. "I've told you before, I don't profess to be a gentleman. And you've already said you are wearing something suitable."

She cleared her throat. Suddenly two chemises layered together did not seem nearly modest enough. Once they entered the water she should be sufficiently covered; it was just a matter of getting to that point.

Heat gathered on her cheeks as she released her buttons, the blouse falling open while his eyes followed her hands. Her nipples tingled as she parted the cloth and slipped the blouse over her shoulders, letting the fabric flutter to the sand. Dear heavens. Her bathing costume felt as insubstantial as clouds—not suitable at all. She could tell as much by the hungry expression on his face.

The air felt marvelous against her bare arms, her neck—as if his gaze had sensitized her skin. She caught her lower lip between her teeth and slipped open the first button of her skirt. Fire leaped in his eyes, and she felt a surge of knowing. He might think he was in command, but she suddenly knew she wielded power over him. Two more buttons, and then she paused.

"Your turn."

His eyes widened a fraction. "It is?"

She gave a slow nod.

Lifting one brow, he mirrored her earlier actions, his hands brown against the white linen. One button, then the next—though, unlike her, there was nothing but Alex, naked, beneath his shirt. Caroline wet her lips, her breath deepening as his sun-darkened skin was revealed. His shoulders were firm with muscle, his ribs and stomach, the vee of hair that arrowed down beneath the waistband of his trousers. . . .

She jerked her head up, met his bright and knowing gaze. Ah, she was no match for him. Heat rushed through her and she was certain he could see the flush on her body, the confusion and desire blazoned on her face.

He bent and pulled off his boots and she took advantage of his distraction to shed her skirts. They fell like a wilted blossom. She unlaced her boots and slipped her feet free, then stepped, barefoot, out of the tumble of cloth. Toward the glittering sea. Toward Alex.

England was worlds away. This was Crete: the soft breeze, the warm sun, the blossom-laden tree. Here the ancient gods had come to earth when the world was new. Alex held out his hand and together they walked down to where the water smoothed the shore.

A wavelet hurried up the sand, pushing past its siblings, and broke over her toes. Caroline gasped and stepped back, out of the water's reach. "It's cold."

"I've never heard you squeal before." He tilted his head, eyes laughing at her.

"I did not squeal. It's just . . . my skin is very sensitive to temperature." She waved at the sea. "You go enjoy a nice swim. I'll stay here in the sun for a bit longer."

"We didn't come so *I* could swim, Caroline."

"But I'm certain you do it very well. I'll just watch from the warm, dry sand." She took another step back.

He followed, a trace of a smile playing about his lips. "This kind of thing is always easier faced head-on. I'll help you."

"Oh, I don't need your help." The wicked light in his eyes signaled his intentions, and she was not going to let him drag her in bodily.

He reached for her. She turned and dashed away, toes digging into the sand, breeze in her hair, the breathless laughter of the chase bubbling through her. "You can't catch me!" She looked over her shoulder to see him standing, shirtless and barefoot, hands on his hips.

"You are only putting off the inevitable, you know."

"Won't it affect your solemn dignity too much to chase an injured woman down the beach?" She paused and glanced at the clear water, the tumbled ochre stones.

Movement made her whirl. Alex was much quicker than

she had given him credit for. She darted, laughing, past his outstretched fingers, and headed back toward the almond tree.

"No, you don't." He sprinted after her, caught her around the waist and pulled her back against him. "I see you require more persuasion." His voice was warm, but his skin warmer, the heat of him pressing through the layers of fabric. She could feel the rise and fall of his chest in counterpoint to her own breath. "Will you go? Or do you need to be carried?"

Some impish whim kept her silent.

"What was that?" He bent his head close to hers, his hair feathering across her cheek.

Heat shot through her, along with the languorous impulse to lay her head back against his shoulder and close her eyes. His arm was still firmly about her, his other hand resting on her hip.

"Very well," she whispered. "I surrender."

"You will not run again?" His breath warmed her ear.

"I promise. . . ."

Slowly he opened his arms.

"I promise to run as fast as I can." She darted away, and he followed, a single laugh pulled from his throat.

"So that's the way of it?" He caught her easily, despite his uneven gait, and scooped her up in his arms. "I can see that someone needs to introduce you to the sea."

Before she could protest, he waded into the surf, still carrying her. The cool water foamed over her feet and curled about her ankles, climbing higher with each step. Now the backs of her thighs, the chemises flapping wetly. She did enjoy swimming, truly. It was just getting *into* the water that was difficult.

"Mr. Trentham!" She tried to scramble up him as he lowered her into the water, but he would not let her go.

At last her feet found the bottom, the ocean surging around her waist.

"All right?" His grip on her hand never faltered. "We need to go deeper."

She nodded, could not help gasping as the layers of cotton wicked moisture up, the fabric damp nearly to her breasts.

"Alex, I'm not sure—"

"You're making it much harder than it needs to be." He led her farther from shore.

They were past where the gentle waves broke, into that place of buoyant swells. She reached for him, and he supported her effortlessly. Water curled around her ribs, lapping up her spine—shockingly pleasant. When it rose past the curve of her breasts, Caroline let out a breath. There. It was not so bad after all. A laugh escaped her.

He looked at her, eyes dark with amusement. "You survived."

"I've finally found the best way to enter the sea. Pity I can't take you with me every time I desire a swim."

The bright sun on the surface dazzled, reflecting the light in an infinite variety of shifting patterns. It was pleasant here in the water, she had to admit. But not as pleasant as it had been in his arms.

Chapter 11

Alex fought the urge to take Caroline back into his embrace and press kisses on her full, tempting lips. It had been foolish to bring her here alone, and even more foolish to have carried her into the sea. God knew he wanted her—wanted to taste her, feel her sweet curves pressed against him. Instead he let the water roll and surge, let the cool weight of the sea take some of the heat from him.

Chasing her down the beach had been one of the best moments he could remember, knowing he would ultimately catch her, sharing her delight as she laughed into the wind. What was it about this woman that made it impossible for him to act sensibly? Every time he thought he had reinforced the barriers, she said or did something that delighted him, that reminded him he was still alive.

"Shall we begin?" She was looking expectantly at him.

Oh yes, her rehabilitation. He forced himself to resume the role of doctor.

"Start by pushing the water away from you. Flex the joint. That's it."

"Goodness, my arm feels like it's made of lead." She swirled the water in front of her, then made great arcs back and forth, nearly losing her footing in the process.

"Steady." He moved to stand behind her, ready to brace her

or fish her out if she went under, but she surprised him. In one smooth movement she launched herself into a breaststroke, heading parallel to the shore. He stood, evaluating her form a moment. Good, she knew how to handle herself in the water, though her arm would tire easily.

It did not take him long to draw even with her; she was a decent swimmer, but he was better. The water was his best friend now, more than the land, where each step recalled him to the burden of the past.

She glanced over and smiled, then stopped moving and let her feet find purchase. "You were right—a dreadful habit of yours, I must say. This feels wonderful."

"How does your elbow feel? Strain? Ache?"

"Fine." She pushed a wet tendril of hair back. "Though a bit noodley."

"Ah, noodley. A well-known medical term for that very condition. Indeed, you have a serious case of noodley arm."

"And what do the medical texts recommend for such a malady?"

He stroked his chin and pretended to ponder. "A bit of butter and garlic, or perhaps a nice tomato basil sauce."

"Do you mock me, sir?" She looked down her nose at him, but her eyes were laughing. He caught the motion of her arm and ducked just as a glittering spray of water arced toward him.

He swam underwater, finally emerging deeper out. She was scanning the water around her, brows drawn together until she caught sight of him.

"There you are! I declare, are you part seal?"

"I was born beside the sea—a far wilder one than this. As a lad I had to be a strong swimmer or the current would drag me away."

She paddled toward him. "A lad? I can hardly imagine you as one."

He shrugged. "I can hardly imagine it either. Come, let's swim to those rocks."

It deflected her, as he knew it would. Miss Caroline Huntington could never resist a challenge. It was not too far to where the rocky arm of the hills curled in to shelter the cove, but Alex was careful to pace her, ready to offer his own strength if hers faltered. A few minutes later she hoisted herself up onto the warm reddish stone.

"Ah," she said, "you must agree it is more pleasant in the sun than in the water. Do climb out."

He could not.

The bathing costume she had fashioned, while scarcely modest when dry, was stunningly inadequate when wet. The garment clung to her, almost transparent despite the double layer of fabric. Her breasts were clearly outlined, the dusky rose of her nipples pressing against the cloth.

He swallowed, his breathing ragged, and not from the exertion of swimming. There was no way he could join her; his aroused state would be immediately obvious, and the cool water did nothing to assuage him. She seemed unaware of his reaction, or of how exposed she was, lying back with one arm pillowed under her head.

No wonder sailors ran their ships aground when they saw mermaids sunning on rocks. Lonely men, long from the company of women.

He cleared his throat. "I'm going to swim a bit longer."

"Very well. I'll just have a nap. Wake me when you're done." She brought her arm up, laying it across her eyes.

Heat pulsed in his groin, and he could not take his gaze from her. Her throat curved down in a graceful line to the dip of her collarbone, and the shape of her breasts made his body ache with wanting. Her belly, her hips, the sweet length of her legs . . .

With a groan Alex pushed off from the rocks and swam away from her—this siren, this temptress who did not even know her own power.

It took two circuits of the cove before he gained enough

control over himself to return. Without looking at her, beyond seeing that her eyes were still closed, he pulled himself onto the rocks beside her and resolutely stared out to sea.

The light was starting to fall into heavy afternoon. This time of day, in summer, everyone would be home, shades drawn, trying to find escape from the heat in dreaming, but that was months away. Now it was perfect, air as warm as his own breath, gentling the touch of the sea from his skin.

"Caroline. Wake up." He turned to her.

She murmured but did not stir. Temptation rose over him in a sudden wave and pulled him under. He bent, pressed a kiss on her shoulder, her cheek, the point of her jaw. When he reached her lips he felt her smile beneath his mouth. She lifted her arm and hooked it about his neck, and he was lost.

The desire he had held in check roared through him, as unstoppable as a rogue wave. His mouth claimed hers, hotly, desperately, and she welcomed him, arching up into the kiss. Impossible, courageous woman. His hand moved to her breast, touching her through the thin layers of cotton, learning her exact curve and how it fitted to his palm.

Her nipple stood erect, and he brushed it lightly with his thumb, back and forth, teasing her, tempting her.

"Ah." Her voice was soft, laden with arousal.

He laid one leg across her thighs and slid over her, covering her. "Siren," he murmured. She had lured him here, all unknowing. It was a welcome doom.

Her hands smoothed down his sides, caressed his ribs. Years of rigidly suppressed need leapt when she touched him, a dark flood that threatened to carry him away. Alex was drowning—in her kiss, in the feel of her softness against him, with only the thin barrier of layered cotton between his skin and hers.

"Caroline," he breathed, then placed urgent kisses down the curve of her throat. He was so full of wanting.

She sighed and arched back, her breasts pushing against him, the flutter of her pulse fast under his hungry mouth. He slid his hands around to brace her, then dipped his head lower, taking one nipple into his mouth through the cloth. She moaned deep in her throat as he curled his tongue around the tight peak and sucked gently.

So lovely, so passionate. He had known she would be, knew it from the fire in her eyes, the way she never backed down from a challenge.

He moved to her other breast, teasing and stroking her with his tongue until the nipple pressed tautly against the damp cotton. She was intoxicating—he could lose himself in the valley between her breasts, or in the rounded rise of her hips, where his hands circled. Or her ripe lips. He kissed her there again and she met him, moving her mouth under his, wanting him as much as he wanted her.

Nothing could cool this fire, not a thousand swims in a thousand seas. He was burning and only the taste of her could quench him. His tongue swept against hers, mouths fused together, and he was acutely aware of her hands splayed across his naked back, the press of her breasts and stomach and thighs. Need coiled through him, tightened his groin to an unbearable ache.

Some sliver of sanity held him back, even as he ravished her mouth and held her hard against him, some awareness that remembered who he was. What he was.

With a harsh groan he broke the kiss, but he could not relinquish her. Not yet. He needed to hold her, needed the feel of her burned into his body. Something to remember during the long nights after she had gone.

She slowly opened her eyes and stared up at him. This close it seemed as though shards of sunlight danced in their brown depths.

"Well." Her voice was unsteady. "Was that part of your cure, too?"

"Was it effective?"

She wet her lips with her tongue. "I must say it was."

"Good." It affected him more than she would ever know. Their kisses already deviled his nights—this would make them nearly unbearable.

An impish smile lit her face. "I presume the treatment will take several applications."

How she tempted him. But he was returned to himself now, no longer a sailor and a captive mermaid, lost in some dreaming shred of myth. He shook his head and rolled off her, then got to his feet. Impossible to stay so close without touching her again.

She sat up and tilted her head at him. "Are we swimming back?" She waved across the cove toward the white foam of the almond tree.

"Unless you fancy a barefoot walk over sharp rocks. Or—I could carry you."

"You would, too." She gave him a measuring look. "That will not be necessary. I suppose I must go back into the water." A delicate shiver ran through her.

"Jump in. Like this." Alex found handholds and climbed up onto the highest rock. "There's a flat spot here," he called, "perfect for diving."

He looked down at the blue waves, a good twenty feet below, then launched himself, spearing cleanly into the water. Into the rushing, cool embrace of the sea, deep blue shading to lightness, then the pure air as he emerged. He shook his wet hair out of his eyes and looked up at her. "Care to try?"

She had her arms clasped around her knees. "I really don't—"

"I'll catch you." He sculled himself backward a few feet as she stood and eyed the water. "Unless, of course, you're afraid."

That did it—she lifted her chin and scrambled up the rocks. She gained the top and stood, her form perfectly silhouetted against the sky.

"Ready for me?" she called.

"Yes." *More than ready.*

"All right." She drew in a deep breath and leaped.

He was there, ducking beneath the surface moments before she submerged. He caught her, held her close, then kicked them up to the air with a powerful thrust of his legs. They broke free in a gust of spray and laughter.

"Oh my! Oh goodness!" Caroline clung to him, her legs scissoring next to his to help keep them afloat. "I never thought I could do that. It seemed so far, and hitting the water so shocking."

"But you're already used to it." He felt himself smiling at her.

She blinked at him. "Why—I am." Droplets clung to her lashes. The touch of her hands, water-slick against his skin, made his pulse begin to drum again, low and insistent.

He made himself pull away from her, then nodded at the beach. "After you, milady."

They went at an easy pace, but partway there he stopped, treading water. He could tell her arm was tiring.

"Hold to me a moment and catch your breath."

She nodded and grasped his shoulders. He could feel her relax, her breathing ease as they floated together on the waves. The cool sea lapped at the warmth where their bodies touched, and her hair swirled loose and free in the water, brushing his arms and chest. Desire flared again, and he closed his eyes, shutting out everything but the feel of her as they moved in the push and pull of the sea. A slow rhythm, insistent. God, he wanted to step out of time and place and let the tide of wanting carry them someplace far away.

They drifted together another long moment, and then she let go and together they swam to shore. The current fought with him, the shifting sand under his feet, but he knew the sea too well to yield to the undertow. He caught her hand in his, felt her stumble, and immediately pulled her up into his arms.

"Carrying me after all?" Her voice was throaty, but she made no protest, just slipped her arms around his neck and laid her head against his shoulder. "I'm getting used to it, I must confess. Dreadfully spoiled of me."

"Yes, you're quite overindulged." He splashed through the low waves and glanced down at her. "Though hasn't it crossed your mind that perhaps I have the better end of the bargain? After all, I get to hold a beautiful woman in my arms."

A blush colored her cheeks and her gaze slipped past his shoulder.

"You don't believe me?" Alex set her on her feet but kept one arm hooked about her waist. The expression on her face was half yearning, half disbelief. It was an endearing combination, and a rare one on the forthright Caroline Huntington. "I'm quite serious."

He lifted his hand to her face, traced the curve of her cheek, then set his fingers under her chin. One last kiss, here, today. The two of them alone against the sea. He could not help himself, any more than he could help the beating of his own heart.

It began lightly, full of soft yearning, but soon the fire rose in him, the hunger he could not leash when he held her. He devoured her mouth, his touch restless over her body as she pressed herself against him. It was not enough. He set his hands to her hips and pulled her close, his hard arousal pressed against her, trying to brand the feel of her into his skin, his bones.

She wrapped her arms about his neck and sighed with pleasure. The sound nearly drove him to bear her down onto the sand, tear the layered chemises from her lovely curves, make her indelibly his. Nearly—but she deserved so much better.

Slowly, he lifted his head, opened his arms and stepped away from her.

"Time to go."

Caroline opened her mouth, as if to argue, but he strode past her to the almond tree. A drift of petals had settled on their clothing. He lifted her skirt and shook it, loosing a flurry of white that could almost be snow, then held it open for her to step into. The touch of her hands on his shoulders, the thin drift of her cotton chemise, her fragrance—all these tangled his senses.

She donned her clothing, unhurriedly fastening the buttons and twisting up that fall of sun-shot brown hair. Something bittersweet settled in him, seeing the goddess that had shared the cove with him transform back into a proper Englishwoman, down to the pointed toes of her laced boots.

His own conversion was quicker. Pull on shirt and coat, shake the sand from his boots, run his fingers through his hair. Neither of them spoke, as though by holding their breaths they could spin the afternoon out a few more moments. Words would break the enchantment, and then they would be nothing but two separate, mortal souls, traveling too quickly away from one another.

Chapter 12

England, April 1848

"Keefe. Come in." Reginald turned from the rain-studded window of his library and waved the viscount to one of the leather-covered armchairs near the fire. "How kind of you to visit. Would you care for a whiskey?"

The blond man draped himself into the indicated chair and drummed his fingers on the arm. His green eyes were watchful. "Just wondering if there has been progress on our current project. Your cousin appears to be delayed."

Caroline had been due back a week ago. She was spoiling his plans, the blasted woman. Keeping the impatience from his face—though the viscount's restlessness mirrored his own—Reginald poured a tumbler and handed it to his guest. He was not surprised Keefe had paid him a call. The trick was to keep him on the hook until the chit actually materialized.

"My father received a letter from her. She is almost healed from her foolish accident and will be on her way home very soon. Patience, my friend, and the prize will be yours."

The viscount shifted, fingers running back and forth over the smooth leather. "I've stretched it damnably far already. I've told my family there's a prospect but they keep demanding to know who she is. And the damned creditors are knocking at my door." He took a long swallow of his drink. "I don't know how much longer I can put them off."

"Your family is your own problem. What would you have me do? Sail to the Mediterranean and drag my cousin back by the ear?" The man's whining was tiresome.

"Surely you can do something?"

"What *we* can do, my friend, is lay the groundwork so she drops into your hand like a ripe plum."

"Into my purse, you mean." There was a glint in Keefe's eye.

"Hand or purse—we can ensure it. The chit's weakness is her blasted orphans and that sinkhole of a school. That is the royal road to her heart. Present yourself as another do-gooder with an inheritance coming." He tilted an eyebrow at the viscount. "Tell her how much you care for the welfare of the despicable little urchins. How much you admire the methods of her school, and how much you admire the woman who sacrifices so much for others."

"Won't she be suspicious?"

"Hardly. She'll be too busy scrambling for money. I've called in a few favors and managed to have the funding for her newest project cut off. She'll be desperate, and you will be there to rescue her, handsome and sympathetic." To think how easily his cousin would be forced onto the path he had made for her. It was a pity he had not thought of it years ago.

The viscount raised his glass. "It seems a brilliant scheme. What is this project of hers I'm supposed to feign interest in?"

"A dispensary addition to her wretched boarding school. Very philanthropic. How could she not turn to you?"

"How, indeed?"

Reginald nodded. The man had few inconvenient morals to get in the way. He preferred working with Keefe's sort, the type of fellow who was completely predictable in his motivations. People talked about morals, but it was their hungers that made them act. Like his own hunger to go on living. And Keefe's inclination for opium. It was the *honorable* gentlemen who were problematic, capable of throwing months of planning awry by their incomprehensible actions. Men like his cousin James.

Fortunately, there were no gentlemen of that ilk involved. This would be a straightforward—and profitable—venture.

"I have something for you to ease your wait." He smiled at Keefe.

"And what would that be?" The viscount's tone was negligent—too negligent. Reginald noted how his fingers had stilled at the first mention of payment. Wonderfully predictable.

Reginald drew a silk-wrapped bundle from his pocket and placed it on the low table between them. Watching the viscount's reaction closely, he unfolded the cloth to reveal a black chunk of solid opium.

Keefe froze, like a setter coming on point. His nostrils flared and a subtle tension seemed to settle over him, a thin mantle of need.

"Or would you prefer some other pleasure?" Reginald made to draw the opium back, amused by the look of loss that ghosted over the viscount's features. It confirmed what he had been told: Keefe was more than a little enamored of the stuff and preferred it in a purer form than the tinctures most opium eaters favored.

"No. This will suffice." The viscount's gaze was still fixed on the drug.

Not until Reginald had pulled a concealing fold of silk back over it did Keefe seem able to look away. He leaned back in his chair and gave a tight smile.

"So, you are aware of my particular pleasures, Huntington." His tone was edged with displeasure. "I trust this information will remain confidential between us."

"Of course. We all have our weaknesses." Reginald rewrapped the opium and slid it toward the viscount.

The man reached for it with fingers that seemed rigidly controlled. "At least it's not the gaming tables for me."

A clumsy allusion to Reginald's own financial difficulties.

Difficulties that would be ended soon enough. He let the remark slide past. After all, *he* was the one who would ultimately reap the full benefit of their scheming.

Crete, April 1848

"This is such fun," Pen said, lifting her face to the light breeze. "What do you think we'll find on the island, Caro?"

Alex bent to the oars of Manolis's fishing boat, but most of his attention was on Caroline. Caroline. It was impossible to think of her as Miss Huntington now. Good thing this was a group outing. Less chance he would lose his head again, lured by her laughing eyes, her tempting mouth. . . .

Stop. Just stop it. He dug into the surface of the sea, channeling his desire down through the oars. Little eddies followed the blades as he dipped and pulled, dipped and pulled. She was not for him—she never could be. She belonged in London. He could never return to England.

If he had spent restless nights replaying her smiles, the feel of her softness under his hands, the taste of her against his mouth, it was no one's business but his. There were more than enough secrets locked behind his eyes. The fact that he could not help thinking of Caroline Huntington day and night was but one more to add to his sins.

"Do you think there's a resident sprite there?" Caroline was trailing her hand in the water, clearly having made her peace with the Mediterranean.

An afternoon of sunshine and water, two bodies melded close in the sea. He shook his head, willing himself not to think of it. He had recommended she and Pen swim together in the future and had pointed out a sheltered area near the village. Not as warm as the cove, but adequate. According to Pen they had gone there the last two afternoons.

Once away from her, the memory of who he was, what he

had done, had smashed down on him. He had no business—none whatsoever—kissing Miss Caroline Huntington, coaxing sweet sighs from her lips, letting his hands explore her body. Blast him, he should stay away, lock himself up with Legault's bones, but he was an idiot and could not resist the excuse to be near her. If it meant indulging Pen's whims and delaying their departure another few days, a week . . .

"The villagers say a Nereid lives on the island," Pen said. "She watches over sailors when storms blow up. Isn't that so, Manolis?"

"It is true." The weather-beaten man adjusted the sail, then nodded toward the little island they were making for. "I bring offerings of respect."

"Oh," Pen said. "I didn't bring anything."

"We will sing to her," Caroline said. "Perhaps 'Stars of the Summer Night' if you can remember your part."

The girl laughed. "I do better with 'The Beautiful Flowers of May.' Besides, it *is* almost May, and the flowers are beautiful."

"Miss Huntington is turning you into a proper lady, Pen." Alex tried to keep his tone light, despite the constant reminders that their departure for England was imminent. He would miss Pen, too, but could only approve Caroline's plan to take her back to London.

"I am merely teaching her some of the songs I know," Caroline said. "Music and poetry are important—for everyone." Her gaze fixed on him, serious and intent.

"For most people, certainly." He excluded himself from that number. It was a torment, having her so close yet knowing she was about to step out of his life forever. No music in that thought. No poetry.

"Caro provides art classes at her boarding school in London," Pen said.

Alex pulled hard at the oars. He did not want to discuss London, or Caroline's projects. The reality of her leaving would come soon enough.

"We are close now," Manolis said. "Stow the oars, *iatros*. The wind will bring us in."

"I hope Mr. Simms does *not* join us," Pen said. She looked back across the bay, to where the houses of the village shimmered white along the shore. "Manolis, how unkind of you to tell him the best fishing was out here by the island. I wanted this to be our afternoon alone."

Alex agreed wholeheartedly. He did not trust the fellow, although he had caused no more trouble. Their earlier meeting on the beach had been amiable enough. Alex could not begrudge Manolis's enthusiasm when Simms had inquired about the best places to cast his line—and Alex had been glad to see the man had left his rifle behind.

"Ready?" Manolis asked. The low island loomed close now, the white crescent of beach waiting just ahead.

Alex pulled off his shoes, rolled his trousers, then went to stand at the prow. As soon as the skiff tumbled past the breakers he leapt into the surf and, splashing, towed them onto the coarse sand. Manolis joined him in heaving the boat high enough that the ladies could disembark without getting their skirts wet.

Pen jumped down. "The island seems larger from shore. But it's just a speck on the sea, isn't it?" She glanced curiously about.

"I don't think you're going to catch sight of the resident Nereid quite yet," Caroline said. She caught Alex's gaze and smiled, accepting his assistance as she stepped over the skiff's side.

"This is but a small part," Manolis said. "The main island is over the rocks." He waved toward the ridge of stone sheltering the beach. "A meadow also. We call it the island of flowers."

"That sounds perfect. Let's go see." Pen hiked up her skirts and began clambering up the small ridge that divided the island.

"Wait for us," Caroline said, laughter in her voice as she followed. She halted at the top with a small exclamation and

Alex hurried to her side. "Oh, look. Isn't it magnificent?" She turned to him and caught his hand.

The contact jolted through him, and for a moment he could not focus on anything but the feel of her skin against his. When his senses cleared he followed her gaze to the meadow and was surprised all over again.

He did not consider himself a plant fancier, but what lay before them was a garden, surely. No natural meadow could boast the swaths of blooms laid out before him. Caroline led him down among the flowers, following Pen, while above them on the ridge he heard Manolis let out a full-bodied laugh.

Red field poppies, daisies, purple iris—those Alex knew. But the tall flags of brilliant color growing in clumps, the sweet herbs he now crushed underfoot, he had no name for these. Or if he did, their only name was joy.

It uncurled painfully in his chest as he stood under the clear eye of the Cretan sun, holding her hand. Their fingers were laced together, the beat of his heart captured against her palm. The surf hummed against the rocks as she turned to him, her hair shot through with golden lights, something he did not know how to name in her eyes.

Awareness moved between them, as heady as the scents thickening the air, the heat that lay welcome across his shoulders. He took a half step forward, uncaring that they were not alone. It did not matter. Nothing mattered except her.

"Caro, come look at the lilies!" Pen called, and the moment was broken.

Caroline smiled at him, a brightness that seemed edged with regret, then slipped her fingers free and went to join the girl.

"Sweet like honey," Manolis said, coming to join him.

"And gone just as soon." Alex cleared his throat. "Is that the shrine?" He indicated a slab of stone at the meadow's edge, near the rough shore.

"It is. Come." Manolis unslung the sack he carried from one shoulder and preceded Alex to the rock.

Seeing what they were about, the women joined them. Pen's fingers were busy crafting a garland of flowers, while Caroline carried a bright bouquet. Silently, Manolis unstoppered a flask of ouzo and poured libations, first on the stone, then the ground, then flung the rest out over the rocks—a glittering arc of liquid meeting the waves. He replaced the flask, then set out an orange, a rough wooden carving of a fish, and a blue hair ribbon. Straightening, he nodded once at the sea.

They stood quietly a moment longer, and then Pen laid her garland on the stone. "Do we . . . say anything?"

"It is not needed," Manolis said. "But what about your song? Now would be good."

Accordingly, the two women began, their voices twining in harmony. Caroline took the low part, singing with a throaty warmth that went right through Alex, while Pen's pleasing, clear tones soared above. The melody was sweet and plaintive, and he felt the words prick against his heart. He turned, looking blindly over the waves, listening.

But when I saw with sad surprise,
The garland fade before mine eyes,
Until the blossoms once so fair,
Were scatter'd in the summer air.

Somewhere near the end, Pen lost the harmony, and to his relief the mood was broken as the song finished in laughter.

"She liked it despite the ending," Caroline said. "What sprite would not?"

Alex shaded his eyes with one hand. "There's a sail."

"Oh, drat, is it Simms?" Pen asked.

Manolis glanced up. "Yes. I think he is having good fishing. He was wise to listen to me."

"As long as he does not stop here." The girl set her hands on her hips.

They watched as the small boat rounded the island and

drew nearer. It was indeed Simms, the man's stocky form unmistakable. Alex observed him closely as the boat approached. The sportsman held one hand up in greeting, then bent and hefted a large sea bass, displaying his catch.

Manolis shouted his approval and Pen and Caroline returned his wave, but Alex merely watched until the man set his fish down and brought the boat around to catch the wind again. It seemed he did not intend to stop, for he turned eastward and soon was out of hailing distance. Shoulders easing, Alex turned away from the sight of that lone sail receding across the water.

Pen had clambered down to the shore—much stonier on this side of the island—and was peering into tide pools, with Caroline close behind. He went to join them. Though he had grown up by the sea, he still enjoyed seeing odd creatures in their miniature ponds waiting for the next tide to surge up and free them. He was as stranded on Crete as one of those fish in their pools—an unsettling thought. No tide was ever going to rise and float him free.

He shoved his hands into his pockets and stared out at the horizon, southward toward invisible Africa. A yellow haze hung low in the watery distance. Maybe it was time for a journey to even farther places once Caroline left.

"Oh my," Pen said, catching the brim of her bonnet. "That was quite a gust. The wind is coming up, isn't it?"

Manolis lifted his head, then let out a cry of alarm. "The *souroko* is coming!" He pointed to the shimmering air hanging far out over the water. "We must go back to the boat—now, now!"

Sudden foreboding shivered over Alex. The southern wind came up quickly this time of year. One had blown last spring and everyone had stayed inside, shutters tight, while the hot and persistent *souroko* raged, pushing dust through any crack it could find. One full day, often two, would pass before the winds died back down. At the first sign, the fishermen brought their boats in to shore. It was perilous to be caught out on the water by that ravening storm.

He whirled, taking Caroline by one arm and Pen by the other, and the three of them ran after Manolis. They skidded to a halt at the top of the ridge.

"My boat!" Manolis shouted. "Look what has been done to my boat!"

A band of fury tightened around Alex's chest as he looked down at the skiff, Manolis pacing beside it in dismay. The sail lay shredded across the bow, rent into long, ragged strips. The stern of the boat—never completely sound—now gaped where boards had been pried open.

"Oh dear!" Pen cried.

On his other side Caroline had gone still with apprehension.

"Simms." Alex spit the name out, then hurried down to see the extent of the damage. "He's a lunatic. Why would anyone do this kind of mischief?"

"Are you certain it was he?" Caroline asked.

"Who else? He knew where we were going." Anger flamed through him, fanned like a brushfire by the approaching winds. "Damn him. He even had the nerve to wave at us after vandalizing our boat."

"Are we stranded?" Pen asked.

"No." God, no. It would be far too dangerous to stay there, for they did not have the supplies or the shelter to survive two days of the *souroko.* "We must beat the storm back to shore."

"My boat. Oh, my little boat." Manolis circled it, shaking his head, then looked to the choppy surface of the sea. "We do not have long, *iatros.*"

"Turn the boat on its side. I don't suppose you have a hammer and nails?"

"No. Fishing line, some hooks. That is all."

"We can pound the boards back in, but . . ." Alex glanced about the shore, then back to the ruined canvas. "Give me the sails."

Manolis handed him the tattered bundle of canvas. "What is your plan?"

"A sling, a tourniquet. I'm going to doctor your boat. We'll winch the cloth tight to keep the boards together."

Caroline watched, lower lip caught between her teeth. The rising breeze gusted strands of her hair across her face. "Manolis, give me the fishing line and hooks. Alex, save me some of the sail if you can."

At least he had a pocketknife. He spread the sail out and half cut, half ripped several long strips of the tough canvas. The rest of the mutilated sail went to Caroline. Together, he and Manolis wrapped the canvas tightly around the keel, binding the boards into place.

"It won't hold long," Alex said. "I hope you have a bailer or two onboard."

"Of course," Manolis said. "This boat was built by my grandfather."

A sudden gust kicked up the sand. Squinting, Alex turned to where the women were bent over the remains of the sail. "We have to go."

Caroline drew her fishhook through the canvas and tied a final knot. Her fingers were pricked, a drop of blood staining the canvas as he watched. "Here." She and Pen held up the partial sail, the worst rents sewn hastily closed with fishing line.

"Good work. We'll have the wind at our backs. Now, into the boat," Alex said.

The women hurried to take their places. Manolis ran up the ragged scrap of sail as Alex pushed the boat into the waves. The repair seemed to be holding—but once beyond the shelter of the islet, the waves grew rough. The bottom of the skiff was soon covered in water.

Alex bent hard over the oars. Fear lent him extra strength. Not fear for himself, but for the women. Pen. Caroline. He dared not lift his head to look at her, only rowed with all his might, lending his strength to the wind in the makeshift sail.

They were making progress, but too slowly. The bend and slosh as the women bailed, the rising waves that tipped water over the side—it was a desperate race.

Could they make it to shore before the boat capsized? The salvaged sail belled wide, the edge of the storm driving them hard before it.

There was no hope of rescue—none of the villagers would venture out into the teeth of the *souroko.* He shot a quick glance at the shore ahead. They might be able to swim for it, though the bay was whipped into a furious froth. He did not like their chances if it came to the boat sinking. If they could only reach the calmer waters ahead. His heart sent his blood pounding in his ears, his hands raw against the oars.

The wind carried a sting now, the first granules of dust overtaking them. Dust from the African desert—carried hundreds of miles by the rough hand of the *souroko* to scour whatever it could find.

"Bail!" Manolis cried.

Everything about them was in motion: the air, the waves, the oars trying to find purchase against the heavy sea, the sail straining, the water taking flight as spray the instant it was tossed from the bailers. Alex's breath rasped in his throat as the world narrowed.

Pull. Breathe, through air thick with dust. The women were both coughing, with their sleeves held over their mouths as they frantically threw water overboard. It made no difference. The boat wallowed low in the water, hungry waves now sloshing over the sides. Even the sail could not pull them forward against the growing weight of the sea.

Though he knew it was hopeless, he kept rowing. Every foot they gained now would be one less length to swim.

"Take off your shoes!" he shouted to the women. Caroline glanced up and he lifted his foot. "Your shoes!"

She nodded and, still bailing with one hand, bent to the laces of her boots. The heavy skirts would be a serious problem, hampering the women once they were forced into the water. But by God he would see them to shore. The alternative was unthinkable. He exchanged a glance with Manolis as another wave spilled over the side.

Voices calling, thin and reedy as the cry of gulls. Alex looked up, blinked in disbelief.

A scattering of boats on the water ahead, and behind them, the shore. He could not believe it. The villagers were coming, despite the risk.

Old Georgios was in the forefront, his son at his side. "A rope!" the lad called, flinging the end straight for them.

Manolis caught it, quickly making it fast to the painter ring, and soon the sinking skiff was in the heart of the flotilla. Safety, just ahead, and willing hands to help them out of the sea the instant the boat surrendered. Alex's heart lifted.

Caroline was still bailing valiantly, a fierce look on her face, but Pen seemed spent. The girl was clutching the side of the boat, white knuckled, her face tight with fear and exhaustion.

"Almost there," he called. The words whipped away in the wind. Almost there.

And suddenly, they *were* there, the damaged boat scraping bottom at the very moment of its sinking. Alex could barely unclench his hands from the oars. Salt stung his raw palms, but they had made it to shore.

Thank God for the villagers.

The wind howled around them now, whirling the beach into a gritty plume. Alex caught Pen by the waist and lifted her out, into the waiting hands of Old Georgios. Caroline stood and Alex took her arm, then the two of them clambered over the side straight into the water. It made no difference—they were wet through.

Around them the fishermen quickly pulled their boats to shore and made them fast. Even the wreck of Manolis's skiff was salvaged from the waves.

"The taverna," Alex called. They needed a fire, shelter. Pen was shaking and Caroline's face was tense as they stumbled up the main street.

The taverna door shut behind them, the shock of being out of the wind making Alex's ears ring. Then hearing returned, the babble of conversation, the commiserations over Manolis's boat.

"But what happened?" Young Georgios asked. "Why was your sail torn and your boat wrapped up?"

Manolis began explaining as Alex stepped up to the rough bar. "Ouzo. For everyone." He took the first two tumblers, pressed one into Pen's hands and the other into Caroline's. "Drink."

Caroline took a sip, then gamely drained the glass, coughing as she handed it back. Her hair was a wild tangle, her fingers cold from the sea. He took the tumbler from her, then sheltered her hands between his own, willing his warmth into her.

"I didn't think. . . ." she began, then glanced at Pen. He knew what she had been about to say; he had not been sure himself they would survive that journey. She gave the girl a strained smile. "Drink it, love. It will stop your shivering."

Pen nodded mutely and took a small swallow, then another. He was glad to see some color seep back into her face.

Reluctantly, he released Caroline's hands and turned to the men. "Simms, the fisherman. Did anyone see him?"

"He did not come back in." Old Georgios quaffed his drink. "And now it is too late."

"Gone," one of the men said. "He took his things away in the boat. His rooms are empty."

Old Georgios nodded. "Gone for good if he stays out on the sea. We will look for wreckage on the coast after the wind dies."

"And send word to the authorities in Agia Galini," Alex said. "I don't want him leaving the island. But for now there's nothing we can do."

"Nothing," Caroline said, "except be grateful we are alive and on dry land."

"The Nereid," Manolis said. "It was our offering on the island that brought us home safe."

Pen looked up, some animation returned to her expression. "But what about the wind? It started rising soon after we finished."

"Hmm." Manolis creased his brow. "I do not think she likes English songs. Only Greek. Next time I will sing the songs myself."

"And I will stay at home," the girl said. She made a face. "I have heard your singing."

The laughter that followed warmed them, despite the angry wind circling outside.

Chapter 13

The *souroko* had blown out the day before and temperate spring was restored to the village. Caroline leaned on the balcony railing and tried not to let England wedge its way into her thoughts. Departure was just days away. She and Pen had tickets on the steamship to Malta, and the girl, in her excitement, had already started packing. Soon enough Caroline would be home, but she wanted to taste every last drop of her time on Crete. Strange how it had become so sweet when at first she had wanted nothing more than to leave the island. Yet even then there had been something indefinable that had drawn her to Alex.

Alex.

Her heart curled around his name. Even now she was watching for him to ride down out of the hills. Today would be their last adventure. Although, to be fair, the last outing had been adventure enough.

But she could not turn down an excursion to the Cave of Zeus, the one place she had wanted to see. This was her last chance—and another day to share with Alex, before the inevitable parting.

She had hoped he would offer to come with them, back to London. Surely his exile must have an end. Yet every time she mentioned England he stiffened, and if she pressed, the haunted look would return to his eyes. She had learned not to speak of it, tried to bury the hope that he would pack his bags, give up his cottage, and come with her back to London.

Whatever lay between the two of them, she could not name it. Only that it was new, and fleeting, and glorious in its brief burning.

And afterward?

The world would be flavored with ashes—but she could not stay. Alex had made her no promises, and what did this quiet village in Crete offer her? A life as a restless foreigner? She thought of the children at the school in London. She knew many of them by name. They needed her. Crete would be a life wasted when she could be helping others.

She shook her head. There was today, tomorrow, the last handfuls of her time here, and she would not taint those days by thinking on what might have been. On what was impossible.

There he was.

She leaned forward and could not help the easing of her heart, the smile that opened like a flower inside her as she watched him ride down the track, sitting easily on his chestnut horse.

"Mr. Trentham is coming," she called behind her, to where Pen was packing away the contents of the desk. Still, she lingered on the balcony. This would be the last time she would see him riding into the village, the last time she would feel that curious rush of nerves and joy at the sight of him coming ever closer.

"Good," Pen said. "Let's get ready to meet him." After a long moment she added, "Are you coming in, Caro?"

"Yes." Caroline watched Alex a heartbeat longer and then, trailing her fingers along the railing, went to join Pen inside.

Her room. Her cell, her haven. She would miss it, she realized with a sudden pang. The bed with its bright blankets, the soft wool rug that greeted her feet each day, the windows open wide to the blue Mediterranean morning.

Her companion turned from the wardrobe. "Pelisse. Bonnet. Do you need anything more?"

"You seem eager to be off." Caroline fastened the bonnet beneath her chin. What a pleasure that was, to be able to dress herself. How quickly one took such things for granted.

"Two days of being shut up inside, listening to the wind blow and the landlady bicker with her husband—aren't you eager, too?" Pen swept up her own bonnet and hurried to the door.

"When you put it that way . . ."

They stepped out of the villa to find Alex in conversation with two young fishermen, each leading a pair of horses. He glanced up to greet the ladies, and it seemed to Caroline that the expression in his eyes deepened when he looked at her, though his face remained somber.

"I have news from Agia Galini. An Englishman matching Simms's description hired a trawler to take him to Italy. We have sent word to the authorities there."

Caroline was glad to hear that the sportsman was off the island—and even gladder that Alex would not be going after the man. The danger had gone.

"Good riddance," Pen said, swinging up on her horse and glancing at the others. "I see Caro gets a real mount today."

"It's a long ride. Agalma would not be up to it. Niko and Young Georgios are coming, too." He nodded to where the two men waited, now mounted on their sturdy horses. The shorter of the two men gave an enthusiastic wave.

"Young Georgios?" Pen groaned. "The most attentive young man on the coast. Once he even offered me his best fish."

The corner of Alex's mouth twitched up. "None of the older men could be enticed from their work today. There is too much to repair after the wind's damage. These two see it as an adventure—and a chance to avoid the extra labor."

The girl sighed but lifted her hand in reply to the young man's salute. "There. Greetings completed. Now can we go? Caro, I expect you to ride beside me and keep Young Georgios at bay."

Despite Pen's predictions, it seemed the young man was content to make eyes at her from afar. As they rode out of the village, Alex bent his head in conversation with the two young men. They nodded, and then the escort split, Niko riding ahead while Young Georgios took the rear, throwing Pen a lovelorn glance as he passed.

She smothered her giggles. "Really, I know it's not funny, but I can't help it."

"Smitten swains—yes, what can one do?" Caroline smiled, letting Pen draw her into conversation about London. It was impossible to withstand the girl's enthusiasm, despite her own resolve not to think of England.

The sun was well into the sky by the time Alex called a halt. The rough path had taken them from the Mediterranean up through folded hills and at last onto a windy plateau presided over by a mountain dusted with white. As they rode closer it began to loom over them. They passed into the shadow of the mountain and Caroline felt anticipation prick her skin.

Alex glanced at her. "The Cave of Zeus is just ahead."

"Yes," Pen said, her voice hushed, "we're approaching the birthplace of gods. Perhaps we'll hear their voices speaking to us from ages past."

"I wouldn't doubt it." Caroline drew in a deep breath. "It's so quiet here—as though our human lives make very little difference."

Another few minutes of riding brought them to a rough cliff face where a huge cleft in the base beckoned, full of shadows and mystery.

"Here we are." Pen slid off her mount and handed the reins to the ever-attentive Young Georgios. "Oh, hurry and come see."

"We have all afternoon to explore," Alex said, a smile in his voice. "Care to dismount, Miss Huntington?"

Caroline blinked at him, abruptly aware she had been sitting her horse and staring, transfixed, at the cavern mouth.

"Yes, of course." She took his offered hand and let him catch her as she slid off the horse. A fleeting sense of rightness as he steadied her. She tried not to lean into his warmth, his solidity.

He stepped back but kept her hand in his. "The going's rough. Shall we catch up to Pen?"

She nodded and they ventured forward. Loose stones shifted under their feet and cool air brushed her cheek, the shadowy exhalation of the cave. The arch of the entrance rose above them until they could peer into the dimness of a huge cavern disappearing into the depths of shadow. The silvery walls shone faintly where moisture trickled, and farther back, just where the light faded, there seemed to be fantastical rock shapes, formed in natural homage to the place a young god was reared.

Alex's hand was warm in hers. "The floor of the main cavern is level, once we get down." He turned and beckoned to one of the lads. "Bring the lanterns. And Pen, wait for Nikos before you go any farther. No exploring on your own."

The girl raised her brows. "What about Young Georgios?"

"He's staying with the horses—and preparing our lunch." Alex accepted one of the lanterns, the warm glow making the cave's interior seem even darker, and they began the descent.

It was a scramble down into another world. The light began to close away from them, like a door swinging shut on an empty room. At the bottom Caroline turned to see Pen and Nikos silhouetted at the entrance, the sky a fierce blue behind them. For a moment she could not quite believe she was here, in the Cave of Zeus. She let go of Alex's hand and took a few careful steps deeper in. Darkness pushed back against the daylight, the shadows nearly tangible, thicker than the questing light.

"It's amazing," she said, voice hushed. "So vast."

It was impossible not to feel as though they were in a great cathedral. In place of votive figures of saints were rock formations, sinuously formed of water and time. The filtered light falling from above did not pass through bits of colored glass, but still there was something holy about it, a sense of quiet presence rooted deep in the earth.

As they stood there, it was easy to imagine countless ages of worship—the uncomfortable powers of nature wrapped in the myths of generations. Here the untamed god Zeus had sprung up, in story if not in fact. Caroline shivered and stepped closer to Alex.

Pen's voice echoed eerily as the girl clambered down. Her words were hushed as she spoke to her escort, the syllables stretched and unintelligible.

"Oh!" Caroline started as a rush of wings eddied overhead, the sound amplified into a flurry of feathered beating.

"Wild pigeons," Alex said, "frightened from their nests. But come, the inner sanctum is a little farther."

The lamp thrust handfuls of light into the darkness as they went, illuminating scattered dark hollows along the walls of the gallery they now traversed.

"Are there more caves opening from this larger chamber?" Caroline kept her voice low, as one would in a church.

"We're going in one now. This is the altar." For a moment the light was blocked by his body as he entered a smaller chamber. Then he turned and the steady lamplight fell over the stone walls, illuminating a small cave nestled within the larger one.

It was a sanctum indeed, and comforting to have the roof closer and fewer shadows collecting at the edges of the light. A slab of smoothed stone ran parallel to the back wall, and it was difficult to tell in the flickering illumination, but Caroline thought she saw symbols inscribed on the rocks above.

"How did you find this place, the Cave of Zeus?"

"It's been part of the local knowledge for centuries. The villagers' ancestors worshipped here, or perhaps the people their ancestors displaced. After I'd been on Crete nearly a year, the villagers entrusted me with the location. I had to make solemn promises to help protect the place from harm, which I think includes forbidding Legault to dig about in here."

"I'd imagine it would."

"Still, I've found . . ." Alex set the lantern on a corner of the altar and knelt, scraping aside pebbles at the base. "Look here."

He offered his hand, palm up, and Caroline set her fingers to the ancient bronze coin cupped there.

"How splendid." She traced the coin, feeling the marks made by a long-ago craftsman. "How old, do you think?"

"Before the Caesars, maybe even longer." He tucked the coin back at the base of the plinth, smoothing the loose pebbles. "Let's make sure Pen and Nikos haven't gone astray."

He rose, gave a cursory brush to the knees of his trousers, then led the way back into the dim outer cathedral.

"Did you feel that?" Caroline stopped short, apprehension a cold breath on the back of her neck. "The floor shifted. Do you think—"

The rest of her words were lost in a deep, rising rumble of earth, a clatter of stone as the cave moved again. She let out a cry and Alex grabbed her shoulder and pushed her toward the cavern wall. She stumbled, the noise of falling rock terrifyingly loud around them, the lantern swinging crazily in his hold, rock dust hanging like smoke in air that seemed too solid to breathe.

"Shelter—go in!" He pushed her forward into a crevice that pierced the wall of the main cavern, one of the small, mysterious openings she had noted earlier.

Blindly thankful, she pressed into it. Stone walls on either side of her, but ahead the way was open. She held out her hands and stepped forward. *Let there not be spiders. They did not like the cold, did they?* She shuddered and kept going, Alex close behind. The earth shivered again. One strong arm looped about her waist and he drew her against him, shielding her from the wild stones tumbling and clattering outside their small refuge. His lips against her hair, the comforting solidity of him in the semidarkness as they waited for the world to be still. Her heart clamored with fear.

A tremendous, earth-thudding crash shook through her

body and she flinched in his embrace. She closed her eyes and pressed her cheek against his chest. No matter what happened, she would be safe with him. Her breath escaped in little, frantic bursts.

"Shh," he breathed, arm tightening around her.

With a last grumble and grind of stone, the quake subsided. She forced her breathing to smooth. "Was that . . . I knew Crete suffered mild tremors . . . but that!"

"That was more than a mild tremor." Concern etched his voice. "Are you unharmed?"

"Yes." Shaken but— "Pen!" She pivoted in his embrace. "We must find her!" Her mind offered up a dreadful image of the girl lying beneath tumbled stones, bruised and bleeding, or worse. . . .

He released her and turned, leading the way back up the tunnel. The lantern cast a circle of dusky light around them.

"Bloody hell." Alex stopped and she craned, trying to see past.

"What? What is it?" *Not Pen, please not Pen.*

He stepped forward over the rubble littering the floor and lifted the lantern. "The way is blocked," he said, voice tight. Where there had been an opening back to the main cave now was only a tumbled matrix of rock.

"But—we have to get back." Her throat was dry, and she tasted dust on her lips.

"Too much stone has fallen from the wall in the main cavern. Here." He thrust the lantern at her. "Maybe I can clear enough at the top to get through."

Taking the light, she retreated, giving him room to throw down the stones he was dislodging. Twice he had to leap clear as his prying released larger rocks. But for every stone he threw down, another took its place. At length he stopped. Caroline saw his hands were dusty and nicked, a long scrape tracing redly down the back of one wrist.

He looked at her, expression set. "Caroline, I don't think we can get through. It's packed solid, and there's a great boulder wedged in the way."

The growing seriousness of their situation was beginning to constrict her, darker even than the shadows cast by their sole lantern. She fought a rising sense of panic and made herself take long, even breaths. They had to get out. Her mind skittered away from the thought they might be trapped. Her hands were cold.

"Do you think yelling will help?"

They tried, but the earth muffled their voices—and who knew if there was anyone to hear? Pen. Fear for the girl lodged in her chest and she redoubled her cries. But variations of *We're in here!* and *Help!* and *Can you hear us?!* could go on only so long.

"I don't think that worked." Hoarse and weary, she slumped against the wall.

"We can't know that." He slid down beside her. "Let's wait a bit and see if there's any response."

He set his arm around her shoulders and she leaned into him, resting her head over his heartbeat and closing her eyes, closing out the sight of stone, stone, stone. The enormity of their predicament seeped like ice into her bones. Even his presence could not warm her.

"Will this be our grave?" She opened her eyes, vision blurred by tears.

"No!" He spoke as if by will alone he could hold back their fate. "No. There's a chance the passage opens up, connects back to the main cavern. If we can't go back, we will go forward."

She nodded and felt his lips brush her cheek.

"Don't lose hope," he said.

No—it was not in her nature. She sat and gave him a wavering smile. "Wandering the labyrinth? But . . . I didn't bring any string."

A brief spark of humor lit his eyes, despite the strain at the corners of his mouth. "If we find the main cavern we won't need string. And if we don't . . ." His voice trailed off.

"We won't need string then, either," she said, filling the pause.

He stood and picked up the lantern. "Let's go, while we still have light to see by."

She shook out her skirts, then followed him. The rough corridor continued a few dozen yards, stone walls close on either side, then began sloping down. What was that ahead? Her heart jolted. Another light? Were they found? She peered around Alex's shoulder.

No. It was no rescue. Only their own light, mirrored in the still surface of an underground pool. She wrapped her arms about herself.

Alex stopped at the edge, the black water silently spreading before them, and lifted the lantern high. The passageway they stood in opened into a larger cave—she could sense the expanse more than see it, but there were no stars reflected in the pool that covered the floor. Only a blind and sightless sky, a roof of stone arching over them.

"Is it very deep?" Dread stirred in her again, woken by the dark, nameless water. Remember to breathe. In. Out.

Think of Hyde Park on a sunny afternoon. The neatly kept rosebushes in her uncle's garden. The wind off the sea, blowing her hair back from her face.

"There's only one way to find out." Alex removed his coat, then began stripping off his shirt.

Her eyes widened at the sight of his chest bared in the lamplight. Shadows in the hollow of his collarbone, tracing the firm lines of his muscled shoulders. He bent to his boots and she took a step forward.

"Alex. Are you sure . . . ?"

He kicked the footwear off and set his hands to his belt. "We don't know how deep it is. And I prefer my clothing dry." His voice was serious as he unfastened his trousers. She turned her eyes away but could not help looking a moment later.

Half illuminated, half shadowed as he set the light at the water's edge, he was naked. He was perfect. She stared at him, this primal creature who had shed his skin of linen and wool to emerge wild and beautiful in the ancient darkness.

"You're not taking the lantern?"

He shook his head. "No. I can't risk sinking over my head and losing the light."

"Be careful." She wet her lips, watching as he waded into the still water. Fire-sparked ripples spread before him as he went deeper, his footsteps wary.

The outrageousness of his undressing had distracted her, but as he went farther into the shadows her fear returned. Darkness crouched at the edge of the small circle of light. Trapped, a mountain of stone between her and the world of the living. What if they did not find a way out? What if Alex slipped under the water and did not return? She could not bear this alone.

A splash, he let out a sound.

"Alex! Are you all right?" Her voice trembled, echoing off invisible walls.

His reply was distant. "There's a deep spot here, but the rest of the pool is not so bad. We'll avoid it next time."

"Next time?" Caroline twisted her hands in her skirts.

For the space of a long minute, perhaps two, she could hear nothing. Then his voice came to her again from over the water.

"Courage. I've found the other side. It's a smooth shore—we'll need the light to see more. I'm coming back now."

At least there was another side—a place to go to. It was enough to keep the dread from overtaking her. She leaned forward, watching for him, listening to him moving through the still water as he returned. Ripples preceded him, the motion drawing her eye until she could see him, striding waist deep in the inky pool. He emerged like some dark god, naked and streaming with water. The lamplight cast a warm glow over him, sparkled off the rivulets and drops. He was a creature of fire and night, so magnificent she could not take her eyes from him.

Without a word he bundled his clothes, secured them with the belt. Then he faced her.

"Your turn."

"I . . . I beg your pardon?"

She could think of nothing else to say. Until that moment she had not thought—had not been able to think—that she would have to cross as well. But there was no way back, only forward, and to cross that water required becoming a different creature altogether.

Her hands went to the buttons of her blouse, paused. She glanced up at him, but he did not turn away to shield her modesty, just as she had not done the same for him. He simply waited for her to shed her clothes and stand beside him in the lamplight, every bit as naked and exposed as he was now.

Caroline swallowed. They were lost in a different world, governed by different rules. It seemed somehow fitting that he should stand there, glorious and bold in his own skin, and watch her with dark and shining eyes. She pushed the top button through, then the next, letting the fabric fall open over the thin cloth of her chemise.

A shrug and the blouse slithered off her shoulders, drifted to the floor. Her skirts were easy enough. Four buttons and they, too, slid down to pool at her feet. Nothing now but the thin slip of her undergarment. No corset—she had never favored them, and here on Crete no one cared if she was laced into a fortress of clothing.

His eyes shone as he watched her, his shoulders back, his black hair gleaming, his body hard and aroused. There was invitation and challenge in his gaze.

Grasping the fabric with both hands, she drew her chemise up, the slide of thin cotton giving way to cool air against her skin. Up, and over her head. Caroline shook her hair free and stood, half defiant, holding the garment in one hand.

The look in his eyes brought heat rushing through her, and a curious sense of freedom. She saw herself suddenly as he did, a goddess made manifest, surrounded by a sphere of light within a sphere of darkness. Persephone to his Hades, light to his shadow.

He knelt and gathered her discarded garments. Without a word she handed him the chemise and he bundled her clothing with his, then stood and held out his hand. She took it, lifted the lantern with her free hand, and let him lead her to the edge of the pool.

In that moment before stepping into the mirror-flat water she caught her own pale reflection. The curve of her hips, her round breasts, the triangle of hair above her sex—and him beside her, a darker shadow on the water. Then they waded forward and the image fractured into ripples.

He led her through the midnight water, avoiding the depths. Her heart was racing, her breath deep and shaky, but not from cold. From the heat of his touch, from the heat within her. Something primal unfurled within her, something called to life by the flickering light, the water-marked quiet. The perfection of her own self inside her own body, the perfection of the man beside her.

When they emerged on the far shore she felt transformed by the passage. A different creature, filled with nameless yearning. Her body hummed with awareness of Alex, naked and magnificent beside her. The ground was softer under her feet, not unyielding stone, as he drew her out of the water.

Chapter 14

Alex released her hand and unfastened the bundle of clothing, then spread the garments to make a nest for them. The circle of lamplight shimmered with the two of them at their center. There was no need for words. Caroline felt it, an inexorable pulse, as if all of time had been distilled down to this one moment, this one breath. She set the lantern down.

Here, in the silence beneath the earth, there was no need for modesty, for shame. Propriety belonged to the surface and the world of the living. Some corner of her mind insisted she ought to blush and cover herself, to pretend a normalcy that was meaningless. The meaning was deeper here—the mysteries of a man and woman. Their separate perfection. Their joining. She still knew very little of it, but the promise of more saturated her senses.

"Come." His voice was low, the single word thrumming through her. He opened his arms and she went, stepped unafraid into the circle of his embrace.

A circle of flame as their bodies met, skin to skin. Thighs, hips, his hardness pressing against her, her breasts against his chest. Their lips meeting, softness to softness and yet it was there the fire burned hottest. Sparks ran through her as his arms tightened, pulling her even closer. She slid her hands around his sides, spreading her fingers across his back.

Taut muscles under the skin. She ran her palms over his body, savoring the feel of him, the magnificence she held in her arms. The taste of him, his breath mingling with hers. He shifted, opened his mouth. The stroke of his tongue over hers, the desire uncoiling within her in response. This was wanting, this heavy heat that lay along her body, that made her want to press even closer, that opened her mouth eagerly beneath his. If not for him holding her she would have fallen, her senses so dizzy, consumed by their kiss.

"Wait," he whispered against her lips.

She opened her eyes, blinked up at him. "Why?"

With a smile that held fierce and tender promises, he took a step back. Her body clamored in protest as the air settled on her skin, replacing his touch.

"I will find a way out for us—I swear it. But we need to save what light we have left. Sit." He nodded to their clothing spread over the cave floor.

As soon as she had settled he bent over the lantern and blew it out. The darkness was immediate and complete. Caroline closed her eyes, then opened them again. There was no difference.

The rustle of cloth as he settled beside her. Moving as confidently as though he could see, he gathered her against him, lips unerring as he brushed them over hers. She sighed, the sound magnified in the darkness, and welcomed his tongue with her own.

Robbed of sight, she was vividly aware of touch. Her skin tingled under the caress of his palms as he ran them over her shoulders, down her back, tracing the dip and curve where her hips flared. Her own hands found their way to the silkiness of his hair, and she wove her fingers through the strands. Mouth raised to his kiss, arms lifted, she was yearning upward, buoyed by the rising sensations within her.

Without warning he grasped her hips and lifted her onto him. She gasped against his mouth. Now she was facing him, straddling his legs, and he pulled her even closer until their hips touched. His hard maleness jutted up, pressed directly against the softness, the heat between her legs. A throbbing began there, low and insistent.

A throbbing that intensified as his hands slid around to cup her breasts, thumbs brushing over the taut peaks. So light, that touch, yet the shock coursed through her. Sweet torment as he circled his fingertips around her nipples, the playful touches drawing soft, breathy sounds from her throat. At last he brought thumb and fingers together, squeezing gently. White fire shot from his touch, and she pressed her hips hard against his as lightning flew through her.

"Yes," he said, his breath warm against her cheek.

Yes. The syllable reverberated inside her, the utter rightness of their bodies, skin to skin, his touch waking sensations she had only half dreamed of.

He bent his head to trail kisses along her neck. She imagined each one shining with heat, shimmering in the darkness like a trail of stars laid across her skin. Along her collarbone, her shoulders. Down the curve of her breast until—

"Oh!" The sharp sound of pleasure escaped her as he set his mouth over her nipple. Already sensitized by his touches, the feel of his lips moving on her and the hot lap of his tongue were nearly unbearable. She could not keep still but arched against him, sending her heated breath up into the darkness, the air escaping her lungs as he caressed her.

The world narrowed to only this. The two of them, male and female, in the darkness. Yearning with desire, the scintillation of touch and breath, mouth and skin, the fire leaping between them. His hands slid to her back, bracing her as he savored her breasts, and she felt his breathing quicken in turn.

He lay back, taking her with him until she lay covering him, legs still wide over his. His mouth returned to hers, urgent kisses in the darkness. Her mouth, the secret place between her legs, all the places where they touched—she was burning.

Deep within her something recognized this, the twining of two lovers in the darkness. It was ancient, it was entirely new.

It consumed her—her body the fuel, the heart of the flame, each caress flaring along her skin.

He turned, pulling her beneath him as their positions reversed. Now he was above her in the sightless air, his hands memorizing her skin, stroking her shoulders, her breasts, her belly. Lower, his palms over her thighs, then moving firmly, inexorably to the center of her. Her heartbeat drowned out the sound of her breathing as she waited, waited to feel him touch her. There, where it seemed a secret star had come to blaze, hidden in her body, burning with a fierce, invisible light.

Then he did, parted her legs, his hands sweeping up and against her, his caress unerring. Right to the center of her. His fingers slid up and down, coaxing long, yearning breaths from her. She had not known how lovely it would feel.

But it was only a prelude. He slipped one finger inside her, still stroking, and a jolt of pure fire flared through her. It was too intimate, too searing a touch, but the darkness forgave everything. A second finger joined the first, and a moan caught in her throat.

This must be how a perfect instrument felt in the hands of a master. Before that touch, dormant, but when played, when put to the use it was made for . . . ah. She rose to the pleasure, she vibrated with the intensity of his knowing strokes. She sang, her body resonating with inaudible music.

He bent over her, his breath mingling with hers. "My beauty," he said, his voice brushing through her.

"Yes," she whispered. Yes and yes.

He pulled back, his glorious touch leaving her, but before she could protest, he was over her again. Now instead of his hands she felt the hard heat of his maleness there, between her legs. In another circumstance she might have been afraid, but there was no room for it here in this hidden cave beneath the earth, with the knowledge of their own mortality so close. This was right, this was inevitable.

It seemed her body knew how to welcome him, for without thinking she spread her legs wider, tilted her hips up to meet him. He pressed against her slick entrance and she felt herself take him in. Slowly, slowly her body stretching until she felt surely she could take no more of him. He was too large, too suddenly overwhelming.

"Shh." His voice stirred her hair.

One hand slid down and began playing against her, light, teasing touches, assuaging, coaxing her pleasure to rise again. Her body, so obedient to his touch. Heat uncoiling again. She let it sweep over her and felt him shift, slide farther in, then stop, letting her become accustomed to him.

He was in her, and over her, laying kisses across her forehead. She could feel the taut stillness, the effort in his shoulders and back, the tight muscles of his buttocks as he held himself quiescent. It was a quiet that held all the promise of a primal storm, the very nature of his stillness a promise of something she could not even name. She only knew it would shake her to the core.

Then he gradually began to move, stroking back and forth as his fingers had stroked, but this was so much more. This was the heart of it, the joining of male and female. His movements beginning to coax the fire forward again, the sensation so different from anything she had ever experienced, but somehow familiar, known in some deep, mystic part of her.

Alex held himself over her, held himself to a slowness that would have been excruciating, but for the dark. But for the mystery of her body, slowly giving its secrets up to him. He felt reverent as he moved in her, easing her tightness, feeling her soften under him. Not all the way in, not yet. He was waiting for her breathy sighs, waiting for the pleasure to outweigh the pain of it before he made that final, deep thrust.

God, but she was beautiful, far beyond any evidence of sight; he did not need his eyes to know it was true. Beautiful, and strong, and brave. The sight of her stripping off her clothes had stolen his breath, the way she had gone fearlessly into the dark water.

And now here, with him. He could no more have kept himself from her than he could have stopped breathing. It was that essential. Though he might have denied it in the bright day, in the air and lavish sunlight, everything had changed now. There was no more denying it. His soul had cracked open and all he could do was take her in his arms and love her.

A fierce joy crossed his face, unseen. She had relaxed beneath him, her hands caressing his shoulders, her hips tilting up to meet the slow slide of his cock. It was time. He drew back farther, lengthening each stroke, felt her fingers tighten as he surged forward. She let out a cry that echoed for a moment over the still water.

Seated deep within her, he stopped and gathered her close. He murmured into her hair, while his body shuddered from the force of his wanting.

"Is it well?" he whispered.

"I . . . yes." Her voice was unsure, and so he kept holding her, his hand moving over her arm, tracing delicate patterns on her skin.

He breathed in the scent of her, so familiar but spiced now with something more intimate, the musk of their bodies together, the heady mix of arousal and need.

At last she let out a slow breath, and he felt her lips along his collarbone, sweet, seeking kisses. He dipped his head and took her mouth with his, letting his tongue move against her the way his cock yearned to do. Soon. Soon now.

A little moan escaped her throat, and he began. She was tight and slick around him as he slid out, in, each stroke sending an exquisite shiver through his nerves. He did not know how long it had been—years, centuries, eternities—but it did not matter now. Time had no meaning here. Only movement, and taste, and touch. Only the pleasure of her body, so soft against his.

She lifted her legs, wrapped them about his hips. His pulse thudded, he tasted her name on his lips. *Caroline. Oh God, Caroline.*

"Alex," she whispered, as if she had heard him, her voice throaty and low.

The pleasure was rising so quickly he could barely contain

it. The piercing sweetness of her, the sound of her breathing quickening in time to his strokes as she held tight to him. Faster, deeper. He groaned, wanting to take her with him, not sure he could hold on long enough.

"Ah," she gasped, something revelatory in her tone. Again. She was moving under him with such urgency that he could not slow, could not deny either of them that headlong rush to completion.

It started low, a smoldering that burst almost immediately into wildfire, sweeping through him, burning over his skin, consuming him in glory, glory, glory.

A shout, their voices combined, reverberating through the cavern, rebounding from stone and water as their bodies twined and strove and, at last, melded into that single, perfect moment. The point where mortal met the divine.

The dark enfolded them, brought them home, at last, to their bodies. Breath, blood, bone. Cool air against the skin, a reminder of their own separateness. Alex levered himself up, fingers finding her face and tracing, as if by feel alone he could discern her thoughts.

Her lips curved, her cheek rounded under his questioning touch, and it was enough. No tears dampened her skin, no frown or sorrow manifest. All was well.

More than well. Something deep within him had eased. He slowly withdrew, rolled off her, and pulled their clothing close, making a burrow for the two of them. With a sigh she moved into his embrace and laid her head on his chest.

No words. Only touch. He held her close and heard her breathing deepen into the edges of sleep. But he could not sleep, not yet. He stared up, imagining the curving stone above them, the earth surrounding them. It was utterly quiet, but for the two of them. He could feel their heartbeats, resonating together in the dark.

Chapter 15

Caroline woke slowly, aware of strong, warm arms around her, the steady rise and fall of Alex's chest at her back. She did not know when she had ever felt so secure, so known and cherished.

Last night had been a revelation. The awakening of her body to such pleasure, the primal knowledge of what it meant to be a woman, joining in that ancient dance with a man. She was changed now, transmuted. She opened her eyes.

Shock held her unbreathing, motionless—and then her heart began to race as she understood, the dizzy blood pushing through her.

"Alex!" She sat bolt upright and set a hand to his shoulder. "Wake up—look!"

"What?" His voice was heavy with sleep, and then it seemed her words penetrated. His eyelids flew open and he sat in one smooth motion. "By God."

Water-dappled light striated the rock above them, and she blinked as she gazed over the pool. A single shaft of sunlight descended, paring the blackness and throwing radiance into the water. Light.

She laughed aloud and flung her arms around him. "There's a way out. We are saved!"

A quick tightening of his arms and then he sobered. "It could be very high up—we may not be able to reach the opening." He rose, gathered his clothes, and dressed with quick efficiency.

She followed more reluctantly, the feeling of her garments closing around her somehow odd and uncomfortable. The act of buttoning her blouse made her more self-conscious than she had felt even lying naked beneath him, taking him into her. The memory warmed her cheeks. She let out a silent sigh and joined Alex at the water's edge.

"Drink before I wade out." He knelt, taking his own advice.

She cupped her hand and scooped water up to her mouth. Cold, flavored with minerals, but welcome. She had not realized how thirsty she was until the moment when liquid filled her mouth. Another handful, another, until at last she sat back on her heels, satisfied. Now hunger woke, but she pressed her lips together. They had nothing to eat. And at any rate they would soon be free. She held tight to the thought.

Alex was prowling the shore, casting glances at the light, then up at the cave ceiling. A delicate fringe of stalactites gleamed, pale white, against the far wall, their reflection a muted lace in the still water.

"Over here." He splashed to the corner and stood, hands on his hips. Light filtered over his upturned face—nothing as strong as full daylight, but strong enough for hope to infuse itself more deeply into her heart.

"Can you see the opening?" Bunching her skirts, she joined him.

"There's a ledge here, and it's definitely lighter up above." He leaped, reaching for the lip of stone, but it was too far and he fell back with a splash.

"Boost me up," she said. "I'll tell you what I see."

He tilted his head, eyes nearly black in the dimness, then nodded. "Grab hold of my shoulders and I'll lift you." He laced his fingers, making a cradle with his hands. "Put your foot there. And up!"

She steadied herself, bracing her hands on his shoulders and hoisting herself a few more inches.

"There's a shelf of rock here, and I think . . ." If he moved over another few feet, she might be able to reach a handhold, maybe even climb and wriggle her way farther back, to where she thought she had glimpsed a slash of whiteness that must surely, surely open to the sky. "We need to go more to the left."

He released her foot and wrapped his arms around her, letting her slide the length of his body. She pressed against him and, overcome by impulse, by his nearness, took his head in her hands and pulled his mouth down to meet hers. Instant heat blossomed between them and he let out a soft groan before opening his lips and returning her kiss.

Dear heavens. Would she never be done with wanting him? Although her body ached in unaccustomed places, she would lie down with him again in a heartbeat and give herself over to that passion, the unbearable blazing sweetness of their two bodies together. She leaned into the kiss, relearning the taste of him, and felt his hands tighten, pull her even closer.

At last they drew apart. She felt as though she had just dashed through Hyde Park, her heart was beating so quickly.

"Caroline." His indigo eyes were serious. "No matter what happens—whether we escape, or not—know that last night was . . ." He halted, as if searching for the right word.

Everything? Her heart was too full, and she could not describe it either. Perhaps there was no way out, no future beyond this cave, this cool air and still water. But the two flames of their bodies would burn long against the night.

"Shall we try again?" she said at length, when the stillness between them had lengthened beyond redeeming. "I think if we come this way I can reach."

She tugged him three steps over, then turned and set her hands to his shoulders. Once again he cradled her foot and hoisted her up, and this time she was close enough to the ledge to reach it.

"I'm going to try to go up." She drew in a quick breath, then let go of his comforting solidity and grabbed for the hard stone.

One scrabbled handhold, then another. Rock scraped her arms as she pulled herself up. Below, she felt Alex wrap his arms around her legs and lift. It was just enough. She levered herself onto the rock shelf, braced both hands flat, and slid forward, legs slipping free of his grasp.

"Caroline! Are you all right?"

"Yes. Let me get my bearings."

She studied the ledge, a rough passage of stone and earth sloping upward. The tunnel narrowed, and at the top . . . surely that must be sky she glimpsed. Not far until freedom. Freedom. She had to see, had to reach that light.

"Caro!" His voice was urgent.

She turned, hampered by her skirts, and leaned over the lip of stone. His expression eased when he saw her.

"Well?" he asked.

"I think . . . it looks promising." She bit her lip. "If you can make it up here."

"Oh, I can. Wait for me."

He splashed across the pool to a tumble of large rocks. It was the work of a few minutes, with a great deal more splashing and some muttered curses, but he managed to pile up smallish boulders under the point the ledge began. He looked up at her.

"Can you wedge yourself in up there, and reach me your hand?"

She wriggled, bracing her feet across. "Yes." Leaning out as far as she dared, she stretched her hand out.

"Coming up now." He balanced on the top of the stone. "All right, hold steady."

He jumped, fingers brushing past hers, and she let out a little cry as he fell back, slipped down into the water.

"Again," he said.

It took three more tries before, their hands clasped tightly,

Alex was able to gain a foothold and swing himself onto the ledge. The force of his final leap laid him half across her. She wrapped her arms about him and took a long, ragged breath.

"We made it. Oh, Alex."

He brushed a kiss over her forehead, then sat up. "Let us hope so, love."

The endearment slipped unguarded off his tongue. Had he even realized what he had said? Caroline smiled at him, unable to deny the warmth rushing through her.

The stone ceiling lowered as they crawled forward, and she bit back a yelp as her hand dislodged a stone. It tumbled and fell with a splash into the pool below. She braced her feet and kept going. This was the way out. Please. It had to be.

The tunnel narrowed further. He gestured for her to stay back as he went on his belly and began to wriggle forward, blocking the light. She pressed her lips together and watched, hands clenched. What if it was solid stone ahead with no space for a living body to pass through? She could not bear to think it.

"Come." His voice was muffled.

She lay down and slithered after him, heedless of the roots tangling in her hair, the rough stone grasping at her skirts. Her lungs clenched, but that was foolish. There was plenty of air to breathe, despite the close earth around them. She forced herself to believe it and dragged in a lungful, exhaled.

Dirt lodged beneath her nails as she scrabbled after Alex. He lay on his side and beckoned for her to come up next to him, reaching a hand to her as she wormed her way forward.

"Is this the end?"

"No." His teeth gleamed in the dimness as he smiled. "I think it's the beginning. Look there." He pointed up.

She turned her head, then nearly wept in relief. A fissure and through it—sky. Bright, fierce blue.

"Can we break through?"

"Yes." His voice was sure. "Ready? Cover your face."

She did, with one arm. The other hand scrabbled alongside

his, pulling down gouts of earth, stones, reaching until the crack widened enough for two hands. Alex gave a shout and covered her with his body as a tumble of rocks and dirt suddenly rained down upon them.

And then it was quiet, and still. She lifted her head, tasting the grit of soil on her lips, and met his eyes. Joy flickered there, and light streamed down over his shoulders.

"Ladies first," he said, laughter in his voice. He set his hands at her waist and eased her past him, up into the breach they had made.

She hardly dared to breathe as her head poked through the crust of earth and ragged grasses. Dear heavens, it was so bright she could barely see. Blinking, she thrust her arms up and through, dislodging more dirt, and levered herself out. Out! She drew her legs up, free of the maw of the earth, and collapsed in a grateful heap. Out, onto the solid ground of a rocky hillside.

"Yes!" Alex clambered out beside her and stretched his arms to the sun. "We are out, Caroline." He grabbed her hand and pulled her to her feet. "Look. Breathe."

She did—senses stunned by the warm wind swirling around them, the impossible sun overhead. Miles below lay the sea, a lacy blue skirt surrounding the island. It felt as though the whole world was laid out before them, enormous and ineffably wonderful.

She scrubbed her sleeve across her eyes, blinking away tears, then started to laugh as he caught her in his arms, scattering kisses over her hair and face.

"We did it! Oh, Alex." She returned his embrace, throat tight with joy. "I tried so hard not to lose hope. . . ."

"We can't be too far from the cave entrance. Come." He planted one last kiss on her lips and let her go, then squinted at the sun, climbing up from morning. "Southeast."

He set off, angling into the new light. The hillside sloped down to a gully lined with scrubby brush and grasses that led roughly in the direction they wanted to go. She could not believe how good it felt to stride out, to feel the sunshine against her skin.

Alex paused and cocked his head, as if listening to something. Wind ruffling the grasses, a hawk's cry high overhead . . . and then she heard it, too. The thump of hoof-beats, snatches of voices ahead and—

"Pen!" she cried, picking up her skirts in both hands and breaking into a run.

Alex was right beside her as they rounded a boulder-strewn curve. There, on the trail below. Pen, unharmed—and what looked to be half the village, leading donkeys laden with shovels and supplies. Relief chased the last chill from her bones.

Caroline dropped her skirts and waved both arms over her head. "Here! We're up here!"

One head, then another turned her way, and with whoops and glad calls the throng began scrambling up the hillside. She felt Alex at her back, a strong, steady presence, and then they were surrounded. Rapid-fire Greek swirled around her, but she let him answer the questions and went to fold Pen into her arms. The girl was pale, her eyes red-rimmed, but she grinned up at Caroline.

"I knew it! Niko was certain you and Mr. Trentham had been crushed, but I wouldn't believe it. I just *knew* you were alive."

"You were right—and you seem to have convinced the villagers of it as well. Heavens, did they all come on the rescue?"

"A few stayed behind." Pen glanced at the cheerful crowd, and then her gaze returned to Caroline. "But where were you? We called and searched but couldn't find any trace. I was so worried."

"Alex and I took cover in a crevice that led to a small cave, then were trapped by the falling rock. This morning we discovered a way out."

It sounded so simple, but in truth those hours together seemed a great divide, separating her past from her future. She had been transformed through water, fire and dark, through the feel of his lips, his hands, the very act of surrendering her body to him and accepting his own surrender in turn.

She raised her head to find him watching her, his dark blue eyes holding a secret only she could read.

"Come in." Caroline caught Alex's hand and tugged him over the threshold of her rooms at the villa. "I'll light the candles and we can sit on the balcony."

Though in truth she wanted nothing more than to lead him straight to her bed, peel the coat and shirt off his broad shoulders, and re-explore every inch of his body. But they were no longer in a world of their own. The villagers still reveled outside and Pen could come up at any time. . . . She let out a sigh, but locked the door behind them.

The bedroom was full of evening shadows, but before she could strike a match Alex caught her up in his arms and placed his mouth over hers. Dear heavens, how quickly her body woke to his touch. She wound her hands behind his neck and pressed against him, demanding more.

Tongues explored, hot and wet, while his hands laid firm caresses up her body, coming to rest over her breasts. Already she could feel the tightness of desire running through her, her nipples taut behind the demure cotton of her dress, her full skirts hiding the heat budding within her. She pressed her hips against him and felt his immediate response.

Bodies fused together, he maneuvered her backward until she felt the edge of the bed bumping her legs. What luxury it would be to come together on a featherbed covered in clean sheets, all the little discomforts melting away in delightful softness.

"Ah," she breathed against his open mouth, and let herself tumble back.

He came down over her, elbows braced to either side, hands

busy sliding out her hairpins. "You are so lovely." His voice was low and rough with emotion. "Caroline, beautiful Caro."

He ran his fingers through her loosened hair, then tugged, tilting her head so her throat was exposed to his hungry kisses. Desire pulsed through her, a deep and utter *need* for this man that two days ago she would have found shocking. How had he so quickly become as essential to her as water, as air?

His lips moved over her skin, trailing heated, tantalizing kisses along the neckline of her dress, and she moaned softly, arching up against him. With one swift motion he set his hands to her hips and scooted her fully onto the bed, then lay beside her, his leg pinning hers. The bulge of his arousal pressed against her hip as he began unfastening the buttons of her dress. Bent to his task, a dark lock fell over his forehead and she smoothed it back, then tangled her fingers through his hair. It was growing too dim to see his face clearly, and she bit back a rueful laugh.

"What is it?" His hands stilled.

She moved restlessly under his touch. "I was wondering if we must always come together in the dark. I'd light a hundred candles to see you by, if I could."

She remembered those glimpses of him in all his nakedness, the lantern light flowing over his tautly muscled skin. She wanted to be able to look deeply into his eyes. There were still so many things unsaid between them, despite how their bodies had spoken. Questions she needed to know the answers to.

But time was running out.

A burst of laughter outside made Alex turn his head toward the window. The festivities were still in full force, the singing, violin-like sound of the lyra, accompanied by bells and drums, voices raised in gladness. On the way back from the cave someone had proposed a full-scale celebration, and so tables had been dragged out into the streets and food laid out in copious amounts.

She had sipped at her glass of ouzo, but the only intoxication she desired was the touch of this man lying beside her. His hands traced her curves, lingering, although he still had his face turned to the window, listening and alert.

She pulled his head down and brushed her lips over his.

Such a light touch, but it was enough to spark flashes of sensation all through her. Him, too, it seemed, for he returned his attention to undressing her. All thought of the outside world banished once again; she gave herself over to the feelings he aroused.

The evening air was a cool breath over her naked skin as he folded back the bodice and pulled her chemise down, baring her breasts to the night, to his touch. A shiver of delicious pleasure went through her as he cupped her and stroked his thumb over, and a glorious shudder when he bent and put his hot mouth on her, laving her nipple to a nearly unbearable tightness. She sighed, a breathy moan caught in the back of her throat, and he responded by moving to lie more fully over her, his legs on either side, his body pressing hers into the soft bedding.

It was perfect, and it was not nearly enough. She tugged at his shirt until she could slip her hands up under the fabric and caress him, setting her palms to his firm stomach, then around, skimming his hips and pulling him closer between her legs. Ah, how good it felt, his hardness pressing just there. And how wanton she was, writhing and sighing and pulling him against her secret, womanly places.

She didn't care, not one whit. In fact, she wanted him even closer, skin to skin, nothing between their two bodies. Her dress was undone to her waist now, his firm hands circling and caressing her.

"I want you," she murmured. "Like in the cave." She squirmed, pushing her dress down until the fabric slid past her hips.

He rose over her and pulled the dress off, leaving her in her thin chemise and shivering—not with the growing coolness of the dusk air, but the anticipation of him touching her, filling her. His face was tense with some emotion she could not name, and he did not stop her when she set her hands to his waist and began slipping his trouser buttons free. Soon he was more naked than she, the straight hardness of him freed. Hot and rigid. She slipped her hand around him and gently squeezed. There was a bead of moisture at the tip, and she smoothed her fingertip over it, heard his sharp intake of breath.

What power, to take a man in her hands and give him—she hoped—the same kinds of sensations, the heat and desire. She began to stroke up and down, his breath keeping time for her, faster, faster. . . .

"Enough," he said, voice hoarse. He pulled her hands away, pinning them together over her head and holding them with one hand. The other slid down, caressing, fondling, skimming over her curves. He caught the edge of her chemise and pulled it up, baring her legs and the throbbing place between. "Your turn."

He began with the inside of her thighs, light strokes that ended tantalizingly close to her center, just short of the place she needed. A little moan escaped her and she tilted her hips, trying to make him touch her *there.*

"Patience." She heard the smile in his voice.

"At least I was not afraid to put my hands right on you."

"Fear has nothing to do with it. I'm only taming you slowly. Very slowly."

"Taming? I'm not wild." Her voice hitched with need.

He brushed his hand across the juncture of her legs, letting his fingers stroke for a bare second against her before moving away again. She felt another moan rise in her throat—a moan, or a growl.

"I meant the opposite—you will be the veriest wild creature under my hand. Starting now." He released her and his touch grew firmer as he took her legs and moved them apart, spreading her wide and wanton across the bed. Now his fingers moved unerringly to caress her, rubbing gently, insistently. Heat sizzled through her, spiraling out from where he touched.

She grabbed the coverlet, bunching the material under her hands as his knowing fingers wound her like a pocket watch. Tighter, tighter . . .

Coolness between her legs as he took his hands away, changed position. The tip of him nudging against her. Filling her as he surged forward.

"Alex," she gasped.

He braced himself over her, then began moving, his hardness stroking back and forth, hips meeting, then pulling away. It was still strange to feel him inside her, and yet so very pleasurable. She rocked her hips, accommodating him, rising to meet each stroke, silently urging him to go deeper, faster. Yes, like that. Pleasure building in her again, rising up from a deeper place this time.

The falling darkness, the fact that she would be leaving impossibly soon—none of it mattered. Only now and here, the two of them breathing fast and low, moving toward a shared star burning on the horizon. Closer, closer until they imploded. Caroline heard him cry out even as she reached that searing heat, the white-hot brightness that meant their coming together was complete.

The room was very quiet. He lay over her, heart beating, skin warm against hers. She must have drowsed, for when she opened her eyes again he was lying beside her and a single candle on the table shed light over the sheets. He smiled at her and began running his hand lightly up and down her arm.

"Alex?" She laid her hand against his cheek.

They had shared so much these last weeks. Flashes of their conversations by the sea, the afternoon he had taken her swimming. The perilous journey across the bay, driven by the southern winds. The way she had begun to feel he was a friend, to know him more deeply each day. And their lovemaking in the cave—the joining that had changed everything.

She could not bear the thought of sailing away without him. She must ask him, she must.

"Hmm?" His voice was relaxed, and fear almost stilled her voice. She did not want to see him withdraw, as he had every time England was mentioned. But she could not leave without asking.

She took a deep breath. "Come with me—back to England. I hate the thought of being so far from you. There must be something for you there and I . . . I want to be with you."

The instant the words left her mouth, she knew it had been a mistake, could feel it in his sudden stillness, the tautness of his face. She pressed her lips together, but it was too late to call the words back, to swallow them unsaid. "I mean—"

"No." The word was like a rock. Unyielding.

She swallowed, her fingers trembling where she touched him. She could feel him pulling away, in spirit if not body, and closed her eyes to shut out the sight of his expression. Distant now. Shadows gathering about him once more.

She had thought what they had experienced together had changed him as much as it had changed her. But she had been a fool, she could see it now. Whatever they had shared, it was not enough. Not enough to remove the haunted look from his eyes. Not enough to ease his pain. Not enough to make him love her.

As she loved him.

Dear heavens, as she loved him. The knowledge sliced through her, pierced her heart and left her gasping silently.

"Please." She had not meant to speak it and bit down hard as the word slipped between her teeth.

He pulled away and began dressing himself, the movements rough and hurried.

"I will not return to England. Ever." His expression was shuttered. "But it is time you left Crete."

If her heart were still whole, the words would have broken like glass inside her. Instead they dropped heavily into the air between them and she had no answer. She watched him pull his shirt on, hopelessness wrapping her, squeezing the breath from her lungs. This was worse than being trapped in a cave beneath the earth. No chance of rescue, no chance of breaking free into brightness. The set of his mouth, the way he thrust his feet into his boots—he would not reconsider.

She sat up, pulling the covers about her, vulnerable and naked. "Why?" The word scraped her throat.

"You will never know. Be grateful for it." His voice was hoarse, filled with old pain. He moved to the door, paused. "Manolis will take you and Pen to Agia Galini tomorrow. Goodbye, Caroline."

No.

It could not end like this. She reached one hand toward him, but he shook his head, his raven-dark hair catching a stray gleam of light.

"Goodbye." The door closed soundlessly behind him.

She was too full of grief to cry, could only curl into the bed, the place where he had lain still warm, the scent of him clinging to the sheets. She burrowed in, trying to hold tight to those last echoes of his memory, but soon the night air stole even those from her. The bed was cold.

She was alone.

Chapter 16

London, May 1848

The city was crowded, hazed with coal smoke and full of the clattering din of wheels over cobblestones. It was so different from Crete that Caroline felt utter relief, even through the weariness of travel. She almost felt she had dreamed her time away—almost, except for the leaden weight she carried where her heart used to beat. The constant ache made her wish she had never left London, never met the dark doctor with his haunted eyes, never let him enfold her in his arms.

The trip back to England had taken a lifetime. They had stopped three days on Malta, where Maggie was completely involved in founding the Valletta Children's Home. Not only had she secured permission for the orphanage, but several prominent local families had committed funds for its construction. She had engaged another companion and a secretary, and it was clear she would remain on Malta for some time yet.

It also had not escaped Caroline's notice that the handsome older captain, attaché to the governor there, had become a valuable ally to her friend—and more, if their shared smiles were any indication. The particular looks she caught between them made her feel hollow and weary.

There had been nothing to keep her on Malta. It was a relief to board the sailing steamer and continue the sad journey home.

Thank heaven for Pen. She had proven a perfect traveling companion, full of enthusiasm for each new sight. She had helped Caroline muster a smile and the energy to rise from her narrow bed each morning. And though she caught the girl giving her thoughtful looks, Pen did not pry, and for that she was grateful.

Perhaps someday she would be able to speak of Alex, to think his name without it piercing her soul. But not now. Not for a long time yet.

Now, finally, they were back in England. Home. As she and Pen disembarked, she saw the familiar figure of Uncle Denby making his way to them through the crowds at the dockside, trailed by two footmen.

"Caroline, my dear." He folded her into a warm embrace of welcome. "I am relieved to have you home safe at last."

She let herself lean against him a moment, but the time had passed when she could take a child's comfort in his steady presence.

"Uncle, it's so good to see you. Let me introduce Miss Penelope Briggs, of whom I wrote you. She is my new companion and secretary, and doing splendidly at both."

"A pleasure to meet you." Uncle Denby took Pen's hand and pressed it between his own. "We owe you a debt of kindness for helping Caroline. You are most welcome to stay with us at Twickenham House, if you would."

Watching him, Caroline felt a pang of memory. This was the man who had taken in two bereft children years ago and had unstintingly made them feel a part of the family. She and her brother owed him much for that kindness. It pleased her to see him treat Pen so, and at the same time she was washed in a thin melancholy. She was grown, changed—seeing Pen's grin of delight only underscored the fact. Uncle Denby and Twickenham House could no longer be the refuge they once were.

"Come, my dears. Home awaits. Along with a large pile of correspondence for you, Caroline." Her uncle waved them toward the waiting carriage emblazoned with the earl's coat of arms, while the footmen loaded their trunks. "I have no doubt you will want to freshen up and get settled."

"Good thing I have my new secretary at hand to assist me." Plunging into a mountain of letters and invitations actually sounded appealing. She was ready for something to occupy her hours.

The carriage pulled up before the warm grey stone of Twickenham House, the familiar sight easing something within her. The entry was spacious and filled with light, and the butler, Jenkins, seemed pleased to see her, in his usual reserved fashion. Mrs. Beale, the housekeeper, was waiting by the stairs to reassure Caroline that her rooms were in order—and yes, they had received her letter and had all in readiness for Miss Briggs as well. Caroline thanked her, then led Pen up to the family wing and her new room, just down the hall.

"Let me wash up," Caroline said. "Then I'll rejoin you and show you a bit more around the house."

Her own rooms seemed familiar, yet strange—smaller, the colors more subdued than she recalled. But they had not changed. She had. The paintings on the walls, the patterned carpet under her feet reminded her of who she had been before. She wished she could slip back into that old self and let Crete fade like a sail receding on the horizon, until finally it was gone. She sighed and closed the door gently behind her.

Pen was ecstatic over her room. "Caro! This is too grand for me—but isn't the sitting area lovely? And the bed . . ." She bounced down on it to show her appreciation. "I'm certain I will sleep exceptionally well."

"If you need anything, make sure to ask Mrs. Beale. Or ask me—I am two doors down. And," she paused for a moment to make sure she had Pen's attention, "I want to remind you once more about my cousin Reggie."

The girl sobered. "I will be on my guard. Is he really so terrible? He is your cousin, and your uncle's son, and you and your uncle are two of the kindest people I have ever met."

"Well, perhaps not *terrible,* but you cannot trust anything he tells you, and he is prone to underhanded tricks and bullying to get his way. And his rows with Uncle. Well, just stay out of his way as much as you can."

Pen nodded. "I'll do my best."

"The fact is . . ." Caroline bit her lip. She disliked airing the family's problems but the girl had to know for her own protection. "He can be utterly charming at times—but that is when you need to be most on your guard. If he seems a delightful fellow, then you can be certain he is up to no good. Luckily he doesn't come here often. He keeps rooms in St. James Square and doesn't call unless he wants something. Usually more money from Uncle."

"Then he's one member of the family I will not look forward to meeting. But what about your brother and his artist wife? I hope they will visit soon."

Strangely, Caroline did not. Or perhaps it was not so strange. James would be able to sense right away that something was troubling her, and she would not—could not—discuss it with him.

Last year he had returned from his travels and she had known immediately that something had happened—something that very nearly broke his heart. She had coaxed the story out of him, and it had all come out right in the end, but . . . She felt a bitter laugh edge her throat. Some things one could not talk about with one's brother. Not and expect him to remain rational.

"Lily is with child," she deflected Pen's hopes, "and James is very protective. I don't think he will let her set foot outside Somergate anytime in the next two months."

The things left unsaid in their letters gave her the impression Lily's pregnancy was not progressing as smoothly as it ought. She felt guilty for being relieved that it kept James at his wife's side. But truly, he needed to be with Lily, and it was better for everyone if Caroline kept out of his way.

"We can visit them after the child comes," she said. "And we'll be busy ourselves—the days will pass in no time."

Despite her words, she feared the days would not pass quickly at all. But at least she was back in grey England, where she could not watch the sun scraping imperceptibly across the sky. Two months until she saw James, maybe more. Long enough for the memory of Crete to become just another place she had visited. And Alex? She closed her eyes.

"Yes, we have so much to do." Pen's voice was bright. "I want to learn everything I can and be the best secretary you've ever had."

Caroline opened her eyes again. "Then let me show you where I do my work. We can investigate the rumored mound of correspondence waiting. That is, if you are ready."

"Of course." Pen jumped up and brushed at her skirts, suddenly transforming into a more serious version of herself. "Are there invitations to balls?"

"Probably." Caroline led the way down the hall to the room she had appropriated years ago as her study. "Balls, and meetings, and picnics, and—well, I've been expected back in London for weeks now. I daresay we'll find all of that waiting. The Season has begun and there's no telling what I've missed. Oh my."

She halted at the door and stared at the papers covering her desk. It was a mystery how none of the stacks of correspondence had yet slid onto the floor, they were piled so high and precariously.

Pen burst out laughing. "Caro! It will take us months to get through all of this. My goodness."

"Well." She went to the bell-pull. "I'll have them send up some tea. There must be some sort of organization to it."

Indeed, she was correct. The piles at the close end of the

desk were most recently received, according to the housekeeper, who accompanied the maid with the tea trolley.

"Thank you, Mrs. Beale. Then that is where we shall begin."

Two hours later Caroline looked up from another invitation to a musicale since past, and stretched. "Put those down, Pen. I'm sure there's nothing pressing in that last stack."

"What about this?" The girl held out an envelope. "From the Ladies' Auxiliary. Aren't they the ones who fund the Twickenham School?"

Caroline opened it and scanned the contents, her stomach tightening as she read. "Pen, you found this one just in time. They are having a board meeting tomorrow to discuss the funding of their various projects, including the dispensary." Or not, if the letter she had received on Crete had been any indication. She wished the hastily scribbled postscript from Mrs. Thorne had been less vague.

"Tomorrow! Goodness, Caro, you almost missed it—and Mrs. Farnsworth isn't even in England to attend."

She dearly wished Maggie were here. The older woman excelled at navigating the political waters and was a forceful advocate for the dispossessed. Well. She would simply have to rise to the occasion.

"It may be a difficult meeting." Caroline bit her lip. "Do you recall the letter from the board I received on Crete? I'm not entirely certain the dispensary project has full approval." How would she be able to explain to Maggie if it failed?

"Will I be attending, too?" Pen looked a bit pale at the thought.

"Of course. I need my secretary with me." And the support of knowing at least one other person in the room was fully in agreement with her.

The girl's hand flew to her mouth. "Oh goodness. What shall I wear?"

"Your blue wool gown will do perfectly for the meeting. And the charity luncheon afterward."

Pen shook her head. "What a ninny I am. I'd forgotten about that already, and here I thought I was keeping track of engagements for *you.*"

"It was one of the first letters you opened, and that was ages ago. But it's vital we attend Lady Wembley's charity luncheon. Everyone in society who even pretends to a cause will be there, as well as those who actually do champion various projects." She set the rest of the letters aside. "Let's leave these until tomorrow. Or the next day—as tomorrow is proving to be rather full of engagements."

Caroline glanced about the meeting room, hoping to catch sight of her friend Mrs. Thorne. She was more unsettled than she would have liked to admit but kept a confident smile on her face, for Pen's sake. Still, she would very much like to know the circumstances that had caused the matron to advise Caroline's immediate return to London—a return that had been impossible at the time.

"Oh my," Pen said in a low voice. "Look at that hat. I've never seen anything remotely like it."

Caroline followed the girl's gaze to where a particularly high contraption featuring artificial grapes and crimson plumes graced a lady's head. "Countess Dunleigh is known for her fashionable flair. If you look closely you'll probably find a stuffed bird in there somewhere as well."

Pen's eyes widened as she continued to gaze at the admittedly eye-catching headwear, but Caroline's attention shifted as she spotted Mrs. Thorne approaching.

"Miss Huntington," the older woman said, her pale blue eyes alight with pleasure, "how very good to see you have returned from your travels. Are you well?"

"Yes, thank you. But you must tell me—what is happening with the funding of the Twickenham School's dispensary?"

"I would be happy to acquaint Mrs. Farnsworth and yourself

with the details, but we must be quick about it. The meeting is about to commence." She blinked. "Where *is* Mrs. Farnsworth?"

"On Malta, establishing an orphanage there."

"How unfortunate." Mrs. Thorne shook her head. "The dispensary project has been pushed aside by Lady Hurston, who is instead advocating we build a fountain in St. Giles. I'm afraid her idea has met with a great deal of approval—and with each success, the plans grow more elaborate. And expensive."

Caroline clenched her fingers together. "I know Lady Hurston has been exceedingly generous to the Auxiliary, but to throw over something so important—"

"Ladies! Attention please—this meeting is now called to order," the secretary raised her voice.

The room flurried into motion as the attendees found seats in the rows of chairs facing the long table. Caroline, flanked by Pen and Mrs. Thorne, found a place near the front. The chairs were as uncomfortable as ever, and she had to school herself to keep from leaning restlessly forward.

The iron-haired chairwoman nodded as the room quieted, then gestured for the secretary to proceed. A brief summary of their agenda followed, and it was with a mixture of relief and dread that Caroline heard project funding would be addressed first.

"We are pleased," the chairwoman said, "to announce that the Ladies' Auxiliary will be a major supporter of the grand memorial fountain proposed by Lady Hurston. At this time she will unveil the architectural plans."

Amid scattered applause the lady rose and unrolled a drawing. "The fountain will show Neptune astride four spouting porpoises. Water will jet from his eyes and ears, falling from the upper basin here"—she pointed—"down to the second tier, where mermaids frolic. They, in turn, will pour water from decorated urns into the bottom tier, where it will cascade munificently over the carved fishes."

Murmurs of "truly inspiring" and "hear, hear" rose from the crowd as Lady Hurston rerolled the plans and took her seat, looking more than a little smug. A pity her violet gown made her complexion so sallow.

"Very good," the chairwoman said. "Are there any questions at this time?"

"Yes." Caroline stood, frustration vibrating through her. "At the meeting in February there was unanimous approval for a dispensary project at the Twickenham School. Will we be able to go forward with that commitment and finance this ambitious fountain project as well?"

"Miss Huntington." The chairwoman's voice was dry. "With Mrs. Farnsworth and yourself on an extended absence from the country, the board felt it advisable to pursue projects whose advocates were more consistently present at our meetings." She peered down her thin nose at Caroline, then shot a look at the preening Lady Hurston.

Calm. Caroline drew in a breath. She must remain collected and rational. Surely she could make the board see sense. "So you are diverting funds from ill children to build this . . . fountain? Please explain to me what benefit, what service, such a thing could possibly—"

"Morale, my dear girl," Lady Hurston said, her voice as cloying as overripe plums. "And beautification. I'm sure a lady of your *breeding* understands the importance of the arts, even for the downtrodden." Her tone made the insult all too clear.

Caroline set her teeth. "Lady Hurston. Members of the board. I agree the less fortunate classes deserve art and beauty—of course they do. But even more they deserve food and shelter. And adequate medical care. It is difficult to appreciate the finer points of a fountain when one is too exhausted, or hungry, or coughing so violently—"

"We take your point," the chairwoman said. "However, the decision has been made. We've had ample time to consider during your absence, and the membership supports this course. The notoriety this project will bring us will benefit our organization for years to come. There will even be a plaque listing the names of all our members in good standing."

"But . . ." Good heavens, this was dreadful. Caroline swallowed, trying to think of something, anything, she could say to convince them. She sent a quick glance at Mrs. Thorne, whose eyes were full of rueful sympathy.

"No doubt you will be able to secure other sources of funding." The chairwoman gave her a smile that was likely meant to be benevolent, but held little warmth. "And we are not withdrawing *all* our support of your laudable school. Now that you have concluded your travels, we have no doubt a young woman of your resources will be able to find additional funding."

The implication she ought to marry and use her husband's money was not lost on Caroline. Just like the simpering Lady Hurston, whose husband's very generous allowance seemed to have given her a free hand over which projects the board would approve—and which it would not.

She straightened her back. "Thank you for your consideration, *and* your ongoing support of the Twickenham School." She nodded stiffly at the chairwoman and let her gaze skim right over Lady Hurston. A lady of her *breeding,* indeed.

"Do let us know how the project proceeds for you," the chairwoman said, already turning her attention to the papers in front of her. "The next meeting on our agenda concerns the efforts of Miss Wimpsey. . . ."

Caroline sat, swathed in heaviness. The rest of the meeting hardly penetrated her awareness as thoughts churned and tumbled in her mind. She had to find a solution—some other source of funding. Maggie would be so disappointed.

Finally the meeting ended, and she was more than glad to leave the stuffy rooms and insincere condolences behind. The rain outside mirrored her mood perfectly. She put up her umbrella and stared into the street, barely registering Pen at her elbow. If only she had not insisted they go to Crete. If only she had returned earlier.

The dispensary project had lost its place to a ridiculous fountain. Neptune with water spouting out his ears—of all the idiotic, goose-headed ideas.

"I can see why, though," Pen said, and Caroline realized she had spoken her thoughts aloud.

"Why?"

"A fountain is much easier, Caro. They don't have to face the fact that people are suffering and they ought to do something about it. Instead they can argue over angels versus cupids, marble or granite. It's much more comfortable."

Caroline paused and looked at her young friend. "That's very perceptive of you. I daresay none of those women have ever lacked for comfort." She squeezed her fingers tightly around the umbrella handle. "If only they could see the need, realize how much it is in their power to help. And their advice to me . . ."

"What did that mean? About you being a woman of resources?"

"Oh, Pen." A painful laugh edged her throat. "They were telling me to find a husband."

The girl was silent a moment, clearly turning the notion over in her mind. "Well, don't worry. Something will work out. Things usually do. Although"—she glanced up at the low clouds sending their insistent drizzle over the city—"I do wish it would stop raining."

"It will, on and off. It's spring, after all. Haven't you noticed the blossoms on the cherry trees outside Twickenham House?"

"Yes—and I'm glad you have, too. Here's the carriage to take us to the luncheon. Are you sure you want to attend, Caro? After that dreadful meeting?"

"I do—I have to. Who knows, maybe we will find some kind benefactor there who cares more for children than fountains." She stepped into the carriage and settled herself on the chilly seat.

It was possible. Lady Wembley's luncheon featured the most active charitable members of Society. Alliances were made and broken, new ideas were speculated about, and a general sense of self-congratulation infused the annual event. Of course there would be serious benefactors there, the kind who enjoyed the recognition and attention their philanthropy bought them. She should see this as an opportunity not to be so beholden to the Ladies' Auxiliary and its capricious patronage.

Caroline, with Pen at her heels, entered the ballroom-turned-tearoom at Lady Wembley's town house and glanced at the gathering. Most of the people she had expected to see—but there, seated at one of the center tables, was a new addition, surrounded by eager supplicants. He was unfamiliar, although there was something arresting about that wealth of blond hair, the elegant features. . . .

He lifted his head as if sensing her regard, amusement in his striking green eyes as he nodded to her, ever so briefly, before returning his attention to the elderly woman seated on his right.

"Do you know him?" Pen asked, clearly having noted the gesture as well. "He is exceptionally handsome."

"I don't, but I have a feeling we'll make his acquaintance soon enough." She nodded as their hostess bustled up. "Lady Wembley looks eager to tell us more."

Indeed, the first words out of the matron's mouth confirmed it. "Hello, Miss Huntington, I am so pleased you could come. And look who is here! Viscount Keefe. What a coup—he is one of the most sought-after bachelors of the Season. And he chose to come to *my* charity luncheon. Can you imagine?"

"I can, since he is sitting right there. But has he any interest in charitable work?"

Caroline supposed he must—a gentleman would not willingly attend this luncheon otherwise. Though there were many ladies present, there was a noticeable lack of young, unmarried ones of the type she supposed a bachelor viscount would prefer. And the food was always wretched.

"You may ask him yourself," said Lady Wembley, towing her forward. "It's high time old Mrs. Sparrowford gave up her spot. She's been monopolizing the poor boy for the last quarter hour or more. Here we are." She halted beside the elderly woman's chair and cleared her throat loudly. "Look who's here—it's Miss Huntington, returned from her travels. May I introduce you? Viscount Keefe, Miss Caroline Huntington."

The gentleman rose immediately and bowed over her gloved hand. "A pleasure." He smiled directly at her, his look warm and engaging.

If she still had a heart, Caroline's would have fluttered, but as it was, she simply smiled in return. Anyone who could endure Mrs. Sparrowford for that long surely had something to recommend him.

"May I offer you my chair?" he asked. "I'd be happy to fetch you a glass of lemonade. And your charming companion as well." He turned and favored Pen with a smile. "If you would care for some refreshment, I stand at the ready."

Likely he was only trying to escape Mrs. Sparrowford, but the thought of some tart-sweet lemonade was appealing. And the eye rolling and head nodding Lady Wembley was performing behind his back surely signified she approved as well.

"Thank you," Caroline said. "That would be lovely."

"Your servant." He inclined his head and headed for the refreshment table.

"Such a charming young man," Mrs. Sparrowford said in her reedy voice. "So kind and agreeable. Why I—"

"Oh, look," Lady Wembley said, taking the elderly woman's arm. "Isn't that your cousin Violet? Come, we must say hello." She hoisted Mrs. Sparrowford from her chair and steered the old woman away. As the two departed, Lady Wembley gave Caroline a significant nod, then shot a glance to where Viscount Keefe was returning with the lemonades.

Pen stifled a giggle. "She's not terribly subtle, is she?"

"A confirmed busybody." Caroline turned as the viscount arrived. "Ah, thank you, my lord. May I offer your chair back? I would offer you a dance as well, were this the right venue for it."

"You think I'm showing my ballroom manners too much?" He smiled at her. "Perhaps not the right thing for a luncheon, but when faced with a pair of lovely ladies, I'm afraid reflex kicks in. My apologies. And no, you may not offer my chair back. Please sit, both of you." He waved to the two empty chairs beside them.

Pen lifted her glass, then let out a little cry of dismay. "Oh dear, how clumsy of me! I've spilled lemonade on my dress. Do excuse me while I go freshen up." She turned a too-innocent expression on Caroline and made a half curtsey to the viscount. "Begging your pardon."

Oh, the schemer. Caroline watched her go, torn between irritation and amusement. It seemed her friend was in the same camp as Lady Wembley, determined to thrust her and Viscount Keefe together, though Pen's motives were probably far more mercenary. Surely the viscount was here to look into becoming a patron of some cause—if he was not one already.

She took the chair he indicated and set her lemonade on the table. "I admit, I don't think I've seen you moving in charitable circles before, Viscount Keefe."

He took the other chair. "I've only recently begun doing so. There's a significant inheritance coming to me, and it seems a shame to just fritter it away on idle amusements when something more meaningful could be accomplished. This has been a most"—he glanced about the room, crowded with knots of well-dressed women—"edifying experience. I've found out a great deal about many different charitable efforts."

The poor man. "I hope you don't feel too much the fox, with hounds baying at your heels. Sometimes those of us who feel passionately about our causes become rather . . . tedious in our conversation."

"I doubt I could ever find you tedious, Miss Huntington, particularly if you were speaking with passion."

Heavens. She had grown unaccustomed to the flirtations of the *ton* during her travels. And now that she had the knowledge to interpret such innuendos, it was difficult to feign unawareness. She took a sip of lemonade.

"You might change your mind, my lord, if I began speaking passionately about the Twickenham Boarding School—how the young women who have graduated from there have gone on to become outstanding citizens who benefit their community in ways too innumerable to list."

She watched to see if his attention would waver, but he returned her gaze, listening with a calmness and an apparent sincerity that surprised her. His fingers traced idle circles on the tabletop as he nodded to her. "Do go on."

"Viscount Keefe, if you could only walk the halls of the school and see what a beneficial place it is. The pupils—orderly, clean, and well nourished. The teachers and headmistress—firm but compassionate. I only wish there were room for more children. When I see the ones on the street, begging, hungry, ill . . . It breaks my heart that we cannot help every one. I've often thought if we could provide day classes, and competent medical care for them, a dispensary . . ." She glanced down at her hands, then back up to his green eyes. "But you see, I have grown enormously tedious."

He leaned forward. "On the contrary. I see you are a soul who feels deeply for others and has the courage and intelligence to do good in this world."

Heat flared against her cheeks at his praise—far more effective than the idle flattery he had practiced earlier. She indicated the gathering about them. "Miss Burdett-Coutts has any number of estimable projects in hand, and there are others here working on behalf of those less fortunate."

He glanced about the room, then settled his gaze on her again. "Yes, but are their causes any more deserving than yours?"

"No." She straightened. "The Twickenham School, a dispensary—they are every bit as deserving."

"Miss Huntington." He had a very charming smile. "Would it be too forward of me to ask if I could see this school of yours? I would like to hear more of your plans and see for myself what you have accomplished—and perhaps speak further of your dispensary project."

Gladness kindled inside her, the first spark she had felt for what seemed a grey eternity. "You would?" She tried not to let her voice sound too eager. "I would be pleased to arrange a tour."

"Where might I find your direction?"

"Twickenham House, in Mayfair."

He nodded. "I should have guessed as much. You are kin to the Earl of Twickenham?"

"He is my uncle. But, my lord, I'm so pleased you are interested in my work."

"I am indubitably interested." His smile thawed her a fraction more. "May I call upon you Wednesday?"

"I . . . yes. That would be most agreeable."

"Then I look forward to continuing our conversation, Miss Huntington." He stood. "And now, if you will excuse me, I will bid farewell to our esteemed hostess." He made her a bow, clear green eyes never leaving her face. "Thank you for being such a bright spot in my afternoon."

Caroline watched as he made his farewells to Lady Wembley and moved with surprising nimbleness through the knots of ladies until he gained the doorway. He looked back, held up a hand in parting, as though he had known she would be watching, and slipped away.

Chapter 17

"Lord Nicholas Havers, Viscount Keefe, has come to call," the butler said, presenting Caroline a polished tray with the viscount's card neatly centered on it. "He is in the gold parlor."

She picked up the card, the cream-colored paper thick and softly napped under her fingers. "Inform him I'll be down momentarily."

"Very good." Jenkins bowed and withdrew, and Caroline resisted the urge to turn to her mirror.

This was a business call—there was no need for her to primp like a debutante. She gave her skirts a brisk shake and descended to the parlor.

Afternoon sun streamed through the tall windows, highlighting the gilt furnishings and the golden brightness of Viscount Keefe's hair. He turned to her with a smile and bowed over her hand.

"Miss Huntington, you are looking well today. That particular shade of russet suits you most admirably."

"Thank you. Shall I ring for tea?"

"Actually, I was hoping to coax you for a drive in the park. This sunshine shouldn't go to waste, and we can discuss your project just as easily in my curricle as here in your parlor."

She rather thought that an exaggeration, but he was right about the weather. It was a glorious spring day, soft and full of blossoms. She had hardly noticed until he pointed it out. Besides, if he wanted to contribute to her school and dispensary, why, she would row him up the Thames if necessary.

"That would be lovely. Let me call for my pelisse and bonnet and tell my uncle where I'm going."

A quarter hour later she was settled in Viscount Keefe's elegant curricle while he drove his matched grays with a light and competent hand. Pale new leaves unfurled from the maples above them and beds of exuberant scarlet tulips edged the road.

"I understand you've been abroad," her escort said. "While England is home, I've found travel can be most stimulating. Tell me, where did you go?"

The sun edged behind a cloud and Caroline drew her pelisse closed. "I was in the Mediterranean, helping found an orphanage on Malta." No need to tell him she had been on Crete, or injured, for that matter. Or under the care of the dark-haired doctor whose face still haunted her dreams. She would stop thinking of him soon. Dear heavens, let it be soon.

Viscount Keefe turned to her, green eyes alight with good humor. "An orphanage on Malta! You seem a busy woman, Miss Huntington. And did you enjoy the journey?"

"The P&O line is quite comfortable, and I did like the climate."

"How clever of you to have escaped the dreary end of winter. Do you have plans to return to the Mediterranean again?"

She looked away from him, across to the gates of Hyde Park. "No. I belong here."

He drew her then into conversation about the Twickenham School. He was surprisingly easy to talk to, and soon Caroline found herself outlining her dreams of what the expanded school and dispensary could be. He seemed interested and engaged, nodding at an idea here, asking a pertinent question there, while deftly guiding the curricle through the park.

They stopped at intervals, conversation interrupted by greetings from various acquaintances, and it was with something of a shock that Caroline realized they had been out for the better part of an hour.

"Heavens, I lost track of the time," she said. "My apologies for keeping you so long, my lord."

"Apologies? Completely unnecessary. It is I who should apologize for monopolizing your time, although I can't say I'm sorry. It is certainly no hardship at all, spending the afternoon in the company of a beautiful and articulate woman like yourself." He gave her one of his charming smiles. "But before we go back, there's one more part of the park I'd like to visit. Have you been down the garden drive recently?"

"I must confess I'm more accustomed to taking the bridle paths."

"Then let me show you one of the chief joys of the park in springtime."

They soon reached a lane edged on either side with blossoming fruit trees. The light wind blew a scatter of blossoms down, a delicate fall of petals to join the profusion already drifted along either side of the track.

"Here we are. I recommend you hold fast to the side of the curricle."

He flicked the reins and gave a sharp call, and the horses burst into motion. Caroline gripped the side of the curricle as it began rocking side to side from their speed, her heart speeding too, and soon she found what the viscount was about. The swiftness of their passing kicked up great flurries of petals and she began to laugh out loud as they swirled up in clouds of blossom.

Viscount Keefe pulled the horses up at the far end of the lane. "I thought you'd like that," he said. "And now you have petals in your hair—the very Queen of the May."

"I wouldn't go that far." She began brushing petals off her skirts. "Still, you were right. That was a delight." An unexpected feeling, as though the clouds that surrounded her in a thin, sad mist were beginning to break apart.

"Here." He leaned over, softly sweeping the last stray

blossoms off her shoulders. She noticed his hands were trembling, as if from a palsy, and he followed her gaze. He curled his fingers closed, then abruptly took up the reins again. "It's time to be getting you home, Miss Huntington."

Oh dear. Was he ill? She made her voice gentle. "Would you care to join me for tea? We can discuss the school."

"I'm afraid I must dash off. I have another appointment." His expression seemed suddenly distant.

"Very well. Thank you again for the outing. It was a very pleasant diversion." She tucked her hands into her pelisse. "I look forward to your next call. And to discussing my projects."

The viscount seemed to give himself a shake, and turned to her with a smile that lit his green eyes. "My apologies—my mind does wander occasionally. Although how it could wander while there's such a lovely occupant in my curricle is beyond me. Of course I want to know more about your school." They broke out from under the trees and warm sunshine settled into the vehicle. "Will you arrange for a tour? My solicitor assures me my inheritance will be accessible very soon."

She gave him a smile made wide with hope. "I would be pleased to show you the school—and the building nearby where I'm hoping to house the dispensary. We can go over some of the figures then, if you like." She and Maggie had always kept detailed notes about the Twickenham School projects. Even without her friend, she felt confident in navigating that aspect of things. Added to the viscount's interest, she was beginning to feel optimism about the project's success. What a relief it would be if she did not have to post a letter to Maggie detailing their failure.

By the time they pulled up to Twickenham House the viscount had agreed to tour the school on Friday. He leaped from his seat and assisted Caroline down from the curricle.

"Miss Huntington, thank you for the pleasure of your company. I enjoyed my afternoon with you. Friday seems an eon away."

She shook her head. "You are an outrageous flatterer, my lord."

"I speak only as my heart commands." His eyes twinkled.

Caroline could only laugh at that. He released her hand, swung up into the curricle, and gave her a jaunty wave before driving away. To think, if he was impressed by the school . . . She was composing a note to the headmistress in her mind as she passed through the entryway.

Her mood dimmed immediately when she encountered her cousin Reggie leaning against the doorjamb of the gold parlor.

"Welcome home, my busy little cousin." He folded his arms. "Losing no time since your return, I see. You look the proper hoyden. There're twigs in your hair."

"They're blossoms." She resisted the urge to reach up and repair the damage. Show no weakness—always the best strategy when dealing with Reggie.

"Was that the feckless Viscount Keefe I saw you with? My dear, your standards are slipping if you're keeping company with him." Her cousin shook his head in mock dismay. "The man is worthless, you know. Flirts uncontrollably with anything in skirts—even you, I would imagine."

The corners of her lips tightened. "He was a perfect gentleman, which is more than I could say for some."

"I wonder what his game is? I suppose your dowry is fat enough to tempt some men. . . ."

"Not everyone plays games, Reginald. Some people grow up and do not behave as overgrown children. Now excuse me, I have a great deal of work to do."

"More of your milquetoast orphans I suppose. A pity you can't find anything useful to do."

His spiteful words followed her up the stairs. Oh, the malicious man—never content unless he was spreading sly innuendo. As far as she was concerned, Reggie's dislike could only make her think more highly of Viscount Keefe.

"Caro!" Pen stepped out of her own room to greet her.

"You're back! Did you have a good time? I'd like you to go over the letters I've written. Oh, and your uncle would like to see you in his study at your convenience."

Caroline smiled at her young friend. "Less than a week here and you are already indispensable. Let me go see what Uncle Denby needs, and then we can work until supper. And I will tell you about my afternoon with Viscount Keefe."

"Is he going to give you all the money you need?"

Caroline laughed. "We aren't quite to that point yet, but I think he's interested. We'll be going to tour the school on Friday, and I'd like you to come as well."

Pen nodded, eyes alight. "I'd like that very much. Especially after seeing the bare beginnings of the project on Malta. Now go, go, your uncle is waiting."

What a mother hen that girl could be. She certainly was taking to life in Twickenham House. Caroline paused before the hall mirror, plucking the last petals from her hair. In truth, Pen was taking to life in London entirely, embracing each new experience with her usual enthusiasm. The theater, the sights—and Caroline had never enjoyed going to the dressmakers as much as when she had taken Pen. The colors and textures of the fabrics had sent the girl into rhapsodies, and they had ordered a number of dresses in various weights and styles. Heavens, at this rate Pen would soon have a top-notch wardrobe by any standard.

Caroline gave her hair a last pat and descended to her uncle's study. The door was ajar, and he had clearly been waiting for her. He beckoned her in.

"My dear." He stood and removed his spectacles. "Getting right back to your projects, I see. And your young protégée seems to be settling in well. What a happy girl she is."

"It's surprising, given her history." She sat in the chair he pulled out for her. "A mother who simply left when she was a child, and a father who has been a ne'er-do-well at best.

Still, she's like one of those wildflowers that can take root and bloom in even the poorest soil."

"I'm glad you have taken her under your wing." Her uncle did not resume his seat. "But that is not what I wanted to discuss with you. Caroline, you know that ever since you and your brother came to live at Twickenham House I have considered you as dear to me as a daughter."

"I know, Uncle. You have been the best of family to me." Heavens, he looked so solemn. "Is anything wrong?"

"Not at all. In fact, I feel I am finally making things completely right." His eyes were misty with unspoken emotion. "I would like to formally adopt you. I want you to be my daughter."

Eyes suddenly hot with tears, Caroline flung herself out of her chair and into his arms. The happy news acted as a key, unlocking the gate of her tears, so that she could not stop. A great flurry of emotions whirled through her, like the swirl of petals she had driven through earlier: she was alone, she belonged, she was brokenhearted, she was whole. It was as if everything she had been holding tightly inside had come loose and swept her away.

Uncle Denby patted her shoulder, then offered his handkerchief when at last she drew in a ragged gulp of air and wiped her eyes.

"I . . . thank you, Uncle. I am, as you see, quite overcome." She gave him a rueful smile. "Now your waistcoat is damp."

"It is a negligible price to pay for your happiness."

"I have always been happy here. You know James and I always, always felt welcome."

He cleared his throat. "It is not the same as having the legal status of family, as being my daughter by law as well as inclination. I have given this a great deal of thought. With your brother now master of Somergate and happily married, I wanted to make sure you were provided for as well. As an heir of the Earl of Twickenham."

She blinked back more tears. "You know I can have no objection, but . . ."

"But what?"

"Reggie will be livid." It was difficult to imagine her cousin being any more intolerable than he already was, but this news would no doubt enrage him.

"He already knows, and has accepted the fact. Besides, I am the earl, am I not? Do not fret, my dear." His voice took on a serious edge. "There is one thing."

"Yes?"

"If he stirs up any trouble for you over it, or behaves abominably, you must inform me. He will be embarked upon a career in India before he can turn about."

"I hardly think it will come to that." Although perhaps she was putting her cousin in a better light than he deserved. Reggie had already proven he considered the earldom and all its benefits as belonging to him and him alone. When her brother, James, had inherited Somergate it had infuriated their cousin. He had gone to despicable lengths to try to prevent the estate passing to James, including threats, sabotage, and blackmail.

"Well then," Uncle Denby gave a satisfied nod. "I think we should host some sort of event to celebrate. Next month, as soon as it becomes official. Would a ball be too much, do you think?"

"We are entering the height of the Season. I think a ball would be just the thing." She leaned into him once more, breathing in his comforting tobacco scent. "And I am honored—beyond honored—to become your daughter."

As for Reggie, she would be on her guard. To what lengths would he go this time? She simply had no idea.

Chapter 18

"Welcome, Viscount Keefe." Mrs. Culbert, headmistress of the Twickenham Boarding School, made him an impeccable curtsey, then turned her amiable smile to Caroline. "And welcome home, mistress. It was not the same with both you and Mrs. Farnsworth gone from London. But please, let me offer you a seat." She hurried over and patted the back of one of the overstuffed chintz chairs in her office.

"Thank you," Caroline said, "but Viscount Keefe is eager to see the school. As I explained in my note, we will be giving him and my new secretary, Miss Briggs, a tour. Were you able to make everything ready? I'm aware you have a busy schedule."

"Oh, there's that much to do, as you know. But this visit is a special occasion, with special guests." The headmistress shot a glance toward the viscount.

"Indeed," Caroline said. "I will attend the next meeting of the staff. We can catch up on business then."

"Miss Huntington is still involved here?" Viscount Keefe asked the matron.

Mrs. Culbert gave an emphatic nod. "We couldn't manage without her. But let's go on—I'm sure you'll want to see the classes before the girls break for lunch."

Caroline stepped into the hallway, noting with approval

that the school seemed as well kept as usual. She hoped the viscount would be able to tell that it was a superior institution.

From a nearby classroom drifted the sound of young voices reciting conjugations. She smiled at the headmistress. "How is the new English teacher coming along?"

"Miss Layton, such a dear. She was surprised to find we don't use the cane or dunce cap here, and the notion the girls get regular baths and proper nutrition—well. It's clear the poor thing has seen the worst of boarding schools, sad to say. But she's more than happy to adopt our ways."

The viscount turned to Caroline. "I take it you have some unusual practices in place here?"

"By unusual you mean that regular waves of typhus don't sweep through, the girls are decently clothed and fed, and we adhere to certain standards of instruction? I am proud to say the Twickenham School is *most* unusual in that regard."

Viscount Keefe nodded. "It seems very laudable."

They spent the next hour looking in on the classrooms, where they were the object of many bright and curious glances. Some of the older girls giggled upon catching sight of the handsome viscount and had to be reprimanded, but overall Caroline felt the tour was going quite smoothly. The viscount asked a few questions about day-to-day activities, which she and the matron answered in turn. Pen, for her part, took it all in with wide eyes. Perhaps she was imagining what her life could have been like here, under different circumstances.

"Where do you find your pupils?" the viscount asked Caroline as they returned to the stairs, where the transom window laid a fan of light on the polished wooden floor.

"They find us, at least now the school's reputation is established." It was a fact she was inordinately proud of. "Given the state of most charity schools, children stay far away from them if they can. The workhouse, even begging on street corners, is considered a better alternative. But word is out that things are different at the Twickenham School. Now we rarely have openings. It's the saddest thing, to turn children away."

"Thus your desire to expand the school."

"Indeed," Mrs. Culbert said, leading them up the stairway. "We are crowded as it is—not *over*crowded, you understand, but more than full. And here is the dormitory." She swung open a wide door.

The clean scent of laundry soap hung over the rows of quiet beds, windows piercing the wall at regular intervals. Viscount Keefe strode over to peer outside.

"I see you have a courtyard and garden."

The headmistress nodded. "Fresh air is very important."

"And the garden helps provide food for the kitchen," Caroline added. "The school does what it can to sustain itself." She shot a quick glance at the viscount, relieved to see approval in his expression.

"Oh, and here's poor little Livvy Brentwick." The matron bustled to one of the far beds, where a small occupant, pale and dark eyed, watched the approaching visitors. "How are you feeling, love?"

"Tired. And hot," came the quiet reply.

Caroline moved to the bedside and gave Mrs. Culbert an inquiring look.

"Fever for the last two days," the headmistress said, "but she's recovering well. Over the worst of it now, I'd say."

"It's tedious to have to spend days in bed, isn't it?" Caroline smiled down at the girl and placed a hand on her cheek. A fever, but not raging, just as Mrs. Culbert had said. She took up a cloth from beside the washbasin, dampened it, and gently laid it across the girl's forehead. "Is that better?"

"Yes, mistress."

She pulled the covers around the girl. "Now you sleep and mend, Miss Livvy Brentwick." Already the child's eyes were half closed. They must have woken her when they entered. Caroline laid a finger to her lips and they departed the dormitory.

As they headed for the foyer Viscount Keefe gave her an appraising look. "So you are the school nurse as well, Miss Huntington?"

"Hardly. I haven't the knowledge or training. But Mrs. Farnsworth and I believe we need to care for these children's bodies if we want to be effective in educating their minds."

"The dispensary project."

"Exactly." She smiled up at him. How perceptive he was. "Not to mention that most of the lower classes go without medical care except in the most dire of circumstances—ones that often can be forestalled by proper treatment early on."

"An excellent notion." They had reached the front door, and he turned to give the matron an elegant bow that made her blush. "I've enjoyed seeing your school. Thank you, Mrs. Culbert, for the tour."

"Thank you so much for coming, my lord," she said. "And we shall see you again soon, Miss Huntington."

"Of course, and Miss Briggs as well. Good day."

They stepped out, the scent of lemon oil and the hubbub of just released classes replaced by the harsh smell of smoke and the racket of carts in the street.

"Well," Viscount Keefe said as they descended the steps. "I must say I'm impressed. Your school seems to be well run and there is no doubt it's making a large difference in the lives of those girls."

She smiled up at him. "I think so, too. But there's always more that can be done. The building we are hoping to use as the dispensary is just across the street. Would you care to see it?"

"Of course."

Caroline nodded to Pen and the three of them paused, waiting for a break in the cabs and carts moving along the busy street. At length the traffic thinned and they started across.

"Caroline!" Pen's warning was shrill.

Caroline glanced up, catching a confused impression of a horse and cab bearing down on her, the clatter of hooves too loud. She tried to hurry out of the way, but the driver veered, coming dangerously close.

Her foot slipped on the slick cobblestones and she tumbled down, landing on her hands and knees on the hard stones. She tried to scramble up, knowing with a dreadful certainty she was too far from the safety of the curb. Too far. In the next moment she would be crushed by the weight of trampling horses, the cruel metal-bound wheels.

She closed her eyes. For an instant the image of sunlight flooding through linen curtains flashed through her mind.

Then strong hands grasped her, hauled her away from the oncoming cab and onto the safety of the sidewalk.

"That cabbie almost made a mess of you. A bit too close for comfort now, weren't it?"

Caroline blinked up in surprise at the large-boned woman who had pulled her out of danger.

"Take more care when crossing, miss," the woman said, extending a calloused hand to help Caroline to her feet. Her voice was deep, her breath flavored with juniper. She brushed at Caroline's skirts, then gave a nod. "You'll be all right now?"

Caroline swallowed. "I . . . think so." She glanced up, looking for her companions. Pen had one hand over her mouth and was white as fresh cotton, while Keefe seemed frozen with shock, eyes wide and fingers trembling.

"Thank you—so very much," She fumbled in her reticule, wanting to give the woman something more than just words.

"Ah, no need for that, miss. I've seen you before." She pointed with her chin to the Twickenham School. "You're to do with the school. That's thanks enough." She collected her abandoned basket from the pavement and settled it on one ample hip, then lifted her hand in farewell, turned, and disappeared back into the fabric of her own life.

"Caro, Caro!" Pen caught her arm.

"Are you injured?" Viscount Keefe's voice was unsteady as he hurried to her side. "Be damned but that was a close call."

"I'm in one piece." Her heart still thudding uncomfortably in her chest, her body trembling, she slowly began to believe she was safe.

"The cab . . ." Pen's voice was tight with fear. "It was Mr. Simms in the cab."

"But that's impossible." Caroline peered down the street and took a quick step back. "Why would he be here in London?"

"I don't know, but he is. How did he find us here?" The girl's hand tightened painfully on Caroline's arm. "He tried to run you down!"

Viscount Keefe laid a hand on Caroline's shoulder. "It's a busy street and there are careless drivers aplenty. Anyone who steps off the curb is in danger—but attempted murder? Before all these witnesses? It hardly seems likely."

"But—"

"I'm sure the viscount is right," Caroline said. It had been frightening enough without imagining Mr. Simms was pursuing her. "There are many people in London. You could have easily seen someone who resembled the man. But it could not have been Mr. Simms. He went to Italy."

The girl shook her head. "I am not mistaken."

Caroline glanced once more down the street. There was no sign of the cab or its reckless driver. She could not believe Mr. Simms would be in London and commanding a cab with the sole intent of running her down. "Don't worry, Pen. We'll just be more careful crossing from now on."

Pen opened her mouth, seeming ready to argue, but Viscount Keefe cut her off. "There's the spirit. Now, it would be best for everyone if I escorted you ladies home."

"No need. Truly, I am quite recovered," Caroline said. "Please, come see the dispensary building. We are here, after all. It will not take long."

He regarded her, green eyes narrowed in concern. "As long

as we do not keep you overlong. You've had a shock, and I daresay will need to recover from it."

"That's very thoughtful of you, my lord." She led them to the stoop of the empty building. "We'll be quick, I promise." She produced the key and unlocked the door. The viscount and Pen followed her inside.

It was a quiet tour, with Caroline outlining her thoughts about the various rooms and what the dispensary could offer. Pen remained silent, but the viscount was encouraging. They paused in one of the south rooms where a stray beam of sunlight slanted between the dust motes.

"What do you think, my lord? It's an ambitious project, I know, but the potential is great."

He gave her one of his charming smiles. "I couldn't agree more. I'd like to consult with my solicitors, Miss Huntington, but to speak candidly, I like your projects very much—and I admire your obvious passion for your cause. I would be pleased to assist you."

She smiled at him, relief and happiness smoothing through her. "That is most kind. It is a great honor to have your support and interest."

He took her hand and pressed it between his own. "You have had my interest from the moment I laid eyes on you, and you shall have my devoted support as soon as the legalities of my inheritance are taken care of. These matters take some time, I fear."

"Of course they do." She refused to let herself be disappointed. "Your support speaks highly of your character, my lord. It means a great deal to the school." She met his eyes. "And to me."

His smile broadened, and she felt warmth touch her cheeks as he held her gaze. Then he released her and reached for his pocket watch. "Oh dear, look what time it is. I must be getting you home at once. I've an appointment with an old friend I simply must keep."

"Of course."

"I do regret that I must rush off." He held the door open for her and Pen. "If I may make so bold, Miss Huntington, may I ask for the pleasure of your company at the opera next week?" When she hesitated—out of surprise, nothing more—he added, "We can further discuss the school and dispensary."

"It would be my pleasure," she said firmly, ignoring Pen's raised eyebrows. It was definitely an invitation that suggested more than a simple business relationship.

She discounted the frown gathering on Pen's face. The girl would learn soon enough the intricacies of these kinds of negotiations.

The next three weeks passed in a whirl of activity. And if some nights found Caroline staring sleeplessly up at the bed canopy while memories of Crete and the man she had left there played through her mind, other nights she tumbled instantly into exhausted dreaming.

Viscount Keefe had been very attentive. In addition to attending the opera, he had squired her to a musicale and an exhibit, and she knew the amount of attention he was paying her was inspiring speculation. Let the gossips talk. He was a fine man. She could do worse. In fact, she *had* done worse, not so long ago.

She had been busy at the Twickenham School and with plans for the dispensary—finding workmen who could set about remodeling the building as soon as the funds became available and interviewing prospective physicians. Although none seemed as capable as the man who haunted her nights.

Dear heavens, Alex Trentham was over a thousand miles away, and never going to be any closer than that. Her battered heart should have learned that lesson, but still she found herself watching the evening sky from her window, finding the band of color that was the exact indigo of his eyes, remembering his rare smile.

She was *not* wrong to accept invitations from the viscount. He was going to sponsor the infirmary, after all. Admittedly, it was easier to forget Alex while laughing at some outrageous flattery of Viscount Keefe's. His company was a relief in so many ways. He was charming, easy to talk with, and certainly more than pleasant in his features. He did not make her feel as though she were about to plunge into the heart of a storm—but that was a good thing. Long-term alliances were built on shared values and mutual esteem. The fact that financial matters were moving so slowly was certainly not his fault.

He came to call on Saturday afternoon. Pen took tea with them, then excused herself to finish up some letters, and Caroline and the viscount went out into the gardens to stroll. Though small compared to the overwhelming verdancy of her brother's country estate, Twickenham House's gardens were impressive enough. A gravel path took them out through the rigid hedges of the knot garden, past a profusion of tight-budded lavender waiting for July, and beyond the yew break to her favorite part of the garden.

The wild walk, despite its appellation, only pretended to wilderness. For a disorienting moment Caroline saw the flower-streaked hillsides of Crete superimposed over the lush plantings. She shook her head. Of a certainty there were some of the same flowers, but the tulips and irises here were contained, not lavishly blooming wherever they happened to take root. This was England, after all. The center of London.

She sighed.

"Are you well, Miss Huntington?" Viscount Keefe stopped and put one hand over hers where it rested on his arm. "You seem a little distracted of late. Do you find my company tiring? Here, let us sit." He guided her to a nearby bench decorated with artichoke finials.

"Forgive me, my lord. There is so very much to do right now, and the invitations for the adoption ball my uncle and I are hosting must go out this week."

"Ah, yes. It is a wonderful thing to celebrate, your formal adoption by a peer of the realm. I fear you will have little time for me after the formal announcement." He gave her a soulful look from those green, green eyes. "You will have too many admirers from which to choose."

"I hardly think so." She smiled at him. "You underestimate yourself. Besides, it's not ladylike to care too deeply for the children of the poor. I think few would desire the company of someone as single-minded as I—earl's daughter or no."

He turned to face her, his look so earnest it made her breath catch. "Now it is you who underestimates yourself. Charity is not named one of the virtues for naught. Your generous nature is worth more than any status your adoption may bestow."

Warmth blossomed inside her at his words and she felt her smile soften. "Would you be my official escort for the ball that evening?"

It was forward of her, but she had given the matter some thought. In spite of their time together he had not seemed assiduous in his wooing. Perhaps he was waiting for her to indicate a willingness to be courted. She had wrestled with the question for days now—*was* she willing to be courted by Viscount Keefe?

Yes, she was. If she waited, there might not be another prospect like this handsome man. He shared her interests and was good company. He came from a fine family, was not at all objectionable in his person or habits, and seemed to like her regardless of her flaws. It was certainly better to spend time with him than alone with her memories.

His eyes gleamed with emotion. "My dear Miss Huntington, nothing would please me better. I know you consider me a gentleman, but in this instance I must give way to less gentle and more manly urges."

He reached and tilted her chin up, leaned in until his lips brushed hers, then pressed more ardently against her own. A pleasant awareness spread through her, and the viscount seemed to be enjoying the kiss, but Caroline found herself waiting for the rush of desire to ignite her body. The viscount's kiss was an altogether different sensation than . . . well, than what she had expected. But not unpleasant. Just less . . . She searched for the word. Tempestuous. And she was relieved at the fact—truly she was.

At length he lifted his head and gave her a lazy smile. "You are a fresh English flower, Miss Huntington. Forgive me if I have bruised your sensibilities."

"Ah, well . . ." She realized she was supposed to be—what? Shocked? Titillated? "That was very nice. Thank you."

A look of disbelief flashed across his face, so quickly replaced by his smile that she thought perhaps she had imagined it. "I look forward to escorting you at the upcoming ball. And I have not forgotten our infirmary project."

Our project. Those words, more than any kiss, melted through her. She could come to love this man, she was certain of it.

"Well, I'm afraid I must be off." He rose. "Time seems to speed all too rapidly when we are together and all too slowly when we are apart. Shall I take you back to the house?"

"No, my lord, thank you. I'll sit a bit longer." She felt fondness touch her smile.

"Then adieu, my dear." He broke off a nearby sprig of roses and presented it to her with an elaborate bow. "I shall call again soon." His step was jaunty as he left the gardens.

That had gone well—at least she thought it had. He had kissed her, yet had not pressed his advantage. A true gentleman. It was wrong of her to hope a single kiss could make her forget . . . everything.

Chapter 19

London, June 1848

Alex descended from the cab and thrust his hands into the folds of his coat. He had forgotten how the chill of England settled to the bone. It even seeped past the impatience firing through him.

Caroline. She was so close.

The carriage ahead of him lingered at the curb, the passengers taking a glacially long time to disembark. He waited, a darker shadow against the night, while footmen with umbrellas hurried forward from the gaily lit mansion that was their shared destination. Light streamed from the Palladian windows on the ground floor, and through them he caught glimpses of brightly hued gowns and cascading tiers of flowers.

He had hastened to London—the sea voyage interminable—wishing he had wings. Only to find, on the day of his arrival, that both Caroline and Pen were away from home and it was the eve of some tremendous ball at Twickenham House. The butler had grudgingly provided pen and paper so Alex could leave a note.

After five minutes of holding the pen above the blank page, he had found he could not write to Caroline what he so desperately needed to ask. In fact, he could not write anything to her at all. Instead he had scribbled a few hasty lines to Pen and left it at that. He would see Caroline soon—though not soon enough to quell his urgency.

The guests had finally entered the grand double doors of Twickenham House. Alex firmed his lips. Caroline had rather downplayed her circumstances, but it did not matter. He had grown up in this world, or one like enough to it, to navigate its waters with ease.

He strode up to the doors, the footmen swinging them open at his approach, and handed over his dripping coat.

"Your invitation, sir?" the butler asked, seeming impervious to the fact that Alex had been there just that afternoon.

"Alex Trentham, of Ravensbridge. I am a late addition to the guest list."

The man nodded stiffly and ran one finger down the list, pausing at the end. "Very good, sir." He bowed and waved Alex toward the ballroom.

Bless Pen. Alex felt his shoulders ease. Although if his name had not been on that list, he would simply have scaled the back wall, or climbed through a window. He would see Caroline. Tonight. For the last two weeks every breath had held the echo of her name, every thought focused on coming here. On speaking with her.

On making her his wife.

He felt one corner of his mouth curl in an ironic smile. Rushing back to England—he never would have thought it. But some things were even stronger than the past.

He had much to thank Pen for. When he had received her letter, standing outside his cottage on Crete, he had felt the oddest shock. As though the sky were a huge, curved bell arching over him that had just been struck. The reverberations of those words echoed through him even now.

Caroline is in trouble. She needs you. Come as soon as you can.

He had.

Alex paused at the edge of the ballroom. It seemed the occasion was going along quite merrily. Huge pots of blue flowers edged the room, and the gas chandeliers threw a brighter light than he was accustomed to over the throng. His gaze skipped across the crowded room, searching for one face, one form . . . ah.

Fire rushed from his soles, leaving a twist of flame burning in his chest. Caroline.

Her garnet satin dress skimmed her shoulders and she was turned half away from him, her brown hair piled artfully atop her head, revealing the sweet length of her neck. It seemed a hundred years since he had seen her, and only a heartbeat. He knew her so intimately—the smell of her, the feel of her smooth skin beneath his hand, the spark of intelligent humor in her amber-flecked eyes.

His gaze traced her slim silhouette. There was no sign of her belly rounding. Of course, the babe would not be showing yet; it had been slightly less than two months.

She was here, in the same room with him, she was carrying his child, and that was all that mattered. He pushed his way into the bright assemblage, gaze never leaving her.

"Are you enjoying your party?" Viscount Keefe asked as he escorted Caroline from one cluster of well-wishers to the next. "Your uncle seems well pleased. I could tell he was proud to make the announcement."

"Yes." A flush of happiness filled her. She had not thought it would matter so much standing at her uncle's side while he announced his plans to adopt her. She belonged.

Even though some of the *ton* might gossip about it behind her back, most of her guests had seemed pleased for her. Cousin Reggie was incensed, of course. He had spent the evening stalking the edges of the room like a wet cat; it was a wonder he was even in attendance. Except for him scowling from the corners, it was a very convivial gathering.

Viscount Keefe gave her his winning smile and set his hand over hers. He had surprised her when he arrived by presenting her with a small box containing the pearl earrings now gracing her ears. It was the kind of gift a suitor would give, and though he had made light of it, the message was clear. Her donning the gift had been a message in return.

It seemed an understanding between them could not be far away.

From the narrow-eyed glances of some of the young ladies, Caroline surmised there was a fair bit of envy. She tilted her head and glanced at her escort. His green eyes and tumbled mane of golden hair, his easy manner and charm were enough to set any number of hearts sighing. Even her own was not immune—what small part of it was left.

Handsome, flattering, attentive—she was certain that in time the viscount would help her forget.

It was unfortunate Pen had come to dislike him, though the girl could not quite explain why. Something about how he had brushed off the incident in the street, about how he was always rushing off at the end of their outings to other "appointments." Caroline could not understand her friend's antipathy, but the girl was young. In time Pen would see that Viscount Keefe was a fine man.

Sound drifted through the room as the musicians on the far dais prepared—the trill of a flute, the answering call of a violin.

"May I count on the pleasure of a dance with you?" he asked. "I want to boast of having such a lovely woman on my arm—the Earl of Twickenham's new daughter."

"Almost new daughter. The Crown is rather slow about these matters, but my uncle did not want to wait any longer to make the announcement. It will be soon."

His gaze sharpened. "I would hope so. Ah, but it seems the

orchestra is ready. Shall we?" His arm came about her waist and he turned them toward the dancing floor.

Caroline took two steps, then halted, her legs refusing to carry her a step farther.

All the warmth drained from her. Ice stilled her blood, closed her lungs. Dear heavens. Dear heavens.

A dark figure was cutting across the room, directly toward her. She swayed, felt the viscount steady her, but all her attention was fixed on this shockingly unexpected guest. Her heart battered her chest as she met his deep indigo eyes.

Alex.

Here. In England. In Twickenham House. In her uncle's very ballroom.

It took no more time for him to cross the room than it did to cock a pistol.

"Miss Huntington." He bowed. His face, that face she could not erase from her dreams, was set, and his eyes blazed into hers. What was he doing here?

Automatic, like a doll on a music box, she held out her hand. He took it, raised it to his lips.

Thank heavens for the formality of her gloves. She would not be able to bear touching him. Not now, not here, in the middle of the ballroom. His presence sparked against her skin, tiny embers flung from some conflagration. Contact like that, skin against skin,would ignite something perilous within her, and she could not—could *not*—acknowledge to herself what it meant. He was here.

Memories pressed against the back of her throat. She pushed words past them.

"Mr. Trentham. What . . ." She swallowed. "What a surprise to see you."

"Is it?" He raised one brow and released her hand. "How could I stay away once I knew?"

Knew what? She was drowning, here in a sea of laughter

and gay chatter, going soundlessly under. She clutched her escort's arm.

"Excuse me," Viscount Keefe said. "I don't believe we've met. Sir?" His voice was wary, as though facing a creature that might be dangerous.

Alex's eyes flicked to the viscount, then back to her.

"Viscount Keefe," she forced the air to move through her lungs, "this is Mr. Alex Trentham. Recently of Crete."

The words splashed like stones into a pool, sending ripples in every direction. Her escort leaned back, as if absorbing their meaning. After a too-long moment he spoke.

"Crete? I take it you know Miss Huntington?"

"I tended her when she was injured during her travels." Although the words were for the viscount, Alex did not release Caroline from his gaze. His eyes carried the memory of just how well he knew her.

He had to leave—she must make him leave.

"Did you?" Viscount Keefe's arm dropped from her waist.

"My lord." Caroline turned to him. "Please—I need a moment to speak with Mr. Trentham." She silently urged him to agree, sure the entreaty was clear on her face.

The viscount's brows drew together as he studied her, his perfect countenance marred by the expression. "Very well. If you insist." Was that a tinge of relief in his voice? "I shall just . . . fetch some refreshment."

As soon as he faded into the crowd, Alex stepped forward. Close, too close. The air around him was going to singe her.

"Alex." She lowered her voice. "Please. You must go. This is not the place to discuss . . . whatever it is you are here to discuss. I will see you soon—tomorrow—whenever you like. But not now."

Not while she was trying to understand that he was truly here, in England. Not while her ball flurried about her. Not while Viscount Keefe's pearls dangled from her ears and her body burned to feel Alex's touch, in spite of everything.

"No." He stood unmoving, his feet planted as though he had grown up from the floor.

They were, both of them, frozen, but Caroline felt it, the inevitable pull forward. Two steps and she would be in his arms. She dragged in a breath, past the yearning that seemed to coalesce in the air around them.

"Well, well." Her cousin Reggie's smooth voice cut through. "What have we here? A damsel in distress? An uninvited guest? Shall I summon the footmen?"

Caroline half turned and her cousin immediately insinuated himself between herself and Alex, his lips set in their usual half smirk. He raised one thin brow at her, clearly waiting.

"Ah. Reggie—Lord Huntington," she amended, "allow me to introduce Mr. Alex Trentham." She continued—better to have it all in the open now than wait for Reggie to pull the information out with his barbed hooks. "He was my doctor when I was injured on Crete. If not for him, I doubt I would have made such an excellent recovery." Her body was mended, at any rate. Her heart felt more fragile than ever.

"Was he?" Her cousin drawled the words. "Your doctor. Imagine." He turned to Alex. "And now you are in England. What brings you all this way, I wonder. Is this still part of the treatment?"

"Of course not." She felt heat color her cheeks. "He was just leaving."

Reggie fingered his diamond stickpin and studied her with eyes dark as coal smoke. "And where is your *escort* for the evening? The oh-so-attentive Viscount Keefe, who is seen at nearly every Society gathering, paying you diligent court."

"He is?" Alex turned to her. "That viscount fellow?"

"Do you find that surprising, Mr. Trentham?" she asked.

A shadow passed over his features. Regret? She could not name it, and it was instantly replaced with something else—a look that burned straight through her. He took a step forward, but Reggie gave no ground.

"The viscount is considered quite a catch." Reggie's voice was like oil. "Although, so is my cousin, now that she's going to be adopted." He curled his lip and glanced at Caroline. "No wonder his lordship looks at you so admiringly."

"Viscount Keefe is not a fortune hunter," she said, voice tight. "I've told you before, he and I met quite before this whole adoption idea of Uncle's came to light."

Alex stepped closer. "You did? When?" There was a dangerous light in his eyes.

"Right after I returned to England." She held his stare without flinching, despite the storm gathering in his expression. He had squandered his chance. He had no claim on her.

"Yes, fortuitous for both of them." Reggie's voice was silkily amused. "Otherwise I'm sure Caroline would be beset by ineligible suitors at every turn. The strangest people seem to turn up out of the woodwork when there's a whiff of money in the air." He brushed a miniscule bit of lint off his sleeve. "But you were just leaving? Don't let me detain you. Sir."

She felt lightning gather about them and gave Alex an imploring look. Go. Just go. Their gazes held for a heartbeat too long.

"Miss Huntington. I'll call on you tomorrow." His eyes darkened and moved to Reggie. "Lord Huntington. It was most . . . instructive to make your acquaintance. Good evening."

Caroline did not release her breath until he had turned and strode away. The air in the room seemed to lighten as he parted the crowds by the door and was gone.

Dear heavens—she did not know how she would endure a private meeting with him. Why had he come to England? And why insist on seeing her? The questions throbbed against her temples.

"Hmm." Reggie's black gaze scanned the room. "No sign of your erstwhile suitor. He's doing a damnable job of things if he left you in the company of that Trentham person. Well, enjoy the rest of your ball, cousin dear." He gave her a mocking bow and left.

She took a breath, trying to still her racing heart. Alex, so unexpected. And, damn him, still with the power to shake her to her very core, a wild wind that snatched her up whether she willed it or no. A part of her reveled in that storm, even as she tried to lock it out, all too aware of what havoc that primal force could wreak.

She smiled and nodded as some of her guests paused with congratulations and well wishes, but she barely heard the words. At last it was not a wild wind that caught up to her, but the breeze of Viscount Keefe. He smiled as he approached, his eyes calm and slightly unfocused.

"I believe we missed our dance, Miss Huntington." He offered his arm. "Shall we try again?"

"Certainly." She owed him that much.

Her head throbbed in time to the music as they stepped onto the floor. She wished the evening would collapse in upon itself and be done, pop like a bubble back into nonexistence. She fixed something that might pass for a smile on her face and let her escort move her into the stream of the dance.

"Miss Huntington. Forgive me for saying so, but I think you should stay clear of Mr. Trentham. He seems a bit . . . uncultured. I hope he realizes this is not Crete."

She missed a step, swallowed the bitter laugh edging her throat. "Thank you for considering my welfare. I assure you, I've no intention of spending time with Mr. Trentham." They had no future together; he had made that adamantly clear when she had left for England.

But he was here.

"I'm glad we're agreed. It's one of the many things I hope we can come to agreement on." The viscount gave her his perfect, easy smile.

She did her best to return it, desperate to will away the memories welling, hot and fresh, too close to the surface.

Chapter 20

"A Mr. Alex Trentham is calling," the butler said, presenting Caroline the gleaming salver with Alex's card neatly centered upon it. "Are you receiving this morning, miss?"

Heat flared through her. Alex here, waiting just downstairs. Her fingers trembled as she lifted his card. Last night, when he had first stepped into the ballroom, she had thought that she was dreaming, that the force of her wanting had somehow summoned him.

"Yes." She swallowed. "I will see him in the gold parlor." Questions burned along her skin. Fear, excitement, her nerves blazed with tension. Dear heavens, why had he come?

She hesitated outside the parlor door, closing her eyes and drawing in a steadying breath. Still, she could not halt the leap of her heart when she crossed the threshold and saw him. Foolish, betraying heart. She schooled her expression to one of politeness, though her blood raced violently through her body.

"Good day, Mr. Trentham."

"Caroline." He crossed the room to her, his stride purposeful, marred only by the slight hitch of his left leg.

She would recognize his walk anywhere. Alex. If he touched her she would be lost. She sidestepped his outstretched hand.

"Shall I ring for some refreshment? Or will you be staying

that long?" She wanted him to leave immediately, she wanted him to stay forever.

"Long enough." He set his hand on her shoulder, a light touch, but enough to scorch her.

She forced herself to step away. It did not matter that she yearned to turn to him, to feel his arms close about her. No. He had refused to come back to England with her. He had broken her heart and let her sail away with the pieces, and it would be years before the painful reconstruction was complete. She tried to summon a core of anger, something to keep her from crumbling.

"I am beyond shocked to see you here." She was surprised at the evenness of her own voice, steady despite the turmoil within her. "What circumstance has brought you to England?" Blast him for returning. For fulfilling her unspoken dreams—dreams that she had tried desperately to deny.

"Do you really have to ask?" His deep blue gaze snared her. "I'm here to marry you."

Suddenly dizzy, she gripped the edge of the wingback chair beside her. Her pulse surged. "I beg your pardon?" He had not said . . . certainly he had not said—

"I am here to make you my wife, Caroline. Marry me." He stepped forward and opened his arms.

Something inside her came free, the shell she had built around her heart breaking open as that part of her remembered how to beat again. How to feel. The world came rushing in at her, full of light and sound and breath.

She was not conscious of moving, but she was in his embrace a moment later. Home. Here, in the shelter of his strong body, the vividly remembered scent of him. The relief of it so intense it was nearly pain, like sensation restoring to a limb that had been numb for far too long. Pinpricks of fire as she came back to life.

"You came." Her voice was broken with tears, her face tracked with them—she didn't care. "You came, after all."

"I did." He bent and kissed her.

Salt mingled with sweetness as his lips touched hers and he gathered her tightly against him. The days apart fell away, replaced by flickering light, sunrise reflecting off the blue, blue sea, the rightness of their bodies together. Caroline clasped her hands around his neck and returned his kiss in equal measure.

All those nights of watching the indigo-shaded sky, all those days of trying to keep the syllables of his name from matching her footsteps, resolved into pure, desire-laced joy. She pressed herself close—she could not get close enough. She wove her fingers through his hair and opened her mouth beneath his.

Alex, her Alex.

Nothing else mattered—not the dismal journey home, not the weeks of aching hollowness she had refused to admit, even to herself. Only this, their bodies joined together in a perfect kiss, their breath mingling, their hearts matching, beat for beat. Standing in the surf on Crete, or on the carpeting of the gold parlor, if she was in the circle of his arms, she was where she belonged. Home was anywhere—as long as it was with him.

He broke the kiss and gazed at her a long moment, a brightness in his eyes she had never seen before. "Did you really think I would stay away after I found out?"

"Found out what?" She kept hold of his shoulders, a thin line of confusion marring her joy, tiny cracks across the surface of a frozen lake.

"My dear." His arms tightened about her. "You don't need to bear the secret alone anymore. I know you're carrying our child."

Her pulse thudded. The cracks in the ice widened, revealing cold water below. "Our child? You think . . . you think I am with child?" The enormity of his mistake hovered at the edge of her consciousness, a black wave waiting to take her under.

"What else would have brought me here?"

What else indeed? Cold, she stepped back, out of the circle of his arms. Alex had only come because, because—

He gave her a smile full of conviction. "I could never let another man take my place beside you—as your husband, as the father of our child. That's why I'm here. To marry you."

"Because of the child."

"Yes. Our child."

The wave hit, so full of despair Caroline could barely breathe through it. She bent forward, trying to contain the knowledge. Not for her. He had not come back for her. He had come because he thought she had something that belonged to him. And she did not.

Not once had any words of love crossed the threshold of his lips. She had been such a fool. He would leave her again. Of course he would. The certainty was like a bitter acid, leaching all color away.

"Caroline!" He placed his hands on her shoulders, his voice laced with tension. "Are you all right? Is it . . . is it the babe?"

She struggled upright. "There is no babe."

"Oh, God." He paled, his eyes searching hers. "Was it terrible? Forgive me, I am too late."

She tore out of his grasp. "Alex! Listen to me. I did not lose the child. There never was a child." Each syllable burned her mouth. "I know that what we—what we did together—could have resulted in it. But no. I never was carrying a child. Your child."

Dear heavens, if only she had been. He would stay, he would marry her.

But it would not have been enough. The knowledge that he had returned only for that would have grown between them, a thorn at first, then a prickle, then a hedge neither of them could see through. Impenetrable—and too painful to ever breach, though she might tear her heart to shreds trying.

He stared at her a long moment while the silence settled thickly around them. Those indigo eyes looked bruised, the confidence fled from them.

"You are certain?" he said at last.

She wrapped her arms around herself. "I wish you had never come."

"There is no child?" His voice was raw.

Mute with despair, she shook her head.

His expression twisted, and then he turned abruptly away from her. The sight of his shoulders, hunched with emotion, loosened her voice. At least he had wanted a child with her. At least he had come—even if it was for the wrong reason.

"Will you stay?" She whispered the words. Yearning, despite herself. She tried to keep the hopelessness from bleeding through her, like dye spilled into clear water. "Now you know there is not a child, will you stay in England? With me?"

He did not look at her, only braced both hands on the mantel and bowed his head. "No." The words were rough and low. "I cannot stay."

She should not have asked.

How could a body remain standing, breathing, yet be so full of pain? She clenched her hands into the folds of her skirts. There was nothing else to hold on to.

I loved you! She opened her mouth but the words were caught in her throat and she could not force them out. All that emerged was a nearly inaudible gasp, a whisper of the enormous shout of despair reverberating through her.

It was enough to turn him. The expression on his face was haunted. He took a half step forward, as if to gather her into his arms, then stopped. Something like self-loathing flickered through his eyes, shadows chasing into midnight.

"I am sorry." His voice was etched with grief. "You are better off without me." He stared at her for one long moment, as if trying to burn her face into memory, and then he bowed. It was the bow of a man who has nothing left to hope for.

"Goodbye, Caroline."

This time truly and inevitably. She could not move, her bones so weighted with the mercury of sorrow. Goodbye. She could not even say the word as he walked to the door, then out. Nothing would bring him back to her.

His footsteps faded down the hall. Muffled voices—the butler fetching Alex's coat and hat. The thud of the front door closing. So final.

She did not know how long she stood there. There was no sunlight to mark time passing over the golden carpet. The clock on the mantel had stopped at five-seventeen—some careless maid had forgotten to wind it. She would have to speak to the housekeeper.

Finally, finally, she took one step. Then another. Down the hall. Up the stairs. Past Pen's room; thank heavens the girl was out in the gardens this morning. Caroline could not bear to see another soul. Not now, not when the container of her body felt so fragile.

At last into her own rooms. She sank down onto the edge of her bed and let herself break. When her sobs grew too loud she turned on her side, grabbed a fistful of covers, and buried her face. She was made of nothing but tears, a jagged weeping that felt as if it would never end.

She must have slept, a thick and dreamless slumber that left her groping and groggy as she opened her eyes to a room grown dim with evening. After a long moment she sat up. Her bones felt too brittle and her chest was empty. Empty of tears, empty of heart.

Outside, she heard a child calling in the street. Closer, Pen's laughter as she spoke with one of the servants.

Suddenly she felt too aware—of herself, of her life. Of the afternoon gone, spent in weeping for something she had lost twice over. Miss Caroline Huntington—soon to be the adopted daughter of the Earl of Twickenham, who sat in her disheveled and tear-stained fine linen, in her suite of rooms in the mansion known as Twickenham House, in the heart of finest London.

Downstairs the cook was preparing dinner, Caroline's horse was tended in the stable, and the maid would soon come in to light the lamps and build a coal fire. And even more than that, she had family and friends—people she cared for and who cared for her in return.

Who was she to weep with such despair? No matter how shattered and irreparable her heart, her life was still pure bliss compared to so many others'. The indelible memory arose again: the orphan girl in that nameless East End street, bone-thin fingers and huge, starving eyes. It might have been her. In another lifetime perhaps it was.

Caroline threw back the covers and stood. No matter how hollow and broken inside she was, others needed her. The school, Pen, Viscount Keefe—so many others, so many plans and projects and alliances. She splashed her face with fresh water from the washbasin, combed her hair. Each breath was a tiny fraction of distance between herself and the perilous meeting that morning. For now, it was enough to simply keep breathing. Keep the thoughts, keep the misery at bay, and only breathe.

Her fragile composure was hard-pressed when she descended for dinner and found her cousin Reggie had joined them. She had, on occasion, wondered if he was clairvoyant; he had such an uncanny knack for showing up when he was least wanted. So she was dismayed, but not overly surprised, when he stood to greet her, his black hair perfectly combed, his shoes sporting a flawless polish. Her cousin prided himself on looking the part of a lord, no matter that the rest of his character was anything but lordly.

"Good evening, cousin." His eyes flicked over her. "Looking a bit worse for wear, aren't you? Well, uninvited guests showing up at grand balls do take a toll."

She tried not to flinch at the words. Despite her resolve, she felt as tattered and despairing as a child alone on the cruel streets of London. But she was not an orphan—though when dealing with Reggie she often wished she could not claim him as family.

It was a relief when the butler announced dinner was

served. Between the distraction of food and the deliberately light conversation her uncle fostered at the table, the meal was bearable. Reggie behaved himself through the dessert course.

"Cousin, may I have a word?" he asked as the servants began clearing the table. "Let us withdraw to the blue parlor."

Caroline twisted her napkin. A private word with Reggie was never a pleasant thing—but of course she must hear what he had to say. Better to know what the viper was thinking than let him take her totally unaware.

Reggie shut the door softly behind them, then turned to her with a scowl. "I understand your fortune-hunting friend from Crete paid you a visit this morning."

"He's not a fortune hunter." Alex. Her heart ached.

Her cousin's eyes narrowed. "You must admit, his appearance on the scene—at the very ball announcing your adoption—is suspect. Now that you're an heiress you'll be besieged by just that kind of blackguard. Receiving gentlemen alone, tsk, tsk. Why, you could be"—he paused, a sudden look of calculation crossing his face—"you could be easily compromised and forced into a match."

"Mr. Trentham would never . . ." She broke off, trying not to recall how it felt to have Alex's arms around her, wrapped in his embrace, his kiss. Heat bloomed in her cheeks.

Reggie's gaze sharpened. "Just what kind of doctoring did he perform while you were on Crete?"

A pox on her cousin. He was far too adept at ferreting out secrets. Caroline moved away. "It's none of your—"

"What kind of doctoring did he do?" Reggie followed, black eyes avid. "Did he overstep his professional bounds? Oh, when I tell father . . ."

Her hands clenched. "There is nothing to tell, you . . . you snake!"

He gave her a slow, virulent smile. "Well, well. Gotten yourself in a bit of trouble, haven't you?"

"I will not stay and listen to this."

Her cousin's low voice mocked Caroline as she turned to go. "Perhaps you should encourage that Keefe fellow to offer for you. Now. Before you start to show."

Anger made a tight ball in her stomach as she escaped the parlor. She was *not* pregnant. She knew if her monthly courses came she was not carrying a child—and they had come with regularity.

Pen met her in the upstairs hallway. "Caro, are you all right?" Concern lit her eyes. "Last night you said you were feeling unwell."

"It's a condition brought on by unpleasant gentlemen, more than anything." She could not make herself smile. "I'm certain I will feel a great deal better in the morning."

The next day started well enough. Caroline could almost convince herself that nothing had happened—that life continued as normal as ever. Pen brought the morning post up after breakfast and the two of them retired to the office.

She drew her shawl close as she sat at her desk. The air held a chill, one of those late spring days that owed more to January than to June. She would ask the maid to lay a fire and bring up a pot of tea, then spend the rest of the day working. At least these were problems she had some control over, things she could solve.

A letter from the Ladies' Auxiliary topped the stack of new correspondence. Perhaps they had relented and abandoned that utterly foolish fountain project—though she pitied herself for even entertaining the notion. She slit the envelope and scanned the page within, fingers tightening on the page with anger the further she read. Of all the . . . With an exclamation of dismay she threw the offending letter down on the desktop.

Pen glanced up. "What is it?"

"Lady Hurston's fountain project is exceeding its budget." Her voice was tight.

"But, isn't that good news? The board will surely see what a folly it is now."

"Oh, no." Caroline rose and began pacing the room. "No, their solution is to cut more funds from the Twickenham School. Listen to this." She swept the letter up and read aloud:

> *"The memorial fountain is going to cost more than expected. In order to fully realize this vision, the board must limit the amount of funding available to the Twickenham School. Furthermore, with the news of your upcoming adoption and increased prospects, the board believes the school should now be able to self-fund to a far greater extent than it has in the past."*

"That's dreadful—those horrible women!" Pen looked as though she had just eaten a raw lemon. "If they knew even half of what you and Mrs. Farnsworth have done with the school, they would be giving you *more* money. Piles of it!"

Her friend's staunch allegiance helped blunt the frustration running through her. "Thank you, Pen. But the fact remains, they have not seen fit to give us piles of money." She tossed the letter down again.

It was a matter of pride that she was able to support the school without being beholden to her uncle. The earldom did not have pots of money to throw about. There were certainly adequate funds, but the estate was still recovering from the mismanagement of her grandfather, who had cared more for his botanical specimens than the proper care of his holdings and investments.

Besides, Reggie would fight her at every step if he saw anything more than the smallest bit of funding going from the Twickenham estate to help support the school.

When was Viscount Keefe due to call again? Perhaps she would be lucky enough to see him today.

Pen picked up the offending missive and scanned it, a

frown between her eyebrows. "What does your 'increased prospects' mean?"

"It means"—Caroline crossed her arms—"they expect me to find a husband very soon. By cutting the funding, I'm certain they are anticipating I will marry to save my projects, and trouble them no further."

"Is that . . . is that your only solution?" Her friend's eyes were wide with concern.

"Not the only one." But there were not many—and it was by far the best solution for saving the school. She couldn't voice the words.

It was nearly impossible to imagine marrying anyone—especially after seeing Alex. After that one perfect kiss, those few glorious minutes when she had felt whole again and full of sheer, shimmering joy. That instant before everything had broken once more. She pressed her lips together.

It was done. He was gone. She must move forward in her life.

"I thought Viscount Keefe was going to help." Pen frowned.

"I'm sure he will. Of course he will. He's just . . . delayed."

"He had better."

She had nothing to say to that. Pen's words cut too close to her own anxious thoughts. "Well—back to work. I'm sure our tea has gotten cold by now."

They labored in silence for the next hour, although Caroline caught her friend giving her thoughtful looks. The rap on the door was a welcome distraction.

"Miss Huntington?" the butler called.

"Yes, Jenkins. Come in." She set aside Maggie's recent letter detailing the progress on Malta. At least *that* project was going well. She rested her fingers a moment on the top of the desk, touching wood.

"You have a caller." He extended the salver. "Viscount Keefe."

Her heart did not leap, but she felt a moment of profound

relief. She shot Pen a glance. The girl's brow creased; she seemed unconvinced.

No matter. The viscount had come.

"Please tell his lordship I will be down momentarily." A minute or two to gather herself, to comb her hair—to don the earrings he had given her. One hand went to her earlobe. "And Jenkins . . ." She pressed her lips together. She could not face another meeting in the gold parlor. Not with Viscount Keefe—not with anyone. "I will receive him in the drawing room."

"Very good, miss." The butler bowed and withdrew.

"Pen, I'll be back soon. And don't worry." Somehow everything would come out right. It must.

The girl nodded, then dropped her gaze to the papers before her. "Good luck," she finally said as Caroline was closing the door.

Viscount Keefe turned with a smile when she stepped into the soothing blue and cream of the drawing room.

"Miss Huntington." He crossed to her and took her hand. "I did enjoy your ball the other night. Thank you for the honor of being your escort."

At least someone had enjoyed it. "I was glad to have you."

His gaze darted to her ears, then back to her face. "You honor me even more by wearing my gift." His voice warmed further and he seemed to relax.

Not that he had been particularly tense before, but she sensed she had pleased him.

"A gift I'm proud to wear."

"Come, sit." He drew her to the nearby settee, coaxing with gentle pressure on her hand until she settled beside him. "I would like to offer more, and I think you know as much. Miss Huntington. Caroline. I admire you a great deal." His green eyes were sincere, his golden hair artfully disheveled.

Her heart began to speed. It was what she had expected. But not so soon.

She dropped her gaze to the floor. She could not agree to

marry him today—not mere days after her own heart and body had betrayed her. She needed time. Time to repent, time to school her heart to love the viscount and him alone. Anything less would be unfair.

"My lord, I must tell you, I received distressing news earlier." Her throat tightened. "I received word this morning that the board is cutting the funding for the Twickenham School and—"

"Oh, my poor dear." His voice was warm, as was his embrace as he gathered her against him. "There now. It's all right." He patted her shoulder, a gesture of comfort, and she leaned into his strength.

So different from being in Alex's arms. So blessedly different. It was easy to let the tears come, here in his arms. Safe and sheltered from the anxiety she had been carrying, however brief the refuge might be.

When she had collected herself, she looked up and gave Viscount Keefe a wavering smile. "Forgive me. It has been a trying few days."

"It's quite all right." He dropped a kiss on her cheek and gave her one of his most charming smiles. "I see you do not wish to speak of our future together quite yet. But dry your eyes. I have news that will take those tears away."

Caroline sat up straighter. Bless him for understanding. "Do you? What news?"

"I have recently met someone who is interested in your work. The widow of a wealthy American industrialist, she has endowed a whole network of schools. She's currently in London, and when she heard about your project she was interested in meeting with you. This could solve so many of your problems, my dear." He gave her a significant look. "At least, until we can come to an understanding between us."

She could not help throwing her arms around his neck and resting her cheek on his shoulder. "Thank you." She had been wrong to doubt him, even for a moment.

He moved back on the settee. A flicker of nervousness crossed his face. "She is, as I said, an American, and you know what a compressed sense of time they have. The thing is, she would like us to join her for luncheon. Tomorrow." He drew an invitation from his pocket and handed it to her.

"Heavens. So immediate—but I cannot conceive of any reason not to go." She scanned the invitation, heart growing lighter with every word. It was beyond providential. "Mrs. Baxter, is it? She would like to meet at one o'clock tomorrow afternoon. You say she has supported many schools?"

"Yes." He flashed that smile again. "Yes, indeed. I will be more than happy to escort you to meet with her. I've no doubt tomorrow will prove to be a turning point—in both our fortunes."

A figure entered the unoccupied town house, slipping like a shadow through the front door and closing it noiselessly behind him. He set a neatly folded handkerchief and a brown medicine bottle on the foyer table, then ghosted past furniture swathed in their dust covers. The place smelled of seclusion and the faint memory of expensive perfume. Although the light was fading, he would not risk a lamp. No need to alert the neighbors to his presence. There was enough illumination for his preparations.

Down the hall, the last door on the right. It swung slowly open, revealing a room dominated by a massive four-poster bed. He pulled sturdy leather straps from his satchel and affixed them to the posts. A quick yank on each—yes, they would hold. Unnecessary perhaps, but it was better to take no chances, especially as his tool had proven so unreliable of late. There was too much at stake.

He left by the side door, stepping out beneath the first stars of evening. As the latch snicked shut behind him, the figure gave a soundless laugh. It would be a luncheon Miss Caroline Huntington would not soon forget.

Chapter 21

Alex stared into the fire, a tumbler of brandy between his hands. He felt hollow, empty. The wet English chill refused to loosen its grip on him, even with his chair pulled close to the hearth and more liquor inside him than was left in the bottle. He could hardly believe the headlong rush to be at Caroline's side had ended in this—sitting alone and hopeless in an anonymous room.

Tomorrow he would leave England again. Forever. Although this time he would not be fleeing, nearly out of his head with grief and fever.

The flames sank lower, and darkness brought the memories.

He had been delirious by the time he reached Southampton but still aware enough to buy himself passage on a ship. He did not care where he was bound as long as it was away. Away from England, away from what he had done. The injury to his leg, untended for days, was beginning to poison his body. It ought to have killed him, but the ship's doctor saved his life. Alex remembered little of that journey, could not recall the man's face through the haze of pain and medication.

By the time he was able to stumble onto deck, once again in possession of his senses, they had reached the Mediterranean.

Crete. It had risen on the horizon like a lost continent from the depths of the ancient sea, its soil soaked in myth and remorse. Flowers burned on the hillsides, and the shore and mountains seemed to offer a rough sanctuary.

It had been his penance. His retreat. Until now.

He dashed the contents of his glass into the embers and they roared up, feeding on the fumes. There was no peace for him now, not after she had made him live again.

No peace on these shores for him, not after what he had done. What he would always be.

A murderer.

Nothing could change that. He had been a fool to imagine that having a child with Caroline would somehow absolve him of his past. There was no absolution. She would have married him, then cursed him for the rest of their bleak lives together. He could not condemn her—either of them—to that.

Thank God there had been no baby. He had nothing to offer. Nothing to give. His lips twisted bitterly as he reached into his breast pocket, then unfolded the well-worn letter from Pen that had summoned him.

Caroline is in trouble.

His heart jolted as he read the familiar line written in the girl's angular hand. There was no baby. Then what the devil could it mean?

The events on Crete—Simms's stray gunshot, rowing for their lives in the froth of the *souroko.* A shiver passed through him, a stirring of urgency blunted by the brandy in his blood. Pen—he had to talk to Pen. He tried to lever himself out of the chair, but the room began to rotate slowly around him.

Tomorrow. He'd send the girl a note. They would meet, somewhere he would not run the risk of seeing Caroline. Tomorrow.

He stared into the gathering shadows, a cold line of foreboding laid over his heart.

The next day Alex found himself once again lifting the heavy brass knocker of Twickenham House.

"Sir," the butler gave him a cold look as he held the door open. "I believe you are expected. Miss Briggs has—"

The girl burst into the foyer. "Alex!" She grabbed him by the arm. "Thank heavens you are here—you must go after her!"

"Who? Pen, calm down and tell me what is going on."

She hauled him over to a sitting area with red velvet upholstered chairs, then paced back and forth, the words tumbling out of her, her hands turning around and around one another.

"A messenger came for Caro a half hour ago—after she had already left for her luncheon appointment—and said it was urgent. I thought . . . her brother's wife, the baby . . . At any rate I knew where she had gone and I told him, even though it was irregular. I shouldn't have, I see that now, but . . ."

"Pen." He caught her by the shoulders, stilling her. "Don't try to explain, just answer me. Caroline is in danger?"

"Yes."

He forced himself to breathe and listen, to keep her panic from infecting him. "And you know where she has gone—you can tell me how to get there?"

The girl nodded, her eyes fixed on his face as though he were the one solid thing in the room. "Kensington. Barberry Lane. I wrote it down. I'm her secretary now, so I keep notes on these things, and I'm so afraid—if Mr. Simms catches her this time—"

Fear began to beat through him, uncontrolled and rising. "Simms? Did you say Mr. Simms? He's here, in London? Why didn't you tell me?" God, the days he had wasted in self-pity when that madman was here. His jaw tightened.

"I was in such a hurry when I sent that letter to you. The ship was leaving for the Mediterranean and I only had time to write a quick note and send the messenger racing down. And"—she dropped her gaze—"no one believed me about seeing Mr. Simms. I was afraid you wouldn't either, if I told you."

"It's all right, Pen. You did the best you could. Now call one of the servants and have them fetch my horse. I'll go after her. Meanwhile, explain as much as you can."

A maid was summoned and dispatched to the stables, and Alex turned to Pen. "Why do you think Simms is after her?"

"The day I wrote you, she was deliberately run down in the street by a cab—a cab with yellow-spoked wheels. And who was in it but Mr. Simms!"

Alex clenched his hands. "The same Mr. Simms from Crete? You're certain?"

"Absolutely." Her eyes were wide. "I know it was. Caroline didn't see him, and Viscount Keefe made light of it. But I know who I saw."

"Has there been anything since then—any other attempts?"

She lowered her voice. "The same cab, the yellow-wheeled one, follows Caroline when she goes out. I know it sounds far-fetched. Caro won't believe me. She thinks I'm being fanciful and am not accustomed to city life."

"And she went out today—with whom?"

"Viscount Keefe. They took his curricle." Pen's voice was unhappy.

"Useless." He was coming to hate Keefe more every minute. "And a messenger came after she left, and . . ."

"And after I told him where she had gone, I went out on the step. Then I saw the same messenger go up to a cab. That cab. The one with the yellow wheels, and right away the driver whipped up the horses and they were gone. He's after her. I can't help feeling she's in terrible danger."

Alex felt it, too, a tightness that gripped his limbs, an urgency that had him pacing as restlessly as Pen. He whirled in relief when the butler pulled the door open. "Here's the groom with my horse. Don't worry, Pen. I'll find her."

"I know." The words were barely a whisper as she followed him to the threshold.

* * *

"Here we are." Viscount Keefe pulled the curricle up outside a respectable-looking town house. "Mrs. Baxter awaits." He jumped down and handed the reins to the footman who had traveled with them, then helped Caroline down from the seat.

She resisted the urge to smooth back her hair. No need to be anxious—or not much, at any rate. Although . . . Americans were different, and there was so very much at stake. Perhaps a little nervousness could be forgiven.

The viscount held out his arm for her. He looked a trifle ill at ease himself, though he gave her his usual charming smile as he led her up the steps. He rapped on the door. There was no answer.

"Did we get the day wrong?" Caroline fished the invitation from her reticule and frowned as she scanned it. "No, we are here at the proper time, and place. This *is* 14 Barberry Lane."

"Well, Americans are not always predictable when it comes to protocol. Maybe we should just peek inside." The viscount set his hand to the knob. There was a slight tremor in his fingers. "Ah, it's open." He waved her forward.

"Are you sure?" Caroline hesitated on the threshold. "I don't think it's quite the thing. Perhaps Mrs. Baxter is expecting us to be late?"

"We can wait in the hall for her butler if that is the case." He set his hand between her shoulders and gave her a gentle push forward.

"My, it's rather dim in here. Our hostess must be a bit of an eccentric." Caroline kept her voice low and peered into the nearby drawing room. "Why look, the furniture is still swathed in dust covers." Unease shivered along her spine, like a spider dropped down her collar. She turned to her escort, who was fumbling with something by the front door. "My lord, I do not think we are expected. There has been some mistake."

"So sorry, my dear." He strode up to her, grabbing the back of her head and bringing a kerchief up to her face. Her unease roared into full panic, flaring like a suddenly overturned lamp in a pool of oil. A noxious odor wafted from the kerchief, and she tried to twist away, but the viscount had a firm hold on her.

What was he doing? Why? There was only time to take one quick breath before her nose was buried in the acrid linen. Caroline fought not to breathe in the fumes, but sudden darkness swathed her senses, the fire of her fear abruptly doused.

Caroline returned to herself in bits, enough presence of mind remaining to feign continued unconsciousness. She was lying on her back, her hands tingling. She cautiously flexed them and found she was bound, arms pulled to either side. Where was she? What had happened? Disbelief and confusion mingled on her tongue with the bitter taste of whatever it was she had breathed. Her eyelids felt like shillings had been stacked on them, they were so hard to open. It was easy to keep her gaze to a mere slit.

A bedroom. A gas lamp, the thick red shade keeping the room more in shadows than light. Movement in the corner of her vision. She slowly turned her head. Viscount Keefe! She almost called his name in relief, before she recalled he was the one who had brought her here.

He was bent over a small table, his hands busy with odd implements. A shiver of fear breathed over her. Dear lord, what kind of trap had she fallen into? The viscount struck a match, the stink of phosphorus burning her nose, then lit a miniature lamp crowned with cut glass. It seemed made for some express purpose, but what that might be she did not know.

Slowly, Viscount Keefe drew a long metal instrument from beneath his coat. She let out a gasp of fear and his head jerked up.

"Awake, I see." He smiled at her—there was nothing leering or sinister about his expression, just his usual disarming smile. "I am very sorry for this circumstance, Miss Huntington—or perhaps I should call you Caroline, since we are soon to be very intimate."

She pulled against the bonds that cut into her wrists. "Why? Why are you doing this?" She worked her left wrist back and forth, trying to keep him distracted with talking.

He gave an apologetic shrug. "Our courtship was proceeding too slowly. It was necessary to speed up matters. While I've no doubt you would have agreed to become my wife in due time, the arrival of that Trentham fellow has muddied the waters."

"My lord. I was more than willing to become your wife." Well, she had been before the bizarre events of the afternoon had begun to unfold. "Untie me—there's no need for . . . whatever it is you are planning." She could not help glancing at the implement he was holding.

He followed her gaze, then let out a sharp laugh. "Oh, don't fear, this particular instrument is not for you. I, however, find it's rather crucial—especially under the circumstances. Give me a moment, and then we can go about our business together."

He set the item down and drew a small pouch from his pocket, the type gentlemen used to carry tobacco. He opened it and removed a shaving of something black and solid. Ah—the metal object was a long, thin pipe, ornamented with filigree. He carefully filled the tiny bowl, sent her a thoughtful glance, and added a bit more. With a nod of satisfaction he licked his fingers and closed the pouch.

Taking advantage of his distraction, Caroline worked her left wrist against the strap imprisoning it. It felt looser. Two or three hard yanks would probably free her, but what then? She slid her gaze back to the viscount.

He was holding the small lamp beneath the bowl of the pipe. As he inhaled, a look of bliss spread over his face. A cloying scent drifted to her—one not completely unfamiliar. She realized she had caught the same faint aroma trapped in his hair and clothing several times before.

"Opium, my lord?" She was not as surprised as she might

have been. It all began to make sense: his sudden tremblings, the way he hurried away after their outings. The clues had been there all along. Certainly some members of the *ton* were firm believers in their tonics and tinctures of laudanum. Still, eating opium was one thing, smoking it was quite another.

He gave her an open smile. "Do you despise me for my vice? You should not. It's very calmative, especially in difficult situations. Not that I don't find you attractive, Caroline, but performing under these circumstances . . . you understand the pressure."

"Did you . . . did you ever care about me at all?"

"Of course." He sounded surprised. "I truly have come to admire you. Although after we are married, I'm afraid your boarding school is going to have to close. I'll be needing the money for my own . . . interests." He smiled down at his pipe.

"After we are married?"

"Here." He stepped unsteadily to the bed. "Take some. It will make this easier for you."

She shook her head emphatically.

"No? A pity to waste it." He set the stem to his mouth and inhaled, long and deep, swirling the lamp beneath. A dreamy look settled over his face, his lids half closed. Finally he set the pipe back on the table. "Time to get to it, my dear. Just imagine it is our wedding night—only a bit early." He swayed and caught himself, one hand on the bedpost. "Our marriage bed."

She watched in horror as he fumbled at his breeches.

"My lord! There is no need to be hasty." She began tugging in earnest at her bonds. "Untie me and I'm sure we can discuss this rationally. You are a gentleman. There is really no need for, for . . ."

"Unfortunately, there is." He blinked down at her, his smile still fixed on his face. "I may be a gentleman, but I'm rather a hard-pressed one at present. You see, I have no money. Don't look so shocked, my dear. It's a common occurrence.

Things have come to a head, and—well, let's just say it's best I secure my interest in you promptly."

Her stomach twisted. How could he? She had believed him to be a good man—but clearly there were things she ought to have known about Viscount Keefe. She jerked her feet, but they, too, were bound tightly. She swallowed back the sharp sting of fear.

"And now . . ." He paused.

Caroline squeezed her eyes shut, then shuddered as his weight came down across her, pressing her into the mattress. She grit her teeth and waited. And waited. It was becoming difficult to breathe.

She opened her eyes. Viscount Keefe's face was inches from her own, his eyes closed, a beatific expression on his face.

"Viscount Keefe?"

The man was unconscious, of all things. The extra opium. He began to snore, the oaf. She had to get free. She bucked, trying to dislodge him, but he was too heavy. Maybe if she wiggled to the side, as far as the tethers would allow . . . Yes. She was only partially trapped by him now. She drew in a deep breath.

One hard yank. Another. She bit her lip as the strap abraded her wrist. *Dear heavens, please, please.* She folded her fingers together and pulled, ignoring the pain as she forced her hand to compress through the confining loop. Tight, too tight, then suddenly slack as her hand slipped free.

Her skin burned, her fingers were squeezed bloodless, but she had her arm back. She wrung her hand out, two sharp shakes, then pushed at the viscount with all her strength, moving him enough that she could turn her body sideways and reach her other hand. Awkward, untying knots with her left hand, but they were not as tight as she had feared.

Her unconscious suitor was still partially pinning her to the bed, but Caroline was able to scoot out from under him. A ripping sound, but she could hardly care about the condition of her skirts. He seemed oblivious to the world, one hand upflung temptingly near the strap she had just untied.

It was easy enough to pull his arm a bit higher. Satisfaction flared through her as she cinched the leather tight about his wrist. There. See how he liked being cooked in his own sauce. Marry him, indeed!

She bent, working to free her ankles. Nearly free . . .

A thud, from the front of the house. The front door closing. Someone was coming. Her heart raced as her fingers fumbled over the knots. She bit back her frustration and tried to keep her hands from trembling as she pulled the last strap off. She sprang to her feet and sent one wild glance at the door. Should she stay?

No. Whoever was coming would be in league with the viscount. A witness to her staged compromise, no doubt. There would be no help from that side of the door.

She pivoted. The window. Thank heavens it opened smoothly. She flung her leg over, barely caring what was below, just thankful she was on the ground floor. A twiggy bush broke her half leap from the sill, and her torn dress caught on the branches. Dratted clothing! She yanked herself free, picked up her ruined skirts, and ran, making for the front of the house, the safety of the street.

Luck was still with her. A hansom cab loitered at the corner. Passengers or no, this was her escape. She hurried up to it.

"Mayfair, quickly," she gasped at the driver. Without hesitating, she opened the door and flung herself inside.

"Unhand my cousin, you blackguard!" Reginald burst into the room, then drew up short at the sight of Keefe snoring on the bed, one hand affixed to the post. "Blast it!" He grabbed the man's shoulder and gave him a rough shake. "Wake up, you incompetent fool. Where is she?"

"What?" The viscount opened his eyes dreamily and blinked

up at Reginald. Saliva had leaked out one corner of the viscount's mouth, wetting his handsome face.

Reginald curled his lip at the apparatus spread out on the small table, then ran to the open window and leaned out. Just in time to see the backside of his cousin disappearing into a cab with yellow wheels. The door had barely closed behind her before the driver whipped up the horse and the vehicle sped out of sight.

He hit his fist against the sill. Bloody hell. Why was he saddled with such an incompetent? His perfectly laid plans dashed for want of proper execution. The jig was up now, at least where his cousin and the viscount were concerned. Reginald was mortally certain she would entertain no further offers from Keefe.

He took a deep, shuddering breath. At least he was not implicated in this—and even if the viscount tried, no one would believe him, the sotted idiot. But damnation, now what? He turned back to the figure on the bed.

"Get up." He prodded the man, finally getting him to sit.

The viscount swayed, then frowned at the strap around his wrist. Memory slowly filtered back into his expression. "The minx. Untie me, and we can go after her."

"There is no going after her. Untie your own damned self, and get out. Go—as far as possible. My father will not be happy once he hears of this little fiasco."

"But . . ." The man stared up at him, his green eyes beginning to clear. "My money. The wedding."

Reginald leaned close. His throat was tight with anger. "There. Is. Nothing. No money, no wedding. You have failed. Our partnership is over." He whirled and stalked to the door. "I suggest France. If your funds can stand the strain."

"Wait. Surely there's some—wait!" The viscount had gained his feet and was straining forward, with little success, as one hand was still firmly attached to the bedpost.

Reginald slammed the door closed behind him.

Chapter 22

Alex rode down yet another street in Kensington, peering through wrought-iron gates and over hedges. He had been quartering the neighborhood for the better part of an hour and had seen neither a curricle bearing Viscount Keefe's arms or the cab with yellow wheels that had so alarmed Pen. The compulsion that had sent him racing out had settled to a dull throb.

One more street, then he would turn back to Twickenham House, where no doubt Caroline was even now sharing a cup of tea and scolding Pen for her fears. The quiet clop of his horse's hooves underscored the peace of the area. Once again he had dashed to the rescue, and once again he was neither needed nor wanted.

What was it that pulled him on, that thin, unbreakable string that tied him to her despite everything? He had thought it was the fact of having a child together, but that had been an excuse for doing the thing his own heart desired. It was her, Caroline, he had come back for. If she had been carrying his child, it only meant there was a hope she might need him, even here in grey London.

A child. It had felt like redemption—as if forgiveness might be possible, his debt somehow paid with love and not suffering.

A false and foolish hope.

Yet he feared Caroline would always be in his thoughts, no

matter how distant he was from her. She was a star in the night sky, one his eyes would always seek out, one that burned more brightly than any other.

One more impossible wound on his heart that he must learn to live with.

The quiet of the neighborhood was suddenly marred by a clatter of hooves and wheels. A cab, barreling down the street toward him. Alex yanked his mount sharply back as the vehicle raced through the intersection—far too quickly for the normal pace of Kensington. His stomach clenched as he registered the wheels blurring past. Yellow spokes.

The urgency he had felt earlier flared back to life. He turned his mount and spurred after. If Simms was behind this, if Caroline was harmed in any way, there would be the devil to pay. He only hoped the man was in the cab—that he had found the right quarry. It was moving too quickly for him to catch up and yank the door open. He would have to settle for keeping it in sight until an opportunity presented itself. Surely the vehicle would reach its destination soon enough.

They entered the crowded thoroughfares bordering Hyde Park. He was just able to keep the vehicle in view, though the press of traffic kept him from getting closer. Then they broke through into the less traveled roads of Paddington, and the driver increased the pace again. They were heading north now, away from the heart of the city.

Alex followed. Until he gained some answers, he would follow.

Caroline lost her balance and tumbled forward as the cab jerked into motion. The door swung shut behind her, and a large hand circled her arm, dragging her onto the worn leather seat.

"Well, well. How fortunate," a familiar voice said.

She glanced up, then froze in recognition, sudden panic fluttering in her chest. Mr. Simms. Good lord! She lunged for the door, but he was quicker, catching the handle and holding it closed. With a snick, he turned the lock.

She gripped the useless handle. "Let me go!"

"I think not. You've cost me plenty, and nearly got my throat slit over it. No, you're a prize bird and I'll not let you fly the cage this time." The smile he gave her was unpleasant, revealing large, yellow teeth. "Very obliging of you to drop into my lap, Miss Huntington."

He rapped on the roof, calling to the driver to make haste, and the vehicle sped forward. She felt like a trapped bird indeed, beating her wings desperately against implacable bars.

"Stop the cab at once! Kidnapping is a capital offense, sir."

The cab rounded a corner, slowed. She darted a glance out the window. The street was full of pedestrians—surely someone would hear her if she screamed. She drew in a deep breath.

"Tsk, tsk. None of that now." Mr. Simms's hand clamped over her mouth.

There was a sharp explosion of pain at the base of her skull, a sudden white flash from within, and then everything was darkness.

It was dim in the cab when Caroline opened her eyes, her cheek pressed against the gritty floorboards. They were still moving, and at some speed if the rocking of the vehicle was any indication. Her head throbbed, a dismal echo of her misery those early days on Crete. But she was in England now—and at the mercy of Mr. Simms. She cautiously looked up. Yes, he was still sitting opposite, arms folded, watching her.

"No more tricks now, missy," he said. "Just sit quiet until we get to where we're going."

"And where is that?" She pulled herself up onto the seat and looked out the window. Empty countryside. No help there. Her hands were cold and she folded them in her lap. In truth, she was cold to the bone. At some point during this dreadful day she had lost her wrap. She remembered now:

Viscount Keefe had fallen on it. A mirthless laugh welled up. And she had thought that situation could not get any worse.

"Where? Just a quiet, out-of-the-way place where we can take care of business."

The way he said the word *business* made her stomach flip. This man was a hundred times more dangerous to her than the viscount. She knew it by the prickles of fear running along her skin, the marrow-deep cold that would not be dislodged. Still, she had to ask.

"I don't understand what 'business' we might have. If it's money you need, I'm sure my uncle—"

He cut her off with a sharp laugh. "Aye, it's your uncle's money the boss is after in the end, but it will do you no good now. Nothing will, I'm afraid." He reached into his coat and pulled out a long blade.

Caroline caught her breath. *No. Please, no.*

He nodded to her, tilting the knife so it caught the red glint of the setting sun. "Pretty, don't you think? Thin, but wicked sharp. Just the thing for . . ." He paused, looking her up and down, then grinned and began to pare his fingernails. "Now sit still and quit your yapping."

She closed her eyes and slumped back against the seat. He was playing with her, a cat with a bird. The thought came, sudden and clear: she was going to die. Tonight, when the cab stopped. Dear lord. She did not know if prayers would help, but she bowed her head and sent a silent plea winging heavenward.

There was so much left undone.

She wished her brother, James, had come to the ball, but he had sent word Lily was in difficult labor, and he would not leave her side. She would never see him again. And her uncle—could it be possible she would never again feel his gentle, fatherly touch on her shoulder? Then there were the children of Twickenham House, Maggie, Pen.

Alex.

Ah, Alex. Death had seemed just as certain when they had

been trapped in the Cave of Zeus, but somehow, with him beside her, she had not felt so utterly lost. If only things could have been different. Regret for that, more than anything, seared through her.

She looked at Mr. Simms, still working with his blade. "Why?"

He glanced at her, then lifted one shoulder. "No reason not to tell. It goes down to the money. Your cousin, Lord Reginald, is, hmm, a wee bit indebted to some powerful people."

"But my uncle—"

His look hardened. "All right then—a great deal indebted. To the tune of mortgaging his entire inheritance in exchange for a bit of the ready. Expensive fellow, your cousin. Very bad judgment when it comes to investments and the like. After his loss of the Somergate estate last year, well"—he wiped the knife on the sleeve of his coat—"the boss thought it best to take matters into his own hands. Or my hands, as it were."

"But why . . ." Caroline trailed off.

Reggie's *entire* inheritance. But if she was adopted, she would be entitled to a handsome portion of the earl's estate herself, leaving her cousin in serious debt. *If* she was adopted. They could stop it, though, if they . . . Comprehension shivered through her.

"You want to kill me to prevent the adoption."

"You're a smart one, Miss Huntington. Though I fooled you readily enough on Crete." He chuckled. "An accident while traveling abroad is not uncommon. Would have been easier than all this rigmarole."

She clenched her hands together. Reggie's entire inheritance. "That is . . . a great deal of money." Oh, how could he have been so stupid!

"It's a shame you're the one paying for it. I'd rather have that black-hearted scoundrel you call cousin sitting across from me, but he's the goose with the golden egg." He shrugged. "Nice of you to nip off with that viscount fellow, though. Makes our work that much easier. He'll be blamed for it when they find you. A man of his vices and low morals, taking a girl like you out to his country house, then getting rough with her. Too bad he killed you after you refused him."

Caroline felt sick. Her mind shied away from those last words. Viscount Keefe. Had everyone known he was a scoundrel but her? And how ironic, that he actually *had* spirited her away to compromise her. She knew Mr. Simms would be much harder to escape. But, dear heavens, she had to try. As soon as the cab stopped.

They traveled on into the darkness. Her captor made no move to light the lamps. Caroline wrapped her arms around herself and tried to think. Where was Viscount Keefe's country manor? In Essex, or was it Suffolk? Not terribly far from London—not nearly far enough. Would there be reinforcements there? It didn't seem likely. Mr. Simms had no way of knowing he would be able to snatch her today. Unless this plot had been a long time in the making. Which perhaps it had.

If only she were not so cold.

The rocking of the cab gentled, slowed as the vehicle turned off the highway. Caroline peered out the window. The driver had lit the exterior lamps. Faint illumination revealed grassy hummocks on either side of a small road, briefly lit the undersides of trees. Were they moving slowly enough she could leap out? She bit her lip.

"Stay where you are." His voice was hard. "And don't touch that door handle you keep eyeing, unless you want to lose your fingers."

A gate flashed by—too quickly for her to make out details. Dread coiled around her, like a snake with its prey. She had to be ready.

The cab slowed further, then came to an abrupt stop. The vehicle tilted as the driver swung down, then righted itself. A knock on the door.

"You ready in there?"

Mr. Simms drew a piece of rope from his pocket. "Aye," he called. "Rouse the lads, and I'll bring her along." He turned his attention to her. "Now, missy, hold your hands out. No use fighting—you must know that."

Caroline nodded, trying to look meek and terrified, which was not at all difficult. She brought her hands up. They trembled as he bound them tightly together.

He undid the lock and turned the handle of the cab door. She was barely breathing. *Soon. Soon.*

The door swung open into the night. Mr. Simms grasped her arm tightly and descended, pulling her out of the cab after him. *Now.* She let herself fall, collapsed on the ground with a moan, tearing free of his grasp. She lay there unmoving. Nothing to alarm him. Nothing to make him grab her again. No movement. No running. Not yet.

"What is it? Get up." He bent over her.

"My leg . . . It's all pins and needles. I can't stand. I can't. Just give me a moment."

He made an exasperated, angry sound in the back of his throat and straightened. "Hurry it up."

Slowly, slowly Caroline sat, then half crouched. Gathered her legs under her—and bolted for freedom.

With a yell, Mr. Simms lunged after her, fingers closing on her sleeve.

Fear gave her strength. She ripped free of his grasp and ran. Away from the house, away from the light. She raced down the drive, breath heaving through her lungs and out her open mouth.

"Come back here!" Mr. Simms sounded as though he was right behind her, his feet loud on the gravel.

She didn't dare risk a glance over her shoulder to see. *Run.*

There was something ahead of her: a rider, closing fast. She veered, trying to find cover—a place to hide. Air rasped her throat as she forced her legs to move faster.

She ducked beneath the trees, brushes dragging at her skirts, branches whipping her face. She lifted her hands, bound together as if in prayer, and plunged on. Behind her, two sets of footsteps. Dear God. She could not outrun them both. Her breath caught on a sob.

"Stop, damn you!" Mr. Simms called out. Close. Too close.

She tripped, stumbled, tried desperately to regain her footing. Trod hard on the hem of her own dress and went down. Inexorably down, the underbrush clawing at her arms and face.

Rough hands hauled her up. There was the glint of that long, thin blade, though the night was dark. Terror beat through her, chasing out everything else, even breath. She squeezed her eyes tightly closed.

"Damn you." Mr. Simms was breathing roughly. "I should just do you in here and drag the body back."

She sensed him raise the knife. Dear God. Not now, not like this.

"Caroline!"

Dear heavens. Her eyes flew open as someone crashed into Mr. Simms and bore him to the ground.

Alex.

Her heart tightened as the two men thrashed, making guttural animal noises. She took a frightened step away from those legs and fists in furious motion.

There. The knife, fallen point first into the ground. She scrambled for it, but with her hands bound it was useless. She hovered, helpless, as the vicious fight continued.

"Ha!" Triumph in his voice, Mr. Simms pinned Alex to the ground, hands closing about his throat.

"No!" She threw herself on Mr. Simms but could not catch hold, and he shrugged her off.

In that moment of distraction, Alex brought his hands up and peeled the man's fingers from his throat, then swiped Mr. Simms's face with his elbow. The man let out a howl of pain, and suddenly Alex was beside her, pulling her to her feet.

He grabbed the knife, used it to slice through the ropes

binding her, then flung it into the underbrush. The blade made a curious singing noise as it flew away, end over end.

"Come." He folded his hand around hers, fingers strong and warm, and she began to cry, soundlessly, the tears scalding her cheeks. "We have to hurry." He pulled her gently after him.

She could see lanterns through the scrim of trees, hear the confused shouts of Mr. Simms's men. Alex angled them away, keeping to the shadows. Ahead, a lighter patch—the drive. As they broke free of the woods she stumbled to a halt behind him and scrubbed a hand across her face. What was he doing? Why had they stopped?

A quiet nicker, the dark bulk of a horse. Alex swung himself into the saddle and pulled her up behind. Skirts bunched around her legs, she found her seat and wrapped her arms tightly about him.

"There they are!" a rough voice called.

"Hold on." Alex set his heels to their mount.

They pelted down the drive while behind them shouting erupted. A shot crackled through the night, but they were too far, already vanishing into the dark. The cries faded behind them as they galloped away. Caroline held tight, breathing in his scent. The night wind dried the tears on her face.

Alex. Impossibly here, bearing her away from danger. Joy ignited through her, as sudden and delirious as a firework over a dark river. Questions sizzled on her tongue, but she could barely draw breath. It was all she could do to stay seated as they raced on.

They reached the main road, pinpricks of stars above them, but instead of turning down it, he guided the horse into the fields. The hedgerows were shadowed hulks, sheltering them from view. There was no moon. The blackness that had given her such despair was now a blessing, covering them, keeping them invisible.

Finally he reined in and turned in the saddle, scanning

the countryside behind them. "We're safe—for now. Are you unhurt? Can you keep going?"

"Yes."

He brushed a kiss across her temple, then urged their mount into motion again.

The next few hours were a blur of fields, lanes, trees. At one point Alex held them silently for a quarter hour before proceeding, although she could not make out what had alerted him. They spared no energy for conversation. Caroline rested her cheek against his wool coat and slipped into a half doze, filled with dream fragments of capture and escape, and recapture.

They rode through the night. Somctimes he would dismount and walk, sparing the tired animal's strength while Caroline slumped in the saddle. At last, when the sky in the east had lightened to the color of wool, they halted in front of an abandoned cottage. The thatch roof had half fallen in and the door was missing, but she had never seen a more welcoming place in her life. With a weary sigh, she slipped off the horse, then clutched at the stirrup when her legs almost buckled under her.

Alex was beside her in a heartbeat. He folded her in his arms as though she were the most precious thing in the world.

"Caroline," he murmured.

She gripped his coat, the questions finally spilling forth. "How did you find me? How did you know?" It was nothing short of miraculous.

"Pen told me about the cab that nearly ran you down—it had yellow wheels. She saw it follow after you left today, and sent me after it."

"Dear Pen." She took a wavering breath. "I should have listened." The girl had been right—about so many things.

His arms tightened. "Thank God she saw it. And that you were able to break free."

"At first I thought you were one of Mr. Simms's men." She leaned her forehead against his solid chest. "But when you called my name and I realized it was you . . ." She would never forget that feeling—joy slicing so cleanly through her terror, like a beam of light, impossibly bright over a black and turbulent sea. A lighthouse calling her home.

"You are safe," he said. "I will never let harm come to you again. I swear it." His voice was so fierce and tender that tears came unbidden.

They held each other quietly and she felt her strength return a little more with each breath, each passing heartbeat.

He brushed his lips over her hair. "We need to rest." He released her and ducked into the dilapidated building, a moment later emerging with cobwebs on his coat. "Not up to the *ton*'s standards, but we won't be noticed here. I'll have to bring the horse in with us."

She nodded. She could accept anything as long as he was there, too.

Alex led her inside, then pulled down some of the thatch, making them a rough bed in the corner. It was rustic and prickly, but as soon as she curled into the shelter of his arms, she felt her whole body relax. Safe.

"Rest now. I'll keep watch."

She wanted to protest that he should sleep too, but exhaustion closed her eyelids, and silenced first her voice, then her thoughts.

Caroline knew a moment's panic when she woke and realized Alex was not beside her. She sat up, heart hammering, then saw him standing at the door with his arms folded, looking out over the fields. He turned his head, and seeing she was awake left his post to sit beside her on the scattered thatching.

"All's quiet," he said. "We covered enough ground last night they have no idea which direction we might have gone. But they'll be watching the road back to London." He took her hand. "What is this about, Caroline? Why has Simms been after you?"

She told him then, told him everything.

He was silent a long moment, his face set and hard. "They wanted you dead to thwart the adoption. Had your uncle only known, he might not have been so quick to give you that gift."

"He couldn't have known. Uncle Denby would never have placed me in danger."

"Not knowingly," Alex said, "but you are in danger still. Grave danger. A broken nose is not going to stop Simms, much less those who pay for the services of a man like him."

"You broke his nose?"

"A nasal fracture with accompanying epistaxis." The corner of his mouth lifted. "And likely some bruising to the testicular area."

"It sounds . . . painful." She gave a short laugh. "Although I'm just as happy not to have a firm grasp of the particulars." It was enough that he had saved her from the murderer's grasp. "They will try again, won't they?"

"Not if I have anything to say about it." His voice was suddenly hard, edged with purpose.

"What happens next?" She set her hand on his arm. "Do we go back to London?"

"No. It's not safe there, even if we could elude Simms and his men. We need a place they won't know of. Somewhere you'll be protected while we resolve things."

"Where?" She caught a haunted expression in his eyes before he looked away.

"I'm taking you to Ravensbridge, in Yorkshire." His voice lowered, grew husky. "The place I used to call home."

Ah. Her fingers tightened on his arm. He did not meet her gaze, only gazed over the fields, mouth tight.

"Thank you," she said when it was clear he was going to remain silent. "I owe you my life, Alex. Many times over."

He stood and offered his hand to help her rise. "Tonight I promise to find us better accommodations, though the going will be hard. And then . . . tomorrow afternoon will see us there."

She shook her tattered skirts down and tried to brush off the worst of the straw. "If we're not taken for gypsies and driven out of town."

"We won't be." The words were clipped.

She hated to see the strain on his face. This was costing him dearly, and she did not know why—could not even begin to guess. He had never spoken the details of his history, but there was plainly something so dreadful he had run all the way to Crete to escape it. She feared what this return might do.

But they could not go back now. Only forward.

Chapter 23

They arrived after dark at a bustling and prosperous-looking inn on the main road to York. Caroline blinked at the light streaming from the windows, too tired to speak, as Alex guided the horse around the side of the establishment. He slid down and handed her the reins.

"I'll be right back." His voice was low. "I need to make sure there's been no sign of Simms. Wait here." Like a shadow, he blended into the night and was gone.

Oh, but she was weary. The thought of sleeping in a bed seemed like heaven. Please, let it be safe. Let them stop here for the night.

Alex returned. "No trace of him. We'll stay here." He took the reins and led their mount around the corner.

The back door was open, a square of golden light illuminating a servant tossing water out of a basin. He glanced up, startled, when Alex hailed him.

"What d'ye want?"

"A room for the night. Supper." Alex stepped forward and dropped a coin into the man's hand. "And no questions. Fetch the innkeeper if you will."

The man peered into the darkness and caught sight of her. A knowing smirk crossed his face as he pocketed the coin and hurried back inside. It was clear he thought her a doxy needing to be smuggled in by the back door, and she was too tired to be discomfited by the thought. She glanced down—her best afternoon dress torn and stained and no doubt her hair in equal disarray. She must look exactly like what the servant took her for, but for a bowl of stew and a bed she would brave worse than a serving man's scorn.

The stout innkeeper stepped out, wiping his hands on a towel. "Aye, sir?" He nodded to Alex, who moved forward and lowered his voice.

Caroline could not catch the whispered conversation but guessed well enough what it concerned.

"Very well." The innkeeper stepped back. "We've the one room available for the, ahem, mister and missus. Smith, was it? I'll show you up and send a man round for your horse."

The back stairs were narrow, shadows elongating wildly on the walls as they followed their host, his lamp held aloft. Smells from the kitchen filtered up: fresh bread, cooking meat. Her stomach clenched with hunger. How long since her last real meal? Alex had procured some cheese and apples that day, but they had avoided people as much as possible. It must have been . . . breakfast, nearly two days ago. The fear and arduous travel had kept hunger at bay, but now she fairly stumbled from the force of it.

The innkeeper opened a door and ushered them into a well-lit corridor. With a quick glance in either direction, he hurried to show them their room.

Alex held his hand out for the key. "Have some water for washing brought up as well." He turned to Caroline. "Go in. I need to arrange for horses for both of us on the morrow. And fresh clothing."

The wavering mirror mounted over the dresser in their room showed all too clearly her wretched state. If she were not about to collapse with hunger she might have been amused at the sight. Hair festooned with bits of straw, straggling over her shoulders, a streak of dirt across one cheek—and her dress. She spread the torn and stained skirts out and shook her head.

A quick rap on the door, and a pair of country maids entered. One bore a pitcher of steaming water, which she poured into the waiting basin on the washstand. Steam and the scent of lavender wafted up. The second girl carried a gown draped over one arm, black hat and veil held carefully between her hands. She bobbed a curtsey and set them on the bed.

"Thank you," Caroline said. "That will be all."

The need to wash off the grime of fear and travel and change into something more respectable eclipsed the growling in her stomach. She pulled off the tatters of her gown.

How lovely warm water was. Clad only in her chemise, she sluiced her arms and face, then ran the sponge over her neck and chest. A pity there was not a tub—but even this simple bath had done wonders. She turned to inspect the dress the maids had brought. Black, clearly mourning garb, with severe black lace edging the neckline. It fit poorly, drooping from her shoulders and obviously meant for a larger woman. But at least it was clean and whole, a sight better than her ruined dress.

She had just finished combing the last bits of straw out of her hair when Alex came in. He paused, gaze resting long on her.

"Caroline."

"I know." She gave him a weary smile. "The dress is hideous."

"I hadn't noticed. Not with you in it." He strode forward and set his hands on her shoulders. "The daughter's Sunday best was too dear to part with, but she was happy enough to be rid of her mourning clothes. And a hat with a veil—under the circumstances it seemed a good idea."

She let out a breath. "I must write my uncle. He and Pen will be frantic with worry. I have to tell them what happened—and that I am unharmed." She bit her lip, imagining the chaos that had surely erupted at Twickenham House.

"Send word, but tell them only that you are alive, and safe.

Nothing of where we are, or where we are going." His eyes searched hers.

It pained that she could not tell them more, but Alex was right. The danger was still too great. She nodded.

"Good," he said. "Now where is our food? I, for one, am about to perish without any assistance from our pursuers."

"If you do, then at least I shall have the proper wardrobe to mourn you in."

It surprised a laugh from him and he bent forward, brushing his lips over hers.

"Supper, sir," a servant called through the door.

"Come." Alex stepped away from her as the man entered, bearing a tray of food. "Set it on the table there."

It was delicious. Caroline had never been overly fond of mutton stew, but she scraped her bowl clean with an extra piece of bread before proclaiming herself too full to move. Alex matched her bite for bite, and ate another half loaf besides. Brown ale quenched the meal, kindling a contented warmth through her.

"Let me see about finding a shaving kit." He pushed back his chair.

"I don't think the daughter will be able to provide that." She waved her hand at him. "Go make yourself presentable, by all means—though it was unkind of you to not think of that *before* supper."

He closed the door softly behind him, and she thought she heard a low chuckle as his footsteps faded.

She penned the letter to her uncle, painfully brief, then blew out the lamp on the table, leaving just the candle burning beside the bed. The one bed. Of course they would share it—the knowledge had been strung taut between them ever since the knowing look of the servant outside. It was foolish to even pretend otherwise. They both needed to sleep soundly in the comfort only a mattress and blankets would afford, and she craved his warmth and touch, the reassurance of his solid presence beside her.

If he harbored any lingering, gentlemanly notions about sleeping on the floor, she would not have it. Especially as she suspected he had not closed his eyes at all in the crofter's hut the night before, but instead kept watch over her through the dark hours. Lines of strain and weariness bracketed his mouth, and his eyes were smudged with exhaustion.

He returned soon enough, freshly shaven, his black hair smoothed back, wet and gleaming. One lock fell over his forehead. She went to him and brushed it aside. He wrapped his arms around her, and she sighed.

"We're sharing the bed, you know," she said.

"Are we?"

"Yes."

Their gazes locked and a charged silence wrapped them. Little fires raced over her skin, circled behind her neck. The air between them shivered with anticipation. Heat glowed inside her, as if she had taken the candle flame between her lips and swallowed it, the dancing fire illuminating her very bones. She could keep that light burning, sustained, forever. As long as he was near.

"You'll have no argument from me," he finally said.

She tangled her fingers through his hair and drew his mouth down to hers, kissing his warm lips, urgent and insistent. With an impatient sound he slid his hand around her back, fingers splayed, pressing her against him. It was not close enough. Not nearly. The folds of the dress bunched between them.

"Wait." She tore free of him a moment, long enough to loosen the top buttons and let the dress slip off her shoulders, down to her feet.

Released from the engulfing fabric, she returned to his arms. He moved his palms along her sides, the touch sliding over her thin chemise. She had left her corset off. Nothing but sheer cotton and the heat of Alex's hands caressing her skin.

The peaks of her breasts tightened as he moved his hands closer, closer. She gasped when he brushed his hands over her, the sensitive nubs tingling. Languid heat uncurled low in her belly, at the secret juncture of her thighs.

"Caroline. You are a goddess, truly." His voice was husky with desire, the words breathed against her neck as she trembled, yearning, under his touch.

She wound her hands through his black hair. "Then I am your goddess, to worship as you please."

His hands fell to her hips and he pulled her against him. The bulge in his trousers pressed between her legs, sending her desire flaring. "Worship you I will. With every tool at my disposal." He stepped backward, nudged her until she was beside the bed, then guided her down. The candlelight flickered across his face, showed clearly the need burning in his eyes as he shrugged out of his coat and knelt over her.

"With my hands." He set his palms on her shoulders and drew his hands down, excruciatingly slowly, fingers spread to cover as much of her as possible.

She arched up to meet his touch, let out a breath as his hands curved over her breasts, thumbs roving back and forth over her tight nipples. Sparks coursed through her, gratifying one hunger, while another built even more steadily.

As if sensing her need he moved his touch down, over her ribs and stomach, cupping her hips. And then, ah, then his hands moved unerringly to the apex of her legs, the hidden, womanly place that bloomed with heat and anticipation. A breath of cooler air as he pulled her chemise up, baring her to his touch.

"Open your legs, my goddess."

She did, and he ran his hands up the inside of her thighs, pressing her even wider. He shifted, moved to kneel between her open legs as his hands caressed her, nimble fingers parting her even more. A jolt of fire as he brushed the hard nub of her desire. She let out a shuddering breath.

"Alex. Come to me." She wanted to feel him over her, their

bodies connected, his hardness stroking into her again and again until she was nothing but a conflagration in his arms. She wanted to burn with him, the two of them the blue heart at the center of the flame.

"Not yet," he said. "I haven't shown you all the ways I'm going to worship you." He rose over her again. "With my mouth."

His kiss was searing and possessive this time—a shiver ran the entire length of her body as his tongue met hers. She slid her hands up to his shoulders and held him tightly against her, the weight of him pressing her into the bed as he took her mouth with his own. They fitted together perfectly, her body curving against his. His trousers were rough against the length of her bare legs, her naked hips, the buttons of his shirt an unexpected hardness along her chest.

When his lips moved to lay a trail of kisses along her jaw she began slipping buttons free.

"Undress," she whispered into the silky darkness of his hair.

"Yes." He rose over her, gripped the hem of her chemise, and pulled it off over her head. His eyes burned as he surveyed her naked body. "That's much better."

"Not me . . . you." She set her fingers to his shirtfront.

He stopped her, pulling her hands away. "Not yet. Not until I am done with you. Now, where was I?" Desire for her was etched across his face. Passion, need, and something more—something she dared not try to name. "Ah, yes. My mouth."

He bent, lips descending to brush over her peaked breast, teasing, sucking until she moaned with pleasure. Ah, he made her feel so wanton, a fiery Aphrodite sighing under his skillful mouth. His hot tongue laved her until her nipple was taut and straining with desire. Then he moved to the other breast, lavishing the same attentions, coiling her tighter and tighter with need.

Need that could not be ignored any longer. She writhed beneath him.

"So impatient, my lovely goddess." There was a smile in his

voice. "But my worship is not complete. I want to taste your secrets." His hand slid down to the juncture of her thighs, pressed lightly. "Do you remember the frescoes on Crete?"

"Yes." Her voice was throaty.

"You wanted to know what they were doing, that last couple. I will show you."

Hot kisses, laid openmouthed against her skin, down her ribs, over her stomach as he traveled down, to the center of her, to the pure heart of her womanhood. He spread her with his hands and then . . . purc heaven . . . the flick of his tongue there, between her legs. She moaned aloud, the molten pleasure as he lapped her, obscuring all thought. Hot and wet, he explored, tracing her folds, moving his tongue over the sensitive bud. She was made of nothing but flame, incendiary, leaping higher, until—until—

A shower of sparks coursed through her, a wall of fire sweeping close behind, her entire body ablaze with unutterable pleasure.

"Ahh . . ." It was her own voice, full of bliss.

She opened her eyes, finally, flashes of heat still sifting along her skin, to find him watching her. Satisfaction and hunger mingled in his expression. When she met his indigo gaze a slow smile spread over his face.

"I believe my offerings at your shrine have been accepted."

"I hope there are more." She reached for him.

Hunger overtook the satisfaction and his smile sharpened. He pulled off his shirt, unfastened the waistband of his trousers, then paused. "There is one more thing I want to worship you with."

Her gaze slipped to the bulge of him, about to be freed. She felt her body clench in anticipation. "Yes."

"With my cock." He slid his trousers down. Half in shadow, golden light flickered against his skin, glinted on the drop of moisture at the head.

Caroline watched the play of muscles in his arms, his

smooth shoulders as he positioned himself over her. So male, and made so perfectly to balance her. She opened her legs wider, felt him nudge against her.

With a soft groan he slid inside. She parted for him, opened her softness and let him in, deeper, deeper, until he filled her completely. Until their bodies were so firmly connected it felt as though nothing could ever come between them.

She slid her arms around him and pulled him close. Desire flared, but eclipsing that, ten times brighter, was love. There was no escaping the knowledge, not now. Not for her. She loved Alex with everything that was in her, and that would never change. No matter how far he might go from her, no matter that his heart was still shackled to his past, she loved him.

It was enough.

Together, they began the dance, the slow circling of the sun, the reflected spiral of the moon. He stroked in and out of her, gentle at first, then faster. The whirl of seasons, long nights filled with fire and stars, storms wracking the sea and subsiding, the sun climbing toward zenith, burning bright, so full of fire.

Hot tears tracked her face as she watched him above her, as she moved beneath him, her hips obeying the tide of love. They rose together, faster, harder, flying for the sun on insubstantial wings held together with hope. But there was no falling into the sea. No. Together they dove upward—straight into the blinding heart of the star.

He shouted her name and she responded, voices tangling as their bodies tangled, burning, consumed until at last there was nothing left but cinders, floating softly down.

She laid her hand against his cheek. Alex. Beloved.

The candle flickered wildly and went out. In the sudden darkness, he gathered her close. She tugged the covers over their nakedness and they slept.

Chapter 24

Alex woke her in the silver light before dawn. All she wanted was to nestle down beneath the covers, curl up next to him and dream, but he was already up and dressed. He rubbed her shoulder.

"Wake up, Caroline."

She made a face and rolled over, but he pulled the blankets back, letting the cool air waft against her sleep-warmed skin.

"I'm awake." With a sigh, she rose, pulled on the black gown, and braided her hair, tucking the ends up to make a respectable bun.

"Here." He set the hat atop her head and pulled the veil down. "No one will recognize you."

"I hardly recognize myself." She studied the somber figure in the glass. The veil set a thin scrim of darkness between herself and the world. She lifted it back up. They were safe enough here. When they met other travelers, then she would draw it closed.

"Come. The horses are ready, and I asked the innkeeper to provide us food for traveling."

Caroline followed him to the threshold, then turned back. "My letter to Uncle Denby." She snatched it from the table.

"We can post it downstairs."

He held open the door to the servant's stairs, narrow and dark, redolent with smells from the early morning kitchen. They emerged to find the innkeeper waiting with their provisions, and a thick wool shawl for her. Behind him, in the kitchen, she glimpsed a woman kneading bread and singing to herself.

Alex paid the man, instructed him to post her letter, then hurried Caroline out the back door. The clear, still air of morning wrapped them as dawn broke, a line of pale orange to the east. A groom was holding two horses. They whickered softly and one stamped its foot on the dew-wet ground.

Alex secured the sack with their provisions behind his saddle, then helped her mount. In moments they were off. She spared a wistful thought for the comfort of the inn's bed. Likely the blankets were still warm.

Mist edged the fields as they rode, bearing north and east. Ahead of them the sky brightened, the road stretching forward, empty.

The hours passed quietly. Alex seemed increasingly wrapped in his own thoughts as he drew closer to his home and whatever waited for him there. Every conversation Caroline began trickled back into silence after a few brief exchanges. The words seemed too heavy to sustain themselves.

Or perhaps it was that they were both exhausted still. They had not spent the entire night in sleeping, after all. Her blood beat with the memory of their lovemaking.

They stopped when the sun was high, and rested in the shade of the hedgerow, sharing the simple fare the innkeeper had provided. The air had warmed, filled with the insect drone of early summer.

Caroline took a hunk of brown bread. "Alex."

He looked up, startled, as if she had interrupted him. "Yes? Would you like more cheese?"

"Tell me about where we are going. Ravensbridge." What had driven him from his home? She could not voice the words. Was there a lost love waiting for him, biding the years until his return? Her heart clenched at the thought. "Did you grow up there?"

Shadows gathered in his eyes. "Yes, until I was sent to school."

"Do you have any brothers? Sisters?" She could not bring herself to ask about his parents—already she felt him withdrawing.

"One brother. Older." He wrapped the cheese back in its packet, his movements controlled. "If you're finished, we need to keep going. We'll skirt York and be on the moors by this afternoon."

Another several hours of riding passed, little but strained silence between them. Caroline tried not to fret, but there were too many problems weighing on her. Her uncle must be mad with worry, and Pen, who knew something of the danger Mr. Simms represented. And what of her school? There would be no endowment now from Viscount Keefe. She shuddered just thinking his name.

The terrain changed, fields giving way to rough heather. Alex shaded his face with one hand, glanced at the sky, then the hills rising on their left. At the next crossroads he turned his mount east and beckoned her to follow. His shoulders were tight, his expression set. Worry squeezed her breath as she prompted her horse after him.

At length they came to a bridge, double arches of stone spanning a dark river. The water moved slowly beneath, reflecting the clouds beginning to stack up in the sky. He drew rein on the near side.

"Pull the veil down." His voice was low, strained. "We're getting close."

She tugged the netting over her face, then looked to him. Face taut, he stared, unmoving, across the bridge.

"Alex?" She prodded her horse next to his, set her hand on his arm. Even through his coat she could feel the tension, the tautness coiling through him. "Are we riding on?"

His lips thinned. “Yes.”

Still, it was another long moment before he urged his mount forward. The horse’s hooves thudded on the weathered stone as they crossed, and on the far side it seemed the air carried a chill.

Or maybe it was the expression in his eyes that made her shiver: cold, remote, as if he were traveling away from her to a place she could not follow.

They left the river behind and the road wound onto the moors. She had not imagined the chill. The wind was beginning to rise, bearing a scent of the sea, and dark clouds were scudding in from the east. Caroline halted a moment, gripped the corners of the sturdy wool shawl, and knotted it more firmly about her. When she looked up she found him watching her, a dark figure against a darkening sky, the wind lashing his black hair.

The road skirted the top of a rough cliff. Alex guided his horse along the edge, glancing constantly down at the tumbled boulders as if searching for something.

“What are you looking for?” she asked.

There was no answer. Perhaps he had not heard. A gust blew her veil, lifted the horses’ manes and tails. The sky was full of dark clouds now, the sun obliterated. Across the rolling expanse of heather a gray curtain of rain moved toward them.

“Alex—”

“There.” He pointed ahead to a sharp bend in the road, then dismounted, leading his horse forward. His limp was more pronounced than she had ever seen it.

Her mount twitched as the first fat drops of rain reached them. The storm was coming, but Alex was intent. He bent and touched the ground as if feeling something that radiated through the earth, and when he rose his cheeks were wet. Rain or tears, she could not tell.

“This place marked me—gave me my limp.” It did not sound like Alex, his voice emerging flat and distant. “It was here I struck the rocks in the dark of night, fleeing the horror of my own making.” He took another step toward the cliff, his coat whipped out behind him by the wind. "I had been driving as fast as the team would pull. More than once the wheels found the edge."

He turned to her then. There was no trace of her lover in those haunted eyes—only a man grimly stepping into the tempest of his own past.

"I wanted to die."

Caroline brought her closed fist to her mouth, her heart clenching. Drops tipped over the brim of her hat and clung to the veil like dew on a spiderweb.

He continued, voice remote. "The carriage upended and the horses dragged it until it caught here. My leg, trapped under me, torn. I clawed my way forward, cut the harness as the carriage tipped." He pointed down over the face of the cliff. "There. I should have gone with it over the edge."

She nudged her mount forward and saw it, the wreckage below, weathered and melting into the landscape, the outlines of what had once been a carriage still clear.

The sky opened then. Sudden, violent, the rain was on them, chains of water flung down from the black clouds. The wind whipped her sodden hair into her eyes. Her mount gave a shrill whinny. They had to find shelter. They had to leave this place.

"Alex!"

He had mounted again, but sat staring down, still trapped in memory. Rigid and unmoving while the storm lashed about him, rain pummeling his shoulders.

Caroline prodded her mount as close as possible to his, then reached for him, lacing her fingers through his hair. She pulled, bringing his face down to hers, fastening her lips over his cold mouth, infusing everything of life she could into a single kiss.

For a heart-stopping instant there was no response. Then he breathed, lips moving against hers, a spark flashing between them. He lifted his head, his expression alive again. Their gazes met. Midnight shadows speared her through with a look more powerful, more frightening than even the elemental fury unleashing around them. He stared at her a moment longer—naked yearning, soul-searing need.

Thunder coiled through the air. He shouted something, then bolted his horse forward, down the winding road into the valley. Her mount was glad to follow. She gave it its head, barely able to see the dark silhouette ahead in the driving rain. Hoofbeats mingled with the drum of her own heart, the rasp of breath, the gather and release of the horse moving beneath her.

They pelted through the storm for what felt an eternity. She was dimly aware of passing hedgerows but did not consider what that meant until her mount turned off the main track, following Alex's horse across a plowed and muddy field. Ahead a shadowy bulk revealed itself—a barn. Shelter.

He was already off his mount and shoving the half door wide. He caught her reins as she rode up, and guided her into the dim, hay-scented safety. Outside, the storm flung itself against the building, the wind pressing through the cracks. She slipped down from her horse, the folds of the black dress sodden and dragging about her, and they waited silently, numbly, for the torrent to spend itself. At last she spoke.

"Why have you come back? You fled so far. You said you would never set foot in England again." She saw in her mind's eye the wrecked carriage at the base of the cliff. What had he fled from that night—and what was he returning to?

He said nothing, his hands clenched into tight fists.

"You can tell me." She let the words carry her trust, her promise of understanding. "I know you are a good man—"

"I am not a good man!" His voice was harsh and raw, driving her back a step.

"You are." Her own heart raced in response. "What could you have done that requires you to live your whole life in shadow? Why must you wall yourself away from those who love you?" She took his hand in hers, cold, unresponsive. "From those you love. Why must this stand between us?"

He jerked his head up. "Can you bear to know the blackness in my heart, Caroline Huntington?" The words were as sharp as broken glass.

"I . . ." Her throat was dry. "I must know."

His eyes burned with despair. "Then I will show you."

Chapter 25

Alex pulled his mount to a halt and stared at the clinic. His pulse clamored in his veins. Dear God. He could not face this. Inside. It waited—his own unforgivable shame. His hands clenched around the reins.

"Alex?"

He glanced at Caroline—the unrelieved black making her a shadow against the evening sky. Veiled and dressed for mourning. He closed his eyes.

Murderer.

The rain-drenched streets had been quiet as they rode into Ravensbridge, lamps in the windows holding back the dusk. And now they were here, the place he had forfeited his soul.

"Come." He flung himself off his horse, wrapped the reins about the post, and stepped forward.

Since crossing the bridge, the pain had intensified, burning more with every mile. Now his leg was on fire—it could barely take his weight. He half stumbled to the door of what had been his waiting room. Locked. No matter. He wrapped the corner of his coat around his fist and smashed the glass, reached through the jagged hole and turned the lock.

Through the clatter of breaking glass he heard Caroline gasp. Sharp pain in his hand. The door swung wide into the darkened room, revealing the chairs, the fringed lamp, the scatter of newspapers, now yellowed. There was a faint smell of medicines, overlaid by years of disuse. He limped forward, pressure growing as if he were diving deep into cold water. Memory swept in, closing over his head.

That night—the farm family had caught him as he was buttoning his coat to leave. Please help their daughter—she was in terrible pain. The child was pale and clutching her stomach. The wife held out a basket of eggs, all they could offer in payment. But he had never refused those in need.

He staggered down the hall, Caroline behind him; he could not turn back. The paneled door wavered in his vision, seemed almost to expand and contract at his approach. Breath rasped painfully through his throat, the air tasted of powdered iron. Feet unable to take another step. The door. The knob.

He shuddered, frozen in place. What had he thought? That he could will away thc past? The girl had had no choice. Why should he deserve one?

Caroline's hand, gentle on his shoulder. Her calm presence beside him. She must know—she must see him for what he truly was.

Alex set his hand to the cold knob, tightened his fingers, and turned. The metal click and release. He could not force himself to step inside.

"She's there." The rough whisper escaped him. "She's waiting—just as on the night I fled."

"Who?"

"The girl. She had braids. The family begged me to help her. She was crying from the pain, a bellyache, or worse. We carried her here."

Hand trembling, he set his palm to the dark wood and pushed. Fear like a noose around his neck. The door opened, revealing what had once been a dispensary, now given over to dust and shadows. Lungs drained of air, he lifted his gaze to the examining table.

Empty.

No white and staring face, no haunted eyes. The pressure around him eased a fraction as he drew in a desperate breath.

"I gave her paregoric, to ease the pain. Told her it would help. I opened a new bottle, fed her a dose, though she turned her head away and had to be coaxed to it. She took it. I promised it would make her feel better. I spooned the medicine into her mouth."

Oh, God. He hunched forward, head in his hands.

The hush of Caroline's skirts, a gentle touch on his arm.

"She stopped breathing. I did everything I could to revive her. I thought it had been the pain in her stomach, and there was nothing I could do to restore life to that frail body. It was not until after . . . until . . ." His voice broke.

The mother's cries of grief, the father's face, ashen, as he had gathered up the limp body of his child and carried her from the room.

He had failed. Despite his skill as a doctor he had not known what was wrong, had not acted in time. There was medicinal brandy in the cupboard. He had drunk straight from the bottle, trying to blunt the edges of his pain. Losing a patient was always excruciating.

But it had been nothing compared to what followed.

"It was later. I drank some brandy and dozed, slumped against the wall. Dark, when I awoke, moonlight coming in. My hand in the puddle of medicine that had spilled. Unthinking, I tasted it. Oh, God."

"Tell me." Caroline's voice, soft and insistent.

He could not stop now. He drew in a ragged breath.

"Laudanum. I gave her laudanum. Twenty-five times stronger than paregoric. The girl did not die. She was killed, killed by an overdose." He made himself say the word. "Murdered."

Her indrawn breath. "But, surely the label—"

"It said paregoric. But I should have tasted it to make sure. I had heard the stories. I knew. I always did." He clenched his fingers through his hair.

The room had turned cold, so cold, as the knowledge of what he had done penetrated. The taste still on his tongue. The back of his neck had prickled, a breath from the grave stealing down his spine. Dream or hallucination brought on by guilt, it did not matter. Her ghost had come.

"I saw her then. Sitting on the table. Her face, so white. And her eyes . . ." They had stared at him, wide and unblinking. Devoid of malice, of accusation—of anything human. "She was lost. Lost to the living, and I bore full responsibility. I had snatched away everything from her, through my own arrogance and carelessness. I had stolen her life." There was no forgiveness, no redemption.

"So you gave up yours in return." Caroline's voice was full of horrified understanding.

"What other payment could I give?"

There. She knew.

He steeled himself for her revulsion, for the moment she would rise and flee. It did not come.

"Is there a lamp?" She spoke softly. "Matches?"

He pointed. The stink of phosphorus, the sudden flame steadying as she re-placed the chimney. The light reflected in her eyes.

"Don't you understand?" His own voice, harsh in his ears. He grabbed her by the shoulders, made her look at him. "I am a murderer!"

"No."

The quiet certainty in her tone rocked him. She did not flinch away, only gripped his arms, as if her touch could anchor him to the present. "Yes, the girl died. Yes, it was from the medicine. That does *not* make you a murderer." Her hands were tight on him, insistent.

"But I—"

"No! Death is not murder." She released him and whirled, swept the room with one arm. "There is no ghost here—because it was an accident. Tragic, yes. Horrible, yes. But murder?" She shook her head. "No."

He began to tremble then, shudders wracking him. Could she be right? He bent over the table, bracing himself. The empty table. There was no ghost. Warm arms came about him, holding him. He turned in her embrace, let her strength buoy him up.

"Alex," she whispered, one hand stroking his hair, "you don't need to run from it anymore. Don't let the mistakes of the past rule your future."

He drew in a shaking breath, bowed his head. He was lost, adrift on a dark sea. But perhaps—perhaps not beyond hope of redemption. Not while her light shone to guide him forward. Not while her calm courage enfolded him.

They stood together for eons. Long enough for his heartbeat to settle to steadiness, for warmth to return to his hands. For a seed of hope to lodge in his heart.

At last he lifted his head. Her amber-flecked gaze, full of understanding and compassion, met his. Caroline.

His love.

He had not been able to think the words, though for months he had known. Known, but could never acknowledge the truth he carried inside him. It had been impossible. He had not had the right to feel, to live.

Did he now?

The idea was so new, so tremulous, he could not absorb it. Not yet. He took up the lamp and held his hand out to her.

"It's time I went home."

The storm had blown away. Overhead, clear stars were flung, glittering, across the sky. Alex pulled in a breath of sea-flavored air. Home. He felt curiously free at the thought.

As they rode higher the view unfolded, the ocean winking darkly, the lights of the village sprinkled warm below the ridge. And the manor, perched above it all. It struck him then how his cottage on Crete had mirrored this, a place removed from the village, set on high ground, with the sea ever present in the distance. Slowing his mount, he let Caroline draw even with him.

"Raven Hall." He opened his hand. Most of the windows were blank reflections of the night, but a half dozen showed light and warmth. There was life within. He had been afraid of finding only a ruin filled with cobwebs and emptiness. "Built by my grandfather after he became owner of the alum works here."

"Did he have a large family then?" Caroline watched the manor.

"No. Just pretensions to nobility. And too much money to indulge his whims. My brother and I rattled about in there."

A sudden memory of riding an imaginary war-steed down the long passageways, through the banquet hall, laying about with a sword fashioned from a stout stick. He had not thought of his childhood for far too long—had locked thoughts of his family, that sense of belonging, behind a huge iron door. Then flung the key into the deeps of the Atlantic as he had traveled away, away from England.

His lungs squeezed with misgiving. Would his mother forgive him? Surely she must have thought him dead these years past. In running from what he had done, had he not set ever-widening circles of pain in motion?

But Caroline was beside him now, and he could face anything. The moonlight washed faintly over her face, her straight nose and high cheekbones. She seemed unaware of his regard, still staring at the hall perched above them. Robbed of color by the night, he could still vividly imagine the brown waves of her hair, tawny streaks laid there by the Mediterranean sun, and flecks of sunlight dancing amber in the depths of her eyes. She turned to him and smiled, and the dimness seemed suddenly full of color and rushing light.

He urged his weary mount forward, the last yards home unrolling with a dreamlike certainty. They left the horses standing—he would send a servant out to tend them—but for now he was pulled inexorably forward.

He did not bother with the heavy iron knocker. This was still his home, no matter how many years had passed. He swung the tall front doors open and the scent of his childhood rushed out to meet him, a blend of wax, peat fires, and flowers. Regrets clogged his throat, the grain of the door familiar under his fingers, and then he stepped inside, beckoning Caroline to follow.

The entryway was unchanged, down to the customary vase of flowers beside the door. It felt as though no time had passed. Yet his vision was overlaid with intervening years, the afterimage of loneliness and isolation jarring against the reality of homecoming. He continued on, through the formal receiving rooms, and deeper into the house. Halfway down a long corridor he stopped and drew in a breath. What if his mother was not at home? What if she was?

A hand, warm and confident, in his. He turned, met Caroline's encouraging gaze, and found the courage to go on, though by the time they reached the family parlor he feared he had squeezed her fingers bloodless. She did not complain, she did not question, only stood beside him, lending him her quiet, unyielding strength.

With trembling fingers, he set his palm to the door and pushed. For a moment the two people inside did not notice the intrusion. He stood, all his attention focused on the woman seated before the fire, lacework in her lap. She looked so much older than three years should have accounted for. His fault—the shockingly silver hair, the lines of grief etched beside her mouth. He drew in a sharp breath. Barely inaudible, but she heard. Her eyes, bluer than his, as blue as the North Sea, lifted to the doorway. Shock limned her face, pulled the blood from her skin.

"Alex?" It was an unbelieving whisper.

"Mother." He stepped into the room, letting go of Caroline's hand.

"Alex!" Astonished joy flashed across her expression. She stood, let the lace tumble unheeded off her lap, and opened her arms wide.

He went forward to his mother and held her while tears spilled down her cheeks.

"My son. You are alive. Oh, Alex, I prayed so often for this day. . . ." Her well-remembered hands smoothed his hair, and he was enveloped in the achingly familiar scent of roses. "I missed you so dearly."

"I am sorry." He swallowed past the ache in his throat. "When I left . . ." He had been more than a little mad; he was beginning to realize that now. Crazed with guilt and despair, then after the accident, pain and fever. It had seemed the only thing he could do was run. But the years on Crete had taught him there was no escaping himself—and that had been a bitter knowledge to bear.

He felt his mother's attention shift to Caroline, watchful and still beside the door. He held his hand out to her, drew her to stand beside him.

"Mother, this is Miss Caroline Huntington. She brought me home."

In so many ways. Without her he would never have returned to England. To Ravensbridge. To himself.

"You have brought my son back to me." She caught Caroline's other hand in her own. "Thank you, my dear. Thank you."

Caroline smiled, and despite the ill-fitting black gown, the grinding days of travel, the storm, the clinic, he thought he had never seen a woman more radiant.

"Mrs. Trentham, I am so very pleased to meet you," she said. "And more happy than I can say that I could be part of Alex's return."

His mother beamed at Caroline, then beckoned to her companion, Lucy, who, it seemed, had borne the years with her usual stoic grace. "Fetch the maid. We must prepare rooms. Alex's suite, of course, and we can put Caroline in the south wing. Have Cook send up a late supper, and . . ."

Home. Alex glanced down at Caroline and squeezed her hand, a fierce conviction flashing through him, so white-hot he was sure she must have felt it run from his fingers to hers. *I love you.*

Their gazes locked, and for a moment it was only the two of them, caught together in the huge, still center of the world.

Chapter 26

Caroline barely recalled following the maid to her room the previous night. After they had reached Raven Hall and she had met Alex's mother, exhaustion had swirled around her, heavy and muffling. She had been so weary she could barely keep her eyes open over the hasty supper prepared for them, and she was certain she had fallen asleep somewhere in between pulling up the sheets and laying her head on the pillow.

Now she felt more rested than she had in days. When she had finally woken, the maid had brought a muslin dress for her—another garment that did not quite fit, but Caroline had been only too happy not to re-don the mourning gown. The time for darkness was over.

Yesterday, learning the dreadful secret that Alex had carried alone for years—her heart twisted at how he had tortured himself for it. He had shut himself away from all joy, all life, in trying to atone. Ah, Alex. She hoped that now . . . But she hardly dared name that hope.

"The breakfast room is this way, miss." The maid—Annie was her name—led her through Raven Hall.

Caroline glanced about, wanting to see everything, to absorb this place that had been his home. It was large—they passed hallways filled with closed doors—but not forbiddingly so. The house was warm and elegant, with a sense of quiet ease, as though nothing truly tragic had ever transpired within its walls.

At the end of one corridor she halted, staring at what could only be called a shrine. A gilt-framed oil painting depicting a smiling young man holding the reins of a horse hung on the wall. Beneath the picture a vase spilled over with fresh peonies, their sweet fragrance rising up like hope. Candles to either side shed a warm, constant light.

She did not need to step any closer to see the rich indigo of his eyes, to know it was a portrait of Alex. They had not forgotten him. He had been loved and remembered every day that he was gone. She moved to the painting and studied it, seeing an Alex she had only caught glimpses of, trapped behind a grimmer self. The face in the painting was open and happy, that of a youth who expects the world to bring him only good things. It wrenched at her to know how little that had proven true for him.

And yet, the man she knew now was truly that. A man. Someone who had plumbed the depths of his own soul, who had known and weathered tragedy. A man who, though he had rarely smiled, had still remembered how.

"Coming, miss?" Annie asked.

"Yes." Caroline gathered herself and followed.

"'Tis late, but the family is still at breakfast. Here we are." The maid bobbed a curtsey at the folded-open doors.

Delicious scents pulled Caroline forward into a sunlit room, where Alex was lingering over his meal. His mother and her companion sat across from him, drinking tea.

"Caroline." He rose the instant he caught sight of her. "Come, sit. I'll fix you a plate." He took her hand and drew her to the chair beside his.

Mrs. Trentham gave her a smile of welcome. "Good morning, Miss Huntington. Did you sleep well? Was the bed comfortable?"

"Very. I know our arrival must have been a shock and—well, I am grateful for your hospitality."

"You needn't worry about that, dear." Mrs. Trentham poured her a cup of tea. "Alex says you need a refuge, and I am delighted to have you here. And my son, of course." Her face softened as she watched Alex at the buffet. "My son."

Caroline blinked at the expression on the woman's face and took a hasty sip of her tea. She would not start weeping, here at the breakfast table. She would not.

"When Mother inquired about luggage I told her we were traveling lightly." Alex slipped a plate of food before her, then took his seat again. "There is a wardrobe and some trunks full of dresses for you to look through, I believe. But no more black."

"No more." She could not help smiling at him.

"I'll have the seamstress come from the village," Mrs. Trentham said. "She can bring along some made-up dresses to fit you with as well. But tell me, Alex says you are a relation of the Earl of Twickenham?"

Caroline finished her bite of toast and nodded. "He is my uncle."

"How splendid! We were acquainted in my youth—before he had the title, of course. You are to be adopted by him?"

A pang against her heart. "No. I'm afraid not."

"It's for your safety." Alex reached and took her hand.

"I know. It's just . . . I worry at how Uncle will take the news. He was so happy at the thought of making me part of the family."

"Caroline, you *are* part of the family. Publicly halting the adoption is the only way you can be free of Simms and his employer." He squeezed her hand. "He will not hesitate to withdraw the petition, knowing it is for your protection. And you know he loves you."

"Yes." That knowledge glowed, a coal of warmth, deep inside her.

"Tell me more of yourself, dear." Mrs. Trentham took up her teacup.

"I am involved in charitable work," Caroline said.

"Yes, she has founded a very successful school for orphans in London," Alex added.

"How good of you." Mrs. Trentham's bright, interested gaze lit on Caroline again. "The world is always in need of generous souls willing to help."

"Which is why I insist you have one of Cook's cakes," Alex said. "Until then you will not know how sadly deprived your life has been." He deposited a round cake before her, lightly dusted with sugar.

"Alex!" his mother said. "I am certain Miss Huntington does not appreciate her orphans being compared to tea cakes."

They laughed together. Caroline was delighted to see him in such a fine mood. She bit into the confection, aware of Alex watching her intently.

She tilted her head, letting a skeptical expression settle on her face, and laughing inwardly at the look in his eyes. "Well . . . I suppose they are not bad."

"Not bad! Cook makes the best cakes in all of England." He took a large bite of his own. "Although, I think one needs to be twelve years old to truly appreciate their finer points."

His mother nodded. "Twelve years old and gangly as a young colt. Heavens, how you could eat, Alex. Cook complained her larder was constantly bare, what with feeding you and your brother."

"How is Percy?" Alex's voice grew serious. "He is well? His family?"

"They are in good health, although Percy works constantly, to hear his wife tell it. Oh, and you have a new niece!"

He smiled at that. "Then a trip to Cumbria will be in order soon. But not yet. Caroline, will you come driving with me today?"

"Of course." She would go anywhere he asked.

* * *

Alex glanced at Caroline, perched beside him as he drove the surrey down the country road. She was carrying a large bouquet of flowers, flowers the two of them had gathered from the gardens. Daisies and peonies, Queen Anne's lace and delphinium, she had named them all for him. She dipped her head and inhaled, closing her eyes. It made him smile. Today almost everything made him smile, though he could not deny the whisper of tension coiling tighter around his spine as they neared their destination.

The morning wind blew lightly off the sea, the sky showing no memory of storms. The roadside was edged with field poppies and the village below seemed a colorful, bustling place. He looked down at Ravensbridge, those well-remembered streets, the marketplace in the center square.

The road meandered along the top of the hill. Ahead the silver-grey walls of the little church became visible, the single bell in its arch over the door. He knew the exact moment Caroline caught sight of it. Her quick, indrawn breath, the sudden stillness of her body as she guessed, then knew, where they were going. Without speaking, she laid her hand over his.

Dear God, she could read him so well. He firmed his lips, his heart tumbling in a whirl of emotion. Gratitude. Fear. Love.

He pulled the surrey to a halt outside the graveyard. It was quiet, and on this light summer day he was beginning to believe the ghost he had seen three years ago had only been inside him, a specter of guilt visible only to his own haunted soul.

He handed Caroline down from the vehicle, then kept hold of her—his living, vibrant talisman. Together they stepped through the gate. The breeze riffled the longer grasses at the edge of the tended graves and the sun lay itself over the headstones. Most were plainly carved. A name, a date. Others were larger—a few ornate crosses studded the yard—but it was not those he was looking for.

There, near the corner. A simple stone. Swallowing, he stepped close enough to read the inscription, his fingers tight over Caroline's.

Adelaide W
1835–1845
Beloved daughter, Blithe spirit
Rest in His love Forever

She read it aloud, her voice steady and clear, though he saw the bright moisture gathering in her eyes. She handed him the bouquet and he knelt, laying it before the stone.

His throat burned with tears, and he let them come. So sorry. He was so sorry.

He did not know how long, but finally a clear peace began filtering through him. The ache eased into something he could bear, the sobs replaced with deep breaths as he returned, cleansed, to the sunlit world.

"Alex." Caroline whispered into his hair, one hand stroking his shoulders.

One final, deep exhalation, the last of old grief slipping free of his body. "I thought that I owed her my hope, my happiness—that somehow by forsaking the sweetness in the world I could right the balance. A life for a life. But now . . ." He pulled her close against him. Caroline, warm and alive and full of sweetness. "Now I know that winding one's self in suffering only brings more of it. The only payment I can offer is to open my heart to the world, not close it away." His voice was rough with the echo of tears. He rose to his feet, drew her up with him. "Come with me."

Beyond the graveyard the grasses grew tall on the bluff, susurrating in the warm breeze. The sea below was clear and flecked with light, and swallows flung themselves through the air in impossible trajectories of joy. He turned to face her, took both her hands in his, warm and strong.

"It ends," he said, "where it began."

"And it begins here as well." Her voice trembled. "All we can ever do is move forward, try to bring a little more light into the world."

"Tend the living." He gazed down at her. Their faces were very close, the amber flecks in her eyes shimmering and golden, something amazed and hopeful in her expression. "Caroline Huntington . . ." Dear God, his heart was hammering in his chest, nearly shaking him with the force of it. "I would ask you something. Something I wish I could have asked a thousand times before this day, but could not." He swallowed. "Today I am a man who is free to love you without bonds or limits. And out of that love I would ask to spend the rest of my life by your side."

Those beautiful eyes now filled with tears, a smile trembling on her lips. He drew her close against him.

"Let us tend the living together, Caroline. I would marry you, heart and soul and strength, if you will have me." He nearly stopped breathing then, standing there, daring to hope.

She searched his face. Finally, finally she spoke.

"Yes, I will have you, Dr. Alex Trentham, for I would have no other."

He lifted her then, laughing with a wild joy that seemed large enough to fill earth and sky. Their lips met in a kiss full of hope and redemption, and there, by the edge of the sea, Alex knew at last what it meant to heal. There would always be scars, but he was becoming a whole man again. More complete than he had ever been, with this woman in his arms.

He felt in his coat pocket and drew the ring out. The faceted topaz caught the sunlight, shone and glinted like warm honey, like her eyes. Diamonds edged it with a harder, brighter fire. "Hold out your hand."

She did, her fingers trembling.

"It was my grandmother's wedding ring. This morning Mother insisted I start carrying it with me everywhere."

Caroline blushed as he slid the ring onto her left hand. "I'm sure she will be relieved. There is no denying the fact we arrived quite outside the bounds of propriety. I'm amazed she didn't say anything."

Amusement ran through him. "You should have heard her before you came down to breakfast. I have not gotten such a thorough scolding since I was six and freed all the chickens from the henhouse."

"Oh?"

"Apparently I have been derelict and rakish in spiriting you away without the benefit of matrimony. She said that any fool could see how it stood between us, and that I had best make my intentions known with all haste."

"Those intentions being?" There was a lilting tease to her voice.

"To give you all the tending you deserve . . ." He bent, brushing another kiss across her lips. "For the rest of our days."

Alex's mother did not miss the significance of the ring on Caroline's finger when they returned to Raven Hall. She was delighted, and he was pleased that she had taken so quickly to Caroline.

"How soon are you planning to have the wedding?" His mother's bright gaze moved between them.

"Ah . . ." Caroline hesitated, her eyes meeting his.

He caught her hand. "For myself, as soon as possible."

For a thousand reasons. Her safety was paramount, but he wanted the freedom to travel openly with Caroline, the freedom to share rooms with his beloved, the freedom to kiss her scandalously in the middle of the town square if he wished. Now that he had set his course, no obstacle would stand in their way.

His mother smiled. "I am well acquainted with the local bishop. He would be able to procure you a special license immediately. That is, if you desire to wed here in Yorkshire. Of course, your fiancée might have different plans."

Caroline bit her lip. "I need to write to London again. I'd like my uncle's blessing—and, oh dear, Alex, he has not even met you! And I still don't know if he'll forgive me for refusing the adoption."

"Of course he'll forgive you. And he'll forgive you for marrying me, once he sees how slavishly devoted I am to you."

That comment made her laugh, as it was designed to do—all the more piquant because of the utter truth shading his words. "Yes, I expect you to cater to my every whim."

He sent her a private look. "I shall certainly find an excuse to indulge you."

Color tinged her cheeks, but she met his eyes steadily.

He set his hand over hers. "Will a week give you enough time? Or—are we to have a large wedding in Town? We could wait if you like, Caroline."

"No . . ." She paused, a thoughtful look in her eyes, then continued with more certainty. "No—if I ever imagined being wed, it was at one of Uncle's summer estates with my family and close friends in attendance. None of those crushing Society events." She shook her head. "The adoption ball was enough for me. I would not relish planning a wedding on that scale. It would take months."

"Excellent!" His mother clapped her hands together, her smile bright enough to outshine the day. "I will speak to the bishop then. The local church is beautiful—it overlooks the bay."

"Yes," Caroline said. "We were just there. It's lovely." She shared a smile with him, a smile full of promise, full of light.

A week. He squeezed her hand. He could hardly wait the span of an afternoon.

Chapter 27

Caroline sat before the fire in her new dressing gown, brushing her hair and waiting. Alex would come—the expression on his face every time he had looked at her today assured her of it. The hunger in his eyes had set little fires burning all through her.

Her room was golden in the extravagant light of a half-dozen lamps, the bed was turned down, and a peat fire infused the air with warmth. She glanced at the wide scalloped lace edging the sleeves of her silk gown, lace that moved gracefully each time she lifted the brush and pulled it through her hair.

The local seamstress, Miss Goodey, had arrived that afternoon, as promised, bringing not only a number of made-up dresses but a selection of undergarments as well. The rest of the day had been spent in measuring and fitting—and in considering what Caroline would be wed in. Mrs. Trentham had declared that none of the simple day dresses would suffice. No, Caroline must be wed in something splendid. She had bade the servants fetch two trunks and watched proudly as they unpacked the contents.

"I am glad my whim to save my favorite gowns is being rewarded. And though styles have changed, Miss Goodey is a marvel with the needle. She will be able to do wonders with any one of these."

The seamstress had nodded thoughtfully as wealth after wealth of ball gowns spilled from the trunks. Sky-blue satin, bronze taffeta, yards of lace, Chinese figured silk in royal purple . . . It was like being at the most stylish of modistes.

"Oh, that one is lovely," Caroline had said, catching sight of an elegant gown of cream and palest rose. She moved forward to run her fingers lightly over the netted silk. "You were quite the height of fashion, were you not?"

Mrs. Trentham blushed. Looking at her, Caroline thought the years were already lying more lightly on her face. It was astounding how joy could so transform a person.

"I was reckoned a beauty in those days, and not a little vain with it. My husband and I would go to London four times a year to take in the sights—which included multiple trips to the milliner's. And then we would have grand balls here at Raven Hall to show off our finery." She smiled, her face softening with memory.

When the seamstress finally left she took the cream and rose gown with her, along with admonishments from Mrs. Trentham to transform it into the pinnacle of the current mode.

Caroline let out a breath and set the brush down. Her only regret was that her family would not be able to attend the wedding, for it was being held in such haste. But this way she could remain at Raven Hall until the adoption was withdrawn, and she would not bring a scandal home with her to London. She could not deny that she was ready—more than ready—to have Alex as her husband.

A feeling of rightness accompanied their decision. It was right she and Alex marry—a completeness that lived in her very soul, that moved through her with each breath.

A quiet rap on the door. Her heart gave a thump of anticipation as she rose to open it.

"Alex." She lifted her gaze to his.

He stepped inside and took her in his arms. The silk of her dressing gown hushed beneath his hands, his touch heating the fine material. For a taut moment they simply stood, sipping one another's breath, gazes locked. Then he lowered his mouth to hers.

Pure fire raced through her. She clutched his shoulders, felt him deepen the kiss, holding nothing back. Their bodies pressed together, her dressing gown slipping against his linen shirt, so tantalizingly near to nakedness.

He pulled her even closer, one hand sliding through her hair, the other at the curve of her back. Heat between her legs, the hardness of him against her there, concealed beneath his trousers. Their mouths open and yearning, tongues melding together the way their bodies would soon be, twining and stroking. So intimate. So perfect.

In a sudden move he gathered her up into his arms.

She laughed and wound her arms around his neck. "Carrying me again, Mr. Trentham?"

He looked down at her, eyes alight with desire. "You are a truly beautiful woman, Caroline Huntington. In every way."

He moved with her to the bed, only the faintest limp in his stride. She did not think he would ever completely lose the trace of what had happened—and that was as it should be. There would always be that echo of great sorrow stirring in the depths, part of what made him who he was.

He laid her down, then stretched beside her on the bed. Tension thrummed in the space between their bodies, his hand resting on her hip, fingers tracing patterns that burned through the silk. She parted her lips, watched his gaze fasten there.

"My love." She opened her arms to him.

A heartbeat later they were pressed tightly together, his hand closing over her hip and pulling her hard against him, her arms around his neck, their legs tangled. Their mouths grazed, meeting in a kiss of passion and prayer.

All the weariness, all the worry fell away, erased like tracks on the beach, the wave of their desire rising, sweeping everything away until the only moment was now. Now, the parting of lips, the sweet taste of his open mouth over hers. Now, the urgent caress of his hand slipping down the curves of her body, heat coursing through her from his touch. Now, her palms sliding around his shoulders, her heart an urgent beat of life.

His hands played in her hair, combing out the long strands. Her hands on his buttons, slipping each one free, tugging his shirt open. Their mouths fused, the pulse moving through them, waves of a silent sea. Ah, how she wanted him. Whole and safe and unhaunted. Alex. Here in her arms. It seemed a miracle.

He wrapped both arms around her and rolled, pulling her on top of him. The curtain of her hair fell about their faces and she laughed, pushing it out of the way.

He pressed gently on her shoulders, coaxing her upright until she was straddling him. "Caroline. I want to see you like this. Fully see you—all of you—in the firelight, in the lamplight. We've been too long in shadows."

It was true—the times they had been together were full of mystery and darkness. Stolen moments. Even at the inn, the light of their single candle had obscured more than it had revealed. But here was a wealth of brightness, steady flames all about them casting a wide, golden light over everything.

She shook her hair back and sat up straight and brazen over him. Her legs were spread on either side of his, her softness pressing him just there. It made her feel powerful and beautiful, to rise above him and know he was as lost to desire as she.

"All of you," he said again, his hands sliding up her sides, then curving around her breasts. "And though I admire this dressing gown, I admire what's beneath even more."

He caught one end of the wide ribbon sash and pulled. The gown parted, falling open at the center. The look in his eyes was intent as he slowly pushed back the silk, exposing her, her nipples standing rosy and erect under his approving gaze.

His hands covered her then, and she tilted her head back, sighing as he stroked her. He raised his hands, sweeping the lightest touches across her breasts, as if she were under a teasing breeze. Then he took her nipples between his fingers and squeezed, gentle but insistent, sending a shock of pure heat between her legs. A moan of pleasure escaped her.

For another torturous, sweet minute he played with her, coaxing spirals of sensation through her. She arched under his touch, encouraging, wordlessly begging for more.

"Yes," he said. He pulled the gown down off her shoulders in one smooth motion, her arms slipping free of the lace sleeves, leaving her bared above him. Eyes never leaving hers, he moved his hands along her legs, tracing her naked thighs beneath the tumbled skirt, his caresses sending delicate shivers over her skin. "Lean forward over me."

She did, and he lifted his head to fasten his lips about one nipple.

"Ahh." The pleasure was incredible after his fondling hands—the contrast of his hot mouth, his tongue moving over the sensitized peaks. She felt as though she were melting into a pool of golden light. His mouth moved to her other breast, and then, in one smooth move, he turned their bodies until she was under him, lips hungry on her skin as he knelt above her.

She kicked the dressing gown off. Naked now except for the fine silk of her drawers, but not bare—not with the sweet brightness covering her body, not with the honey of desire wrapping her round.

"You," she murmured, pushing the shirt off his shoulders. Dear heavens, he was beautiful, all male and muscled, disheveled hair black as a raven's wing. She let her hands rove over him, smoothing up his strong arms, tracing the firm planes of his chest, the contours of his ribs.

When her fingers went to the fastening of his trousers he gently pushed them aside. "All of you—first."

His smile was wicked as he slid down to trail kisses over her chest, her stomach. At the top of her drawers he paused, then licked, a line of sweet fire where her skin met the silk. She thought he would pull them off, but instead he moved even lower, his mouth brushing over the cloth, then veering to her thigh.

Another tease of his tongue, this time pushing the silk up with his mouth. His legs on either side of hers, holding her closed. She was pulsing with desire, with anticipation, all her senses focused there, where he played between her legs. A nibble along her other thigh.

And then, at last, his open mouth above the source of her pleasure. She could feel his breath through the thin silk. Slowly, so slowly that she could barely breathe from it, he lowered his mouth.

Pure fire, even through the barrier of her drawers, his tongue lapping her, sending waves surging through her, sparkling and insistent. The wet silk clung to her as he licked and her every breath released on a sigh.

"All of you." It was a whisper. He stripped her drawers off, then spread her legs, hands pressing her wide. "All of you."

He bent to taste her again, and the wave rose as his lips moved over her, his tongue touching that one, searing point of pleasure, coaxing the pleasure to wind tight. Tight. Tighter. She was open to his mouth, at his mercy as he steered her, unerring, right into the peak of blinding bliss.

It was a crashing glory, a tide pulsing, pulsing, pulsing. Finally receding.

She opened her eyes to see Alex watching her, pleasure and desire clear in his expression.

"Beautiful." He swept his hands over her. "My golden goddess."

"And you are my midnight god. Show yourself to me." He never had, not completely. Always some part of him had been hidden by the shadows. But after today there could be no more hiding between them.

"Yes." There was a brief hesitation, and then he unbuttoned his trousers and let them fall to the floor.

His cock jutted up in striking arousal, but her gaze was

momentarily distracted. The light also revealed the scar on his left leg, a pale line, an indelible reminder of the past.

"My turn to worship you."

She slid down, trailing kisses over his muscled chest, the flat plane of his stomach. She paused at the wiry tangle of hair between his legs and wrapped one hand around the hot hardness there. Then slowly she bent to taste the salty bead of moisture at his tip.

He let out a soft groan and his pleasure made her bolder. The skin of his cock was supple under her tongue as she lapped the underside, traced the head, then fitted her mouth over him. He groaned again and she could feel the blood pulsing through him where her hand caressed.

It was a slow exploration, learning the shape of him, feeling him inside her mouth. His turn, and yet she was the one in power, holding him captive with his own pleasure.

"Stop." He breathed the word, ragged.

"Mmm." She continued sliding her mouth up and down, impishly ignoring his command. He was engorged, and she tasted salt again.

"Woman." He caught her by the shoulders and pulled her up, then wrapped his arms tightly around her to keep her from wriggling back down his body. "Another time you may continue to your heart's content—and mine. But not tonight."

"No?" She loved the feeling of being pressed so close to him, skin to skin.

"Tonight I want to be in you."

"Then come."

Golden lamplight burnished him as he moved over her. She opened her legs and he slid himself smoothly inside, filling her, the two of them fitting together perfectly. For a long moment he was still, all hard and trembling tension over and in her. And then he moved. Long, sensuous strokes that rocked the two of them, as though they were on the surface of the sea. A warm, welcoming sea. But beneath the surface, the depths.

She tilted her hips up, moving to his rhythm, taking him deeper, accepting him heart, body, and soul. Her hands on his shoulders, urging him faster.

"Not yet." He stilled, pressing her to the bed. "We have time. All the time we need." His voice was steady, but she could see the desire hot in his eyes, could feel the effort to hold himself back in his corded arms, the set of his mouth.

"Kiss me." She reached, tangled her fingers in his dark hair and pulled his head down. Gentle at first, lips brushing, his tongue lightly tracing the seam of her mouth. Then open mouths, breath mingling, the sweet, hot taste of him. She felt him thrust into her, his tongue, then his cock taking up the pulse, insistent. This time there would be no stopping. They would ride the steep, curving wall of pleasure together until it crested and pulled them under.

She wanted him, wanted all of him, and he gave it, unstintingly. Nothing held back now, only this, two naked souls meeting in the heart of the fire. The heart of a promise.

He was moving faster now, urgent above her, and she felt the molten heat uncoil. She moved with him, bodies locking and unlocking, the ebb and surge of a primal tide sweeping through them. His jaw was tight, his gaze locked on hers, and she felt desire building to the breaking point. Almost. Almost.

Now.

He threw his head back, the release shuddering through him as her own pleasure peaked again, pulsing through her in a hard current. The two of them riding the wave across sunlit water, tumbled by the force of passion until at last they fetched up on the shore.

He lay on her, breathing hard, a pleasant heaviness as she stroked his back. It seemed their hearts shared a single beat, their lungs a single breath. Joy welled up inside her, pressed against her throat, against her eyes until a tear rolled down either cheek.

"I love you, Alex," she whispered.

His arms tightened around her and he rolled them both onto their sides, faces just inches apart. There was something so heartbreakingly vulnerable in his expression that she had to say it again.

"I love you—all of you. Everything that you are. Past and present."

"And future." His voice vibrated with hope.

"Yes. Future." But for now, the present was enough. She held him close, the warm, still air all around them, the last ripples of their lovemaking shivering through her.

"Caroline." He smiled, his eyes oddly shy. "I never thought to have such sweetness in my life and be able to accept it. You are . . ." He shook his head. "It took me a long time to realize what I really felt."

He fell silent, staring at her as though memorizing her face. One hand lifted to stroke her hair.

"And that is?"

"Love." He kissed her forehead. "Love." Her cheek. "Love." Her chin. "I love you, Caroline Huntington. I think I must have from the first moment I saw you, fighting to keep your feet when the world was spinning around you."

She smiled at the memory. "You were so forbidding. I almost wished they *had* taken me to another doctor."

"I will always be grateful they did not."

He pulled her close and she nestled her head into the curve of his shoulder and closed her eyes.

It was nearly dawn when she woke. The fire had burned down to coals and the room was suffused with the pearly grey of early morning. She was still in Alex's arms and could feel he was awake. Had he lain there unsleeping, content to hold her all through the dark hours? His eyes met hers and he smiled.

"Good morning, love."

"Yes." Any morning waking with him lying beside her could only be good.

"I need to leave soon, before the servants are up. But

first . . ." A wicked light in his eyes, he set his hands to her hips and pulled her against his unmistakable arousal.

"Insatiable, are you?" She felt an answering warmth kindle through her.

"For you? Yes."

He kissed her, demonstrating just how insatiable he was, hands roving over her body, coaxing sparks of desire back into flame. Playful, teasing touches that grew insistent until she was breathless with wanting him again.

When he slid inside her she sighed, then arched to meet him. Faster this time. The sheets bunched and pulled, the covers tangling about them. She was dimly aware of sliding near the edge, the hungry force of their movements propelling them until, with a gasp, she felt nothing but air beneath her shoulders.

"Alex!" She wrapped her arms around him, breathless, holding on. "Ahh . . . don't stop."

He growled low in his throat, and her response soared to meet him. It was a sweet explosion, sparks tingling all through her, a feeling of being suspended. . . .

And then the two of them were laughing as they toppled off the bed in a twist of covers and pure, satisfied joy.

"Shh." She clapped her palm over his mouth but could not restrain her own giggles.

He gently removed her hand and smiled that rare, enormous smile, the one that smote her straight to the heart. She quieted.

"Back into bed with you, milady."

"I'd rather you were there, too." She sighed and clambered back onto the mattress, let him arrange the covers over her.

"I know." He dropped a kiss on her mouth, then gathered his clothing. "Soon."

Chapter 28

Today.

She was marrying Alex today. The knowledge rang through Caroline, even before she opened her eyes to yet another flawless Yorkshire morning. Gladness was a sweet taste on her lips as she stretched beneath the covers.

She glanced out the window at the blue June sky, softer than the dome of blue over Crete. No length of linen cloth filtering the sunlight here. She thought back to that first waking in his spare cottage. Mediterranean light had filled the room that morning, but now the light was inside her. How far they had come, she and Alex.

The shadows that had haunted his eyes were gone, the hard cast to his face had eased. His smiles came more frequently now, though they still had the power to leave her shaken and amazed. He was full of life and hope, playful and vigorous. . . . She blushed, though no one was there to see her.

He had come to her every night, stolen kisses aplenty, and there had been one delightful interlude in the garden. She sighed at the memory of his hands moving over her, his mouth laying passionate kisses down her whole body, impatience in his touch as he undid buttons, pushed her clothing aside. And her own urgency as she stroked him, freed him from his trousers, and felt him gasp with desire for her. Ah, the wicked intimacy of their two bodies coming together half clothed, in the *garden* of all places—a secluded bower, but anyone might have stumbled over them. It had added an unexpected thrill to their lovemaking, as though they had stepped away from a summer party, the illicit strength of their hunger for each other enough to obscure any of the proprieties.

Afterward she had lain against him, happiness glowing through her as deeper in the foliage a thrush had burst into song.

She was glad they were not waiting. What bliss it would be to wake next to him, day after day after day, to turn and smile at one another, sleepy and utterly content, gazing into the eyes of the beloved.

Today she would stand before him in the little chapel overlooking the sea and pledge her heart.

"Miss?" A quiet knock at the door. "Are you awake? I've some chocolate."

Caroline sat up and pulled her dressing gown over her shoulders. "Come in, Annie." A cup of chocolate in the morning was one of her favorite indulgences, a pleasure that Alex had discovered upon their second morning here and that Cook had spoiled her with ever since.

"Good morning, dear." Mrs. Trentham followed the maid in. "Our bride-to-be. Are you ready to see your dress? The seamstress just brought it." Her blue eyes were lit with excitement as she smiled at Caroline.

"Very much." She slipped out of bed and cinched the dressing gown tight while Alex's mother stepped out to fetch Miss Goodey.

They returned, bearing the gown between them. It was wrapped in tissue paper, rustling as they carried it. Miss Goodey, who had struck Caroline as a very demure and serious woman, had a definite lilt in her step.

"Lay it on the bed," Mrs. Trentham said. "Now, let us see what Miss Goodey has wrought. Come, stand here, Caroline—yes, right in front."

It would be lovely. It must be lovely. She was certain it

would be lovely. Caroline bit her lip as the seamstress drew the paper away, revealing the gown beneath.

For a moment there was a reverent silence and then Caroline stepped forward. "Oh my. Oh, it is gorgeous."

Miss Goodey had transformed an already lovely dress into something that surely the Queen herself would be envious of. The rich cream-colored skirts spilled from the fashionable V-pointed bodice, and the off-the-shoulder neckline was edged with fine lace embroidered with roses, the same embroidery echoed in the pale pink gauze netting of the overskirt.

"Try it on, miss, do!" Annie had lingered in the room, and her squeal of excitement made them all laugh.

Drawers, chemise, corset, crinolines, and finally the gown itself. Annie fastened the back and let out a soft sigh. "Oh, miss, but you look fine."

"Indeed you do," Alex's mother said. "How is the fit? Miss Goodey brought her needles if we need to make any last-minute adjustments."

Caroline took a few experimental steps, skirts hushing and elegant about her. She turned to the seamstress and performed her best court curtsey. "It's perfect. Thank you, Miss Goodey."

The woman brought her hand to her mouth, covering her smile, and dipped a curtsey in return.

Caroline swirled the skirts around her. The gown was truly exquisite. She fetched up before Alex's mother and caught her hands. "I must thank you, Mrs. Trentham. For everything."

"My dear. I have always wanted a daughter, and I am so pleased. . . ." Her eyes were bright with emotion. "I am so pleased to welcome you into the family. You must call me Gertrude. Or mother, if you would like."

Now Caroline felt her own eyes fill. She sniffed. "I mustn't get tear stains on my dress."

"Here, miss." Annie held out a handkerchief, which Caroline accepted gratefully.

"Mother? Are you there?"Alex's voice from the hall, his footsteps coming closer. "I need to ask you something."

Mrs. Trentham and Caroline shared one startled glance, then both rushed to the door and slammed it shut. Just in time, too, if Alex's confused exclamation was any indication. He pounded, and Caroline leaned against the door while Gertrude turned the lock.

They looked at each other again and broke into laughter.

"What the dev—er, what is going on in there?" Alex's voice sounded through the door. "Is everything all right? Caro?"

"Yes," she called back. "Everything is just fine."

"Alex!" His mother's voice was stern, but mirth spoiled the effect. "The groom is *not* supposed to see the bride on the wedding day!"

"Well then, how am I supposed to marry her?" He sounded aggrieved.

"I meant, not until you are at the church. Now give me a moment. I will meet you in the parlor." She turned to Caroline. "I'll have breakfast and a bath sent up, and we shall spend the rest of the morning making you the most beautiful bride in all of England."

"In all the world, I'd think," Annie said, nodding vigorously.

After that the day accelerated at an alarming pace. Gertrude and Annie spent the next two hours devoted to Caroline's toilette. She was bathed in warm water, given a variety of perfumes from which to choose—she settled on lavender with a hint of gardenia—her hair was combed and curled, and then she was dressed in the lovely gown.

At last they let her look in the mirror, and she caught her breath. It was said that any bride on her wedding day was transformed, but she could not quite believe the woman looking back at her. Her honey-brown hair was caught up in a chaplet of rosebuds, the pale pink matching her gown, and her cheeks were flushed with pleasure and anticipation. She was beautiful—and today she wanted, more than anything, for Alex to see her like this. Beautiful.

"Oh, you are a vision." Gertrude tilted her head to one side, considering. "Perfect, except for jewelry. A necklace, hmm . . . let me go and see what I have."

She returned carrying a velvet box. "I was thinking. . . . Do you like this?" She held up a double strand of pearls interspersed with pink tourmalines, the brighter gems sparkling between the rich satin of the pearls.

Caroline drew in her breath. "It's beautiful." She took the necklace, the smooth pearls warming under her fingers. The colors matched her gown to perfection.

Gertrude smiled. "It was a gift to me from Alex's father. I would like you to have it as the first of your wedding gifts." She gently fastened it about Caroline's neck.

"I . . ." Caroline lifted her hand to a throat suddenly tight with tears. She turned to embrace Alex's mother. "Thank you," she whispered.

"The thanks are yours, my dear. Without you I would not have my son again." Her voice was filled with soft conviction. "You brought him back. You were the light he followed home."

The carriage bore them over the country lanes. Caroline rubbed her thumb across the band of her ring, over and over, though it felt comfortable now after a week of constant wear. Bound for her wedding, with a light and a heavy heart. She missed her uncle, her brother, Pen. But it was no use wishing, and they were all miles away. Somehow she would make it up to them. She glanced out at the flower-bright meadows. Perhaps later in the summer she would ask her uncle to host a garden party and they could all celebrate together.

She released her breath, let the regrets fall away. For now, it was enough to be joined with Alex. More than enough—it was remarkable in the very best way.

The track wound up past the village and soon she glimpsed the silver stone walls of the chapel. It was modest, no huge Gothic steeples or medallions of stained glass, but graceful in its own proportions, the single bell set above the doorway pealing out merrily. Arched windows ran the sides of the building, and inside Caroline knew it was light and airy and filled with peace. She smoothed her skirts once more and caught Gertrude's empathetic smile.

A crowd had gathered outside the front door, eagerly awaiting their arrival. As the carriage slowed she recognized Annie and the other servants, quiet Miss Goodey, friends of the Trentham family. Certainly there were many well-wishers from the village and surrounding estates who had come to see the return of the county's most prominent prodigal son.

And then she glimpsed a familiar face, then another. Caroline blinked—surely she was only wishing, hoping to see them. . . . But no, they were there. Her family.

With a glad cry, she threw open the door and leapt out of the carriage into the arms of Uncle Denby.

"Uncle! You are here!"

He held her tightly a moment, then set her back and gave her an intent look. "My dear, of course we came. But is this indeed your will—to marry Alex Trentham?"

"Oh, yes. Willingly, with all my heart."

He nodded. "I have never had reason to doubt your judgment or good intent before, and I shall not begin now. If this is what you truly want, then you have my blessing, Caroline."

"Are you going to monopolize my sister all day?" James stepped forward and embraced her. "Caro, we couldn't miss your wedding."

"But where is Lily? Is she well?" She craned but could not find James's wife in the happy throng.

He smiled, a look of sheer joy and relief crossing his face. "She is at Somergate—with our new son. They are both well."

"Oh, James!" She squeezed his shoulders. "You look happier than I have ever seen you. Although a bit tired."

"Yes," Pen pushed forward, her grin lighting her face. "That's Alex's fault. The letter telling us to come barely arrived in time. Lord Denby sent for your brother—and here we are!" She linked arms with Caroline. "But don't you look beautiful! Wherever did you get that dress?"

"I can hardly believe you are all here." Caroline blinked, still not convinced she was not dreaming it. "When did you arrive?"

"Yesterday evening," Pen said. "The gentlemen stayed at the inn in Ravensbridge, and I with a friend of Alex's mother. We saw Alex and his mother last night, too. The idea of marrying you has quite transformed him."

"The wretch—he said they were going to procure the license."

"And so he was," her uncle said. "License from your family."

James cocked an eyebrow at her. "Really, Caro, did you think we would let you marry a Yorkshire man sight unseen? Even if his mother turned out to be the younger sister of the Marquess of Edgerton."

"So you do know Mrs. Trentham." Caroline turned to her uncle.

He gave a dry smile. "Yes. Although our relationship consisted primarily of her stuffing turf down the neck of my jacket when she was seven. She thought it quite amusing at the time." He set his hand on Caroline's shoulder. "James and I both found your Alex to be a satisfactory gentleman, sincere in his intentions and affection for you."

"Oh, it's good you didn't meet him months ago," Pen said. "He was quite dreadful then." They all laughed.

"In truth," James said, "Miss Briggs has proved herself a formidable advocate on his behalf. But look, the crowd is clearing. It must be nearly time."

"Here, Caro." Pen held out her hand, a silver sixpence glinting in her palm. "Good luck and joy for all your days. I know it's more a country tradition, but . . ." She tilted her head. "It goes in the left shoe."

"Allow me." Uncle Denby took the coin.

Holding to his arm, Caroline slipped off her shoe and, balancing on one foot, held it out. He tucked the shilling into the lining by the heel, and she re-placed her shoe. "Quite comfortable."

James offered his arm to Pen. "I will escort Miss Briggs to our seats and await your grand entrance."

"My dear." Her uncle cleared his throat. "Are you entirely sure about withdrawing the petition for the adoption? I would not want you to feel—"

"Uncle." She took his hands in her own. "You've always been the family of my heart, and I could have asked for no better. But I will have Alex now, family of my own. I don't need a piece of paper to know you love me."

"I do indeed. Are you ready, then, to be escorted down the aisle by the father of your heart?" His eyes held a suspicious brightness.

She leaned up and kissed his cheek. "Yes. I am ready."

The chapel stilled as she stepped inside, one hand on her uncle's arm, the other holding her bridal bouquet of pink roses twined with ivy. Light streamed in through the windows, and at the head of the nave was Alex. His dark blue eyes were serious and he looked almost forbidding in his formal dark clothes. For a moment she recalled him on that first night on Crete, when he stood in the doorway black as a thundercloud.

Now he saw her and smiled, and was transformed.

The look in his eyes, the way his gaze followed her as she made her way down the aisle—it was as if they were the only two people in the room. Her heart ached with joy. Joy that took wing even as she released her uncle's arm. She stepped forward, taking her place beside Alex. The long journey was over. She smiled up at him and was rewarded with a deepening warmth in his expression, the love so clear in his eyes that she caught her breath.

They clasped hands as the vicar spoke of return and redemption, and when she said the words *I will,* no words had ever felt more true. His in return sent a thrill of pure belonging through her.

The ceremony passed in a happy rush until the vicar gave

them a final benediction, and the chapel bell began to ring again, the church organ sounding out glorious music. Alex swept her into his embrace and kissed her, their lips together sealing the promises they had just made.

"I love you," he murmured.

Then they were down the aisle, catching quick glimpses of Alex's mother weeping happily into her kerchief, James's approving nod, and Pen grinning with glee. They paused to sign the registry, her hand surprisingly steady, and then forward into the perfect June day.

The guests followed them out of the church. Amid the hubbub of congratulations, she pressed one rose into Pen's palm, another into Mrs. Trentham's. Then her husband—her husband!—handed her up into the carriage and slid in beside her.

He nodded to the driver to set off, back to the house for the wedding breakfast, and amid good-natured cheering he once again lowered his mouth to hers.

There are kisses, and then there are *kisses*. This one reverberated with the peal of happiness chiming through her, his name ringing in all the spaces of her body as he pulled her close. Lip to lip, sharing the same breath, the same heartbeat. The same wild coursing of love through them. Despite—or perhaps because of—all they had gone through together.

She was breathless when at last he let her go.

"So, wife, are you glad?" His voice held an undertone of joy she had never heard before.

"I am beyond gladness."

"Gladder than that day when two lost souls emerged from the Cave of Zeus into the light?"

"Even that. Because that joy was shadowed with an ending, where this one . . ." She put her hand to his cheek, studying those beloved features. "This one is made brighter still by a beginning."

Chapter 29

Caroline lay on her side and watched her husband reading the *Times* in bed next to her. It had taken no getting used to at all, sharing a bedchamber with Alex, though for the past week they had been frightfully indolent.

It was not that they were *waking* late, it was just that, finding themselves in bed together, well . . . one thing led to the next. She smiled privately. Sometimes it was a wonder they made it downstairs before noon.

She set her hand on Alex's chest—his naked chest, the muscles of his arms admirably displayed. Her glance strayed down to the sheet. She could say with authority that his lower half was as unclothed as his upper. Unlike her, he had soon stopped wearing nightclothes to bed, arguing that since they seemed to have a problem staying on he may as well dispense with them altogether.

He glanced at her, something serious in his eyes. "Your uncle's announcement is in the notices."

"Let me see." She curled closer to him and he tilted the paper so she could read:

At the request of Mrs. Alex Trentham, née Miss Caroline Huntington, the petition for adoption by Lord Charles

Denby Huntington, Earl of Twickenham, shall void ab initio.

"Does it make you sad?" He settled his arm around her.

"No. It's only the adoption that's been canceled, not my uncle's affection. Besides, this means Mr. Simms will have no reason for additional attempts on my life."

Alex's mouth hardened. "Attempts or no, if I ever see him again, so help me . . ."

She dropped a kiss on his collarbone. "It will be good to move freely again, to return to London. To our new home."

Alex had made inquiries and they had taken a house in Belgrave Square. It should have come as no surprise to her that he was in possession of a decent fortune—after all, his family clearly had wealth.

But most surprising of all had been his mother's contribution. Pen had stayed on at Raven Hall with them, and she and Gertrude had taken to one another as kindred spirits, despite the decades separating them. The girl had quickly involved Alex's mother in all the particulars of Caroline's project—including the financial complications facing the dispensary.

One evening at dinner Alex's mother had made the announcement. She would like to become the Twickenham School's benefactor. She would notify her solicitor, if Caroline and Alex agreed.

Agreed? Caroline had flown up out of her chair and embraced Gertrude right there, at the dinner table, the soup course forgotten. And she had to admit, she was delighted to be free of the Ladies' Auxiliary Board and their fountain-filled schemes.

Alex folded the paper and set it aside. "Back to London, yes. How soon would you like to leave Raven Hall?"

Never. Immediately. Caroline shook her head at her own conflicted reaction. "Part of me would love to stay here forever—while the other part is anxious to return." She let out a soft breath. "I worry I have been away from the school too long, especially as things have been so unsettled."

He smiled at her, and again she thought how very handsome he was, the sun glossing his dark hair, his eyes reflecting a hard-won serenity. Very handsome. She smoothed her hand over his chest, warmth kindling through her again.

"Then we shall leave the day after tomorrow," he said. "That should give us time to pack."

She nodded. "Not that I have a great deal in my own possession. I suppose you have things you'd like to bring from Raven Hall." Though she couldn't imagine him filling trunks with childhood mementos. Not after seeing the unadorned simplicity of his cottage in Crete.

His smile turned mysterious. "I'll make the arrangements."

If they were going to be leaving soon, she had best take advantage of the time they had left. She gave him a wicked grin. "Mm. I think you have some arrangements to make with your wife right now." She slipped her leg against his beneath the covers, then laughed out loud as he rolled her into his arms.

The day of their departure was overcast, which was all to the good. Another perfect, sun-drenched day would have made leaving Yorkshire too much like abandoning paradise.

At breakfast—attended at the true hour this time—Alex's mother had been hard put not to break into weeping. She kept dabbing her eyes with her kerchief and reaching to clasp her son's hand.

"Mother, you know you are welcome to come with us. There is more than enough room in the house and we would be happy to have you and Lucy there."

Caroline nodded. "You are easy company, Gertrude, and we're not best pleased at the thought of leaving you alone here."

"It is exceedingly kind of you both, but you need time to

establish your household. I will visit, of course. I need to see your school and finalize arrangements with my solicitor."

"You must come soon," Caroline said, "and we will take you about London."

"Oh, yes." Pen nodded. "There is a milliner's shop that has the most splendid dresses."

"And in addition to the school I would also like to see the—"

"Don't spoil the surprise, Mother," Alex said. He took a last gulp of tea, then stood. "I'm going to check on the luggage. Come out as soon as you're ready."

Caroline finished her toast and again assured Mrs. Trentham of a warm welcome any time she chose to visit. "And I've no doubt we'll come back to Raven Hall as often as we can. I've come to love Yorkshire—and not only because I married your son here."

Gertrude smiled at that and the two of them, followed by Pen, proceeded to the front doors. Caroline stepped outside, blinked at what she was seeing, then blinked again.

There was the coach to take them to London, but behind it were two wagons, heavily loaded and covered with thick canvas.

"What is this?" She looked from the wagons to Alex.

He was grinning—a most unusual expression on his face. "The furnishings and equipment for the dispensary. I will need them if I am to return to the practice of medicine."

"You're . . ." She looked again and felt a bubble of happiness form in her chest. It was . . . he had brought . . . The bubble expanded, rose, carrying her words with it. "Your clinic? You have packed up your entire clinic?"

"And am transporting it to London. If you still need a physician, I would be honored to offer my services."

She flung her arms around him, for surely this lightness of spirit would otherwise carry her off, buoyed as she was by joy.

"Oh, Alex!" A moment later she stepped back to study his face. "Are you certain?" It had been a topic left unsaid between them. She had not wanted to press, and it seemed too demanding, the potential for reopening old wounds too great. "I did not expect—"

"No, you did not, which is most satisfying, since it was meant to be a surprise. I am choosing this freely, Caroline." He snared her gaze. "What are we here for, after all, if not to make life easier for one another?"

London, September 1848

The gardens at their new home were nearly overflowing with people. Caroline took another sip of lemonade and shook her head.

"What is it?" Pen glanced curiously about. "Did someone come who was not invited?"

"No, it is the number of *invited* guests I find amusing. I had envisioned something, well, something much smaller."

"Hmm." The girl's voice was matter-of-fact. "Who would you have left out? The headmistress and faculty of the school? Alex's new assistants? Your brother and his family?"

Caroline's gaze sought James, standing near the rose arbor with Lily, their three-month-old son cradled in his arms. The babe lay quietly, watching the proceedings with large eyes.

"You're right, Pen. There is no one here I would wish uninvited. And how fortunate that Maggie has returned for a visit and brought her captain with her."

"It's very romantic, their surprise wedding in Spain." Pen twirled her parasol, still reviewing the guests. "Of course, Mrs. Trentham and Lucy—and how grand that Alex's brother was able to come." She nodded to the tall, dark-haired gentleman. Percy seemed to share the same serious nature as Alex, from the few conversations Caroline had had with him. A man much involved in his business, nevertheless he had been quietly astounded to see Alex again and seemed glad to be in attendance.

"There are a few people I am frankly relieved are *not* here."

Thankfully, though she was half expecting to glimpse Reggie skulking in the shrubbery, it was impossible. Uncle Denby had bought him a position with the East India Company and had sent him away. He had been gone by the time she and Alex returned to London.

"I hear Viscount Keefe has taken an extended tour of the Continent," Pen said.

For a moment the afternoon darkened and Caroline repressed a shudder. "Good riddance. I would be happy never to hear that name again." She had no sympathy for the man, or the weakness that had led him to such abominable behavior.

Servants moved to light the lamps scattered about the garden, and in one corner the string quartet resumed playing, the graceful strains of Haydn drifting into the evening air. Caroline let out a breath. Everything had ultimately come out right, and she could only be thankful for it.

Who would have thought being thrown from a horse would have resulted in such a happy ending? It had certainly seemed unreasonable at the time. She smiled, remembering her first view of Alex—all stormy and forbidding male in the flickering torchlight.

But they had met their match in one another.

As if her thoughts had summoned him, Alex strode onto the terrace and came directly to her side. He slipped an arm about her waist. "Are you pleased with your party?"

"Yes." She leaned against him, and he dipped his head, pressing a gentle kiss on her neck, just behind her ear. A shiver ran through her at the caress. Ah, the rogue—he knew her sensitive spots all too well.

"I'll just . . . um, go and fetch more lemonade then," Pen said brightly. "You two seem well occupied." A knowing glance, and the girl took herself off.

"Wasn't her glass mostly full?" Alex asked.

"Perhaps she was overcome by a raging thirst."

"She is not the only one." His other hand came to rest on her hip and he pulled her lightly against him. "It's cool inside the parlor. And . . . private."

She laughed. "You are incorrigible."

"I am also married. Why not take advantage of the fact that a brief absence on our part will not cause a scandal? One kiss Caroline, that's all I ask."

"Only one?" She raised her brows. "Then it's hardly worth the bother."

"A dozen then." He was already leading her inside.

Two steps into the quiet parlor and they were in one another's arms, silently affirming the vows between them, the promise of two lives twined together. And a dozen kisses, twelve thousand kisses, more kisses than the petals in the fields would not be enough to express how deeply she loved him, her thunderstorm, her husband.

Deep indigo eyes met hers. "Caroline. I love you more than night loves the day." He kissed her then, so sweetly, so perfectly that she felt her heart would break from it.

A million years, a heartbeat later, a discreet knock sounded at the door.

"The toasts are about to begin." James's voice, amused. "Perhaps the happy couple—incidentally the subject of those toasts—would like to join us?"

"Ah, yes," she called back. "We'll be right there." She smoothed her skirts, then turned to Alex.

He smiled and held his arm out to her and together they went, out of the shadows and into the sunshine. Forward. Into life.